Blind Lake

Tor Books by Robert Charles Wilson

Bios
Blind Lake
The Chronoliths
Darwinia
A Hidden Place
The Perseids and Other Stories

Blind Lake

Robert Charles Wilson

TOR®

A TOM DOHERTY ASSOCIATES BOOK

NEW YORK

BLIND LAKE

Edited by Teresa Nielsen Hayden

A Tor Book
Published by Tom Doherty Associates, LLC
175 Fifth Avenue
New York, NY 10010

www.tor.com

Tor® is a registered trademark of Tom Doherty Associates, LLC.

Library of Congress Cataloging-in-Publication Data

Wilson, Robert Charles, 1953–
    Blind Lake / Robert Charles Wilson.—1st ed.
        p. cm.
    "A Tom Doherty Associates book."
    ISBN 0-765-30262-4 (alk. paper)
    I. Title.
PR9199.3.W4987B59   2003
813'.54—dc21

                                   2003047345

First Edition: August 2003

Printed in the United States of America

0   9   8   7   6   5   4   3   2   1

PART ONE

The New Astronomy

Telescopes of surpassing power revealed to her the unrevealed depths of the cosmos on polished mirrors of floating mercury. The dead worlds of Sirius, the half-formed worlds of Arcturus, the rich but lifeless worlds whirling around vast Antares and Betelgeuse—these she studied, without avail.

—Polton Cross,
"Wings Across the Cosmos," 1938

One

It could end at any time.

Chris Carmody rolled into a zone of warmth in an unfamiliar bed: a depression in the cotton sheets where someone had lately been. *Someone*: her name was elusive, still lost in layers of sleep. But he craved the warmth of her recent presence, the author of this lingering heat. He pictured a face, benevolent and smiling and a little bit walleyed. He wondered where she had gone.

It had been a while since he had shared anyone's bed. Strange how what he relished, as much as anything, was the heat she left behind. This space he entered in her absence.

It could end at any time. Had he dreamed the words? No. He had written them in his notebook three weeks ago, transcribing a comment from a grad student he had met in the cafeteria at Crossbank half a continent away. *We're doing amazing work, and there's a kind of rush, knowing it could end at any time . . .*

Reluctantly, he opened his eyes. Across this small bedroom, the woman with whom he had slept was wrangling herself into a pair of pantyhose. She caught his glance and smiled cautiously. "Hey, baby," she said. "Not to rush you, but didn't you say you had an appointment somewhere?"

Memory caught up with him. Her name was Lacy. No surname offered. She was a waitress at the local Denny's. Her hair was red and long in the current style and she was at least ten years younger than Chris. She had read his book. Or claimed to have read it. Or at least to have heard of it. She suffered from a lazy eye, which gave her a look of constant abstraction. While he blinked away sleep, she shrugged a sleeveless dress over freckled shoulders.

Lacy wasn't much of a housekeeper. He noted a scattering of dead flies on the sunny windowsill. The makeup mirror on the side table, where, the night before, she had razored out skinny, precise lines of cocaine. A fifty-dollar bill lay on the carpet beside the bed, rolled so tightly it resembled a budding palm leaf or some bizarre stick-insect, a rust spot of dried blood on one end.

It was early fall, still warm in Constance, Minnesota. Balmy air turned gauzy curtains. Chris relished the sense of being in a place he had never been and to which he would in all likelihood never return.

"You're actually going to the Lake today, huh?"

He reclaimed his watch from a stack of the print edition of *People* on the nightstand. He had an hour to make his connection. "Actually going there." He wondered how much he had said to this woman last night.

"You want breakfast?"

"I don't think I have time."

She seemed relieved. "That's okay. It was really exciting meeting you. I know lots of people who work at the Lake but they're mostly support staff or retail. I never met anybody who was in on the big stuff."

"I'm not in on the big stuff. I'm just a journalist."

"Don't undersell yourself."

"I had a good time too."

"You're sweet," she said. "You want to shower? I'm done in the bathroom."

The water pressure was feeble and he spotted a dead cockroach in the soap dish, but the shower gave him time to adjust his expectations. To ramp up whatever was left of his professional pride. He borrowed one of her pink disposable leg razors and shaved the ghostly image of himself in the bathroom mirror. He was dressed and at the door by the time she was settling down to her own breakfast, eggs and juice in the apartment's tiny kitchenette. She worked evenings; mornings and afternoons were her downtime. A tiny video panel on the kitchen table played an interminable daytime drama at half-volume. Lacy stood and hugged him. Her head came up as far as his breastbone. In the gentle embrace there was an acknowledgment that they meant essentially nothing to each other, nothing more than an evening's whim recklessly indulged.

"Let me know how it goes," she said. "If you're back this way."

He promised politely. But he wouldn't be back this way.

He reclaimed his luggage from the Marriott, where *Visions East* had thoughtfully but needlessly booked him a room, and caught up to Elaine Coster and Sebastian Vogel in the lobby.

"You're late," Elaine told him.

He checked his watch. "Not by much."

"Would it kill you to be punctual once in a while?"

"Punctuality is the thief of time, Elaine."

"Who said that?"

"Oscar Wilde."

"Oh, *there's* a great role model for you."

Elaine was forty-nine years old and immaculate in her safari clothes, a digital imager clipped to her breast pocket and a notebook microphone dangling from the left arm of her zirconium-encrusted sunglasses like a stray hair. Her expression was stern. Elaine was a working science journalist almost twenty years Chris's elder, highly respected in a field where he himself was lately regarded with a certain disdain. He liked Elaine, and her work was top-notch, and so he forgave her tendency to address him the way a grade-school teacher might address the kid who planted the whoopee cushion.

Sebastian Vogel, the third member of the *Visions East* expeditionary force, stood silently a few feet away. Sebastian wasn't really a journalist at all; he was a retired professor of theology from Wesleyan University who had written one of those books that becomes an inexplicable bestseller—*God & the Quantum Vacuum*, it was called, and it was that ampersand in place of the conventional "and," Chris suspected, that had made it acceptably fashionable, fashionably elliptical. The magazine had wanted a spiritual take on the New Astronomy, to complement Elaine's rigorous science and Chris's so-called "human angle." But Sebastian, who might be brilliant, was also terminally soft-spoken. He wore a beard that obscured his mouth, which Chris took as emblematic: the words that found their way out were sparse and generally difficult to interpret.

"The van," Elaine said, "has been waiting ten minutes."

The van from Blind Lake, she meant, with a young DoE functionary at the wheel, one elbow out the open window and a restless expression on his face. Chris nodded and tossed his luggage in back and took a seat behind Elaine and Sebastian.

It was past one in the afternoon, but he felt a wave of exhaustion sweep over him. Something to do with the September sunlight. Or last night's excesses. (The coke, although he had paid for it, had been Lacy's idea, not his. He had shared a couple of lines for the sake of companionability—more than enough to keep him buzzed nearly until dawn.) He closed his eyes briefly but refused himself the indulgence of sleep. He wanted a glimpse of Constance by daylight. They had come in late yesterday and all he had seen of the town was the Denny's, and later a bar where the local band played requests, and then the inside of Lacy's apartment.

The town had done its best to reinvent itself as a tourist attraction. As famous as the Blind Lake campus had become, it was closed to casual visitors. The curious had to make do with this old grain-silo and rail-yard hamlet, Constance, which served as a staging base for Blind Lake's civilian day employees, and where the new Marriott and the newer Hilton occasionally hosted scientific congresses or press conferences.

The main street had played up to the Blind Lake theme with more gusto than taste. The two-story brick commercial buildings appeared to date from the middle of the last century, yellow brick pressed from local river-bottom clay, and they might have been attractive if not for the wave of hucksterism that had overtaken them. The "lobster" theme was everywhere, inevitably. Lobster plush toys, holographic lobster window displays, lobster posters, lobster cocktail napkins, ceramic garden lobsters . . .

Elaine followed his gaze and guessed his thought. "You should have had dinner at the Mariott," she said. "Lobster fucking *bisque*."

He shrugged. "It's only people trying to make a buck, support their families."

"Cashing in on ignorance. I really don't get this whole lobster thing. They don't look anything at all like lobsters. They don't have an exoskeleton and God knows they don't have an ocean to swim around in."

"People have to call them something."

"People may have to call them something, but do they have to paint them onto neckties?"

The Blind Lake work had been massively vulgarized, undeniably so. But what bothered Elaine, Chris believed, was the suspicion that somewhere among the nearer stars some reciprocal act might be taking place. Plastic caricatures of human beings lolling behind glazed windows under an alien sun. Her own face, perhaps, imprinted on a souvenir mug from which unimaginable creatures sipped mysterious liquids.

The van was a dusty blue electric vehicle that had been sent from Blind Lake. The driver didn't seem to want to talk but might be listening, Chris thought, trying to feel out their "positions"—the public relations office doing a little undercover work. Conversation was awkward, therefore. They rolled out of town along the interstate and turned off onto a two-lane road in silence. Already, despite the lack of obvious markers beyond the PRIVATE ROAD—U.S. GOVERNMENT PROPERTY and DEPARTMENT OF ENERGY signs, they were in privileged territory. Any unregistered vehicle would have been stopped at the first (hidden) quarter-mile checkpoint. The road was under constant surveillance, visual and electronic. He recalled something Lacy had said: at the Lake, even the prairie dogs carry passes.

Chris turned his head to the window and watched the landscape scroll past. Dormant farmland gave way to open grassland and rolling meadows sprinkled with wildflowers. Dry country, but not desert. Last night a storm had rumbled through town while Chris sheltered with Lacy in her apartment. Rain had swept the streets clean of oil, filled the storm drains with soggy newsprint and rotting weeds, provoked a late blush of color from the prairie.

A couple of years ago lightning had ignited a brush fire that came within a quarter mile of Blind Lake. Firefighters had been shipped in from Montana, Idaho, Alberta. It had all looked very photogenic on the news feeds—and it emphasized the fragility of the fledgling New Astronomy—but the risk to the facility had never been great. It was just another case, the scientists at Crossbank had grumbled, of Blind Lake grabbing the headlines. Blind Lake was Crossbank's glamorous younger sister, prone to fits of vanity, hypnotized by the paparazzi. . . .

But any evidence of the fire had been erased by two summers and two winters. By wild grass and wild nettles and those little blue flowers Chris couldn't name. By nature's enviable talent for forgetting.

They had started at Crossbank because Crossbank should have been easier.

The Crossbank installation was focused on a biologically active world circling HR8832—second planet from that sun, depending on how you tallied up the ring of planetesimals circling half an AU inward toward the star. The planet was an iron-cored, rocky body with 1.4 times the mass of the Earth and an atmosphere relatively rich in oxygen and nitrogen. Both poles were frigid agglutinations of water ice at temperatures occasionally cold enough to freeze out CO_2, but the equatorial regions were warm, shallow seas over continental plates and rich with life.

That life was simply not glamorous. It was multicellular but purely photosynthetic; evolution on HR8832/B seemed to have neglected to invent the mitochondria necessary for animal life. Which is not to say that the landscape was not often spectacular, particularly the huge stromatolite-like colonies of photosynthetic bacteria that rose, often two or three stories tall, from the green sea-surface mats; or the fivefold symmetry of the so-called coral stars, anchored to the sea-beds and floating half-immersed in open water.

It was an exquisitely beautiful world and it had captured a great deal of public attention back when Crossbank was the only installation of its kind. The equatorial seas yielded stunning sunsets every 47.4 terrestrial hours on average, often with stratocumulus clouds billowing far higher than any on Earth, cloud-castles extracted from a Victorian bicycle ad. Time-adjusted twenty-four-hour video loops of the equatorial seascape had been popular as faux windows for a few years.

A beautiful world, and it had yielded a host of insights into planetary and biological evolution. It continued to produce extraordinarily useful data. But it was static. Nothing much moved on the second world of HR8832. Only the wind, the water, and the rain.

Eventually it had been labeled "the planet where nothing happens," a phrase coined by a *Chicago Tribune* columnist who considered the whole New Astronomy just one more federally funded font of gaudy but useless knowledge. Crossbank had learned to be wary of journalists. *Visions East* had negotiated at length to get Chris, Elaine, and Sebastian inside for a week. There had been no guarantee of cooperation, and it was probably only Elaine's rep as a solid science journalist that had finally sold the public relations staff. (Or Chris's reputation, perhaps, that had made them so difficult to convince.)

But the Crossbank visit had been generally successful. Both Elaine and Sebastian claimed to have done good work there.

For Chris it had been a little more problematic. The head

of the Observation and Interpretation Department had flatly refused to speak to him. His best quote had come from the kid in the cafeteria. *It could end at any time.* And even the kid in the cafeteria had finally leaned forward to eyeball Chris's name badge and said, "You're the guy who wrote that book?"

Chris had confessed that he was, yes, the guy who wrote that book.

And the kid had nodded once and stood up and carried his half-eaten lunch to the recycling rack without saying another word.

Two surveillance aircraft passed overhead during the next ten minutes, and the van's dashboard all-pass transponder began to blinking spastically. They had crossed any number of checkpoints already, well before they reached the steel and accordion-wire fence that snaked into the prairie in both directions, the steel and cinderblock guardhouse from which a uniformed officer stepped to wave them to a stop.

The guard examined the driver's ID and then Elaine's and Sebastian Vogel's, finally Chris's. He spoke into his personal microphone briefly, then supplied the three journalists with clip-on badges. At last he waved them through.

And they were inside. As simple as that, barring the weeks of negotiation between the magazine and the Department of Energy.

So far it was just one stretch of rolling wild grass separated from another by chain-link fence and barbed wire. But the entry was more than figurative; it carried, at least for Chris, a genuine sense of ceremony. This was Blind Lake.

This was practically another planet.

He looked back as the van gathered speed and saw the gate glide shut with what he would remember, much later, as a terrible finality.

Two

There really was a lake in Blind Lake, Tessa Hauser had learned. She thought about that as she walked home from school, following her own long shadow down the sparkling white sidewalk.

Blind Lake—the lake, not the town—was a muddy swamp between two low hills, full of cattails and wild frogs and snapping turtles, herons and Canada geese and stagnant green water. Mr. Fleischer had told the class about it. It was called a lake but it was actually a wetland, ancient water trapped in the stony, porous land.

So Blind Lake, the lake, wasn't really a lake. Tess thought that made a certain kind of sense, because Blind-Lake-the-town wasn't really a town, either. It was a National Laboratory, built here in its entirety, like a movie set, by the Department of Energy. That's why the houses and shops and office buildings were so sparse and so new and why they began and ended so abruptly in a vast and empty land.

Tess walked by herself. She was eleven years old and she hadn't made any friends at school yet, though Edie Jerundt (whom the other children called Edie Grunt) at least spoke to her once in a while. But Edie walked the other way home, toward the mallway and the administrative buildings; the tall cooling towers of Eyeball Alley, far away to the west, were Tessa's landmark. Tess—when she was with her father, at least, which was one week out of four—lived in one of a row of pastel-colored town houses pressed up one against the next like soldiers at attention. Her mother's house, though even farther west, was almost identical.

She had stayed twenty minutes late at school, helping Mr. Fleischer clean the boards. Mr. Fleischer, a man with a white-brown beard and a bald head, had asked her a lot of questions about herself—what she did when she was home, how she got along with her parents, whether she liked school. Tess had answered dutifully but unenthusiastically, and after a while Mr. Fleischer had frowned and stopped asking. Which was perfectly okay with her.

Did she like school? It was too early to tell. School had hardly started. The weather wasn't even cool yet, though the wind that brushed the sidewalk and flapped her skirt had a touch of autumn in it. You couldn't tell about school, Tess thought, until at least Halloween, and Halloween was still a couple of weeks away. By then you knew how it would be—for better or worse.

She didn't even know if she liked Blind Lake, the town-not-a-town near the lake-not-a-lake. Crossbank had been better, in some ways. More trees. Autumn colors. Snow on the hills in winter. Her mother had said there would be snow here, too, and plenty of it, and maybe this time she would make friends to go sledding with. But the hills seemed too low and gentle for proper sledding. Trees were sparse here, mostly saplings planted around the science buildings and the shopping concourse. Like trees imperfectly wished-for, Tess thought. She passed some of these on the lawns of the town houses: trees so new they were still staked to the earth, still trying to take root.

She came to her father's small house and saw that his car wasn't in the driveway. He wasn't home yet. That was unusual but not unheard-of. Tess used her own key to let herself inside. The house was ruthlessly tidy and the furniture still smelled new, welcoming but somehow unfamiliar. She went to the narrow, gleaming kitchen and poured herself a glass of orange juice from the refrigerator. Some of the juice spilled over the lip of the glass. Tess thought about her father, then took a paper towel and wiped the tiled counter clean. She deposited the balled-up evidence in the bin under the sink.

She carried her drink and a napkin into the living room, stretched out on the sofa, and whispered "Video" to turn on the entertainment panel. But there was nothing except static on any of the cartoon channels. The house had saved a couple of programs for her from yesterday, but they were dull ones— *King Koala, The Unbelievable Baxters*—and she wasn't in the mood. She guessed there must be something wrong with the satellite, because there was nothing else to see, either . . . only the closed-circuit feed from the downloads, Lobster City nighttime, the Subject motionless and probably asleep under a naked electric light.

Her phone buzzed deep in her schoolbag on the floor at her feet, and Tess sat up abruptly. A mouthful of orange juice went down the wrong way. She fumbled the phone out and answered, hoarsely.

"Tessa, is that you?"

Her father.

She nodded, which was useless, then said, "Yes."

"Everything okay?"

She assured him she was fine. Daddy always wanted to know whether she was okay. Some days he asked more than once. To Tess it always sounded like: *What's the matter with you? Is something wrong?* She never had an answer for that.

"I'm working late tonight," he said. "I can't take you to Mom's. You'll have to phone her and have her pick you up."

Tonight was the night she changed over to her mother's house. Tess had a room in each house. A small, neat one at Daddy's. A big messy one at her mother's. She would have to pack her school stuff for the change. "Can't you call her?"

"It's better if you do it, sweetie."

She nodded again; then said, "All right."

"Love you."

"You too."

"Keep your chin up."

"What?"

"I'll call you every day, Tess."

"Okay," Tess said.

"Don't forget to call your mother."

"I won't."

Dutiful, and undistracted by the blank video panel, Tess said good-bye, then whispered "Mom" at the phone. There was an interlude of insect sounds, then her mother picked up.

"Daddy says you have to come get me."

"He does, huh? Well—are you at his place?"

Tess liked the sound of her mother's voice even over the phone. If her father's voice was distant thunder, her mother's was summer rain—soothing, even when it was sad.

"He's working late," Tess explained.

"According to the agreement he's supposed to bring you. I have work of my own to finish up."

"I guess I can walk," Tess said, though she made no effort to conceal her disappointment. It would take her a good half hour to walk to her mom's place, past the coffee shop and the teenagers who gathered there and who had taken to calling her Spaz because of the way she jerked her head to avoid their eyes.

"No," her mother said, "it's getting late. . . . Just have your stuff together. I'll be there in, oh, I guess twenty minutes or so. 'Kay?"

"Okay."

"Maybe we'll get takeout on the way home."

"Great."

After she deposited the phone back in her schoolbag, Tess made sure she had all the things she needed to bring to Mom's: her notebooks and texts, of course, but also her favorite shirts and blouses, her plush monkey, her plug-in library, her personal night-light. That didn't take long. Then, restless, she put her stuff in the foyer and went out back to watch the sunset.

The nice thing about her Dad's place was the view from the yard. It wasn't a spectacular view, no mountains or valleys or anything as dramatic as that, but it looked out over a long stretch of undeveloped meadowland sloping toward the road into Constance. The sky seemed immensely large from here, free of any borders except the fence that encircled Blind Lake. Birds lived in the high grass beyond the neatly trimmed lawn, and sometimes they rose up into the huge clean sky in flocks. Tess didn't know what kind of birds they were—she didn't have a name for them. They were many and small and brown, and when they folded their wings they flew like darts.

The only man-made things Tess could see from her father's backyard (as long as she faced away from the mechanical line of the adjoining town houses) were the fence, the road that led across the rolling hills to Constance, and the guardhouse at the gate. She watched a bus driving away from Blind Lake, one of the buses that carried day workers home to their houses far away. In the fading dusk the windows of the bus were warm with yellow light.

Tess stood silently watching. If her father were here, he would have called her inside by now. Tess knew that she sometimes stared at things too long. At clouds or hills or, when she was in school, out the spotless window to the soccer field where white goalposts clocked the hours with their shadows. Until someone called her back to the world. *Wake up, Tessa! Pay attention!* As if she had been asleep. As if she had *not* been paying attention.

Times like this, with the wind moving the grass and curling around her like a huge cool hand, Tess felt the world as a second presence, as another person, as if the wind and the grass had voices of their own and she could hear them talking.

The yellow-windowed bus stopped at the distant guardhouse. A second bus pulled up behind it. Tess waited for the guard to wave the buses through. Almost a thousand people worked days at Blind Lake—clerks and support staff and the people who ran the stores—and the guard always waved the buses through.

Tonight, however, the buses stopped and stayed stopped.

Tess, the wind said. Which made Tess think about Mirror Girl and all the trouble that had caused her back at Crossbank. . . .

"Tess!"

She jumped involuntarily. The voice had been real. Her mother's.

"Sorry if I scared you—"

"It's okay." Tess turned and was pleased and reassured by the sight of her mother coming across the broad, neat lawn.

Tessa's mother was a tall woman, her long brown hair some-what askew around her face, her ankle-length skirt flirting with the wind. The setting sun turned everything faintly red: the sky, the town houses, her mother's face.

"You have your stuff?"

"At the front door."

Tess saw her mother glance away toward the distant road. Another bus had come up behind the first two, and now all three were motionless at the gate.

Tess said, "Is something wrong with the fence?"

"I don't know. I'm sure it's nothing." But she frowned and stood a moment, watching. Then she took Tessa's hand. "Let's go home, shall we?"

Tess nodded, suddenly eager for the warmth of her mother's house, for the smell of fresh laundry and takeout food, for the reassurance of small enclosed spaces.

Three

The campus of the Blind Lake National Laboratory, its scientific and administrative offices and supply and retail outlets, had been constructed on the almost imperceptibly gentle slope of an ancient glacial moraine. From the air it resembled any newly built suburban community, peculiar only in its isolation, served by a single two-lane road. At its center, adjacent to a partially enclosed retail strip called the mallway, was an O-shaped ring of ten-story concrete buildings, Hubble Plaza. This was where the interpretive work of the Blind Lake facility was done. The Plaza, with its narrow escutcheon windows and its grassy enclosed park, was the brain of the installation. The beating heart was a mile east of the inhabited town, in an underground structure from which two massive cooling towers rose into the brittle autumn air.

This building was officially the Blind Lake Computational Array, but it was commonly called Eyeball Alley, or the Alley, or simply the Eye.

Charlie Grogan had been chief engineer at the Alley since it had been powered up five years ago. Tonight he was working late, if you could call it "working late" when it was his regular custom to stick around well after the day shift had gone home. There was, of course, a night shift, and a supervising engineer to go with it (Anne Costigan, whose abilities he had come to respect). But it was precisely this relaxation of his official vigilance that made the after-hours shift rewarding. He could catch up on paperwork without risk of interruption. Better, he could go down into the hardware rooms or the O/BEC gallery and hang out with the hands-on guys in a non-official capacity. He enjoyed spending time in the works.

Tonight he finished filling out a requisition form and told his server to transmit it in the morning. He checked his watch. Ten to nine. The guys in the stacks were due for a break. Just a walk-through, Charlie promised himself. Then home to feed Boomer, his elderly hound, and maybe catch some downloads before bed. The eternal cycle.

He left his office and rode an elevator two levels deeper into the underground. The Alley was quiet at night. He passed no one in the sea-green lower-level hallways. There was only the sound of his footsteps and the chime of the transponder in his ID tag as he crossed into restricted areas. Mirrored doors offered him unwelcome reminders of his age—he had turned forty-eight last January—the creeping curvature of his spine, the paunch that ballooned over his belt buckle. A fringe of gray hair stood out against his dark skin. His father had been a light-skinned Englishman, taken by cancer twenty years ago;

his mother, a Sudanese immigrant and Sufi scholar, had survived him by less than a year. Charlie resembled his father more than ever these days.

He detoured through the O/BEC gallery—though, like "staying late," it was probably wrong to call it a "detour." This was one of the stations of his habitual nightly walk.

The gallery was constructed like a surgical theater without the student seating, a ring-shaped tiled hallway fitted with sealed glass windows on its inner perimeter. The windows overlooked a circular chamber forty feet deep. At the bottom of the chamber, serviced by columns of supercooled gases and bundles of light pipes and monitoring devices, were the three huge O/BEC platens. Inside each tubular platen were rank upon rank of microscopically thin gallium arsenide wafers, bathed in helium at a temperature of $-451°$ Fahrenheit.

Charlie was an engineer, not a physicist. He could maintain the machines that maintained the platens, but his understanding of the fundamental process at work was partial at best. A "Bose-Einstein Condensate" was a highly ordered state of matter, and the BECs created linked electron particles called "excitons," and excitons functioned as quantum gates to form an absurdly fast and subtle computing device. Anything beyond that *Reader's Digest* sketch he left to the intense and socially awkward young theorists and graduate students who cycled through Eyeball Alley as if it were a summer resort. Charlie's job was more practical: he kept it all working, kept it cool, kept the I/O smooth, fixed little problems before they became big problems.

Tonight there were four maintenance guys in sterile suits down in the plumbing, probably Stitch and Chavez and the new hands cycling through from Berkeley Lab. More people than usual . . . he wondered if Anne Costigan had ordered some unscheduled work.

He walked the circumference of the gallery once, then followed another corridor past the solid-state physics labs to the data control room. Charlie knew as soon as he stepped inside that something was up.

Nobody was on break. The five night engineers were all at their posts, feverishly scrolling systems reports. Only Chip McCullough looked up as Charlie came through door, and all he got from Chip was a glum nod. All this, in the few hours since his shift had officially ended.

Anne Costigan was here, too. She glanced up from her handheld monitor and saw him standing by the door. She held up a finger to the junior supervisor—*one second*—and strode over. Charlie liked this about Anne, her economy of motion, every gesture purposeful. "Christ, Charlie," she said, "don't you ever *sleep?*"

"Just on my way out."

"Through the stacks?"

"Came for coffee, actually. But you guys are busy."

"We had a big spike through the I/O's an hour ago."

"Power spike?"

"No, an *activity* spike. The switchboard lit up, if you know what I mean. Like somebody fed the Eye a dose of amphetamine."

"It happens," Charlie said. "You remember last winter—"

"This one's a little unusual. It settled down, but we're doing a systems check."

"Still making data?"

"Oh, yeah, nothing *bad*, just a blip, but . . . you know."

He understood. The Eye and all its interrelated systems hovered perpetually on the brink of chaos. Like a harnessed wild animal, what the Eye needed was not maintenance so much as grooming and reassurance. In its complexity and unpredictability, it was very nearly a living thing. Those who understood that—and Anne was one of them—had learned to pay attention to the small things.

"You want to stick around, lend a hand?"

Yes, he did, but Anne didn't need him; he would only get underfoot. He said, "I have a dog to feed."

"Tell Boomer hello for me." She was clearly anxious to get back to work.

"Will do. Anything I can get you?"

"Not unless you have a spare phone. Abe's out on the coast again." Abe was Anne's husband, a financial consultant; he made it to Blind Lake maybe one month out of three. The marriage was troubled. "Local calls are okay, but I can't get through to L.A. for some reason."

"You want to borrow mine?"

"No, not really; I tried Tommy Gupta's; his didn't work either. Something wrong with the satellites, I guess."

Strange, Charlie thought, how everything seemed to have gone just slightly askew tonight.

For the fifth time in the last hour, Sue Sampel told her boss she hadn't been able to put his call through to the Department of Energy in Washington. Each time, Ray looked at her as if she had personally fucked up the system.

She was working way late, and so, it seemed, was everybody else in Hubble Plaza. Something was up. Sue couldn't figure out what. She was Ray Scutter's executive assistant, but Ray (typically) hadn't shared any information with her. All she knew was that he wanted to talk to D.C., and the telecoms weren't cooperating.

Obviously it wasn't Sue's fault—she knew how to punch a number, for God's sake—but that didn't prevent Ray from glaring at her every time he asked. And Ray Scutter packed a killer glare. Big eyes with pinpoint pupils, bushy eyebrows, flecks of gray in his goatee . . . she had once thought he might be handsome, if not for his receding chin and slightly pouchy cheeks. But she didn't entertain that thought anymore. What was the expression? *Handsome is as handsome does.* Ray didn't *do* handsome.

He turned away from her desk and stalked back to his inner office. "Naturally," he growled over his shoulder, "I'll be blamed for this somehow."

Y^3, Sue thought wearily. It had become her mantra in the months she'd been working for Ray Scutter. Y^3: *Yeah, yeah, yeah.* Ray was surrounded by incompetents. Ray was being ignored by the research staff. Ray was thwarted at every turn. Yeah, yeah, yeah.

Once more, for good measure, she attempted the Washington connection. The phone popped up an error message: SERVER UNAVAILABLE. Same message came up for any phone, video, or net connection outside the local Blind Lake loop. The only call that *had* gone through was to Ray's own house, here in town—letting his daughter know he'd be late. Everything else had been incoming: Security, Personnel, and the military liaison.

Sue might have been worried if she'd been a little less tired. But it was probably nothing. All she wanted to do right now was get back to her apartment and peel off her shoes. Microwave her dinner. Smoke a joint.

The terminal buzzed again—according to the screen announcement, a call from Ari Weingart over at Publicity and Public Relations. She picked up. "Ari," she said, "what can I do for you?"

"Your boss around?"

"Present but not keen to be disturbed. Is this urgent?"

"Well, yeah, kind of. I've got three journalists here and nowhere to put them."

"So book a motel."

"Very funny. They're on a three-week pass."

"Nobody penciled this into your calendar?"

"Don't be obtuse, Sue. Obviously, they ought to be sleeping in the guest quarters in the Visitor Center—but Personnel filled those beds with day workers."

"Day workers?"

"Duh! Because the buses can't get out to Constance."

"The *buses* can't get out?"

"Have you been in an isolation booth the last couple of hours? The road's closed at the gatehouse. No traffic in or out. We're in total lockdown."

"Since when?"

"Roughly sunset."

"How come?"

"Who knows? Either a plausible security threat or another drill. Everybody's guessing it'll be sorted out by morning. But in the meantime I have to billet these folks somewhere."

Ray Scutter's reaction to the problem would be more indignant fuming, certainly nothing helpful. Sue thought about it. "Maybe you could call Site Management and see if they'll open up the gym in the rec center. Put in some cots for the night. How's that sound?"

"Fucking brilliant," Ari said. "Should have thought of it myself."

"If you need authority, cite mine."

"You're a gem. Wish I could hire you away from Ray."

So do I, Sue thought.

Sue stood and stretched. She walked to the window and parted the vertical blinds. Beyond the roofs of the worker housing and the darkness of the undeveloped grassland she could just make out the road to Constance, the lights of emergency vehicles pulsing eerily by the south gate.

Marguerite Hauser thanked whatever benevolent fate it was that had put her into a town house (even if it was one of the smaller, older units) on the northeastern side of the Blind Lake campus, as far as possible from her ex-husband Ray. There was something reassuring about that ten-minute drive as she took Tess home, closing space behind her like a drawbridge over a moat.

Tess, as usual, was quiet during the ride—maybe a little quieter than usual. When they picked up chicken sandwiches at the drive-through outlet in the commercial strip, Tess was indifferent to the menu. Back home, Marguerite carried the food and Tess hauled her tote bag inside. "Is the video working?" Tess asked listlessly.

"Why wouldn't it be?"

"Wasn't working at Daddy's house."

"Check and see. I'll put the food on plates."

Eating in front of the video panel was still a novelty for Tess. It was a habit Ray had not permitted. Ray had insisted on eating at the table: "family time," inevitably dominated by Ray's daily catalogue of complaints. Frankly, Marguerite thought, the downloads were better company. The old movies especially. Tess liked the black-and-white ones best; she was fascinated by the antique automobiles and peculiar clothing. *She's a xenophile*, Marguerite thought. *Takes after me.*

But Marguerite's video panel proved as useless as Ray's had presumably been, and they had to make do with whatever was in the house's resident memory. They settled on a hundred-year-old Bob Hope comedy, *My Favorite Brunette*. Tess, who would ordinarily have been full of questions about the twentieth century and why everything *looked* like that, simply picked at her food and gazed at the screen.

Marguerite put a hand on her daughter's forehead. "How do you feel, kiddo?"

"I'm not sick."

"Just not hungry?"

"I guess." Tess scooted closer, and Marguerite put an arm around her.

After dinner Marguerite cleaned up, put fresh linen on the beds, helped Tess sort out her schoolbooks. Tess flicked through the blue-screen entertainment bands in a moment of misplaced optimism, then watched the Bob Hope movie a second time, finally announced she was ready for bed. Marguerite supervised her toothbrushing and tucked her in. Marguerite liked her daughter's room, with its small west-facing window, the bed dressed in a pink fringed comforter, the watchful ranks of stuffed animals on the dresser. It reminded her of her own room back in Ohio many years ago, minus the well-meaning volumes of *Bible Stories for Children* her father had installed in the vain hope that they might provoke in her a piety she had conspicuously lacked. Tessa's books were self-selected and tended toward popular fantasy and easy science. "You want to read a while?"

"Guess not," Tess said.

"I hope you feel better in the morning."

"I'm okay. Really."

Marguerite looked back as she switched the light off. Tessa's eyes were already closed. Tess was eleven but looked younger. She still had that baby-fat cushion under her chin, the full cheeks. Her hair was darkening but still a dirty blond. Marguerite supposed a young woman was emerging from this childhood cocoon, but her features were still indistinct, difficult to predict.

"Sleep well," Marguerite whispered.

Tess curled into her comforter and arched her head against the pillow.

Marguerite closed the door. She crossed the hall to her office—a converted third bedroom—determined to get a little more work done before midnight. Each of her department heads had flagged video segments for her to review from the last twenty-four hours with the Subject. Marguerite dimmed the lights and queued the reports to her wall screen.

Physiology and Signalling was still obsessed with the Subject's lung louvers. "Possible Louver Gesturing in Social Interaction," the subhead proclaimed. There was a clip of the Subject in a food well conclave. Subject stood in the dim green light of the food well in apparent interaction with another individual. The Subject's ventral louvers, pale whitish slits on each side of his thoracic chamber, quavered with each inhalation. That was standard, and Marguerite wasn't sure what the Physiology people wanted her to notice until new text scrolled up. *The louver frills palpate in a distinct vertical pattern of some complexity during social behavior.* Ah. Yes, there it was in an enlarged subscreen. The louver frills were tiny pink hairs, barely visible, but yes, they were moving like a wheat field in the wind. For comparison there was an inset of Subject breathing in a non-social environment. The louver frills flexed inward with each breath but the vertical quaver was absent.

Potentially very interesting, Marguerite thought. She flagged the report with a priority notice, which meant Physiology and Signalling could send it up to the compilers for further analysis. She added some notes and queries of her own (*Consistency? Other contexts?*) and bumped it back to Hubble Plaza.

From the Culture and Technology group, screen shots of Subject's latest addition to his chamber walls. Here was the Subject, stretched to full height, his squat lifting legs erect as he used a manipulating arm and something that looked like a crayon to add a fresh symbol (if it *was* a symbol) to the symbol-string that adorned the walls of the room. This one was part of a string of sixteen progressively larger snail-shell whorls; the new one terminated with a flourish. To Marguerite it looked like something a restless child might doodle in the margin of a notebook. The obvious inference was that the Subject was writing something, but it had been established early on that the strokes, lines, circles, crosses, dots, etc., never repeated. If they were pictographs, the Subject had never written the same word twice; if they were letters, he had yet to exhaust his alphabet. Did that mean they were art? Perhaps. Decoration? Possibly. But Culture and Technology thought this latest string suggested at least some linguistic content. Marguerite doubted it, and she flagged the report with a priority that would stack it up on the peer-review desk with a dozen similar documents.

The rest of the backlog consisted of progress reports from the active committees and a couple of brief segments the landmarks survey team thought she might like to see: balcony views, the city stretching away beyond the Subject in a pastel afternoon, sandstone-red, layer on layer, like an empire of rusty wedding cakes. She stored these images to look at later.

She was finished by midnight.

She switched off her office wall and walked through the house turning off other lights until the soft dark was complete. Tomorrow was Saturday. No school for Tess. Marguerite hoped the satellite interface would be back up by morning. She didn't want Tess to be bored, her first day back home.

It was a clear night. Autumn was coming fast this year. Marguerite went to bed with the curtains parted. When she moved in last summer she had pushed her big, futile double bed close to the window. She liked to look at the stars before she fell asleep, but Ray had always insisted on keeping the blinds shut. Now she could indulge herself. The light of the crescent moon fell across a reef of blankets. She closed her eyes and felt weightless. Sighed once and was asleep.

Four

Ari Weingart, Blind Lake's PR guy, carried a big digital clipboard. Chris Carmody worried a little bit about that. He'd seldom had good experiences with people who carried clipboards.

Clearly, things weren't going too well for Weingart. He had met Vogel, Elaine, and Chris outside Hubble Plaza and escorted them to his small office overlooking the central plaza. They had been halfway through a tentative first-week itinerary when Weingart took a call. Chris and company retired to a vacant conference room, where they sat until well after sunset.

When Weingart returned he was still toting the dreaded clipboard. "There's been a complication," he said.

Elaine Coster had been simmering behind a months-old print edition of *Current Events*. She put the magazine down and gave Weingart a level stare. "If there's a problem with the schedule, we can work it out tomorrow. All we need right now is a place to unpack. And a reliable server. I haven't been able to get a link through to New York since this afternoon."

"Well, that's the problem. The facility is in lockdown. We have some nine hundred day workers with homes off-site, but they can't get out and I'm afraid they have a prior claim on the guest quarters. The good news is—"

"Hang on," Elaine said. "Lockdown? What are you talking about?"

"I guess you didn't run into this problem at Crossbank, but it's part of the security regs. If there's any kind of threat against the facility, no traffic is allowed in or out until it's cleared up."

"There's been a threat?"

"I'm assuming so. They don't tell me these things. But I'm sure it's nothing."

He was probably right, Chris thought. Both Crossbank and Blind Lake were designated National Laboratories, operated under security protocols that dated back to the Terror Wars. Even idle threats were taken terribly seriously. One of the drawbacks of Blind Lake's high media profile was that it had attracted the attention of a broad spectrum of lunatics and ideologues.

"Can you tell us the nature of the threat?"

"Honestly, I don't know myself. But this isn't the first time this has happened. If experience is any guide it will all be cleared up by morning."

Sebastian Vogel stirred from the chair where he had been sitting in sphinxlike repose for the last hour. "And in the meantime," he said, "where do we sleep?"

"Well, we've set up—cots."

"Cots?"

"In the gymnasium at the recreation facility. I know. I'm terribly sorry. It's the best we can do on short notice. As I said, I'm sure we'll have it all sorted out by morning."

Weingart frowned into his clipboard as if it might contain a last-minute reprieve. Elaine looked primed to explode, but Chris preempted her: "We're journalists. I'm sure we've all slept rough one time or another." *Well, maybe not Vogel.* "Right, Elaine?"

Weingart looked at her hopefully.

She bit back whatever she had been about to say. "I've slept in a tent on the Gobi Plateau. I suppose I can sleep in a fucking gym."

There were ranks of cots in the gym, some already occupied by displaced day workers overflowing from guest housing. Chris, Elaine, and Vogel staked out three cots under the basketball hoop and claimed them with their luggage. The pillows on the beds looked like deflated marshmallows. The blankets were Red Cross surplus.

Vogel said to Elaine, "The Gobi Plateau?"

"When I was writing my biography of Roy Chapman Andrews. *In the Footsteps of Time: Paleobiology Then and Now.* Admittedly, I was twenty-five. You ever sleep in a tent, Sebastian?"

Vogel was sixty years old. He was pale except for the hectic red of his cheeks, and he wore shapeless sweaters to disguise the awkward generosity of his stomach and hips. Elaine disliked him—he was a parvenu, she had whispered to Chris, a fraud, practically a fucking spiritualist—and Vogel had compounded the sin with his unfailing politeness. "Algonquin Park," he said. "Canada. A camping trip. Decades ago, of course."

"Looking for God?"

"It was a coed trip. As I recall, I was looking to get laid."

"You were what, a divinity student?"

"We didn't take vows of chastity, Elaine."

"Doesn't God frown on things like that?"

"Things like what? Like sexual intercourse? Not so far as I have been able to discern, no. You should read my book."

"Ah, but I did." She turned to Chris. "Have you?"

"Not yet."

"Sebastian is an old-fashioned mystic. God in all things."

"In some things more than others," Sebastian said, which struck Chris as both cryptic and typically Sebastian.

"Fascinating as this is," Chris said, "I'm thinking we should get some dinner. The PR guy said there's a place in the concourse that's open till midnight."

"I'm game," Elaine said, "as long as you promise not to pick up the waitress."

"I'm not hungry," Vogel said. "Go on without me. I'll guard the luggage."

"Fast, St. Francis," Elaine said, shrugging her jacket on.

Chris knew about Elaine's Roy Chapman Andrews biography. He had read it as a freshman. Back then she had been an up-and-coming science journalist, shortlisted for an AAAS Westinghouse Award, charting a career path he hoped one day to follow.

Chris's one and only book to date had also been a biography of a sort. The nice thing about Elaine was that she had not made an issue of the book's stormy history and seemed to have no objection to working with him. Amazing, he thought, what you learn to settle for.

The restaurant Ari Weingart had recommended was tucked between an interface store and an office-supply shop in the open-air wing of the mallway. Most of these stores were closed for the evening, and the concourse had a vaguely derelict aspect in the cooling autumn air. But the diner, a franchise Sawyer's Steak & Seafood, was doing a brisk business. Big crowd, lots of talk in the air. They grabbed a vinyl booth by the wide concourse window. The decor was chrome and pastel and potted plants, very late-twentieth-century, the fake reassurance of a fake antiquity. The menus were shaped like T-bones.

Chris felt blissfully anonymous.

"Good God," Elaine said. "Darkest suburbia."

"What are you ordering?"

"Well, let's see. The All-Day Breakfast? The Mom's Comfort Meat Loaf?"

A waiter approached in time to hear her name these offerings in a tone of high irony. "The Atlantic Salmon is good," he said.

"Good for *what*, exactly? No, never mind. The salmon will do. Chris?"

He ordered the same, embarrassed. The waiter shrugged and walked away.

"You can be an incredible snob, Elaine."

"Think about where we are. At the cutting edge of human knowledge. Standing on the shoulders of Copernicus and Galileo. So where do we eat? A truck stop with a salad bar."

Chris had never figured out how Elaine reconciled her close attention to food with her carefully suppressed middle-age spread. Rewarding herself with quality, he guessed. Sacrificing quantity. Balancing act. She was a Wallenda of the waistline.

"I mean, come on," she said, "who exactly is being snobbish here? I'm fifty years old, I know what I like, I can endure a fast-food joint or a frozen dinner, but do I really have to pretend the apple-brown-betty is crème brulée? I spent my youth drinking sour coffee from paper cups. I *graduated* from that." She added, "You will, too."

"Thanks for the vote of confidence."

"Confess. Crossbank was a washout for you."

"I picked up some useful material." Or at least one totemic quote. *It could end at any time.* Almost a Baptist piety.

"I have a theory about you," Elaine said.

"Maybe we should just eat."

"No, no, you don't escape the obnoxious old harridan quite as easily as that."

"I didn't mean—"

"Just be quiet. Have a breadstick or something. I told you I read Sebastian's book. I read yours, too."

"Maybe this sounds childish, but I'd really prefer not to talk about it."

"All I want to say is, it's a good book. You, Chris Carmody, wrote a good book. You did the legwork and you drew the necessary conclusions. Now you want to blame yourself for not flinching?"

"Elaine—"

"You want to flush your career away, pretending to work and not working and blowing deadlines and screwing waitresses with big tits and drinking yourself to sleep? Because you can totally do that. You wouldn't be the first. Not by a country mile. Self-pity is such an absorbing hobby."

"A man died, Elaine."

"You didn't kill him."

"That's debatable."

"No, Chris, it's *not* debatable. Galliano went over that hill either accidentally or as a willed act of self-destruction. Maybe he regretted his sins or maybe not, but they were *his* sins, not yours."

"I exposed him to ridicule."

"You exposed work that was dangerously shoddy and self-serving and a threat to innocent people. It happened to be Galliano's work, and Galliano happened to drive his motorcycle into the Monongahela River, but that's his choice, not yours. You wrote a good book—"

"Jesus, Elaine, how badly does the world need one more fucking *good book*?"

"—and a *true* book, and you wrote it out of a sense of indignity that was not misplaced."

"I appreciate you saying this, but—"

"And the thing is, you obviously got nothing useful from Crossbank, and what worries me is that you'll get nothing here, and blame yourself for it, and you'll blow off the deadline in order to conduct more efficiently this project of self-punishment you've embarked on. And that's so goddamn unprofessional. I mean, Vogel is a crackpot, but at least he'll produce copy."

For a moment Chris entertained the idea of getting up and walking out of the restaurant. He could go back to the gym and interview some of the stranded day workers. They would talk to him, at least. All he was getting from Elaine was more guilt, and he'd had enough, thank you.

The salmon arrived, congealing in drizzled butter.

"What you have to do—" She paused. The waiter dangled an enormous wooden pepper mill over the table. "Take that away, thank you."

The waiter fled.

"What you have to do, Chris, is stop acting like you have something to be ashamed of. The book you wrote, *use* it. If someone's hostile about it, *confront* them. If they're afraid of you because of it, use their fear. If you're stonewalled, you can at least write the story of *how* you were stonewalled and how it felt to walk around Blind Lake as a pariah. But don't blow this opportunity." She leaned forward, her sleeves dangling perilously close to the butter sauce. "Because the thing is, Chris, this is *Blind Lake*. Maybe the great unwashed public has only a vague notion of what goes on here, but we know better, right? This is where all the textbooks get rewritten. This is where the human species begins to define its place in the universe. This is the fulcrum of who we are and what we'll become."

"You sound like a brochure."

She drew back. "Why? You think I'm too wrinkled and cynical to recognize something genuinely awesome when I see it?"

"I didn't mean that. I—"

"For what it's worth, you caught me in a moment of sincerity."

"Elaine, I'm just not in the mood for a lecture."

"Well, I didn't really think you were in the *mood* for it. Okay, Chris. Do what you think is best." She waved at his plate. "Eat that poor assaulted fish."

"A tent," he said. "The Gobi Plateau."

"Well, sort of a tent. An inflatable habitat airdropped from Beijing. Rechargeable fuel cells, heat at night, all the satellite channels."

"Just like Roy Chapman Andrews?"

"Hey," she said. "I'm a journalist, not a martyr."

Five

To Marguerite's dismay, and Tessa's grave disappointment, video and download reception did not improve over the weekend. Nor was it possible to put a call or net connection through beyond the fenced perimeter of Blind Lake.

Marguerite assumed this was some new incarnation of Blind Lake's elaborate security protocols. There had been several such shutdowns back at Crossbank during the time Marguerite had worked there. Most had lasted only a few hours, though one such occasion (an unauthorized overflight that turned out to be nothing more than a private pilot who'd burned out both his nav chips and his transponders) had created a minor scandal and sealed the security perimeter for nearly a week.

Here at Blind Lake the shutdown was, at least for Marguerite, not much of an inconvenience, at least so far. She hadn't planned to go anywhere, and there was nobody on the outside to whom she urgently needed to speak. Her father lived in Ohio and called her every Saturday, but he was savvy about security issues and wouldn't worry unduly when he couldn't get hold of her. It was a problem for Tessa, however.

Not that Tess was one of those kids who lived in front of the video panel. Tess liked to play outside, though she mostly played alone, and Blind Lake was one of the few places on Earth where a child could wander unaccompanied with negligible fear of drugs or crime. This weekend, though, the weather wasn't cooperating. A crisp, sunlit Saturday morning gave way by noon to rolling asphalt-colored clouds and brief, violent squalls of rain. October sounding the horn of winter. The temperature dropped to a chilly ten degrees Centigrade, and although Tess ventured out once—to the garage, to root through a box of dolls not yet unpacked from the move—she was quickly back inside, shivering under her flannel jacket.

Sunday was the same, with wind gusting around the eaves troughs and piping through the bathroom ceiling vent. Marguerite asked Tess if there was anyone from school she'd like to play with. Tess was dubious at first but finally named a girl called Edie Jerundt. She wasn't certain about the spelling, but there were, thank goodness, only a few J's in the Blind Lake intramural access directory.

Connie Jerundt, Edie's mother, turned out to be a sequence analyst from Imaging who promptly volunteered to bring Edie over for a play date. (Without even asking Edie, who was, Marguerite had to assume, just as bored as Tess.) They arrived within the hour. Mother and daughter looked so much alike they might have been Russian dolls, one nesting comfortably inside the other, distinct only in their dimensions. Both were mousy and wide-eyed and tousle-haired, features softened by Connie's adulthood but concentrated, grotesquely, in Edie's small face.

Edie Jerundt had brought along a handful of recent downloads, and the two girls settled down immediately in front of the video panel. Connie stayed a quarter of an hour, making nervous conversation about the lengthy security shutdown and how inconvenient it was proving—she had hoped to make a trip into Constance for some early Christmas shopping—then excused herself and promised to stop by and pick up Edie before five.

Marguerite watched the two girls as they sat in the living room staring at the video panel.

The downloads were a bit babyish for Tess, *Panda Girl* adventures, and Edie had brought along those image-synched glasses that were supposed to be bad for your eyes if you wore for them for more than a few hours. Both girls flinched from the enhanced 3-D action sequences.

Apart from that they might have been alone. They sat at opposite ends of the sofa, inclined at contrasting angles against plump pillows. Marguerite felt immediately and obscurely sorry for Edie Jerundt, one of those girls designed by nature to be picked on and ostracized, arms and legs awkward as stilts, her grasp approximate, her words halting, her embarrassment perpetual and profound.

It was nice, Marguerite reflected, that Tess had befriended a girl like Edie Jerundt.

Unless—

Unless it was Edie who had befriended Tess.

After the downloads the girls played with the dolls Tess had liberated from the garage. The dolls were a motley bunch, most collected by Tess at outdoor flea markets back when Ray used to make weekend drives from Crossbank into the New Hampshire countryside. Sun-paled fashion dolls with strangely twisted joints and mismatched clothes; oversized baby dolls, a majority of them naked; a scattering of action figures from forgotten movies, arms and legs frozen akimbo. Tess tried to enlist Edie in a scenario (*this is the mother, this is the father; the baby is hungry but they have to go to work so this is the babysitter*), but Edie quickly grew bored and was reduced to parading the dolls across the coffee table and giving them nonsense monologues (*I'm a girl, I have a dog, I'm pretty, I hate you*). Tess, as if gently nudged aside, retired to the sofa and watched. She began to bump her head rhythmically against the sofa cushion. About one beat per second, until Marguerite, passing, steadied her head with her hand.

This ryhthmic bumping, plus a worrisome speech-delay, had been Marguerite's first clue that there was something different about Tessa. Not something *wrong*—Marguerite would not accede to that judgmental word. But, yes, Tess was different; Tess had some problems. Problems none of the well-intentioned therapists Marguerite had consulted were ever quite able to define. Most often they talked about idiosyncratic threshold-level autism or Asperger's Syndrome. Which meant: we have a labelled bin in which to toss your daughter's symptoms, but no real treatment.

Marguerite had taken Tess for physiotherapy aimed at correcting her clumsiness and "poor proprioception," had tried her on courses of drugs designed to modify her supply of serotonin or dopamine or Factor Q, none of which had made any perceptible change in Tess's condition. Which implied, perhaps, only that Tess had an unusual personality; that her skewed aloofness, her social isolation, were problems she would have to carry indefinitely or overcome as an act of personal will. Fooling with her neurochemical architecture was counterproductive, Marguerite had come to believe. Tess was a child; her personality was still a work-in-progress; she should not be drugged or bullied into someone else's notion of maturity.

And that had seemed like a plausible compromise, at least until Marguerite left Ray, until the trouble back at Crossbank.

There had not even been a newspaper this weekend. Usually it was possible to e-print sections of the *New York Times* (or most any other urban paper), but even that meager connection to the outside world had been clipped. And if Marguerite missed the papers, how the news junkies must be suffering! Cut off from the great global soap opera, left to simmer in ignorance about the Belgian Accords or the latest Continental Court appointment. The silence of the video panel and the periodic sputtering of the rain gave the afternoon a yawning lassitude, made Marguerite content to sit in the kitchen and leaf through old issues of *Astrobiology and Exozoology,* her attention fluttering mothlike over the dense text, until Connie Jerundt returned for Edie.

Marguerite rooted the girls out of Tess's room. Edie was sprawled on the bed, her feet against the wall, picking through Tess's shoebox of faux jewelery, ornamental combs, and tortoiseshell barrettes. Tess sat at her dresser, in front of the mirror.

"Your mom's here, Edie," Marguerite said.

Edie blinked her froggishly large eyes, then scurried downstairs to hunt for her shoes.

Tess remained at the mirror, twining her hair around her right forefinger.

"Tess?"

The hair made a glossy curl from fingernail to knuckle, then fell away.

"Tess? Did you have a good time with Edie?"

"I guess."

"Maybe you should tell her so."

Tess shrugged.

"Maybe you should tell her now. She's downstairs, getting ready to go."

But by the time Tess had loped down to the front door, both Edie and her mother were already gone.

By Monday, what had begun as a tedious inconvenience began to feel more like a crisis.

Marguerite dropped Tess off at school on her way to Hubble Plaza. The crowd of parents in the parking lot—including Connie Jerundt, who waved at Marguerite from her car window—boiled with rumors. Since there was no local emergency to account for the shutdown, something must have happened outside, something big enough to create a security crisis; but what? And why hadn't anyone been told?

Marguerite refused to take part in the speculation. Obviously (or at least it seemed obvious to Marguerite), the logical thing to do was to get on with the work at hand. It might not be possible to talk to the outside world, but the outside world was still providing Blind Lake's power and presumably still expected Blind Lake's people to go about their business. She kissed Tess good-bye, watched her daughter walk a long stochastic loop through the playground, and drove off when the bell sounded.

The rain had stopped but October had taken charge of the weather, a cold wind blowing out of a gem-blue sky. She was glad she had insisted on a sweater for Tess. For herself she had selected a vinyl windbreaker, which proved inadequate on the long hike from the Hubble Plaza parking facility to the lobby of the east wing. Snow before long, Marguerite thought, and Christmas coming, if you looked past the looming headland of Thanksgiving. The change in the weather made the quarantine that much more unsettling, as if isolation and anxiety had rolled in with the thin Canadian air.

As she waited for the elevator Marguerite caught a glimpse of Ray, her ex-husband, ducking into the lobby convenience shop, probably for his morning fix of DingDongs. Ray was a man of fiercely regular habits, one of them being DingDongs for breakfast. Ray used to go to amazing lengths to guarantee his supply, even during business trips or on vacation. He packed DingDongs in Tupperware in his carry-on luggage. A day without DingDongs brought out the worst in him: his petulance, his near-tantrums at the slightest frustration. She kept her eye on the shop entrance while the elevator inched down from the tenth floor. Just as the bell chimed, Ray emerged with a small bag in his hand. The DingDongs, for sure. Which he would devour, no doubt, behind the closed door of his office: Ray didn't like to be seen eating sweets. Marguerite pictured him with a DingDong in each fist, nibbling at them like a mad squirrel, dribbling crumbs over his starched white shirt and funereal tie. She stepped into the elevator with three other people and punched her floor promptly, making sure the door closed before Ray could run for it.

Marguerite's own work—though she loved it and had fought hard to get it—sometimes made her feel like a voyeur. A paid, dispassionate voyeur; but a voyeur nonetheless.

She hadn't felt that way at Crossbank; but her talents had been wasted at Crossbank, where she had spent five years distilling botanical details from archival surveys, the kind of scutwork any bright postgraduate student could have done. She could still recite the tentative Latin binomials for eighteen varieties of bacterial mats. After a year there she had grown so accustomed to the sight of the ocean on HR8832/B that she had imagined she could smell it, smell the near-toxic levels of chlorine and ozone the photochromatic assays had detected, a sour and vaguely oily smell, like drain cleaner. She had been at Crossbank only because Ray had taken her there—Ray had worked administration at Crossbank—and she had turned down several offers to transfer to Blind Lake, mostly because Ray wouldn't countenance the move.

Then she had sucked up her courage and initiated the divorce, after which she had accepted this Obs position, only to discover that Ray had also had himself seconded to Blind Lake. Not only that, but he moved west a month *before* Marguerite was scheduled to do so, establishing himself as a fixture at the Lake and probably sabotaging Marguerite's reputation among the senior administrators.

Still, she was doing the work she had trained for, longed for: the closest thing to field astrozoology the world had ever seen.

She picked her way through the maze of support-staff desks, said hello to the clerks and secretaries and programmers, stopped by the staff kitchen to fill her souvenir Blind Lake lobster-motif cup with overcooked coffee and half-and-half, then closed herself into her office.

Paper covered her desk, e-paper littered her virtual desktop. This was work pending, most of it the kind of procedural checkmarking that was necessary but frustratingly tedious and time-consuming. But she could clean up some of that later, at home.

Today she wanted to spend time with the Subject. Raw time, realtime.

She closed the blinds over the window, dimmed the sulfur-dot ceiling lights, and illuminated the monitor that comprised the entire west wall of the office.

Good timing. UMa47/E's seventeen-hour day had just begun.

Morning, and the Subject stirred from his pallet on the warren's stone floor.

As usual, dozens of smaller creatures—parasites, sym-
biotes, or offspring—scuttled away from his body, where they
had been nursing at the sleeping Subject's exposed blood-
nipples. These small animals, no larger than mice, many-
legged and sinuously articulated, disappeared into gaps where
the sandstone walls met the floor. Subject sat up, then stood to
his full height.

Estimates put the Subject's height at roughly seven feet.
Certainly he was an impressive specimen. (Marguerite used
the masculine pronoun privately. She would never dare commit an assumption of gender in her official writing. The gender
and reproductive strategies of the aliens were still wholly unre-
solved.) Subject was bipedal and bilaterally symmetrical, and
from a great distance, in silhouette, he might have been mistaken for a human being. But there the resemblance ended.

His skin—*not* an exoskeleton, as the ridiculous "lobster"
nickname implied—was a tough, red-brown, pebble-textured
integument. Because of this dense moisture-conserving skin,
and because of the lung louvers exposed on his ventral surface
and such details as the multiple jointing of his legs and arms and
the tiny food-manipulating limbs that grew from the sides of
his mandibles, some had speculated that Subject and his kindred might have evolved from an insect-like form. One scenario pictured a strain of invertebrates attaining the size and
mobility of mammals by burying their notochord in a chiti-
nous spinal column while losing their hard carapace in favor of
a thick but lighter and more flexible skin. But little evidence
had emerged for this or any other hypothesis. Exozoology was
difficult enough; exopaleobiology was a daydream of a science.

Subject was clearly visible in the light cast by the string of incandescent bulbs suspended across the ceiling. The bulbs were small, more like Christmas lights than household lamps, but otherwise they seemed ridiculously familiar, *were* familiar: the filaments were of ordinary tungsten, spectroscopy had revealed. Dumb, rugged technology. At intervals, other aboriginals would arrive to replace exhausted bulbs and check the insulated copper wire for gaps or irregularities. The city boasted an elaborate, reliable maintenance infrastructure.

Subject did not dress nor did he eat; he had never been observed to eat in his sleeping quarters. He did pause to evacuate liquid waste over an open drain in the floor. The thick greenish liquid cascaded from a cloacal gap in his lower abdomen. There was, of course, no sound to accompany the image, but Marguerite's imagination supplied the splash and gurgle.

She reminded herself that these events had happened half a century ago. It lessened her sense of invasion. She would never speak to this creature, never interact with him in any way; this image, however mysteriously it had traveled, was in all likelihood limited to the speed of light. The parent star 47 Ursa Majoris was fifty-one light years from Earth.

(And by the same token, if anyone elsewhere in the galaxy were watching *her,* she would be safely in her grave long before her observers could attempt to interpret her bathroom functions.)

Subject left his warren without preamble. His two-legged gait looked awkward by human standards, but it covered ground efficiently. This part of the day could be interesting. Subject did essentially the same thing every morning—walked to the factory where he assembled machine parts—but he seldom took the same route to work. Enough evidence had accumulated to suggest that this was a cultural or biological imperative (i.e., most others did the same thing), perhaps out of an atavistic instinct to avoid predation. Too bad; Marguerite would have preferred to think of it as Subject's idiosyncrasy, an individual preference, a discernible choice.

In any case, the observation program tracked him precisely and predictably. When Subject moved, the apparent point of view (the "virtual camera," folks in Image Acquisition called it) followed him at a constant distance. Subject was centered in the screen but his world was visible around him as he traveled. He strode with others of his kind through the incandescently lit corridors of his warren, everyone moving in the same direction, as if the passages were one-way streets, though their "wayness" varied day by day. In a crowd, she had learned to identify Subject not just by the centrality of his image (he was sometimes, briefly, obscured from view) but by the vivid orange-yellow of his dorsal-cranial crest and the rounded contour of his shoulders.

She glimpsed daylight as he passed balconies and rotundas that opened to the air. The sky today was powdery blue. Lobsterville got most of its rain during the mild winter season, and it was high summer now, the very middle of the southern latitude's long dalliance with the sun. The planet possessed a gentle axial tilt but a very lengthy orbit around its star: it would be summer in the Subject's city for another two terrestrial years.

In summer it was more often dust than rain clouds that darkened the sky. UMa47/E was drier than the Earth; like Mars, it could generate vast electrically charged dust storms. There was always fine dust suspended in the atmosphere, and the skies were never as clear as a terrestrial sky. But today was calm, Marguerite surmised. Warm, judging by the flourish of the Subject's cooling cilia. The colored-chalk blue of the sky was as good as it got. (Marguerite blinked and imagined Arizona or New Mexico, cliffside pueblos in a still noon.)

At last the Subject emerged onto one of the broad exterior ways that wound down to the floor of the city.

The original high-altitude survey had identified no less than forty of these large stone cities, and twice as many significantly smaller ones, scattered across the surface of UMa47/E. Marguerite kept a globe of Subject's planet on her desk, the cities marked and named only by their latitude and longitude. (No one wanted to give them proper names for fear of seeming arrogant or anthropocentric—"Lobsterville" was only a nickname, and you learned not to use it in front of administrators or the press.)

Maybe it was even an error of attribution to call this community a "city." But it looked like a city to Marguerite, and she loved the sight of it.

There were over a thousand sandstone ziggurats in the city, and each one was enormous. As the Subject wound his way downward—his sleeping chamber was high up this particular structure—Marguerite's view was panoramic. The towers were all very similar, nautilus-shell spires coiling upward from red tiled plazas, the industrial structures distinguished by the smokestacks erupting from their peaks and the streams of light or dark smoke dispersing in the still air. All over the city, freshly wakened natives filled the external ways and crowded the open spaces. The sun, rapidly rising, sent fingers of yellow light down the east-facing canyons. Beyond the city Marguerite glimpsed irrigated agricultural lands; beyond that, brown scrubland and a horizon jagged with distant mountains. (And if she closed her eyes she could see the afterimage lingering in contrary colors as if unmediated by a billion dollars' worth of incomprehensible technology, as if she were actually there, breathing the thin atmosphere, fine dust burning her nostrils.)

Subject reached ground level, walked on through parallel

bands of light and shadow to the industrial tower where he spent his days.

Marguerite watched, ignoring her desk work. She was not a primary viewer nor was it likely she would notice anything pertinent that the five focal committees had missed. Her job was to integrate their observations, not to make her own. But that could wait at least until after lunch. The security shutdown meant that exterior agencies couldn't read her reports in any case. She was free to watch.

Free, if she wanted, to dream.

She grabbed lunch at the Plaza's west-wing staff cafeteria. Ray wasn't there, but she caught a glimpse of his assistant Sue Sampel picking up coffee at the checkout. Marguerite had met Sue only once or twice but felt genuinely sorry for her. She knew how Ray treated his employees. Even back at Crossbank, Ray's staff had cycled pretty quickly. Sue had probably already applied for a transfer. Or soon would. Marguerite waved; Sue absently nodded back.

After lunch Marguerite buckled down to her paperwork. She vetted a particularly interesting report from a Physiology team leader who had put a thousand hours of video through a graphics processor, marking the motile parts of Subject's body and correlating its changes with time of day and situation. This approach had yielded surprising amounts of hard data, which would need to go out to all the other divisions in a high-priority FYI bulletin. She'd have to compose it herself, with input from Bob Corso and Felice Kawakami of Physiology whenever they got back from the Cancun conference . . . a bullet-point summary, she supposed, with hints for follow-up, keeping it as succinct as possible so the various team bosses wouldn't bitch about the added infoload.

She kept Subject on the wall panel so she could look up from her work and see the Subject doing his. Subject worked in what was almost certainly a factory. He stood at a pedestal in a vast enclosed space under a spotlight that illuminated his station. Similar beams of light demarked similar aboriginals, hundreds of them, arrayed behind him like phosphorescent pillars in a gloomy cavern. Subject took modular parts (cylindrical devices as yet unidentified) from a bin at the side of the pillar and inserted them into prepunched disks. The disks rose from a chamber in his pedestal on an elevated platform and subsided again once he had completed them. The cycle repeated every ten minutes or so. To call it monotonous, Marguerite thought, was pushing the limits of understatement.

But something had caught her attention.

Because the Subject was more or less stationary, the virtual camera had rotated to image him head-on. She could see Subject's face, stark in the overhead light. If you could call it a face. People had called it "horrifying," but it wasn't, of course; only intensely unfamiliar. Shocking at first because one recognized some of the component parts (the eyes, for instance, which sat in cups of bone like human eyes, though they were white through and through) while other features (the feeding arms, the mandibles) were insectile or otherwise unfamiliar. But you learned to transcend those distressing first impressions. More disturbing was the inability to see past them. To see *meaning*. Humans were wired to recognize human emotion reflected in human faces, and with some skill a researcher could learn to understand the expressions of apes or wolves. But Subject's face defied interpretation.

His hands, though—

They *were* hands, disturbingly humanlike. The long, flexible fingers numbered three, and the "thumb" was a fixed bony protruberance erupting from the wrist. But all the parts made instant sense. You could imagine grasping something with those hands. They moved in a fast, familiar fashion.

Marguerite watched them work.

Were they trembling?

It seemed to Marguerite that the Subject's hands were trembling.

She forwarded a quick note to the Physiology team:

> Tremor in Subject's hands? Looked like it (3:30 this P.M. on direct feeds). Let me know. M.

Then she went back to her own work. It was pleasant, somehow, tapping at her keyboard with the image of the Subject over her shoulder. As if they were working together. As if she had company. As if she had a friend.

She picked up Tess on the way home.

It was a gym day, and on gym days Tess inevitably left school with her blouse buttoned off-kilter or her shoes untied. Today was no exception. But Tess was subdued, huddling against the autumn chill in the passenger seat, and Marguerite said nothing about her clothes. "Everything okay?"

"I guess," Tess said.

"From what I hear, the data pipes are still shut down. No video tonight."

"We watch *Sunshine City* on Mondays."

"Yeah, but not tonight, sweetie."

"I have a book to read," Tess volunteered.

"That's good. What are you reading?"

"A thing about astronomy."

Home, Marguerite fixed dinner while Tess played in her room. Dinner was a frozen chicken entree from the Blind Lake grocery store. Dull but expedient and within the range of Marguerite's limited culinary skills. The chicken was rotating in the microsteamer when her phone buzzed.

Marguerite dug the talkpiece out of her shirt pocket. "Yes?"

"Ms. Hauser?"

"Speaking."

"Sorry to bother you so close to dinnertime. This is Bernie Fleischer—Tessa's homeroom teacher."

"Right." Marguerite disguised the sudden queasiness she felt. "We met in September."

"I was wondering whether you might be able to stop by and have a talk sometime this week."

"Is there a problem with Tess?"

"Not a problem as such. I just thought we should touch base. We can talk about it in more detail when we get together."

Marguerite set a date and replaced the phone in her pocket.

Please, she thought. Please, don't let it be happening again.

Six

School ended early on Wednesday.

The final bell rang at 1:30, so that the teachers could hold some kind of meeting. It had been homeroom all morning, Mr. Fleischer talking about wetlands and geography and the different kinds of birds and animals that lived around here; and Tess, although she had stared out the window most of the time, had been listening closely. Blind Lake (the lake, not the town) sounded fascinating, at least the way Mr. Fleischer described it. He had talked about the sheet of ice that had covered this part of the world, thousands upon thousands of years ago. That in itself had been intriguing. Tess had heard of the Ice Age, of course, but she had not quite grasped that it had happened *here*, that the land right under the school's foundations had once been buried in an unbearable weight of ice; that the glaciers, advancing, had pushed rocks and soil before them like vast plows, and, retreating, had filled the land's declivities and depressions with ancient water.

Today was cloudy and cool but not rainy or unpleasant. Tess, with the afternoon before her like an unopened gift, decided to visit the wetlands, the original Blind Lake. She came across Edie Jerundt in the playground and asked whether she'd like to go too. Edie, punching a tetherball, frowned and said, "Unh-uh." The tetherball chimed dully against its metal post. Tess shrugged and walked away.

The ice had been here ten thousand years ago, Mr. Fleischer had said. Ten thousand summers, growing cooler if you imagined travelling backward toward the glaciers. Ten thousand winters merging into winter uninterrupted. She wondered what it had been like when the world had just begun to warm, glaciers retreating to reveal the land underneath ("ground moraine," Mr. Fleischer had said; "washboard moraine," whatever that meant), far-carried soil dropped from the ice to block bedrock valleys and muddy the new rivers and make fresh sod for the grasslands. Maybe everything had smelled like spring back then, Tess thought. Maybe it had smelled that way for years at a time, smelled like muck and rot and new things growing.

And long before that, before the Ice Age, had there been a global autumn? There must have been. Tess was sure of it. A whole world made like right now, she thought, with patches of frost in the morning and being able to see your breath when you walked to school.

She knew the wetlands lay beyond the paved spaces of town and at least a mile east, past the cooling towers of Eyeball Alley, and farther on beyond the low hill where (Edie Jerundt had told her) there was sledding in winter but the older kids were mean and would crash into you unless you came with an adult.

It was a long walk. She followed the sidewalkless access road that led east from the town houses toward the Alley, turning aside when she reached the perimeter of that cluster of buildings. Tess had never been inside Eyeball Alley, though she had been on a school tour of the similar building back at Crossbank. To be honest, she was a little scared of the Alley. Her mother said it was just like the one at Crossbank—a duplicate of it, in fact—and Tess had not liked those deep enclosed corridors or the huge racks of O/BEC platens or the loud cryopumps that kept them cold. All these things frightened her, more so because her then-teacher Mrs. Flewelling kept saying that these machines and processes were "not well understood."

She understood, at least, that images of the ocean planet at Crossbank and Lobsterville here at the Lake were generated at these places, at Eyeball Alley or what they had called at Crossbank the Big Eye. From these structures arose great mysteries. Tess had never been much impressed with the images themselves, the Subject's static life or the even more static ocean views—they made boring video—but when she was in the mood she could stare at them the way she might stare out a window, feeling the exquisite strangeness of daylight on another planet.

The cooling towers at Eyeball Alley emitted faint trails of steam into the afternoon air. Clouds moved above them like nervous herd animals. Tess skirted the building, keeping well clear of its perimeter fences. She cut west along a trail through the wild grass, one of the innumerable trails that had been scythed into the prairie by Blind Lake's children. She buttoned the collar of her jacket against a rising wind.

By the time she reached the top of the sledding hill she was already footsore and ready to turn back, but her first view of the wetlands fascinated her.

Beyond the hill and past a grassy perimeter lay Blind Lake, a "semipermanent wetland," Mr. Fleischer had said, a square mile of watery meadow and shallow marshes. The land was overgrown with humps of grass and broad stands of cattails, and in the patches of open water she could see resting Canada geese like the ones that had passed overhead in noisy V-formation all this autumn.

Beyond that was another fence, or rather the same fence that surrounded all of the Blind Lake National Laboratory and the wetlands too. This land was enclosed, but it was also wild. It lay within the so-called perimeter of security. Tess, if she wandered into these marshes, would be safe from terrorist attack or espionage agents, though perhaps not from snapping turtles or muskrats. (She didn't know what a muskrat looked like, but Mr. Fleischer had said they lived here and Tess disliked the sound of the name.)

She walked downhill a little way farther, until the ground oozed under the pressure of her feet and the cattails loomed before her like brown sentinels with woolly heads. In a pool of still water to the left of her she could see her own reflection.

Unless it was Mirror Girl looking back at her.

Tess was barely willing to entertain that possibility even in the privacy of her own mind. There had been so much trouble back at Crossbank. Counselors, psychiatrists, all those endless and maddeningly patient questions she had been asked. The way people had looked at her; the way even her father and mother had looked at her, as if she had done something shameful without being aware of it. No, not that. Not again.

Mirror Girl had only been a game.

The problem was, the game had seemed real.

Not *real* real, the way a rock or a tree was real and substantial. But more real than a dream. More real than a wish. Mirror Girl looked just like Tess and had inhabited not only mirrors (where she had first appeared) but also empty air. Mirror Girl whispered questions Tess would never have thought to ask, questions she couldn't always answer. Mirror Girl, the therapist had said, was Tessa's own invention; but Tess didn't believe she could invent a personality as persistent and frequently annoying as Mirror Girl had been.

She risked another glance at the reflective water at her feet. Water full of clouds and sky. Water where her own face looked back at an oblique angle and seemed to smile in recognition.

Tess, said the wind, and her reflection vanished in a corrugation of ripples.

She thought of the astronomy book she had been reading. Of the deepness of time and space in which even an Ice Age was only a moment.

Tess, the cattails and the rushes whispered.

"Go away," Tess said angrily. "I don't want any more trouble with you."

The wind gusted and died, though the sense of unwanted presence remained.

Tess turned away from the suddenly forbidding wetlands. When she faced west she found the sun peeking out from a rack of cloud almost level with the hilltop. She glanced at her watch. Four o'clock. The house key she kept on a chain around her neck felt like a ticket to paradise. She didn't want to be out in this lonely wetness anymore. She wanted to be home, with this leaden knapsack off her back, curled into the sofa with something good on the video panel or a book in her hands. She felt suddenly doubtful and guilty, as if she had done something wrong just by coming here, though there were no rules against it (only Mr. Fleischer's passing remark that it was possible to get lost in the marshes and that the shallow water wasn't always as shallow as it looked).

A huge blue heron rose into the air from the rushes only a few yards away, cracking the air with its wings. It carried something green and wiggling in the vise of its beak.

Tess turned and ran to the top of the ridge, anxious for the reassuring sight of Blind Lake (the town). Wind whistled in her ears, and the shush-shush noise of her trouser legs brushing together sounded like urgent conversation.

She was comforted by the towers of the Alley as she hurried past them, comforted by the smooth blackness of the asphalt road as it wound into the town houses, comforted by the nearness of the tall buildings of Hubble Plaza.

But she didn't care for the sound of police-car sirens down by the south gate. Sirens always sounded to Tess like wailing babies, hungry and lonely. They meant something bad was happening. She shivered and ran the rest of the way home.

Seven

Wednesday morning, Sebastian Vogel joined Chris at one of the tiny makeshift tables in the community center cafeteria.

Breakfast consisted of croissants, watery scrambled eggs, orange juice, and coffee, free of charge to involuntary guests. Chris started with the coffee. He wanted a little neurochemical fortification before he even glanced at the steam table.

Sebastian ambled up and dropped a copy of *God & the Quantum Vacuum* on the tabletop. "Elaine said you were curious. I inscribed it for you."

Chris tried to look grateful. The book was a premium edition, printed on real paper and bound in boards, sturdy as a brick and about as heavy. He imagined Elaine suppressing a smile when she told Sebastian how "anxious" Chris was to read it. Sebastian must have carried a suitcase full of these into Blind Lake, as if he were on a promotional tour.

"Thanks," Chris said. "I owe you one of mine."

"No need. I downloaded a copy of *Weighted Answers* before the links were cut. Elaine recommends it highly."

Chris wondered how he could repay Elaine for this. Strychnine in her breakfast cereal, perhaps.

"She seems to think," Sebastian went on, "this security crisis may work to our advantage."

Chris leafed through Vogel's book, scanning the chapter heads. "Borrowing God," he read. "Why Genes Make Minds & Where They Find Them." The pernicious ampersand. "To our advantage how?"

"We see the institution in crisis. Especially if the lockdown goes on much longer. She says we can get past Ari Weingart's publicity machine and talk to some real people. See a side of Blind Lake that's never been explored in the press."

Elaine was right, of course, and for once Chris was ahead of her. For a couple of days now he had been interviewing the stranded day workers, getting their take on the security shutdown.

He hadn't needed Elaine's pep talk the other night. He knew this was in all likelihood his last chance to salvage his career as a journalist. The only question was whether he wanted to take it. As Elaine had also pointed out, there were other options. Chronic alcoholism or drug abuse, for instance, and he had come close enough to both of those to understand the attraction. Or he could take some inconspicuous job writing ad copy or tech manuals and slide into a sedate, respectable middle age. He wasn't the first adult to face diminished expectations and he didn't feel entitled to sympathy for it.

The assignment to Crossbank and Blind Lake had come

like a childhood dream too long deferred. A dream gone stale. He had grown up in love with space, had relished the images from the early NASA and EuroStar optical interferometers— tentative, crude pictures that had included the two gas giants of UMa47's system (each with enormous, complex ring systems) and the tantalizing smudge that was a rocky planet inside the habitable zone of the star.

His parents had indulged his enthusiasm but never really understood it. Only his younger sister Portia had been willing to listen to him talk about it, and she treated these discussions as bedtime stories. Everything was a story, as far as Portia was concerned. She liked to hear him talk about these distant and freshly envisioned worlds but always wanted him to go beyond the established facts. Were there people on these planets? What did they look like?

"We don't know," he used to tell her. "They haven't discovered that yet." Portia would pout in disappointment—couldn't he have made something up?—but Chris had acquired what he would later think of as a journalistic respect for the truth. If you understood the facts they needed no embroidery: all the wonder was already there, the more spellbinding because it was true.

Then the NASA interferometer had begun to lose signal strength, and the newly designed O/BEC devices, quantum computers running adaptive neural nets in an open-ended organic architecture, were enlisted to strain the final dregs of signal from noise. They had done more than that, of course. Out of their increasingly deep and recursive Fourier analysis they had somehow derived an optical image *even after the interferometers themselves ceased to function.* The analytic device had replaced the telescope it was meant to augment.

Chris was spending his last year at home when the first images of HR8832/B were released to the media. His family hadn't paid much attention. Portia by that time was a bright teenager who had discovered politics and was frustrated that she hadn't been allowed to go to Chicago to protest the inauguration of the Continental Commonwealth. His parents had withdrawn from one another into their own pocket universes—his father into woodworking and the Presbyterian church, his mother into a late-blooming bohemianism marked by Mensa meetings and Madras blouses, psychic fairs and Afghan scarves.

And although they had marveled at the images of HR8832/B they hadn't truly understood them. Like most people, they couldn't say how far away the planet was, what it meant that it orbited "another star," why its seascapes were more than abstractly pretty, or why there was so much fuss over a place no one could actually visit.

Chris had wanted desperately to explain. Another nascent journalistic impulse. The beauty and significance of these images were transcendent. Ten thousand years of humanity's struggle with ignorance had culminated in this achievement. It redeemed Galileo from his inquisitors and Giordano Bruno from the flames. It was a pearl salvaged from the rubble of slavery and war.

It was also a nine-day-wonder, a media bubble, a briefly lucrative source of income for the novelty industry. Ten years had passed, the O/BEC effect had proven difficult to understand or reproduce, Portia was gone, and Chris's first attempt at book-length journalism had been a disaster. Truth was a hard commodity to market. Even at Crossbank, even at Blind Lake, internecine squabbling over target images and interpretation had almost engulfed the scientific discourse.

And yet, here he was. Disillusioned, disoriented, fucked-over and fucked-up, but with a last chance to dig out that pearl and share it. A chance to relocate the beauty and significance that had once moved him nearly to tears.

He looked at Sebastian Vogel over the breakfast-stained plastic tabletop. "What does this place mean to you?"

Sebastian shrugged amiably. "I came here the same way you did. I got the call from *Visions East*, I talked to my agent, I signed the contract."

"Yeah, but is that all it is—a publishing opportunity?"

"I wouldn't say that. I may not be as sentimental about it as Elaine, but I recognize the significance of the work that goes on here. Every astronomical advance since Copernicus has changed mankind's view of itself and its place in the universe."

"It's not just the results, though. It's the process. Galileo could have explained the principle behind the telescope to almost anyone, given a little patience. But even the people who run the O/BECs can't tell you how they do what they do."

"You're asking which is the bigger story," Sebastian said, "what we see or how we see it. It's an interesting angle. Maybe you should talk to the engineers at the Alley. They're probably more approachable than the theorists."

Because they don't care what I told the world about Galliano, Chris thought. Because they don't consider me a Judas.

Still, it was a good idea. After breakfast he called Ari Weingart and asked him for a contact at the Alley.

"Chief engineer out there is Charlie Grogan. If you like, I'll get ahold of him and try to set up a meet."

"I'd appreciate it," Chris said. "Any new word on the lockdown?"

"Sorry, no."

"No explanation?"

"It's unusual, obviously, but no. And you don't have to tell me how pissed-off people are. We've got a guy in Personnel whose wife went into labor just before the gates closed Friday. You can imagine how happy he is about all this."   ·

His situation wasn't unique. That afternoon Chris interviewed three more day workers at the Blind Lake gym, but they were reluctant to talk about anything except the shutdown—families they couldn't reach, pets abandoned, appointments missed. "The least they could do is give us a fucking audio line out," an electrician told him. "I mean, what could happen? Somebody's going to bomb us *by phone?* Plus there are rumors starting to go around, which is natural when you can't get any real news. There could be a war on for all we know."

He could only agree. A temporary security block was one thing. Going most of a week without information exchange in either direction bordered on lunacy. Much longer and it would look like something truly radical must have happened outside.

And maybe it had. But that wasn't an explanation. Even in times of war, what threat could a web or video connection pose? Why quarantine not only the population of Blind Lake, but all their data conduits?

Who was hiding what, and from whom?

He intended to spend the hour before dinner putting his notes in some kind of order. He was beginning to imagine the possibility of a finished article, maybe not the twenty thousand words *VE* had asked for but not far short of it. He even had a thesis: miracles buried under the human capacity for indifference. The somnolent culture of UMa47/E as a distant mirror.

A project like this would be good for him, maybe restore some of his faith in himself.

Or he could wake up tomorrow in the usual emasculating fog of self-revulsion, the knowledge that he was kidding absolutely nobody with his handful of half-transcribed interviews and fragile ambitions. That was possible too. Maybe even likely.

He looked up from the screen of his pocket server in time to see Elaine bearing down on him. "Chris!"

"I'm busy."

"There's something happening at the south gate. Thought you might want to see."

"What is it?"

"Do I know? Something big coming down the road at slow speed. Looks like an unmanned vehicle. You can see it from the hill past the Plaza. Can that little gizmo of yours capture video?"

"Sure, but—"

"So bring it. Come on!"

It was a short walk from the community center to the crest of the hill. Whatever was happening was unusual enough that a small group of people had gathered to watch, and Chris could see more faces leaning into the windows of the south tower of Hubble Plaza. "Did you tell Sebastian about this?"

Elaine rolled her eyes. "I don't keep track of him and I doubt he's interested. Unless that's the Holy Ghost rolling down the road."

Chris squinted into the distance.

The sinuous road away from Blind Lake was easily visible under a ceiling of close, tumbling clouds. And yes, something was approaching the locked gate from outside. Chris thought Elaine was probably right: it looked like a big eighteen-wheel driverless freight truck, the kind of drone vehicle the military had used in the Turkish crisis five years ago. It was painted flat black and was unmarked, at least as far as Chris could tell from here. It moved at a speed that couldn't have been more than fifteen miles per hour—still ten minutes or so away from the gate.

Chris shot a few seconds of video. Elaine said, "You in good shape? Because I mean to jog down there, see what happens when that thing arrives."

"Could be dangerous," Chris said. Not to mention cold. The temperature had dropped a good few degrees in the last hour. He didn't have a jacket.

"Grow some balls," Elaine scolded him. "The truck doesn't look armed."

"It may not be armed, but it's armored. Somebody's anticipating trouble."

"All the more reason. Listen!"

The sound of sirens. Two Blind Lake Security vans sped past, headed south.

Elaine was spry for a woman of her age. Chris found himself hurrying to keep up.

Eight

Marguerite left work early Wednesday and drove to the school for her interview with Mr. Fleischer, Tessa's homeroom teacher.

Blind Lake's single school building was a long, low two-story structure not far from the Plaza, surrounded by playgrounds, an athletic field, and a generous parking lot. Like all of the buildings in Blind Lake, the school was cleanly designed but essentially anonymous—it might have been any school, anywhere. It looked much like the school at Crossbank, and the smell that greeted Marguerite when she stepped through the big front door was the smell of every school she had ever been inside: a combination of sour milk, wood shavings, disinfectant, adolescent musk, and warm electronics.

She followed the corridor into the west wing. Tess had entered grade eight this year, a step away from the hopscotch and Barbie crowd, tottering on the brink of adolescence. Marguerite had suffered through her own high school years, and still felt a conditioned wave of apprehension amidst these rows of salmon-colored lockers, though the school was largely empty—the students had been sent home early to allow for this round of parent-teacher interviews. She imagined Tess already at the house, maybe reading and listening to the hum of the floorboard heaters. *Home safe,* Marguerite thought a little enviously.

She knocked at the half-open door of Room 130, Mr. Fleischer's room. He waved her in and rose to shake her hand.

She didn't doubt Mr. Fleischer was an excellent teacher. Blind Lake was a flagship federal institution, and a key part of its employment package was the availability of a first-class school system. Marguerite was sure Mr. Fleischer's credentials were impeccable. He even looked like a good teacher, or at least the kind of teacher you could safely confide in: tall, somewhat doe-eyed, well but not intimidatingly dressed, with a trim beard and a generous smile. His grip was firm but gentle.

"Welcome," he said. The room was equipped with child-sized desks, but he had imported a pair of parent-friendly chairs. "Have a seat."

Funny, Marguerite thought, how awkward all this made her feel.

Fleischer glanced at a sheet of notes. "Good to meet you. Meet you again, I should say, since we were introduced at Tessa's orientation. You work in Observation and Interpretation?"

"Actually, I'm the department head."

Fleischer's eyebrows levitated briefly. "Here since August?"

"Tess and I moved here in August, yes."

"Tessa's father was here a little earlier, though, wasn't he?"

"That's right."

"You're separated?"

"Divorced," Marguerite said promptly. Was it paranoia, or had Ray already discussed this with Fleischer? Ray always said "separated," as if the divorce were a temporary misunderstanding. And it would be just like Ray to describe Marguerite as "working in Interpretation" rather than admit she was heading the department. "We have joint legal custody, but Tess is in my care the majority of time."

"I see."

Maybe Ray had failed to mentioned that, too. Fleischer paused and added a note to his files. "I'm sorry if this is intrusive. I just want to get a sense of Tessa's situation at home. She's been having some trouble here at school, as I'm sure you're aware. Nothing serious, but her marks aren't where we'd like them to be, and she seems a little, I don't know how to say it, a little *vague* in class."

"The move—" Marguerite began.

"No doubt that's a factor. It's like an army base here. Families move in and out all the time, and it's hard on the kids. The kids can be hard on newcomers, too. I've seen it far too often. But my concerns about Tess go a little bit beyond that. I had a look at her records from Crossbank."

Ah, Marguerite thought. Well, that was inevitable. Raking these old coals again. "Tess had some problems last spring. But that's all over now."

"This was during the process of the divorce?"

"Yes."

"She was seeing a therapist at that time, right?"

"Dr. Leinster, at Crossbank. Yes."

"Is she seeing anyone now?"

"Here at Blind Lake?" Marguerite shook her head decisively. "No."

"Have you thought about it? We've got people on staff who can provide absolutely first-rate counseling."

"I'm sure you do. I don't feel it's necessary."

Fleischer paused. He tapped a pencil against his desk. "Back at Crossbank, Tess had some kind of hallucinatory episode, is that correct?"

"No, Mr. Fleischer, that's not correct. Tess was lonely and she talked to herself. She had a made-up friend she called Mirror Girl, and there were times when it was a little hard for her to distinguish between reality and imagination. That's a problem, but it's not a *hallucination*. She was tested for temporal-lobe epilepsy and a dozen other neurological conditions. The tests were uniformly negative."

"According to her file, she was diagnosed with—"

"Asperger's Syndrome, yes, but that's not a terribly uncommon condition. She has a few tics, she was language-delayed, and she's not very good at making friends, but we've known that for some years now. She's lonely, yes, and I believe her loneliness contributed to the problem at Crossbank."

"I think she's lonely here, too."

"I'm sure you're right. Yes, she's lonely and disoriented. Wouldn't you be? Parents divorced, a new place to live, plus all the usual cruelties a child her age endures. You don't have to tell me about it. I see it every day. In her body language, in her eyes."

"And you don't think therapy would help her deal with that?"

"I don't mean to be dismissive, but therapy hasn't been a

huge success. Tessa's been on and off Ritalin and a host of other drugs, and none of them has done her any good. Quite the opposite. That should be in the file too."

"Therapy needn't involve medication. Sometimes just the talking helps."

"But it didn't help Tess. If anything it made her feel more unique, more alone, more oppressed."

"Did she tell you that?"

"She didn't have to." Marguerite discovered her palms were sweating. Her voice had tightened up, too. *That defensive whine of yours*, Ray used to call it. "What's the point, Mr. Fleischer?"

"Again, I'm sorry if this seems intrusive. I like to have some background on my students, especially if they're having trouble. I think it makes me a better teacher. I guess it also makes me sound like an interrogator. I apologize."

"I know Tess has been slow with her written work, but—"

"She comes to class, but there are days when she's, I don't know how to describe it—emotionally absent. She stares out the window. Sometimes I call her name and she doesn't respond. She whispers to herself. That doesn't make her unique, much less disturbed, but it does make her difficult to teach. All I'm saying is, maybe we can help."

"Ray's been here, hasn't he?"

Mr. Fleischer blinked. "I've talked to your husband—your ex-husband—on a couple of occasions, but that's not unusual."

"What did he tell you? That I'm neglecting her? That she complains about being lonely when she's with me?"

Fleischer didn't respond, but his wide-eyed look gave him away. Direct hit. Fucking Ray!

"Look," Marguerite said, "I appreciate your concern, and I

share it, but you should also know that Ray isn't happy with the custody arrangements and this isn't the first time he's tried to set me up, make me look like a bad parent. So let me guess: he came in here and told you how *reluctant* he was to raise the issue, but he was worried about Tess, what with all the problems back at Crossbank, and maybe she wasn't getting the kind of parental attention she deserves, in fact she'd said a thing or two to him . . . is that the gist?"

Fleischer held up his hands. "I can't get involved in this kind of discussion. I told Tessa's father the same things I'm telling you."

"Ray has an agenda of his own, Mr. Fleischer."

"My concern is with Tess."

"Well, I—" Marguerite restrained an urge to bite her lip. How had this gone so badly wrong? Fleischer was looking at her now with patient concern, *patronizing* concern, but he was a grade eight teacher, after all, and maybe that big-eyed frown was just a defensive reflex, a mask that slid into place whenever he was confronted with an hysterical child. Or parent. "You know, I, obviously, I'm willing to do whatever will help Tess, help her focus on her schoolwork . . ."

"Basically," Fleischer said, "I think we're on the same wavelength here. Tess missed a good deal of school at Crossbank—we don't want to repeat that."

"No. We don't. Honestly, I don't think it will happen again." She added, hoping it didn't sound too obviously desperate, "I can sit down with her, talk to her about being more thorough with her work, if you think that would be a good idea."

"It might help." Fleischer hesitated, then: "All I'm saying, Marguerite, is that we both need to keep our eyes open where Tess is concerned. Stop trouble before it happens."

"My eyes are all the way open, Mr. Fleischer."

"Well, that's good. That's the important thing. If I think we need to touch base again, can I call you?"

"Anytime," Marguerite said, ridiculously grateful that the interview seemed to be drawing to a close.

Fleischer stood up. "Thank you for your time, and I hope I didn't alarm you."

"Not at all." An outrageous lie.

"My door is always open if you have any concerns of your own."

"Thank you. I appreciate that."

She hurried down the corridor to the school door as if she were leaving the scene of a crime. Mistake to mention Ray, she thought, but his fingerprints were all over this encounter, and what a slick setup it had been—and how like Ray to use Tessa's problems as a weapon.

Unless, Marguerite thought, I'm kidding myself. Unless Tessa's problems went deeper than a mild personality disorder; unless the whole Crossbank circus was about to repeat itself . . . She would do anything to help Tess through this difficult passage, if only she knew *how* to help, but Tessa's own refractory indifference was almost impossible to breach . . . especially with Ray running interference, playing mind games, trying to position himself for some hypothetical custody battle.

Ray, seeing every conflict as a war and driven by his own dread of losing.

Marguerite pushed through the doors into autumn air. The afternoon had cooled dramatically, and the clouds overhead were closer, or seemed so in the long light of the sun. The breeze was frigid but welcome after the claustrophobic warmth of the schoolroom.

As she let herself into her car she heard the wail of sirens. She drove cautiously to the exit and stopped long enough to let a Blind Lake Security vehicle roar past. It looked like it was heading for the south gate.

Nine

Sue Sampel, Ray Scutter's executive assistant, tapped on his door and reminded him that Ari Weingart was scheduled for a meeting in twenty minutes. Ray looked up from a stack of printed papers and pursed his lips. "Thank you, I'm aware of that."

"Plus the guy from Civilian Security at four o'clock."

"I can read my own day planner, thanks."

"Okay, then," Sue said. *Screw you, too.* Ray was in a dark mood this Wednesday, not that he was ever sweetness-and-light. She supposed he was chafing under the lockdown like everybody else. She understood the need for security, and she could even imagine that it might be necessary (though God knows *why*) to make it impossible to place so much as a phone call outside the perimeter. But if this went on much longer people were going to get seriously PO'd. Many already were. The day workers, for sure, who had lives (spouses, children) outside the Blind Lake campus. But the permanent residents, too. Sue herself, for example. She lived in the Lake but she dated off-campus, and she had been anxious to get that all-important second phone call from a man she'd met at a Secular Singles group in Constance, a man her age, mid-forties, a veterinarian, with thinning hair and gentle eyes. She imagined him with a phone in his hand, gazing sadly at all those NO SIGNAL or SERVER UNAVAILABLE tags and eventually giving up on her. Another lost opportunity. At least this time it wouldn't be her fault.

Ari Weingart popped into the office at the appointed hour. Good old Ari: polite, funny, even *prompt*. A saint.

"The boss is in?" Ari asked.

"As luck would have it. I'll let him know you're here."

Ray Scutter's window looked south from the sixth floor of Hubble Plaza, and he was often distracted by the view. Usually there was a constant stream of traffic in and out of the Lake. Lately there had been none, and the lockdown had made his window view static, rendered the land beyond the perimeter fence as blank as brown paper, no motion but gliding cloud-shadows and the occasional darting flock of birds. If you stared long enough it began to look as inhuman as the landscape of UMa47/E. Just another imported image. It was all *surface*, wasn't it? All two-dimensional.

The lockdown had created a number of irritating problems. Not the least of which was that he appeared to be the senior civilian authority on campus.

His status in the Administration hierarchy was relatively

junior. But the annual NSI Conference on Astrobiology and Exocultural Science had been held in Cancun this weekend past. A huge delegation of academic staff and senior administrators had packed their swimsuits and left Blind Lake a day before the lockdown. Pull those names out of the flow chart and what remained was Ray Scutter floating over the various department heads like a loose balloon.

It meant that people were coming to him with problems he wasn't empowered to resolve. Demanding things he couldn't give them, like a coherent explanation of the lockdown or a special exemption from it. He had to tell them he was in the dark too. All he could do was carry on under the standing protocols and wait for instructions from outside. Wait, in other words, for the whole shitting mess to reach a conclusion. But it had already gone on for an uncomfortably long time.

He looked away from the window as Ari Weingart knocked and entered.

Ray disliked Weingart's cheery optimism. He suspected it disguised a secret contempt, suspected that under his hale-fellow exterior Weingart was peddling influence as enthusiastically as every other department head. But at least Weingart understood Ray's position and seemed more interested in coping than complaining.

If he could only suppress that smile. The smile bore down on Ray like a klieg light, teeth so white and regular they looked like luminous mahjong tiles. "Sit," Ray said.

Weingart pulled up a chair and opened his pocket desktop. Down to business. Ray liked that.

"You wanted a list of situations we'll have to address if the quarantine goes on much longer. I drew up some notes."

"Quarantine?" Ray said. "Is that what people are calling it?"

"As opposed to a standard six-hour lockdown, yeah."

"Why would we be quarantined? No one's sick."

"Talk to Dimi." Dimitry Shulgin was the Civilian Security chief, due here at four. "The lockdown follows an obscure set of regs in the military manual. He says it's what they call a 'data quarantine,' but nobody ever really expected it to come into effect."

"He hasn't mentioned this to me. I swear to God, he's like some fucking Slavic clam. What exactly is a 'data quarantine' meant to accomplish?"

"The regs were written back when Crossbank was just beginning to pull images. It's one of those paranoid scenarios from the congressional hearings. The idea was that Crossbank or Blind Lake might download something dangerous, obviously nothing physical, but a virus or a worm of some kind . . . you know what steganography is?"

"Data encrypted into photographs or images." He didn't remind Weingart that he, Ray, had testified at those hearings. Information warfare had been a hot topic at the time. The Luddite lobby had feared that Blind Lake might import some pernicious alien self-replicating digital program or, for God's sake, a deadly meme, which would then spread through terrestrial data routes wreaking unknowable havoc.

Wary as he often was of Blind Lake's groping into the unknown, the idea was preposterous. The aboriginals of UMa47/E could hardly know they were being spied on . . . and even if they did, images processed at the Lake had traveled, however mysteriously, at the conventional speed of light. It would need both an impossible perceptivity and a ridiculously patient desire for revenge for them to react in any hostile way. Still, he had been forced to admit, dangerous steganography was not an absolute impossibility, at least in the abstract. So a series of contingency plans had been written into the already immense web of security plans surrounding the Lake. Even though, in Ray's opinion, it was the biggest crock of astronomical shit since Girolamo Fracastoro's theory that syphilis was caused by the conjunction of Saturn, Jupiter, and Mars.

Had those bullshit edicts actually been called into effect? "One problem with that idea," he told Weingart. "No provocation. We haven't downloaded anything suspicious."

"Not yet, anyway," Weingart said.

"You know something I don't?"

"Hardly. But let's say if there was a problem at Crossbank—"

"Come on. Crossbank is looking at oceans and bacteria."

"I know, but if—"

"And we're imaging completely different targets in any case. Their work doesn't reflect on ours."

"No, but if there was a problem with the *process* somehow—"

"Something endemic to the Eye, you mean?"

"If there was some kind of problem with the O/BECs at Crossbank, DoE or the military might have decided to put us under a precautionary quarantine."

"They could at least have warned us."

"Information jamming is two-way. No in, no out. We have to assume they don't want so much as a carrier wave getting through."

"That doesn't preclude a warning."

"Unless they were in a hurry."

"This is ridiculously speculative, and I hope you and Shulgin haven't been spreading it around. Rumors can cause panic."

Weingart looked like he wanted to say something, but bit it back.

"Anyway," Ray said, "it's out of our hands. The pressing question is what we can do for ourselves until somebody unbuttons the fence."

Weingart nodded and began to read from his list. "Supplies. We pipe in our drinking water, and that hasn't been interrupted, but without intervention we'll run short of some foodstuffs before the end of the week and face a starvation-level crisis by the end of November. I'm assuming we'll be resupplied, but it might be a good idea to segregate our surplus and maybe even post guards over it in the meantime."

"I can't imagine this . . . *siege* . . . going on until Thanksgiving."

"Well, but we're talking 'what-if' here—"

"All right, all right. What else?"

"Medical supplies, same deal, and the on-campus clinic isn't set up to deal with serious or widespread illness or injuries. If we had a fire we'd have to ship burn victims to a major hospital or suffer needless fatalities. Not much we can do about that, either, except ask the medical staff to make contingency plans. Plus, if the quarantine is prolonged, people are going to need emotional counselling. We already have some folks with urgent family matters on the outside."

"They'll live."

"Lodging. There are a couple hundred day workers sleeping in the gym, not to mention visiting journalists, a handful of contractors, and anybody who happened to be here on a day pass. Long-term, if this *is* a long-term quarantine, it might be better to see if we can billet those people out. There are people living on-campus who have spare rooms or guest quarters available, and it wouldn't be hard to round up volunteers. With a little luck we could have everybody sleeping on a bed, or at least a pullout sofa. Sharing bathrooms instead of fighting over the showers at the community center and lining up for the jakes."

"Look into it," Ray said. After a moment's thought he added, "Put together a list of volunteers, but bring it to me before you talk to them. And we'll have to compile an inventory of day workers and guests to go with it."

There was more of this—minutiae that could be easily delegated, for the most part, all predicated on a prolonged lockdown Ray couldn't seriously envision. A month of this? *Three* months? It was unimaginable. His certainty was tempered only by the nagging fact that the lockdown had already gone on an unreasonably long time.

Sue Sampel tapped at the door while Weingart was summing up. "We're not finished," Ray called out.

She leaned into the room. "I know, but—"

"If Shulgin is here, he can wait a few minutes."

"He's not here, but he called to cancel. He's headed down to the south gate."

"The south gate? What's so fucking important about the south gate?"

She smiled infuriatingly. "He said you'd understand if you took a look out your window."

The huge eighteen-wheeled vehicle—powder-black and heavily armored—crawled along the road toward Blind Lake like an immense pill bug, timid for all its layered defenses. Where the driver's cab should have been there was only a blunt cone fitted with sensors. The truck was reading the road, gauging its location according to buried transponders and GPS numbers. There was no human driver. The truck was driving itself.

By the time Chris and Elaine neared the south gate the road was already mobbed with off-duty day workers and office staff and a gaggle of high school kids. A pair of Civilian Security vans pulled up and discharged a dozen men in gray uniforms, who began waving the crowd back to what they deemed a safe distance.

The fence surrounding Blind Lake's innermost perimeter was a state-of-the-art "containment device," Elaine had told Chris. Its posts were reinforced alloy cores sunk deep into the earth; its chains and links were carbon composites stronger than steel, their exposed surfaces slicker than Teflon and studded with sensors; atop all this was a double concertina of razor wire inclined at ninety degrees. The whole thing could be electrified to a lethal voltage.

The gate that barred the road was hinged to swing open on a signal from the guardhouse or from a coded transponder. The guardhouse itself was a concrete bunker with slit windows, sturdy as bedrock but currently vacant; the resident guard had been pulled out when the lockdown went into effect.

Chris wormed his way to the front of the crowd, Elaine following with her hands on his shoulders. At last they came up against the highway barriers the security men were muscling into place. Elaine pointed out a car just arriving: "Isn't that Ari Weingart? And I think the guy with him is Raymond Scutter."

Chris took note of the face. Ray Scutter was an interesting story. Fifteen years ago he had been a prominent critic of astrobiology, "the science of wishful thinking." The Martian disappointment had lent Ray's point of view a great deal of credibility, at least until the Terrestrial Planet Finders began to yield interesting results. The Crossbank/Blind Lake breakthroughs had made his pessimism look shortsighted and mean-spirited, but Ray Scutter had survived through a combination of graceful backpedalling and a convert's enthusiasm. The genuinely solid contributions he made to the first wave of geological and atmospheric surveys had not only rescued his career but allowed him to move up through the bureaucracy to important administrative positions at Crossbank and now the Lake. Ray Scutter would have made an interesting subject, Chris thought, but he was supposed to be hard to approach, and his public pronouncements were so predictably banal that better journalists than Chris had written him off as a lost cause.

Right now he was scowling, butting heads with the Security chief. Chris couldn't hear the conversation but he zoomed in his pocket recorder and archived a few seconds of video. Just a few, though. He was saving the bulk of the memory for the apparently inevitable collision of the robotic truck with the gate.

The truck had crept to within a hundred yards of the guardhouse. It looked unstoppably massive.

Elaine shaded her eyes and stared intently along the line of the fence. The setting sun had come under a rack of cloud and spilled a raking light across the prairie. She put her mouth against Chris's ear: "Am I seeing things, or are there pocket drones out there?"

Startled, Chris followed her line of sight.

Bob Krafft, a contractor who had come into Blind Lake with a team of engineers to survey the high ground east of the Alley for the construction of new housing, had spotted the truck shortly after noon, when it was still a pea-sized dot on the wide southern horizon.

He had done some time in the Turkish wars and he recognized it as the kind of driverless resupply vehicle more commonly found in a combat zone. But the truck didn't alarm him. Quite the opposite. Incongruous as it might be, the truck was still inbound traffic. Which meant the south gate would have to swing open to admit it. And that was a golden opportunity. He knew immediately what he had to do.

He found his wife Courtney among the cots set up in the Blind Lake gymnasium where they had languished for most of a week. He told her to wait right here but be ready to travel. She looked at him nervously—Courtney was nervous at the best of times—but kept her mouth shut and gave him a terse nod.

Bob walked two blocks (quickly, but not quickly enough to attract attention) to his car in the visitors' lot under Hubble Plaza. He got in, double-checked the charge gauge, sparked the motor, and drove at a deliberate speed back to the rec center. His pulse was up but his palms were dry. Courtney, wandering through the big front doors even though he had told her stay put, spotted him and climbed into the passenger seat. "Are we going somewheres?" she asked.

He had always hated this about her, her Missouri trailer-park grammar. There were days when he loved Courtney more than anything in the world, but there were also days when he wondered what had possessed him to marry a woman with no more culture than the raccoons who used to raid her trash. "I don't think we have a choice, Court."

"Well, I don't see what the hurry is."

With any luck she never would. Bob was quarter-owner of a respectably successful landscaping and foundation business operating out of Constance. Thursday morning—tomorrow morning—he was supposed to meet Ella Raeburn, a nineteen-year-old high school dropout who worked in reception, and drive her to the Women's Clinic in Bixby for a D&C. Although it was not Bob's fault that the vacuous Ella had neglected to use any form of birth-control or morning-after pill—unless you considered his predilection for brick-stupid women a fault—he did have to own up to responsibility for the condition she was in. So Thursday morning he would drive her to Bixby, buy her a few days in a motel to recuperate, write her a check for five thousand dollars, and that would be the end of it.

If he refused—or if this government-inspired Blind Lake fuck-up kept him confined here another day—Ella Raeburn would FedEx a certain video recording to Bob's wife Courtney. He doubted Courtney would divorce him over it—the marriage wasn't a bad deal for her, all in all—but she would hold it over his head for the rest of his life, the fact that she'd been treated to the sight of her own husband with his face buried between Ella Raeburn's generous young thighs. The video had been his own half-baked idea. He hadn't realized Ella would burn a copy for herself.

And that wasn't the worst of it. Not by half. If Bob failed to arrange for an abortion, Ella would be forced to throw herself on the mercy of her father. Her father was Toby Raeburn, a hardware salesman, a deacon at the Lutheran church, and a part-time basketball coach. His nickname was "Teeth," because he had once knocked out the left bicuspid of a would-be car thief and then had the souvenir embedded in Lucite so he could carry it around as a good-luck charm. Toby "Teeth" Raeburn might be willing to extend Christian forgiveness to his daughter, but surely not to a middle-aged contractor who (as Ella would mention) had introduced her to the barbiturates that always put her in a cooperative mood.

He didn't bear Ella Raeburn any particular grudge over the matter. He was more than willing to pay for her D&C. She was dumb as a bag of hammers, but she knew how to look out for herself. He kind of admired that.

Courtney had been one of those before he married her. She had dulled down into a perpetual sullen snit, though, and that wasn't the same.

"Did they call off the siege or something?" Courtney asked.

"Not exactly." He headed toward the south gate, reminding himself to maintain an inconspicuous speed. Certainly the black transport was in no hurry. It hadn't crept more than a quarter of a mile since he'd first spotted it, judging by the view from the rise past the Plaza.

"Well, *what*, then? We can't just leave."

"Technically, no, but—"

"Technically?"

"You want to let me finish a thought? They shut down places like this for security reasons, Court. They don't want the bad guys getting in. People aren't allowed to just come and go because that would make it hard to enforce. But basically they don't care about *us*. All we want to do is go home, right? If we break the rules we get, what, a lecture?" More likely a fine, and probably an expensive one, but he couldn't tell Courtney why it was worth taking that risk. "They don't care about us," he repeated.

"The gate's *locked*, dummy."

"Won't be in a little while."

"Who says?"

"I say."

"How do you know?"

"I'm psychic. I have psychic powers of prediction."

There was already a crowd gathering. Bob drove off the road onto the trimmed grass of the verge and parked as close as possible to the right side of the gate. He turned the motor off. Suddenly he could hear the wind whistling through gaps in the bodywork. The wind was getting colder—winter cold—and Courtney shivered pointedly. She hadn't brought winter clothes to Blind Lake. Bob had, and he was punished for that foresight: he had to lend his jacket to whining Courtney and sit behind the wheel in a short-sleeve cotton shirt. The sun dropped down below a big raft of turbulent gray clouds, casting a sickly light over everything. A couple of months and all this prairie would be balls-deep in snow. It was melancholy weather. This kind of weather always made him feel sad and somehow bereft, as if something he loved had been carried away by the wind.

"Are we just going to sit here?"

"Till the gate opens," he said.

"What makes you think they'll let us through?"

"You'll see."

"See what?"

"You'll see."

"Huh," Courtney said.

She had dozed off—warm, he guessed, with her arms lost in his oversized leather jacket and her chin tucked down into the collar—when the immense black truck paused in its crawl not more than ten yard from the gate. It was past dusk now, and the truck's headlights pivoted to sweep the ground ahead of it in restless arcs.

The crowd had grown considerably. Just before Courtney fell asleep a couple of on-campus Security vehicles had come from town with their sirens howling. Now guys in what looked like rent-a-cop uniforms were waving the crowd back. Courtney was motionless and Bob hunkered down in the driver's seat, and in all the commotion and darkness the car passed for an empty vehicle someone had parked and left. Within moments, Bob was delighted to see, the bulk of the crowd was actually behind him.

And the gate began to open. On some command from the truck, he guessed. But it was a beautiful sight. That nine-foot-tall reinforced barrier began to swing outward with an oiled ease so smooth it looked digitally rendered. *Jackpot*, Bob thought. "Buckle your seat belt," he told Courtney.

Her eyes blinked open. "What?"

He made a mental estimate of the clearance ahead of him. "Nothing." He sparked the engine and stepped hard on the accelerator.

Pocket drones, Elaine explained, were self-guided flying weapons about the size of a Florida grapefruit. She had seen them in use during the Turkish crisis, where they had patrolled no-go lines and contested borders. But she had never heard of them being deployed outside of a war zone.

"They're simple and pretty dumb," she told Chris, "but they're cheap and you can use lots of them and they don't sit in the ground forever like land mines, blowing legs off kids."

"What *do* they do?"

"Mostly they just lie there conserving energy. They're motion-sensitive and they have a few logic templates to identify likely targets. Walk into a no-go zone and they'll fly up like locusts, target you, spit out small but lethal explosives."

Chris looked where Elaine had pointed, but in the gathering dusk he could see nothing suspicious. You had to be quick to catch them, Elaine said. They were camouflaged, and if they hopped up without finding an allowed target—disturbed, say, by the rumbling of that huge automated truck on the pavement—they went dormant again very quickly.

Chris thought about that as the truck approached and the increasingly nervous security men shooed gawkers farther back from the road. Made no sense, he decided. The innermost fence around Blind Lake was only one of dozens of security measures already in place. What threat was so formidable that it would require wartime ordnance to keep it out?

Unless the idea was to keep people *in*.

But that made no sense either.

Which didn't mean the pocket drones hadn't been deployed. Only that he couldn't figure out why.

The crowd grew quieter as darkness fell and the truck crawled up within range of the gate and idled for a moment. Some few began to drift away, apparently feeling more vulnerable, or cold, than curious. But a number remained, pressed against the rope restraints the Security people had thrown up. They seemed not to mind the increasingly cutting wind or the unseasonable snowflakes that began to swirl into the truck's high beams. But they gasped and withdrew a few feet when the gate itself began to swing silently open.

Chris looked behind him at Elaine and caught a passing glimpse of Blind Lake beginning to light up in a mist of flurries, the concentric slabs of Hubble Plaza, the blinking navigation lights on the towers of Eyeball Alley, the warmer light of resident housing in neat, logical rows.

He turned back at the sudden sound of an electric motor much closer than the rumble of the idling truck.

"Video," Elaine barked. "*Chris!*"

He fumbled with the little personal-server accessory. His fingers were cold and the controls were the size of flyspecks and fleabites. He had only ever really used the thing for dictation. At last he managed to trigger the RECORD VID function and point the device approximately toward the gate.

A car sprang forward onto the tarmac from somewhere down by the guardhouse. Its lights were out, its occupants invisible. But the intention was clear. The vehicle was making a run for the half-opened gate.

"Somebody wants to go home and feed the dog," Elaine said, and then her eyes went wide. "Oh, Jesus, this is bad."

The drones, Chris thought.

It seemed that the vehicle might not make it past the guardhouse, but the driver had estimated the widening gap pretty well. The car—it looked to Chris like a late-model Ford or Tesla—squeezed through the space with millimeters of clearance and swerved hard left to avoid the grille of the robotic truck. The car's headlights came on as it bounced onto the margin of the road and began to pick up serious speed.

"Are you getting this?" Elaine demanded.

"Yes." At least, he hoped so. It was too late to check. Too late to look away.

"Home free!" Bob Krafft yelled as his rear bumper swung past the bulk of the black truck. It wasn't true, of course. Probably they'd be intercepted by a military vehicle, maybe even spend the night getting lectured and threatened and charged with violating small-print regulations, but he wasn't an enlisted man and he'd never signed an agreement to spend a fucking eternity in Blind Lake. Anyway, the open land rolling out beyond his headlights was a welcome sight. "Home free," he said again, mostly to drown out the sound of Courtney's breathless screeches of fear.

She sucked in enough air to call him an asshole. He said, "We're out of there, aren't we?"

"Jesus, *yeah*, but—"

Something out the side window caught her eye. Bob caught a glimpse of it, too. Some small thing leaping out of the tall grass.

Probably a bird, he thought, but suddenly the car was full of cold air and hard little flakes of snow, and his ears hurt, and there was window glass everywhere, and it seemed like Courtney was bleeding: he saw blood on the dashboard, blood all over his good leather jacket. . . .

"Court?" he said. His own voice sounded strange and underwatery.

His foot stabbed the brake, but the road was slippery and the Tesla began to swerve despite the best efforts of its overworked servos. Something caused the engine to explode in a gout of blue fire. The body of the car rose from the road. Bob was pressed against his seat, watching the tarmac and the tall grass and the dark sky revolve around him, and for a fraction of a second he thought, *Why, we're flying!* Then the car came down on its right front fender and he was thrown into Courtney. Into the sticky ruin of her, at least: into Courtney gone all red and licked with flames.

"The fuck?" Ray Scutter asked when he saw the fireball. Dimitry Shulgin, the Civilian Security chief, could only mumble something about "ordnance." Ordnance! Ray tried to grasp the significance of that. A car had run the fence. The car had caught fire and rolled over. It came to a stop, top-down. Then everything was still. Even the crowd at the gate was momentarily silent. It was like a photograph. A frozen image. Halted time. He blinked. Pellet snow blew into his face, stinging.

"Drones," Shulgin pronounced. It was as if he had broken the crust of the silence. Several people in the crowd began to scream.

Drones: those objects hovering over the burning automobile? Winged softballs? "What does that mean?" Ray asked. He had to shout the question twice. Spectators began to dash for their cars. Headlights sprang on, raking the prairie. Suddenly everybody wanted to go home.

Heedless as a bad dream, the gate continued gliding open until it was parallel to the road.

The black robotic truck inched forward again, past the barrier and into the Lake.

"Nothing good," Shulgin replied—Ray, by this time, had forgotten the question. The Security chief edged away from the tarmac, seeming to fight his own urge to run. "*Look.*"

Out beyond the gate, in the hostile emptiness, the driver's-side door of the burning car groaned open.

Now that the car had come to rest Bob registered little more than the need to escape from it—to escape the flames and the bloody, blackened object Courtney had somehow become. At the back of his mind was the need to *get help*, but there was also, dwelling in the same place, the unwelcome knowledge that Court was beyond all human help. He loved Courtney, or at least he liked to tell himself so, and he often felt a genuine affection for her, but what he needed now more than anything else in the world was to put some distance between himself and her ravaged body, between himself and the burning car. There was no gasoline in the motor, but there were other flammable fluids, and something had ignited all of them at once.

He scrambled away from Courtney to the driver's-side door. The door was crumpled and didn't want to open; the latch-handle came off in his hand. He braced himself against the steering wheel and the seatback and kicked outward, and though it hurt his feet hellishly, the door did at last creak and groan a little way open on its damaged hinges. Bob forced it wider and then tumbled out, gasping at the cold air. He rose to his knees. Then, shaking, he stood upright.

This time he saw quite clearly the device that popped out of the tall grass at the verge of the road. He happened to be looking in the right direction, happened to catch sight of it in a moment of frozen hyperclarity, this small, incongruous object that was in all likelihood the last thing he would ever see. It was round and camouflage-brown and it flew on buzzing pinwheel wings. It hovered at a height of about six feet—level with Bob's head. He looked at it, eyeball to eyeball, assuming some of those small dents or divots were equivalent to eyes. He recognized it as a piece of military equipment, though it was like nothing he had ever encountered in his weekends with the Reserves. He didn't even think about running from it. One doesn't run from such things. He stiffened his spine and began, but had no time to finish, the act of closing his eyes. He felt the sting of snow against his skin. Then a brief, fiery weight on his chest, then nothing at all.

This final act of bloody interdiction was more than enough for the crowd. They watched the dead man, if you could call that headless bundle of exposed body parts a man, crumple to the ground. There was an absolute silence. Then screams, then sobs; then car doors slamming and kids wheeling their bikes around for a panicked trip back through the snowy dusk toward the lights of Blind Lake.

Once the spectators had cleared out, it was easier for Shulgin to organize his security people. They weren't trained for anything like this. They were bonded nightwatchmen, mostly, hired to keep drunks and juveniles out of delicate places. Some were retired veterans; most had no military experience. And to be honest, Ray thought, there was nothing much for them to do here, only establish a mobile cordon around the slowly-moving truck and prevent the few remaining civilians from getting in the way. But they did a presentable job of it.

Within fifteen minutes of the events beyond the gate the black transport truck came to a stop inside the perimeter of Blind Lake.

"It's a delivery vehicle," Elaine said to Chris. "It was designed to drop cargo and go home. See? The cab's disengaging from the flat."

Chris watched almost indifferently. It was as if the attack on the fleeing automobile had been burned into his eyes. Out in the darkness the fire had already been reduced to smoldering embers in the wet snow. A couple of people had died here, and they had died, it seemed to Chris, in order to communicate a message to Blind Lake in the bluntest possible way. You may not pass. Your community has become a cage.

The truck cab reversed direction, pulling itself and its sheath of armor away from the conventional aluminum cargo container shielded within. The cab kept moving, more quickly than it had arrived, back through the open gate along the road to Constance. When it reached the smoldering ruins of the automobile it pushed them out of its way, shoveled them onto the verge of the road like idle garbage.

The gate began to swing closed.

Smooth as silk, Chris thought. Except for the deaths.

The cargo container remained behind. The overworked security detail hurried to surround it . . . not that anyone seemed anxious to get close.

Chris and Elaine circled back for a better view. The rear of the container was held closed by a simple lever. There was some dialogue between Ray Scutter and the man Elaine had identified as the Lake's security chief. At last the security man stepped through the cordon and pulled down the lever decisively. The container's door swung open.

A half-dozen of his men played flashlight over the contents. The container was stacked high with cardboard boxes. Chris was able to read some of the printing on the boxes.

Kellogg's. Seabury Farm. Lombardi Produce.

"Groceries!" Elaine said.

We're going to be here awhile, Chris thought.

PART TWO

Polished Mirrors of Floating Mercury

Having an intelligence of a vastly different order than that of Man, the decapods were unable to conceive the fact that an Earth-man was a thinking entity. Possibly to them Man was no more than a new type of animal; his buildings and industry having impressed them no more than the community life of an ant impresses the average man—aside from his wonder at the analogy of that life to his own.

—Leslie Frances Stone, "The Human Pets of Mars," 1936

Ten

"Chris Carmody? What'd you do, walk here? Brush off that snow and come in. I'm Charlie Grogan."

Charlie Grogan, chief engineer at Eyeball Alley, was a big man, more robust than fat, and he put out a beefy hand for Chris to shake. Full head of hair, gone white at the temples. Confident but not aggressive. "Actually," Chris said, "yeah, I did walk here."

"No car?"

No car, and he had arrived in Blind Lake without winter clothes. Even this unlined jacket was borrowed. The snow tended to get down the collar.

"When you work in a building without windows," Grogan said, "you learn to pick up clues about the weather outside. Are we still this side of a blizzard?"

"It's coming down pretty good."

"Uh-huh. Well, you know, December, you have to expect a little snow, this part of the country. We were lucky to get through Thanksgiving with only a couple of inches. Hang your coat over there. Take off those shoes, too. We got these little rubber slippers, grab a pair off the shelf. That thing you're wearing, is that a voice recorder?"

"Yes, it is."

"So the interview's already started?"

"Unless you tell me to turn it off."

"No, I guess that's what we're here for. I was afraid you wanted to talk about the quarantine—I don't know any more about it than anyone else. But Ari Weingart tells me you're working on a book."

"A long magazine article. Maybe a book. Depending."

"Depending on whether we're ever allowed outside again?"

"That, and whether there's still an audience to read it."

"It's like playing let's-pretend, isn't it? Pretend we still live in a sane world. Pretend we have useful jobs to do."

"Call it an act of faith," Chris said.

"What I'm prepared to do—my act of faith, I guess—is show you around the Alley and talk about its history. That's what you want?"

"That's what I want, Mr. Grogan."

"Call me Charlie. You already wrote a book, didn't you?"

"Yes, I did."

"Yeah, I heard about that. Book about Ted Galliano, that biologist. Some people say it was character assassination."

"Have you read it?"

"No, and no offense, but I don't want to. I was introduced to Galliano at a conference on bioquantum computing. Maybe he was a genius with antivirals, but he was an asshole, too. Sometimes when people get famous they also get a little celebrity-happy. He wasn't content unless he was talking to media or big investors."

"I think he needed to feel like a hero, whether he deserved it or not. But I didn't come here to talk about Galliano."

"Just wanted to clear the air. I don't hold your book against you. If Galliano decided to drive his motorcycle over that cliff, it surely wasn't your fault."

"Thank you. How about that tour?"

Eyeball Alley was a replica of the installation at Crossbank, which Chris had also visited. Structurally identical, at least. The differences were all in the details: names on doors, the color of the walls. Some halfhearted seasonal decor had lately been installed, a festoon of green and red crepe over the cafeteria entrance, a paper wreath and menorah in the staff library.

Charlie Grogan wore a pair of glasses that showed him things Chris couldn't see, little local datafeeds telling him who was in which office, and as they passed a door marked ENDO-STATICS Charlie had a brief conversation (by throat microphone) with the person inside. "Hey there, Ellie . . . keeping busy . . . nah, Boomer's fine, thanks for asking . . ."

"Boomer?" Chris asked.

"My hound," Charlie said. "Boomer's getting on in years."

They took an elevator several stories down, deep into the controlled environment of the Alley's core. "We'll get you suited up and into the stacks," Charlie said, but when they approached a wide door marked STERILE GEAR there was a flashing red light above it. "Unscheduled maintenance," Charlie explained. "No tourists. Are you prepared to wait an hour or so?"

"If we can talk."

Chris followed the chief engineer back to the cafeteria. Charlie had not had lunch; nor, for that matter, had Chris. The food on the steam tables was the same food they served back at the community center, the same prefabricated rice pilaf and chicken curry and wrapped sandwiches delivered by the same weekly black truck. The engineer grabbed a wedge of ham-on-rye. Chris, still a little chilled by his walk to the Alley, went for the hot food. The air in the cafeteria was pleasantly steamy and the smell from the kitchen rich and reassuring.

"I go a fairly long way back in this business," Charlie said. "Not that there are any novices at the Lake, apart from the grad students we cycle through. Did Ari tell you I was at Berkeley Lab with Dr. Gupta?"

Tommy Gupta had done pioneering work on self-evolving neural-net architectures and quantum interfaces. "You must have been an undergraduate yourself."

"Yup. And thank you for noticing. This was back when we were using Butov chips for logic elements. Interesting times, though nobody knew exactly how interesting it was going to get."

"The astronomical application," Chris said, "you were in on that, too?"

"A little bit. But it was all unexpected, obviously."

In truth, Chris didn't need this playback. The story was familiar and every general astronomy and pop-science journalist of the last several years had recounted some version of it. Really, he thought, it was only the latest chapter of mankind's long ambition to see the unseeable, embellished with twenty-first-century technology. It had begun when NASA's first generation of spaceborne planet-spotting observatories, the so-called Terrestrial Planet Finders, identified three arguably earthlike planets orbiting nearby sunlike stars. The TPFs begat the High Definition Interferometers, which begat the greatest of all the optical interferometer projects, the Galileo Array, six small but complex automated spacecraft all operating beyond the orbit of Jupiter, linked to create one virtual telescope of immense resolving power. The Galileo Array, it was said at the time, could map the shapes of continents on worlds hundreds of light years away.

And it had worked. For a while. Then the telemetry from the Array began to deteriorate.

The signal faded slowly but relentlessly over a period of months. After an intensive review NASA pinpointed the source of the failure as a few lines of bad code so deeply embedded in the onboard Galileo architecture that they couldn't be overwritten. This was a risk NASA had assumed from the beginning. The Array was both complex and radically inaccessible. It couldn't be repaired in place. A technological triumph was on the way to becoming an insanely expensive joke.

"NASA didn't have an O/BEC processor back then," Charlie said, "but Gencorp offered them time on their unit."

"You worked at Gencorp?"

"I baby-sat their hardware, yeah. Gencorp was getting good results doing proteinomics. You could do the same stuff with a standard quantum array, of course. Engineers used to think of the O/BECs as unnecessarily complicated and unpredictable, a fancy kludge—like a vacuum cleaner with an appendix, people used to say. But you can't argue with results. Gencorp got faster results with a O/BEC machine than MIT could coax out of a standard BEC device. Spooky ones, too."

"Spooky?"

"Unexpected. Counterintuitive. Anybody who works with adaptive self-programming will tell you it's not like running raw BECs, and BECs can be pretty strange all by themselves. What I can't really say, because I'm supposed to be a level-headed and factually oriented kind of guy, is that an O/BEC just plain *thinks* strange. But that's as good an explanation as any, because nobody really knows why a BEC processor with an open-ended organic architecture can outthink a BEC processor alone. It's the fucking ghost in the machine, pardon my French. And what we do in the pit, it isn't just amps and volts. We're tending something that's very nearly alive. It has its good days and its bad days . . ."

Charlie trailed off, as if he realized he'd overstepped the bounds of engineering propriety. He doesn't want me quoting this, Chris thought. "So you went to NASA with the O/BEC processor?"

"NASA ended up buying a few platens from Gencorp. I was part of the package. But that's another story. See, basically, the problem was this: as the Galileo Array's output got fainter, it was increasingly harder to separate the signal from the noise. Our job was to extract that signal, hunt it down, subtract it from all the rest of the random radio garbage the universe belches out. People ask me, 'So how'd you do it?' And I have to tell them, we *didn't* do it, nobody did it, we just posed the problem to the O/BECs and let them generate tentative answers and bred them for success . . . hundreds of thousands of generations per second, like this big invisible Darwinian evolutionary race, survival of the fittest, where the definition of 'fittest' is success at extracting a signal from a noisy input. Code writing code writing code, and code withering and dying. More generations than all the people who ever lived on the earth, almost more generations than *life* on the earth. Numbers complexifying themselves like DNA. The beauty is the unpredictability of it, you understand?"

"I think so," Chris said. He liked Charlie's eloquence. He always liked it when an interviewee showed signs of passion.

"I mean, we made something that was beautiful and mysterious. Very beautiful. Very mysterious."

"And it worked," Chris said. "Signals out of noise."

"Whole world knows it worked. Of course, we weren't sure of that ourselves, not while it was happening. We had a few what we called threshold events. We'd almost lose everything. We'd have a good clean image, then we'd start to lose it, almost pixel by pixel. That was the noise winning out. Loss of intelligibility. But each time, the O/BECs pulled it back. Without our intervention, you understand. It drove the math guys nuts, because there's obviously a level where you just *can't* extract a meaningful signal, when there's just too much lost, but the machines kept on pulling it out, rabbit out of a hat, presto. Until one day . . ."

"Until one day?"

"Until one day a man in a suit came into the lab and said, 'Boys, we got confirmation from upstairs, the Array just stopped broadcasting altogether, shut down entirely, you can get ready to close up shop and go home.' And my boss at the time—that was Kelly Fletcher, she's at Crossbank now—she turned away from her monitor and said, 'Well, that may be, but the fact is, we're still making data.'"

Charlie finished his sandwich, wiped his mouth, pushed his chair away from the table. "We can probably get into the stacks now."

Back at Crossbank, Chris had toured the O/BECs from the gallery level. He hadn't been invited into the works.

The sterile suit was comfortable as such things went—cool air piped in, a wide and transparent visor—but Chris still felt a little claustrophobic inside it. Charlie led him through an access door into the eerily quiet O/BEC chamber. The platens were white enameled cylinders each the size of a small truck. They were suspended on isolation platforms that would filter out any groundborne vibration short of a major earthquake.

Strange, delicate machines. "It could end at any time," Chris murmured.

"What's that?"

"Something an engineer at Crossbank told me. He said he liked the rush, working with a process that could end at any time."

"That's part of it, for sure. These are technologies of a whole new order." He stepped over a bundle of Teflon-insulated wires. "These machines are looking at planets, but ten years after that first NASA connection we still don't know how they're doing it."

Or *if* they're doing it, Chris thought. There was a fringe of hard-core skeptics who believed there was no real data behind the images: that the O/BECs were simply . . . well, dreaming.

"So," Charlie said, "we really have two research projects going on at once: guys at the Plaza trying to sort out the data, and people here trying to figure out how we *get* the data. But we can't look too closely. We can't take the O/BECs apart or dose them with X-rays or anything invasive like that. You measure it, you break it. Blind Lake didn't just duplicate the Crossbank installation; we had to walk our machines through the same development process, except we used the old high-def interferometers instead of the Galileo Array, deliberately stepping down the signal strength until the machines learned the trick, whatever that trick is. There are only two installations like this in the world, and efforts to create a third have been consistently unsuccessful. We're balanced on the head of a pin. That's what your guy at Crossbank was talking about. Something absolutely strange and wonderful is happening here, and we don't understand it. All we can do is nurse it along and hope it doesn't get tired and turn itself off. It could end at any time. Sure it could. And for any reason."

He led Chris past the last of the O/BEC platens, through a series of chambers to a room where they stripped off their sterile suits.

"What you have to remember," Charlie said, "is that we didn't design these machines to do what they do. There's no linear process, no A then B then C. We just set them in motion. We defined the goals and we set them in motion, and what happened after that was an act of God." He folded the sterile suit crisply and left it on a rack for cleaning.

Charlie walked him through the busiest sector of the Alley, two huge chambers wallpapered with video surfaces, rooms full of attentive men and women hovering over mutable desktops. Chris was reminded of the old NASA facilities at Houston. "Looks like Mission Control."

"For good reason," Charlie said. "NASA used to control the Galileo Array with interfaces like these. When the problems got unmanageably bad they routed this stuff through the O/BECs. This is where we talk to the platens about alignment, depth of field, magnification factors, things like that."

Down to the finest detail. A monitor on the far wall showed raw video. Lobsterville. Except Elaine was right. It was a ridiculous misnomer. The aboriginals didn't look remotely like lobsters, except perhaps for their roughly textured skin. In fact Chris had often thought there was something bovine about them, something about their slow-moving indifference, those big blank cueball eyes.

Subject was in a food conclave, deep inside a dimly lit food well. Mossy growth and vegetable husks everywhere, and grublike things crawled through the moist refuse. Watching these guys eat, Chris thought, was a great appetite killer. He turned back to Charlie Grogan.

"Yeah," Charlie said, "it could end at any time, that's the truth. You're staying at the community center, Ari tells me?"

"For now, anyway."

"You want a ride back? I'm basically done here for the day."

Chris checked his watch. Almost five o'clock. "Sounds better than walking."

"Assuming they plowed the road."

A good couple of inches of fresh snow had come down while Chris was inside the Alley, and the wind had picked up. Chris flinched from it as soon as he stepped outside. He had been born and raised in Southern California, and despite all the time he'd spent in the East, these harsh winter days still shocked him. It wasn't just bad weather, it was weather that could kill you. Walk the wrong way, get lost, die of hypothermia before dawn.

"It's bad this year," Charlie admitted. "People say it's the shrinking ice cap, all that cold water flowing into the Pacific. We get these supercharged Canadian fronts rolling through. You get used to it after a while."

Maybe so, Chris thought. The way you get used to living under siege.

Charlie Grogan's car was parked in the roofed lot, plugged into a charge socket. Chris slipped into the passenger seat gratefully. It was a bachelor's car: the backseat was full of old *QCES* journals and dog toys. As soon as Charlie pulled out of the parking compound the tires slipped on compressed snow and the car fishtailed before it finally gripped the asphalt. Harsh sulfur-dot light columns marked the way to the main road, sentinals cloaked in vortices of falling snow.

"It could end at any time," Chris said. "Kind of like the quarantine. It could end. But it doesn't."

"Have you turned off that little recorder yet?"

"Yes. You mean, is this for the record? No. It's conversation."

"Coming from a journalist . . ."

"I don't work for the tabloids. Honest, I'm just mumbling. We can go on talking about the weather if you like."

"No insult intended."

"None taken."

"You got a little burned on that Galliano thing, right?"

Now who's pushing? But he felt he owed this man an honest response. "I don't know if you can say that or not."

"I guess if you say unflattering things about a national hero, you're taking a certain risk."

"I didn't set out to tarnish his reputation. Much of it is deserved." Ted Galliano had made national news twenty years ago by patenting a new family of broad-spectrum antiviral drugs. He had also made a fortune founding a next-generation pharmaceutical trust to exploit those patents. Galliano was the prototype of the twenty-first century scientist-entrepreneur—like Edison or Marconi in the nineteenth, also products of the commercial environment of their day, also brilliant. Like Edison or Marconi, he had become a public hero. He had attracted the best genomic and proteinomic people to him. A child born today in the Continental Commonwealth could expect a lifetime of one hundred years or more, and no small part of that was due to Galliano's antiviral and antigeriatric drugs.

What Chris had discovered was that Galliano was a ruthless and sometimes unscrupulous businessman—as Edison had been. He had lobbied Washington for extended patent protection; he had driven competitors out of the market or absorbed them through dubious mergers and leverage schemes; worse, Chris had uncovered several sources who were convinced Galliano had engaged in blatantly illegal stock manipulation. His last big commercial effort had been a

genomic vaccine against artheriosclerotic plaque—never per-
fected but much discussed, and the prospect of it, however
inflated, had driven Galtech stocks to dizzying heights. Ultimately the bubble had burst, but not before Galliano and
friends cashed out.

"Could you prove any of this?"

"Ultimately, no. Anyhow, I didn't think of it as a muckrak-
ing biography. He *was* a brilliant scientist. When the book
came out it got a good initial reaction, some of it just *schaden-
freude*—rich people have enemies—but some of it balanced.
Then Galliano had his accident, or committed suicide,
depending on who you listen to, and his family made an issue
of the book. Yellow Journalism Drives Benefactor to His Death.
That makes a nice story too."

"You were in court, right?"

"I testified at a congressional inquiry."

"Thought I read something about that."

"They threatened to jail me for contempt. For not revealing
my sources. Which wouldn't have helped, anyway. My sources
were all well-known public figures and by the time of the
inquiry they had all issued statements siding with Galliano's
estate. By that time, in the public mind, Galliano was a dead
saint. Nobody wants to conduct an autopsy on a dead saint."

"Bad luck," Charlie said. "Or bad timing."

Chris watched the curtains of snow beyond the passenger-
side window, snow trapped on the car's exposed surfaces, snow
piling up behind the mirrors. "Or bad judgment. I took a tilt at
one of the biggest windmills on the planet. I was naive about
how things worked."

"Uh-huh." Charlie drove in silence for a while. "You got a
good one this time, though. The story of the Blind Lake quarantine, told from the inside out."

"Assuming any of us ever get to tell it."

"You want me to drop you in front of the community center?"

"If it's not too far out of your way."

"I'm in no hurry. Though Boomer's probably getting hungry. I thought they were getting all you stray day-timers billeted with locals."

"I'm on the waiting list. Actually, I've got a meeting tomorrow."

"Who'd they set you up with?"

"A Dr. Hauser."

"Marguerite Hauser?" Charlie smiled inscrutably. "They must be putting all the pariahs in one place."

"Pariahs?"

"Nah, forget it. I shouldn't talk about Plaza politics. Hey, Chris, you know the nice thing about Boomer, my hound?"

"What's that?"

"He doesn't have a clue about the quarantine. He doesn't know and he doesn't care, as long as he gets fed on a regular schedule."

Lucky Boomer, Chris thought.

Eleven

Tess woke at seven, her usual weekday morning time, but she knew even before she opened her eyes that there wouldn't be school today.

It had snowed all day yesterday and it had been snowing when she went to bed. And now, this morning, even without pulling back the lacy blinds that covered her bedroom window, she could hear the snow. She heard it sifting against the glass, a sound as gentle and faint as mouse whispers, and she heard the silence that surrounded it. No shovels scraping driveways, no cars grinding their wheels, just a blanketing white nothing. Which meant a *big* snow.

She heard her mother bustling in the kitchen downstairs, humming to herself. No urgency there, either. If

Tess went back to sleep her mother would probably let her stay in bed. It was like a weekend morning, Tess thought. No jolting awake but letting the world seep in slowly. Slowly, willfully, she opened her eyes. The daylight in her room was dim and almost liquid.

She sat up, yawned, adjusted her nightgown. The carpet was cold against her bare feet. She scooted down the bed closer to the window and drew back the curtain.

The windowpane was all white, opaque with whiteness. Snow had mounded impressively on the outside sill, and, inside, moisture had condensed into traceries of frost. Tess immediately put out her hand, not to touch the icy window but to hover her palm above it and feel the chill against her skin. It was almost as if the window were breathing coolness into the room. She was careful not to disturb the delicate lines of ice, the two-dimensional snowflake patterns like maps of elfin cities. The ice was on the inside of the window, not the outside. Winter had put its hand right through the glass, Tess thought. Winter had reached inside her bedroom.

She stared at the frost patterns for a long time. They were like written words that wouldn't reveal their meanings. In class last week, Mr. Fleischer had talked about symmetry. He had talked about mirrors and snowflakes. He had showed the class how to fold a piece of paper and cut patterns into the fold with safety scissors. And when you opened the paper up, the random slashes became beautiful. Became enigmatic masks and butterflies. You could do the same thing with paint. Blot the paper, then fold it down the middle while the paint was still wet. Unfold it and the blots would be eyes or moths or arches or rainbow rays.

The frost patterns on the window were more like snowflakes, as if you had folded the paper not once but two times, three times, four . . . but no one had folded the glass.

How did the ice know what shapes to make? Did the ice have mirrors built into it?

"Tess?"

Her mother, at the door.

"Tess, it's after nine . . . There's no school today, but don't you want to get up?"

After nine? Tess looked at her bedside clock to confirm it. Nine oh eight. But hadn't it been seven o'clock just moments ago?

She reached out impulsively and put a melting palm print on the window. "I'm coming!" Her hand was instantly cold.

"Cereal for breakfast?"

"Cornflakes!" She almost said, *Snowflakes*.

At breakfast Tessa's mother reminded her that there was a boarder coming by today—"Assuming they clear the roads by noon." This interested Tess immensely. Tessa's mother was working from home today, which made it even more like a weekend, except for the possibility of this new person coming to the house. Her mother had explained that some of the day workers and visitors were still sleeping in the community center gym, which wasn't very comfortable, and that people with room to spare in their homes had been asked to volunteer it. Tessa's mother had moved her exercise equipment, a treadmill and a stationary bike, out of the small carpeted room in the basement next to the water heater. There was a folding bed in there now. Tess wondered what it would be like to have a stranger in the basement. A stranger sharing meals.

After breakfast Tessa's mother went upstairs to work in her office. "Come and get me if you need me," she said, but in fact Tess had seen less of her mother than usual the last few days. Something was happening with her work, something about the Subject. The Subject was behaving strangely. Some people thought the Subject might be sick. These concerns had absorbed her mother's attention.

Tess, still in her nightgown, read for a while in the living room. The book was called *Out of the Starry Sky*. It was a children's book about stars, how they first formed, how old stars made new stars, how planets and people condensed out of the dust of them. When her eyes got tired she put down the book and watched snow pile up against the plate-glass sliding door. Noon inched by, and the sky was still dark and obscure. She could have fixed herself a sandwich for lunch, but she decided she wasn't hungry. She went upstairs and dressed herself and knocked at her mother's door to tell her she was going outside for a while.

"Your shirt's buttoned crooked," her mother said, and came into the hallway to fuss it into place. She ruffled Tessa's hair. "Don't go too far from the house."

"I won't."

"And shake off your boots before you come back in."

"Yes."

"Snow pants, not just the jacket."

Tess nodded.

She was excited about going out, even though it meant struggling into her snowsuit in the warm, sweaty hallway. The snow was so deep, so prodigious, that she felt the need to see and feel it up close. Overnight, Tess thought, the world beyond the door had become a different and much stranger place. She finished lacing her boots and stepped out. The air itself wasn't as cold as she had expected. It felt good when she drew it deep into her lungs and let it out again in smoky puffs. But the falling snow was small and hard this afternoon, not gentle at all. It bit against the skin of her face.

Rows of town houses stretched off to the right and left of her. Next door, Mrs. Colangelo was shoveling her driveway.

Tess pretended not to see her, worried that Mrs. Colangelo would ask her to help. But Mrs. Colangelo paid no attention to Tess and seemed lost in her work, red-faced and squinty-eyed, as if the snow were her own personal enemy. White clouds leapt from the shovel blade and dispersed in the wind.

The undisturbed snow on the front lawn came up almost to Tessa's shoulders. *I'm small,* she thought. Her head rose above the mounded dunes only a few feet, making her feel no taller than a dog. A dog's-eye view. She restrained an urge to leap and bury herself in whiteness. She knew the snow would get down the collar of her jacket and she would have to go back inside that much sooner.

Instead she walked in big labored moonsteps to the sidewalk. The main road had been plowed, though fresh snow had already deposited a thin new blanket over the asphalt. The plows had pushed up windrows too tall to see over. The tree in the front yard was so freighted with snow that its limbs had drooped into cathedral arches. Tess pushed her way underneath and was delighted to find herself in a sort of perforated cavern of snow. It would have been a perfect hideout, except for the cold air that wormed its way under her snowsuit and made her shiver.

She was under the tree when she saw a man walking up the street—the sidewalks were impassable—toward the house.

Tess guessed at once that this was the boarder. He wasn't dressed very warmly. He paused to check the snow-encrusted, semilegible numbers of the town houses. He walked until he was in front of Tessa's house; then he took his hands out of his pockets, wallowed through the windrows, and made his way to the door. Tess shrank back in the tree shadow so he wouldn't notice her. By the time he rang the bell there was snow up past the knees of his denim pants.

Tessa's mother answered the door. She shook hands with

the stranger. The man brushed off the snow and went inside. Tessa's mother lingered on the doorstep a moment, tracing out Tessa's footprints. Then she spotted Tess under the tree and aimed her finger at her, pistol-style. *Gotcha, cowgirl,* Tessa's mother always said at times like this. This time she mouthed the words.

Tess stayed under the sheltering tree for a while. She watched Mrs. Colangelo finish shoveling her driveway. She watched a couple of cars come down the street at a careful, tentative speed. She decided she liked snowy winter days. Every surface, even the big front window of the house, was opaque and textured, not at all reflective. And in this dearth of mirror surfaces she was not afraid of suddenly seeing Mirror Girl.

Mirror Girl often posed as a reflection of Tess. Tess, caught unawares, would find Mirror Girl gazing back at her from the bathroom or bedroom mirror, indistinguishable from Tessa's own reflection except in the eyes, which were questioning and urgent and intrusive. Mirror Girl asked questions no one else could hear. Idiotic questions, sometimes; sometimes adult questions Tess couldn't answer; sometimes questions which left her feeling troubled and uneasy. Just yesterday Mirror Girl had asked her why the plants inside the house were green and alive while the ones outside were all brown and leafless. ("Because it's *winter*," Tess had said, exasperated. "Go away. I don't believe in you.")

Thinking about Mirror Girl made Tess uneasy.

She began to make her way back to the house. The front lawn was still full of unspoiled white expanses of snow. Tess paused and pulled off her gloves. Her hands were already cold, but since she was going inside it didn't matter. She pushed both hands into the paper-white unbroken snow. The snow took the imprints impeccably, mirror images of her hands. *Symmetrical,* Tess thought.

When she got to the door she heard voices from inside. Raised voices. Her mother's angry voice. Tess eased inside. She shut the door gently behind her. Her boots dropped clots of icy snow on the carpet runner. Her woolen cap was suddenly itchy and uncomfortable. She pulled it off and dropped it on the floor.

Her mother and the boarder were in the kitchen, invisible. Tess listened carefully. The boarder was saying, "Look, if it's a problem for you—"

"It *creates* a problem for me." Tessa's mother sounded both outraged and defensive. "Fucking *Ray*—!"

"Ray? I'm sorry—who's Ray?"

"My ex."

"What does he have to do with this?"

"Ray Scutter. The name is familiar?"

"Obviously, but—"

"You think it was Ari Weingart who sent you here?"

"He gave me your name and address."

"Ari means well, but he's Ray's puppet. Oh, *fuck*. Excuse me. No, I know you don't understand what's going on . . ."

"You could explain," the boarder said.

Tess understood that her mother was talking about her father. Usually when that happened Tess didn't pay attention. Like when they used to fight. She put it out of her mind. But this was interesting. This involved the boarder, who had taken on a new and intriguing status simply by being the object of her mother's anger.

"It's not you," Tessa's mother said. "I mean, look, I'm sorry, I don't know you from Adam . . . it's just that your name gets thrown around a lot."

"Maybe I should leave."

"Because of your book. That's why Ray sent you here. I don't have a lot of credibility in Blind Lake right now, Mr. Car-.

mody, and Ray is doing his best to undermine what support I do have. If word gets around that you're rooming here it just confirms a lot of misperceptions."

"Putting all the pariahs in one place."

"Kind of. Well, this is awkward. You understand, I'm not mad at *you*, it's just . . ."

Tess imagined her mother waving her hands in her *well-what-can-I-do?* gesture.

"Dr. Hauser—"

"Please call me Marguerite."

"Marguerite, all I'm really looking for are accommodations. I'll talk to Ari and see if he can set up something else."

There was the kind of long pause Tess also associated with her mother's periodic unhappiness. Then she asked, "You're still sleeping in the gym?"

"Yes."

"Uh-huh. Well, sit down. At least get warm. I'm making coffee, if you like."

The boarder hesitated. "If it isn't too much trouble."

Kitchen chairs scraped across the floor. Quietly, Tess stepped out of her boots and hung her snowsuit in the closet.

"Do you have a lot of luggage?" Tessa's mother asked.

"I travel pretty light."

"I'm sorry if I sounded hostile."

"I'm used to it."

"I didn't read your book. But you hear things."

"You hear a lot of things. You're head of Observation and Interpretation, right?"

"The interdepartmental committee."

"So what does Ray have against you?"

"Long story."

"Sometimes things aren't what they look like at first."

"I'm not judging you, Mr. Carmody. Really."

"And I'm not here to put you in a difficult position."

There was another silence. Spoons clicking in cups. Then Tessa's mother said, "It's a basement room. Nothing fancy. Better than the gym, though, I guess. Maybe you can stay there while Ari makes other arrangements."

"Is that a real offer or a pity offer?"

Tessa's mother, no longer angry, gave a little laugh. "A guilt offer, maybe. But sincere."

Another silence.

"Then I accept," the stranger said. "Thank you."

Tess went into the kitchen to be introduced. Secretly, she was excited. A boarder! And one who had written a book.

It was more than she had hoped for.

Tess shook hands with the boarder, a very tall man who had curly dark hair and was gravely courteous. The boarder stayed drinking coffee and chatting with Tessa's mother until almost sunset, when he left to get his things. "I guess we have company at least for a little while," Tessa's mother told her. "I don't think Mr. Carmody will bother us much. He might not be here for too long, anyway."

Tess said that was all right.

She played in her room until dinner. Dinner was spaghetti with canned tomato sauce. The black truck delivered food every week, and the food was distributed according to ration points through the supermarket where people used to shop before the quarantine. That meant you couldn't pick and choose your favorites. Everybody got the same weekly allotment of fruits and vegetables and canned and frozen food.

But Tess didn't mind spaghetti. And there was buttered bread and cheese to go with it, and pears for dessert.

After dinner, Tessa's father called. Since the quarantine it was impossible to phone or e-mail outside the fence, but there was still basic communication through Blind Lake's central server. Tess took the call on her own phone, a pink plastic Mattel phone without a screen or much memory. Her father's voice over the toy phone sounded small and far away. The first thing he said was, "Are you all right?"

He asked the same thing every time he called. Tess answered as she always did: "Yes."

"Are you sure, Tessa?"

"Yes."

"What did you do today?"

"Played," she said.

"In the snow?"

"Yes."

"Were you careful?"

"Yes," Tess said, though she wasn't sure what she was supposed to be careful about.

"I hear you had a visitor today."

"The boarder," Tess said. She wondered how her father had heard about it so quickly.

"That's right. How do you feel about having a visitor?"

"It's okay. I don't know."

"Is your mother looking after you all right?"

Another familiar question. "Yes."

"I hope so. You know, if there's ever a problem over there, you just have to call me. I can come pick you up."

"I know."

"Anyway, next week you're back home again with me. Can you wait another week?"

"Yes," Tess said.

"Be a good girl till then?"

"I will."

"Call me if there's any problem with your mother."

"I will."

"Love you, Tessa."

"I know."

Tess put the pink phone back in her pocket.

The boarder came back that evening with a duffel bag. He said he'd already had dinner. He went to the basement to do some work. Tess went to her room.

The embroidery of ice had melted from the windowpane during the day but had reformed after sunset, new and different symmetries growing like a private garden. Tess imagined crystal roads and crystal houses and crystalline creatures inhabiting them: ice cities, ice worlds.

Outside, the snow had stopped falling and the temperature had dropped. The sky was very clear, and when she rubbed away the ice Tess could see a great many winter stars beyond the snow-bent tree limbs and the towers of Hubble Plaza.

Twelve

Chris met Elaine for dinner at the Sawyer's restaurant in the mallway. Despite the rationing, Ari Weingart had lobbied to keep the local restaurants open as meeting places and for the sake of the town's morale. Hot meals strictly at lunch, just sandwiches after 3 P.M., no alcoholic drinks, no seconds, but no bill, either: since no one was getting paid it would have been futile to try to keep the local economy running on a cash basis. Staff had been told their wages would be totalled and paid at the end of the quarantine, and customers with pocket change were encouraged to tip whatever they deemed appropriate.

This evening Chris and Elaine were the only customers—yesterday's snowfall was keeping people at home.

The single waitress who had shown up was a teenage part-timer, Laurel Brank, who spent most of her time in the far corner of the room reading *Bleak House* from a pocket display and picking at a bowl of Fritos.

"Heard you got billetted," Elaine said.

A cold front had followed the storm. The air was clear and bitter and the wind had picked up, rearranging yesterday's snowfall and rattling the restaurant windows. "I'm in the middle of something I don't entirely understand. Weingart signed me up with a woman named Marguerite Hauser who lives with her daughter in the housing west of town."

"I know the name. She's a recent arrival from Crossbank, heads up Observation and Interpretation." Elaine had been interviewing all the important Blind Lake committee people— the kind of interviews Chris tended not to get, given his reputation. "I haven't talked to her directly, but she doesn't seem to have many friends."

"Enemies?"

"Not enemies exactly. She's just a newbie. Still kind of an outsider. The big deal with her is—"

"Her ex-husband."

"Right. Ray Scutter. I gather it was an acrimonious divorce. Scutter's been talking her down. He doesn't think she's qualified to head a committee."

"You think he's right?"

"I wouldn't know, but her career record's impeccable. She was never a big hitter like Ray and she doesn't have the same academic credentials, but she hasn't been as spectacularly *wrong* as Ray's been either. You know the debate over cultural inteligibility?"

"Some people think we'll eventually understand the Lobsters. Some don't."

"If the Lobsters were looking at us, how much of what we

do could *they* figure out? Pessimists say, nothing—or very little. They might work out our system of economic exchange and some of our biology and technology, but how could they possibly interpret Picasso, or Christianity, or the Boer War, or *The Brothers Karamazov,* or even the emotional content of a smile? We aim all our signalling at each other, and our signals are predicated on all kinds of human idiosyncracies, from our external physiology down to our brain structure. That's why the research people talk about the Lobsters in weird behavioral categories—food-sharing, economic exchanges, symbol-making. It's like a nineteenth-century European trying to work out Kwakiutl kinship systems, without learning the language or being able to communicate . . . except that the European shares fundamental needs and urges with the Indian, and we share nothing at all with the Lobsters."

"So it's futile to try?"

"A pessimist would say yes—would say, let's collect and collate our information and learn from it, but forget the idea of ultimate comprehension. Ray Scutter is one of those guys. In a lecture, he once called the idea of exocultural understanding 'a romantic delusion comparable to the Victorian fad for table-rapping and spirit chambers.' Sees himself as a hard-core materialist."

"Not everybody in Blind Lake takes that point of view," Chris said.

"Obviously not. There's another school of thought. Of which Ray's ex happens to be a charter member."

"Optimists."

"You could say. They argue that, while the Lobsters have unique physiological constraints on their behavior, those are observable and can be understood. And culture is simply learned behavior modified by physiology and environment—learnable, hence comprehensible. They think if we know enough about the daily life of the Lobsters, understanding will inevitably follow. They say all living things share certain common goals, like the need to reproduce, the need to feed and excrete, and so forth—and that's enough commonality to make the Lobsters more like distant cousins than ultimate aliens."

"Interesting. What do you think?"

"What do *I* think?" Elaine seemed startled by the question. "I'm an agnostic." She canted her head. "Let's say it's 1944. Let's say some E.T. is examining the Earth, and let's suppose he happens to drop in on an extermination camp in Poland. He's watching Nazis extract the gold from the teeth of dead Jews, and he's asking himself, is this economic behavior or is it part of the food chain or what? He's trying to make sense of it, but he never will. Never. Because some things just don't make sense. Some things make no fucking sense at all."

"This is what's between Ray and Marguerite, this philosophical debate?"

"It's far from just philosophical, at least as far as Blind Lake politics go. Careers are made and broken. The big thing about UMa47 was the discovery of a living, sentient culture, and that's where most of the time and attention gets lavished. But if Lobster culture is static and ultimately incomprehensible, maybe that's wrong. There are planetologists who'd rather be studying the geology and the climate, there are even exozoologists who'd like to get a closer look at some of the other local fauna. We're ignoring a lot in order to stare at these bugs—the five other planets in the system, for instance. None of them is habitable but they're all novel. Astronomers and cosmologists have been demanding diversification for years."

"You're saying Marguerite's in a minority?"

"No . . . the plurality of opinion has been on the side of

studying Lobsterville, at least so far, but support isn't nearly as strong as it used to be. What Ray Scutter's been doing is trying to swing support for diversification. He doesn't like being locked onto a single subject, which has been Marguerite's pet policy."

"All that's beside the point, isn't it—since the siege, I mean?"

"It just takes a different form. Some people are starting to argue for shutting down the Eye altogether."

"You shut it down, there's no guarantee it'll ever function again. Even Ray must know that."

"So far these are just whispers. But the logic is, we're under siege because of the Eye, because of what somebody is afraid we'll see. Shut down the Eye and the problem disappears."

"If the people outside wanted us shut down they could turn off the power supply. A word to Minnesota Edison is all it would take."

"Maybe they're willing to keep us up and running just to see what happens. We don't know the logic of it. The argument goes, maybe we're guinea pigs. Maybe we should pull the plug on the Eye and see if that makes them open the cage."

"It would be an incredible loss to science."

"But the day workers and the civil staff don't necessarily care about that. They just want to see their kids or their dying parents or their fiancées. Even among the research staff, people are starting to talk about 'options.'"

"Including Ray?"

"Ray keeps his opinions to himself. But he was a late convert to the cause of astrobiology. Ray used to believe in an uninhabited, sterile universe. He jumped on the bandwagon when it made career sense, but I suspect some part of him still dislikes all this messy organic stuff. According to my sources he hasn't breathed a word of support for switching off the Eye. But he hasn't said anything against it, either. He's a consummate politician. He's probably waiting to see which way the wind blows."

Wind rattled the window. Elaine smiled.

"From the north," Chris said. "Briskly. I'd better get back."

"Which reminds me. I got you something." She reached into the bag at her feet. "I raided the community center lost-and-found."

She pulled out a brown knit scarf. Chris accepted it gratefully.

"To keep the wind out of your collar," Elaine said. "I hear you trekked out to the Alley and talked to Charlie Grogan."

"Yes."

"So you're working again?"

"After a fashion."

"Good. You're too talented to hang it up."

"Elaine—"

"No, don't worry. I'm finished. Stay warm, Chris."

He tipped for both of them and stepped out into the night.

Marguerite hadn't given him a key. He rang the bell at the door of the town house after his walk from Sawyer's. He appreciated the scarf Elaine had given him, but the wind was almost surgical, knifing from a dozen angles. Stars rippled in the brutally clear night sky.

He had to ring twice, and it wasn't Marguerite who finally answered, it was Tessa. The girl looked up at him solemnly.

He said, "Can I come in?"

"I guess so." She held the inner door ajar.

He shut it hastily behind him. His fingers burned in the warm air. He stripped off his jacket, his snow-encrusted shoes. Too bad Elaine hadn't scavenged a pair of boots for him, too. "Your mom's not home?"

"She's upstairs," Tess said. "Working."

The girl was cute but uncommunicative, a little chubby and owl-eyed. She reminded Chris of his younger sister Portia—except that Portia had been a nonstop talker. She watched closely as Chris hung his jacket in the closet. "It's cold out," she said.

"That it is."

"You should get warmer clothes."

"Good idea. You think it would be all right with your mom if I made coffee?"

Tess shrugged and followed Chris to the kitchen. He counted teaspoons into the filter basket, then sat at the small table while the coffee brewed, warmth seeping back into his extremities. Tess pulled up a chair opposite him.

"Did they open the school today?" Chris asked.

"Only in the afternoon." The girl put her elbows on the table, hands under her chin. "Are you a writer?"

"Yes," Chris said. Probably. Maybe.

"Did you write a book?"

The question was guileless. "Mostly I write for magazines. But I wrote a book once."

"Can I see it?"

"I didn't bring a copy with me."

Tess was clearly disappointed. She rocked in the chair and nodded her head rhythmically. Chris said, "Maybe you should tell your mom I'm here."

"She doesn't like to be bothered when she's working."

"Does she always work this late?"

"No."

"Maybe I should say hello."

"She doesn't like to be bothered," Tess repeated.

"I'll just tap at the door. See if she wants coffee."

Tess shrugged and stayed in the kitchen.

Marguerite had given him a tour of the house yesterday. The door to her home office was ajar, and Chris cleared his throat to announce himself. Marguerite sat at a cluttered desk. She was scribbling notes on a handpad, but her attention was focused on the screen on the far wall. "Didn't hear you come in," she said without looking up.

"Sorry to interrupt your work."

"I'm not working. Not officially, anyhow. I'm just trying to figure out what's going on." She turned to face him. "Take a look."

On the screen, the so-called Subject was climbing an upward-sloping ramp by the light of a few tungsten bulbs. The virtual viewpoint floated behind him, keeping his upper half-torso centered. From behind, Chris thought, the Subject looked like a wrestler in a red leather burka. "Where's he going?"

"I have no idea."

"I thought he had pretty regular habits."

"We're not supposed to use gendered pronouns, but just between us, yes, he's a creature of very regular habits. By his clock he ought to be sleeping—if 'sleeping' is what they're doing when they lie motionless in the dark."

This was the kind of carefully hedged clinical talk Chris had come to expect from Blind Lake staff.

"We've been following him for more than a year," Marguerite said, "and he hasn't varied from his schedule by more than a few minutes. Until lately. A few days ago he spent two hours in a food conclave that should have lasted half that time. His diet has changed. His social interactions are declining. And tonight he seems to have a case of insomnia. Sit down and watch, if you're interested, Mr. Carmody."

"Chris," he said. He cleared a stack of *Astrobiological Review* off a chair.

Marguerite went to the door and shouted, *"Tess!"*

From below: "Yeah?"

"Time for your bath!"

Footsteps pattered up the stairs. "I don't think I *need* a bath."

"You do, though. Can you run it yourself? I'm still kind of busy."

"I guess so."

"Call me when it's ready."

Moments later, the distant rush of running water.

Chris watched the Subject climb another spiral walkway. The Subject was entirely alone, which was unusual in itself. The aboriginals tended to do things in crowds, though they never shared sleeping chambers.

"These guys are pretty regularly diurnal, too," Marguerite said. "Another anomaly. As for where he's going—hey, *look*."

Subject reached an open archway and stepped out into the starry alien night.

"He's never been here before."

"Here *where*?"

"A balcony platform, way up on top of his home tower. My God, the view!"

Subject walked to the low barricade at the edge of the balcony. The virtual viewpoint drifted behind him, and Chris could see the Lobster city spread out beyond the Subject's grainy torso. The elongated pyramidal towers were illuminated at their portals and balconies by lights in the public walkways. Anthills and cowrie shells, Chris thought, threaded with gold. When Chris was little his parents used to cruise up along Mulholland Drive one or two evenings a year to see the lights of Los Angeles spread out below. It had looked kind of like this. Almost this vast. Almost this lonely.

The planet's small, quick moon was full, and he could make out something of the dry lands beyond the limits of the city, the low mountains far to the west and a reef of high cloud rolling on a quick wind. Spirals of electrostatically charged dust rolled across the irrigated fields, quickly formed and quickly dissipated, like immense ghosts.

He saw Marguerite give a little shiver, watching.

Subject approached the balcony's eroded barricade. He stood as if hesitating. Chris said, "Is he suicidal?"

"I hope not." She was tense. "We've never seen self-destructive behavior, but we're new here. God, I hope not!"

But the Subject stood motionless, as if intent.

"He's looking at the view," Chris said.

"Could be."

"What else?"

"We don't know. That's why we don't attribute motivation. If I were there, I'd be looking at the view; but maybe he's enjoying the air pressure, or maybe he was hoping to meet somebody, or maybe he's lost or confused. These are complex sentient creatures with life histories and biological imperatives no one even pretends to understand. We don't even know for sure how good their vision is—he may not see what we're seeing."

"Still," Chris said. "If I had to lay a bet, I'd say he's admiring the view."

That won him a brief smile. "We may think such things," Marguerite admitted. "But we must not say them."

"*Mom!*" From the bathroom.

"I'll be there in a second. Dry yourself off!" She stood. "Time to put Tess to bed, I'm afraid."

"You mind if I watch this a little longer?"

"I guess not. Call me if it gets exciting. All this is being recorded, of course, but there's nothing like a live feed. But he may not do anything at all. When they stand still they often stay that way for hours at a time."

"Not a great party planet," Chris said.

"It would be nice if we could take advantage of his static time and look around the city. But training the Eye to follow a single individual was a minor miracle in itself. If we looked away we might lose him. Just don't expect much."

She was right about the Subject: he stood absolutely motionless before the long vista of the night. Chris watched distant dust-devils, immense and immaterial, ride the moonlit plains. He wondered if they made a sound in the relatively thin atmosphere of that world. He wondered if the air was warm or cool, whether the Subject was sensitive to the temperature. All this anomalous behavior and no way to divine the thoughts circulating in that perfectly imaged but perfectly inscrutable head. What did loneliness mean to creatures who were never alone except at night?

He heard the pleasant sound of Marguerite and Tessa talking in low voices, Marguerite tucking her daughter into bed. A flurry of laughter. Eventually Marguerite appeared in the doorway once more.

"Has he moved?"

The moon had moved. The stars had moved. Not the Subject. "No."

"I'm making tea, if you feel like a cup."

"Thanks," Chris said. "I'd like that. I—"

But then there was the unmistakable sound of breaking glass, followed by Tessa's high, shrill scream.

Chris came into the girl's bedroom behind Marguerite.

Tess was still shrieking, a high, sustained sob. She sat at the edge of her bed, her right hand pressed into the waist of her flannel nightgown. There were spatters of blood on the bedspread.

The bottom pane of the bedroom window was broken. Shards of glass stood jagged in the frame and bitterly cold air gusted inside. Marguerite knelt on the bed, lifting Tessa away from the litter of glass. "Show me your hand," she said.

"*No!*"

"Yes. It'll be all right. Show me."

Tess turned her head away, squeezed her eyes shut and extended her clenched fist. Blood seeped between her fingers and ran down her knuckles. Her nightgown was stained with fresh red blood. Marguerite's eyes went wide, but she resolutely peeled back Tessa's fingers from the wound. "Tess, what happened?"

Tess sucked in enough breath to answer. "I leaned on the window."

"You leaned on it?"

"*Yes!*"

Chris understood that this was a lie and that Marguerite acquiesced to it, as if they both understood what had really happened. Which was more than he understood. He balled up a blanket and stuffed it into the gap in the window.

More blood welled from the exposed palm of Tessa's right hand—a small lake of it. This time Marguerite couldn't conceal a gasp.

Chris said, "Is there glass in the wound?"

"I can't tell . . . no, I don't think so."

"We need to put pressure on it. She'll need to be stitched, too." Tess wailed in fresh alarm. "It's okay," Chris told her. "This happened to my little sister once. She fell down with a glass in her hand and cut herself up—worse than you did. She bragged about it later. Said she was the only one who *wasn't* scared. The doctor fixed it up for her."

"How old was she?"

"Thirteen."

"I'm eleven," Tess said, gauging her courage against this new standard.

"There's gauze in the bathroom cupboard," Marguerite said. "Will you get it, Chris?"

He fetched the gauze and a brown elastic bandage. Marguerite's hands were shaking, so Chris pressed the gauze into Tessa's palm and told her to clench her fist over it. The gauze immediately turned bright red. "We have to drive her to the clinic," he said. "Why don't you give me your keys; I'll start the car while you bundle her up."

"All right. Keys are in my purse, in the kitchen. Tess, can you walk with me? Watch out for the glass on the floor."

She left blood spots on the carpet all the way down the stairs.

The Blind Lake Medical Center, a suite of offices just east of Hubble Plaza, kept its walk-in clinic open at all hours. The nurse on desk duty looked briefly at Tess, then hustled her and Marguerite off to a treatment room. Chris sat in reception, leafing through six-month-old print editions of travel magazines while gentle pop songs whispered from the ceiling.

From what he had seen, Tessa's injury was minor and the clinic was equipped to handle it. Better not to think what might have happened if she had been more seriously hurt. The clinic was well-equipped, but it wasn't a hospital.

She had "leaned on" the window. But you don't break a window like that by leaning on it. Tess had lied, and Marguerite had recognized the lie for what it was. Something she hadn't wanted to talk about in front of a stranger. Some ongoing problem with her daughter, Chris supposed. Anger, depression, post-divorce trauma. But the girl hadn't seemed angry or depressed when he spoke to her in the kitchen. And he remembered the sound of her easy laughter from the bedroom just moments before the accident.

It's none of my business, he told himself. Tess reminded him a little of his sister Portia—there was some of the same guileless amiability about her—but that didn't make it any concern of his. He had given up comforting the afflicted and afflicting the comfortable. He wasn't good at it. All his crusades had ended badly.

Marguerite came out of the treatment room shaken and spotted with her daughter's blood, but obviously reassured. "They've got her cleaned up and sutured," she told Chris. "She was actually very brave, once we saw the doctor. That story about your sister helped, I think."

"I'm glad."

"Thank you for your help. I could have driven her myself, but it would have been much trickier. Scarier for Tess, too."

"You're welcome."

"They gave her a painkiller. The doctor said we can go home when it takes effect. She'll have to keep the hand immobilized for a few days, though."

"Have you called her father?"

Marguerite was instantly downcast. "No, but I guess I ought to. I just hope he doesn't go ballistic. Ray is—" She stopped. "You don't want to know my problems."

Frankly, no, he didn't. She said, "Excuse me," and took her phone to a distant corner of the waiting room.

Despite his best intentions Chris overheard a little of the

conversation. The way she talked to her ex-husband was instructive. Carefully casual at first. Explaining the accident gently, understating it, then cringing from his response. "At the clinic," she said finally. "I—" A pause. "No. No." Pause. "It isn't necessary, Ray. *No*. You're blowing this way out of proportion." Long pause. "That isn't true. You know that isn't true."

She clipped off without saying good-bye and took a moment to steady herself. Then she came across the waiting room between the rows of generic hospital furniture, her lips compressed, her hair askew, her clothing bloodstained. There was a stiff dignity in the way she carried herself, an implicit rejection of whatever it was Ray Scutter had said to her.

"I'm sorry," she said, "but would you please go out and start the car? I'll fetch Tess. I think she'll be better off at home."

Another polite lie, but with an unspoken urgency under it. He nodded.

The walkway between the clinic and the parking lot was cold and windswept. He was glad enough to climb inside Marguerite's little car and start the motor. Heat wafted up from the floor ducts. The street was empty, swept with sinuous lines of blowing snow. He looked at the lights of the Plaza, the shopping concourse. The stars were still bright, and on the southern horizon he could see the running lights of a distant jet. Somewhere planes were still flying; somewhere the world was still conducting its business.

Marguerite came out of the clinic with Tess some ten minutes later, but she had not reached the car when another vehicle roared into the lot and screeched to a stop.

Ray Scutter's car. Marguerite watched with obvious apprehension as her ex-husband left the vehicle and came toward her with a rapid, aggressive stride.

Chris made sure the passenger door was unlocked. Better to avoid a confrontation. Ray had that mad-bull look about him. But Marguerite didn't make it to the car before Ray got a hand on her shoulder.

Marguerite kept her eyes on her ex-husband but pushed Tess behind her, protecting her. Tess cradled her injured hand under her snow jacket. Chris couldn't make out what Ray was saying. All he could hear over the whine of the motor was a few barked consonants.

Time to be brave. He hated being brave. That was what people used to say about his book, at least before Galliano's suicide. *How brave of you to write it.* Bravery had never gotten him anywhere.

He stepped out of the car and opened the rear door for Tess to climb in.

Ray gave him a startled look. "Who the fuck are you?"

"Chris Carmody."

"He helped drive Tess here," Marguerite said hurriedly.

"Right now she needs to get back home," Chris said. Tess had already scooted into the backseat, quick despite the clumsiness of her bandaged hand.

"Clearly," Scutter said, his eyes narrow and fixed on Chris, "she's not safe there."

"Ray," Marguerite said, "we have an agreement—"

"We have an agreement written before the siege by a divorce counselor I can't contact." Ray had mastered the vocal tones of bull-male impatience, equal parts whining and imperious. "There's no way I can trust you with my daughter when you permit things like this to happen."

"It was an accident. Accidents happen."

"Accidents happen when children aren't supervised. What were you doing, staring at the fucking Subject?"

Marguerite stumbled over an answer. Chris said, "It happened after Tess went to bed." He motioned discreetly for Marguerite to get into the car.

"You're that tabloid journalist—what do you know about it?"

"I was there."

Marguerite took the hint and climbed in. Ray looked frustrated and doubly angry when he heard the door slam. "I'm taking my daughter with me," he said.

"No, sir," Chris said. "Not tonight, I'm afraid."

He maintained eye contact with Ray as he slid behind the wheel. Tess began quietly crying in the backseat. Ray leaned against the car door, but whatever he was shouting was inaudible. Chris put the vehicle in drive and pulled away, not before Scutter aimed a kick at the rear bumper.

Marguerite soothed her daughter. Chris drove cautiously out of the clinic lot, wary of ice. Ray could have jumped in his own car and followed but apparently chose not to; last he saw of him in the rearview mirror, he was still standing in impotent rage.

"He hates for anyone to see him like that," Marguerite said. "I'm sorry. I'm afraid you made an enemy tonight."

No doubt. Chris understood the alchemy by which a man might be charming in public and brutal behind closed doors. Cruelty as the intimacy of last resort. Men generally didn't like to be witnessed in the act.

She added, "I have to thank you again. I'm truly sorry about all this."

"Not your fault."

"If you want to find a new place to room, I understand."

"The basement's still warmer than the gym. If that's okay with you."

Tess snorted and coughed. Marguerite helped her blow her nose.

"I keep thinking," Marguerite said, "what if it had been worse? What if we'd needed a real hospital? I'm so tired of this lockdown."

Chris pulled into the driveway of the town house. "I expect we'll survive," he said. Clearly, Marguerite was a survivor.

Tess, exhausted, went to sleep on Marguerite's bed. The house was cold, icy air rivering in through the broken window in Tessa's room, the furnace struggling to keep up. Chris rummaged in the basement until he found a heavy plastic drop cloth and a wide piece of maplewood veneer. He duct-taped the plastic over the empty window frame in Tessa's bedroom, then tacked up the veneer for good measure.

Marguerite was in the kitchen when he went downstairs. "Nightcap?" she said.

"Sure."

She poured him fresh coffee laced with brandy. Chris checked his watch. After midnight. He didn't feel remotely like sleeping.

"I guess you're tired of hearing me apologize."

"I grew up with a younger sister," Chris said. "Things happen with kids. I know that."

"Your sister. You mentioned Portia."

"We all call her Porry."

"Do you still see her? Before the siege, I mean."

"Porry died a while back."

"Oh. I'm sorry."

"Now you *do* have to stop apologizing."

"I'm—oh."

"How much trouble do you expect Ray to make over this?"

She shrugged. "That's a question and a half. As much as he can."

"It's none of my business. I'd just like some warning if you expect him to show up at the door with a shotgun."

"It's not like that. Ray is just . . . well, what can I say about Ray? He likes to be right. He hates to be contradicted. He's eager to pick fights but he hates to lose them, and he's been losing them most of his life. He doesn't like sharing custody with me—he wouldn't have signed the agreement, except his lawyer told him it was the best deal he was going to get—and he's always threatening some new legal action to take Tess away. He'll see tonight as more evidence that I'm an unfit parent. More ammunition."

"Tonight wasn't your fault."

"It doesn't matter to Ray what really happened. He'll convince himself I was either responsible for it or at least grossly negligent."

"How long were you married?"

"Nine years."

"Was he abusive?"

"Not physically. Not quite. He'd shake his fist, but he never threw it. That wasn't Ray's style. But he made it clear he didn't trust me and he sure as hell didn't approve of me. I used to get calls from him every fifteen minutes, where was I and what was I doing and when would I be home and I'd better not be late. He didn't like me, but he didn't want my attention focused on anyone but him. At first I told myself it was just a quirk, a character flaw, something he'd get over."

"You had friends, family?"

"My parents are charitable people. They accommodated Ray until it became obvious he didn't want to be accommodated. He didn't like me seeing them. Didn't like me seeing friends, either. It was supposed to be just the two of us. No countervailing forces."

"Good marriage to get out of," Chris said.

"I'm not sure he believes it's over."

"People can get hurt in situations like that."

"I know," Marguerite said. "I've heard the stories. But Ray would never get physical."

Chris let that pass. "How was Tess doing when you said good night?"

"She looked pretty sleepy. Worn out, poor thing."

"How do you suppose she happened to break that window?"

Marguerite took a long sip of her coffee and seemed to inspect the tabletop. "I honestly don't know. But Tess has had some problems in the past. She has a thing about shiny surfaces, mirrors and things like that. She must have seen something she didn't like."

And put her hand through the glass? Chris didn't understand, but Marguerite was obviously uncomfortable talking about it and he didn't want to press her. She'd been through enough tonight.

He said, "I wonder how the Subject is doing. Sleepless in Lobsterville."

"I left everything running, didn't I?" She stood up. "Want to have a look?"

He followed her upstairs to her office. They tiptoed past the room where Tess was sleeping.

Marguerite's office was exactly as they had left it, lights burning, interfaces lit, the big wall screen still dutifully following the Subject. But Marguerite gasped when she saw the image.

It was morning again on Subject's patch of UMa47/E. Subject had left the high balcony and made his way to a surface-level street. Last night's winds had given every exposed surface a coating of fine white grit, fresh texture under the raking light of the sun.

Subject approached a stone arch five times his height, walking into the sunrise. Chris said, "Where's he going?"

"I don't know," Marguerite said. "But unless he turns around, he's leaving the city."

Thirteen

"Charlie Grogan called," Sue Sampel said as Ray passed through the outer office. "Also Dajit Gill, Julie Sook, and two other department heads. Oh, and you have Ari Weingart at ten and Shulgin at eleven, plus—"

"Forward the agenda to my desktop," Ray said. "And any urgent messages. Hold calls." He disappeared into his *sanctum sanctorum* and closed the door.

Bless silence, Sue thought. It beat the sound of Ray Scutter's voice.

Sue had left a cup of hot coffee on his desk, a tribute to his punctuality. Very good, Ray thought. But he was facing a difficult day. Since the Subject had set out on his pilgrimage last week, the interpretive committees had been in a state of hysteria. Even the astrozoologists were divided: some of them wanted to keep the focus in Lobsterville and tag a new and more representative Subject; others (and Marguerite was one of these) were convinced the Subject's behavior was significant and ought to be followed to its conclusion. The Technology and Artifacts people dreaded losing their urban context, but the astrogeologists and climatologists welcomed the prospect of a long detour into the deserts and mountains. The committees were squabbling like fishwives, and absent Blind Lake's senior scientists or a line to Washington there was no obvious way to resolve the conflict.

Ultimately, these people would look to Ray for guidance. But he didn't want to assume that responsibility without a great deal of consultation. Whatever decision he made, sooner or later he'd be forced to defend it. He wanted that defense to be airtight. He needed to be able to cite names and documents, and if some of the more hotheaded committee partisans thought he was "dodging the issue"—and he had heard those words bandied about—too bad. He had asked them all to prepare position papers.

Best to start the day in a positive mood. Ray unfolded a paper napkin and used his key to open the bottom drawer of the desk.

Since the lockdown began Ray had been keeping a stash of DingDongs locked in his desk drawer. It was embarrassing to acknowledge, but he happened to like baked goods and he especially liked DingDongs with his breakfast coffee, and he could live without the inevitable smart-ass commentary about Polysorbate 80 and "empty calories," thank you very much. He liked peeling back the brittle wrapper; he liked the sugar-and-cornstarch smell that came wafting out; he liked the glutinous texture of the pastry and the way hot coffee flensed the slightly chemical aftertaste from his palate.

But DingDongs weren't included in the weekly black truck deliveries. Ray had been canny enough to buy up the remaining inventory from the local grocer and the convenience shop in the Plaza lobby. He had started with a couple of cartons, but they'd be gone before long. The last six DingDongs in the entire quarantined community of Blind Lake, as far as Ray could determine, were currently residing in his desk drawer. After that, nothing. Cold turkey. Obviously, it wouldn't kill him to do without. But he resented being forced into it by this ongoing bureaucratic fuck-up, this endless mute lockdown.

He pulled a DingDong out of the drawer. Take one away: that left five, a business-week's-worth.

But all he could see were four packages lingering in the shadows.

Four. He counted again. Four. He searched the drawer with his hand. Four.

There should have been five. Had he miscalculated?

Impossible. He had recorded the count in his nightly journal.

He sat immobile for a moment, processing this unwelcome information, working up a solid righteous anger. Then he buzzed Sue Sampel and asked her to step inside.

"Sue," he said when she appeared in the doorway. "Do you happen to have a key to my desk?"

"To your desk?" She was either surprised by the question or faking it very plausibly. "No, I don't."

"Because when I came here the support people told me I'd have the only key."

"Did you lose it? They must have a master somewhere. Or they can replace the locks, I guess."

"No, I didn't *lose* it." She flinched from his voice. "I have the key right here. Something's been stolen."

"Stolen? What was stolen?"

"It doesn't matter *what* was stolen. As it happens, it was nothing very important. What matters is that somebody gained access to my desk without my knowledge. Surely even you can grasp the significance of that."

She glanced at the desktop. Ray realized, too late, that he had left this morning's DingDong lying unopened next to his coffee cup. She looked at it, then at Ray, with a you-must-be-kidding expression on her face. He felt blood rush to his cheeks.

"Maybe you could talk to the cleaning staff," Sue said.

Now all he wanted was for her to disappear. "Well, all right, I suppose it doesn't matter . . . I shouldn't have mentioned it . . ."

"Or Security. You have Shulgin coming in later."

Was she concealing a smile? Was she actually *laughing* at him? "Thank you," he said tightly.

"Anything else?"

"No." *Get the fuck out.* "Please close the door."

She closed it gently. Ray imagined he could hear her laughter floating behind her like a bright red ribbon.

Ray considered himself a realist. He knew some of his behavior could be labeled misogynistic by anyone who wanted to smear him (and his enemies were legion). But he didn't hate women. Quite the opposite: he gave them every opportunity to redeem themselves. The problem was not that he hated women but that he was so consistently disappointed by them. For instance, Marguerite. (Always Marguerite, forever Marguerite . . .)

Ari Weingart came in at ten with a series of morale-enhancing proposals. Cayti Lane from the PR department wanted to put together a local video ring for news and social updates—Blind Lake TV, in effect—which she would host. "I think it's a good idea," Ari said. "Cayti's bright and photogenic. What I also want to do is pool the individual downloads people have residing in their house servers so we can rebroadcast them. No-choice scheduled television, very twentieth century, but it might help hold things together. Or at least give people something to talk about at the water cooler."

Fine, all this was fine. Ari went on to propose a series of live debates and lectures Saturday nights at the community center. Also fine. Ari was trying to reconfigure the siege as a church social. Let him, Ray thought. Let him distract the whining inmates with dog-and-pony shows. But all this boosterism was ultimately tiresome, and it was a relief when Ari finally packed up his grin and left the room.

Ray counted his DingDongs again.

Of course, it could have been Sue who had broken into his desk. There was no sign that the mechanism had been tampered with—maybe he'd been careless about locking the drawer and she had taken advantage of his lapse of attention. Sue often worked later than Ray, especially when Tess was in his care; unlike Marguerite, he didn't like leaving his daughter alone in the house after school. Sue was the prime suspect, Ray decided, though the cleaning staff weren't entirely above suspicion.

Men were easier to deal with than women. With men it was a matter of barking loud enough to command attention. Women were slyer, Ray thought, overtly yielding but easily subverted. Their loyalties were tentative and too quickly revoked. (Marguerite, for instance . . .)

At least Tess wouldn't grow up to be one of those kind of women.

Dimi Shulgin showed up at eleven, crisp in a gray tailored

suit, a welcome distraction even though he was full of ominous news. Shulgin had mastered the art of Baltic inscrutability, his doughy face impassive as he described the mood prevailing among the day workers and salaried staff. "They've endured the siege this long," Shulgin said, "with minimal problems, probably because of what happened to unfortunate Mr. Krafft when he tried to run the fence. That was a blessing in disguise, I think. It frightened people into acceptance. But discontent is growing. Casual and support staff outnumber the scientific and management people by five to one, you know. Many of them are demanding a voice in decision-making, and not a few of them would like to shut down the Eye and see what happens."

"It's all talk," Ray said.

"So far, it's all talk. In the long run—if this lockdown continues—who knows?"

"We should be seen to be doing something positive."

"The appearance of action," Shulgin said, any irony safely buried under his turgid accent, "would be helpful."

"You know," Ray said, "my desk was broken into recently."

"Your desk?" Shulgin's caterpillar eyebrows rose. "Broken into? This was vandalism, theft?"

Ray waved his hand in what he imagined was a magnanimous gesture. "It was trivial, office vandalism at most, but it got me thinking. What if we launched an investigation?"

"Into the vandalism of your desk?"

"No, for Christ's sake, into the *siege*."

"An investigation? How could we? All the evidence is on the other side of the fence."

"Not necessarily."

"Please explain."

"There's a theory we're under lockdown because something happened at Crossbank, something dangerous, something connected with their O/BECs, something that might as easily happen here."

"Yes, which is why there's a growing movement to switch off our own processors, but—"

"Forget about the O/BECs for a minute. Think about Crossbank. If Crossbank had a problem, wouldn't we have heard about it?"

Shulgin considered. He rubbed a finger against his nose. "Possibly, possibly not. All the senior administrators were in Cancun when the gates closed. They would have been the first to know."

"Yes," Ray said, gently urging the idea to its conclusion, "but messages might have stacked up on their personal servers before the quarantine went into effect."

"Anything urgent would have been forwarded . . ."

"But copies would still reside in the Blind Lake servers, wouldn't they?"

"Well . . . presumably. Unless someone took the trouble to erase them. But we can't break into the personal servers of senior staff."

"Can't we?"

Shulgin shrugged. "I would have thought not."

"In ordinary circumstances the question wouldn't even arise. But circumstances are a long way from ordinary."

"Crack the servers, read their mail. Yes, it's interesting."

"And if we find anything useful we should announce the results at a general meeting."

"If there *are* any results. Apart from voicemail from wives and mistresses. Shall I talk to my people, find out how difficult it would be to break into our servers?"

"Yes, Dimi," Ray said. "You do that."

He liked this better the more he thought about it. He went to lunch a happier man.

Ray's moods were mercurial, however, and by the time he left the Plaza at the end of the day he was feeling sour again. The DingDong thing. Sue had probably shared the story with her friends in the staff cafeteria. Every day, some fresh humiliation. He liked DingDongs for breakfast: was that so fucking funny, so laughably aberrant? People were assholes, Ray thought.

He drove carefully through flurries of hard snow, trying unsuccessfully to time the stoplights on the main street.

People were assholes, and that was what the exocultural theorists always missed, people like Marguerite, blind little featherweight optimists. One world full of assholes wasn't enough for them. They wanted more. A whole living universe of assholery. A shiny pink organic cosmos, a magic mirror with a happy face beaming out of it.

Dusk closed around the car like a curtain. How much cleaner the world would be, Ray thought, if it contained nothing but gas and dust and the occasional flaring star—cold but pristine, like the snow enshrouding the few high towers of Blind Lake. The real lesson of Lobsterville was the politically incorrect one, the unspeakable but obvious fact that sentience (so-called) was nothing but a focused irrationality, a suite of behaviors designed by DNA to make more DNA, empty of any logic but the runaway mathematics of self-reproduction. Chaos with feedback, $z \rightarrow z^2 + c$ blindly repeated until the universe had eaten and excreted itself.

Including me, Ray thought. Better not to shy from that caustic truth. Everything he loved (his daughter) or thought he had loved (Marguerite) represented nothing more than his participation in that equation, was no more or less sane than the nocturnal bleeding of the aboriginals of UMa47/E. Marguerite, for instance: acting out flawed genetic scripts, the possessive if unfit mother, a walking womb claiming equality under the law. How quickly she still came to mind. Every insolence Ray suffered was a mirror of her hatred.

The garage door rolled open as it sensed the approach of the car. He parked under the glare of the overhead light.

He wondered what it would be like to break free of all these biological imperatives and see the world as it truly was. To our eyes horrible, Ray thought, bleak and unforgiving; but our eyes are liars, equally as enslaved to DNA as our hearts and our minds. Maybe that was what the O/BECs had become: an inhuman eye, revealing truths no one was prepared to accept.

Tess had come back to him this week. He called hello as he entered the house. She sat in the living room in the chair next to the artificial Christmas tree, hunched over her homework like a studious gnome. "Hi," she said listlessly. Ray stood a moment, surprised by his love for her, admiring the way her dark hair curled tightly to her skull. She wrote on the screen of a lap pad, which translated her babyish scrawls into something legible.

He shed his coat and overshoes and drew the blinds against the snowy dark. "Have you called your birth mother yet?"

It was in the agreement he had signed with Marguerite after arbitration, that Tess would phone the absent parent daily. Tess looked at him curiously. "My *birth* mother?"

Had he said that aloud? "I mean, your mother."

"I called already."

"Did she say anything disturbing? You know you can tell me if your mother causes problems for you."

Tess shrugged uncomfortably.

"Was the stranger with her when you called? The man who lives in the basement?"

Tess shrugged again.

"Show me your hand," Ray said.

It didn't take a genius to know that Tessa's problems back at Crossbank had been Marguerite's fault, even if the divorce mediator had failed to figure it out. Marguerite had consistently ignored Tess, had focused exclusively on her beloved extraterrestrial seascapes, that Tess had made several desperate bids for attention, transparent in their motivation. The frightening stranger in the mirror might as well have been Marguerite's Subject—oblique, demanding, and omnipresent.

Glumly, head lowered in embarrassment, Tess held out her right hand. The sutures had been removed last week. The scars would disappear with time, the clinic doctor had said, but now they looked ghastly, pink new skin between angry divots where the stitches had been. Ray had already taken a few photographs in case the issue ever arose in court. He held her small hand in his, making sure there was no sign of infection. No small life eating the life from his daughter's flesh.

"What's for dinner?" Tess asked.

"Chicken," Ray said, leaving her to her books. Frozen chicken in the freezer. Subject removed from cold storage the butchered flesh of a ground-dwelling bird and began to sear it in a pan of extracted vegetable oil. Plus garlic and basil, salt and pepper. The smell of it flooded his mouth with saliva. Tess, drawn by the odor, wandered into the kitchen to watch him cook.

"Are you worried about going back to your mother tomorrow?"

Your birth mother. Half your genetic bag of tricks. The lesser half, Ray thought.

"No," Tess said, then, almost defiantly, "why do you always keep *asking* me that?"

"Do I?"

"Yes! Sometimes."

"Sometimes isn't always, though, is it?"

"No, but—"

"I just want everything to be okay for you, Tess."

"I know." Defeated, she turned away.

"You're happy here, aren't you?"

"It's okay here."

"Because you never know with Mom, isn't that right? You might have to come live here all the time, Tess, if anything happens to her."

Tess narrowed her eyes. "What would happen to her?"

"You never know," Ray said.

Fourteen

Before he left the city, Subject's life had been a repetitive cycle of work, sleep, and food conclaves. It had reminded Marguerite dismayingly of the Hindu idea of the kalpas, the sacred circle, eternal return.

But that had changed.

That had changed, and the circle had become something different: it had become a narrative. A *story*, Marguerite thought, with a beginning and an end. That was why it was so important to keep the Eye focused on the Subject, despite what the more cynical people in Interpretation thought. "The Subject is no longer representative," they said. But that was what made this so interesting. Subject had become an individual, something more than the sum of his functions in aboriginal society. This was clearly some kind of crisis in Subject's life, and Marguerite couldn't bear the idea of not seeing it through to its conclusion.

Even to the Subject's death, if it came to that. And it might.

Early on, she conceived the idea of writing the Subject's odyssey, not analytically, but as what it had become: a story. Not for publication, of course. She'd be violating the protocols of objectivity, indulging all kinds of conscious and unconscious anthropocentrism. Anyway, she wasn't a writer, or at least not that kind of writer. This was purely for her own satisfaction . . . and because she believed the Subject deserved it. After all, this was a real life they had invaded. In the privacy of her writing she could give him back his stolen dignity.

She began the project in a spiral-bound blue school notebook. Tess was asleep (she had come back from her father's two days ago, after a disappointing Christmas) and Chris was downstairs messing up the kitchen or raiding her library. It was a precious moment, hallowed in silence. A time when she could practice the black art of empathy. When she could freely admit that she cared about the fate of this creature so unknowable and so intimately known.

> Subject's last days in the city [Marguerite wrote] were disturbed and episodic.
>
> He manned his workstation at the usual time, but his food conclaves became briefer and more perfunctory. He descended the stairs into the food well slowly, and in the dim light of the evening conclaves he took less than the customary amount of cultivated crops. He spent more time scraping moldlike growths from the damp well walls, sucking the residue from his food claws.
>
> Normally this was a time of intense social interaction; the wells were crowded; but the Subject kept his face to the stone

wall, and his visible signaling motions (cilia-waving, head gestures) were minimal.

His sleep was disturbed, too, which in turn seemed to disturb the small creatures that fed on his blood nipples at night.

The place of these wall-dwelling animals in Subject's culture or ecology is not well understood. They might have been parasites, but since they were universally tolerated they were more likely symbionts or even a stage in the reproductive cycle. Perhaps their feeding stimulated desirable immune responses—at least, that was one theory. Shortly before his departure, however, the feeders seemed repelled by the sleeping Subject. They tasted him, skittered away, then came back to try again with the same result. Meanwhile, Subject was restless and moved several times during the night in an uncharacteristic manner.

He spent his last night in the city in a sleepless vigil on a high exterior balcony of the communal tower in which he lived. It was tempting to read both loneliness and resolve into these behaviors. [*Forbidden, but tempting*, Marguerite thought.] Subject's life had clearly changed, and perhaps not for the better.

Then he left the city.

It looked like a spontaneous decision. He left his warren, left his home tower, and walked directly through the eastern gate of the aboriginal city into a clear blue morning. In the sunlight his thick skin glittered like polished leather. Subject was a dusky shade of red over most of his body, a dark red merging into black at the major body joints, and his yellow dorsal crest stood up like a crown of flame as he walked.

The city was surrounded by an enormous acreage of agricultural land. Canals and aqueducts carried irrigation water from the snowy mountains in the north to these fields.

The system lost enormous amounts of moisture to evaporation in the dry, thin air, but the trickle that remained was enough to nourish miles-long avenues of succulent plants. The plants were thick-skinned, olive-green, and consisted of a few basic and similar types. Their stems were sturdy, the leaves as broad as dinner plates and as thick as pancakes. Taller than the Subject, they cast variegated shadows over him as he walked.

Subject followed the dirt-pack road, a wide avenue lapped with drainage ditches and verdant midsummer crops. He displayed no social interaction with either the sap-stained laborers in the fields or the foot traffic along the way. Shortly after he left the city he detoured into a cultivated plot of ground, where he was ignored by farm laborers as he pulled several large leaves from a mature plant, wrapped them in a broader, flatter fan leaf, and tucked them into a pouch in his lower abdomen. A picnic lunch? Or provisions for a longer journey?

For much of the morning he was forced to walk along the less-busy margin of the road, out of the way of traffic. According to planetary maps prepared before the O/BECs focused on a single Subject, this road ran east into the drylands for almost a hundred kilometers, veered north through a line of low mountains (foothills of a taller range) and east again until, after a few hundred kilometers of sparsely vegetated high plains it reached another aboriginal city, the as-yet-unnamed 33° latitude, 42° longitude urban cluster. 33/42 was a smaller city than Subject's own but an established trading partner.

Big trucks passed in both directions—huge platforms equipped with simple but refined and effective motors, riding on immense solid rollers rather than wheels. (This might have been an example of aboriginal efficiency. The trucks

maintain the pressed-earth roads simply by driving on them.)
And there was plenty of foot traffic, pairs and triads and
larger clusters of waddling individuals. But no other soli-
taries. Did a unique journey imply a unique destination?

By midday Subject reached the end of the agricultural
land. The road widened as the walls of succulent plants
dropped behind. The horizon was flat dead ahead and moun-
tainous to the north. The mountains shimmered in waves of
rising heat. When the sun reached its apex Subject stopped for
a meal. He left the road and walked a few hundred yards to a
shady formation of tall basaltic stones, where he urinated
copiously into the sandy soil, then climbed one of the rocky
pedestals and stood facing north. The atmosphere between
Subject and the mountains was white with suspended dust,
and the snowy peaks seemed to hover over the desert basin.

He might have been resting, or he might have been sensing the air or planning the next stage of his journey. He was
motionless for almost an hour. Then he walked back to the
road and resumed his journey, pausing to drink from a road-
side ditch.

He walked at a steady pace through the afternoon. By
nightfall he had passed the last evidence of cultivation—old
fields gone fallow, irrigation canals filled and obscured with
windblown sand—and entered the desert basin between the
northern mountains and the far southern sea. Traffic on the
road moved in diurnal surges, and he had fallen behind
the last of the day's vehicular traffic. He was alone, and his
pace slowed with the approach of night. It was an unusually
clear evening. A fast, small moon slid up from the eastern
horizon, and Subject looked for a place to sleep.

He scouted for some minutes until he found a sandy
depression sheltered in the lee of a rocky outcrop. He curled
into an almost fetal posture there, his ventral surfaces pro-

tected from the cooling air. His body slowed to its usual nightly catatonia.

When the moon had crossed three-quarters of the sky a number of small insectile creatures emerged from a nest hidden in the sand. They were immediately attracted by the Subject, by his smell, perhaps, or the rhythm of his breathing. They were smaller than the nocturnal symbionts of his native city. They carried distinct thoracic bulges and they moved on two extra sets of legs. But they fed in the same fashion, and without hesitation, from the Subject's blood-nipples.

They were still there (sated, perhaps) when Subject woke to the first light of morning. Some of them still clung to his body as he stood up. Carefully, fastidiously, Subject picked them off and tossed them away. The discarded creatures lay motionless but uninjured until the sun warmed their bodies; then they burrowed back into the sand, pink fantails vanishing with a flourish.

Subject continued to follow the road.

When she looked at her first entry Marguerite was unhappy with what she had written.

Not because it was incorrect, though of course it was—it was outrageously, deliciously incorrect. Errors of attribution everywhere. The social scientists would be appalled. But she was tired of objectivity. Her own project, her private project, was to put herself in the Subject's place. How else did human beings understand one another? "Look at it from my point of view," people said. Or, "If I were in your place . . ." It was an imaginative act so commonplace as to be invisible. People who couldn't do it or refused to do it were called psychotics or sociopaths.

But when we look at the aboriginals, Marguerite thought, we're supposed to pretend to indifference. To an aloofness almost Puritanical in its austerity. Am I tainted if I admit I care whether the Subject lives or dies?

Most of her colleagues would say yes. Marguerite entertained the heretical idea that they might be wrong.

Still, the narrative was missing something. It was hard to know what to say or, especially, how to say it. Who was she writing for? Herself alone, or did she have an audience in mind?

A couple of weeks had passed since the Subject left the city—the time when Tess had cut her hand so badly. If she carried on with this there would be a great deal more to write. Marguerite was alone in her study, bent over her notebook, but at the thought of Tess she raised her head, sampling the night sounds in the town house.

Chris was still awake downstairs. Chris had made his own space in the house. He slept in the basement, was gone most of the day, took his evening meals at Sawyer's and used the kitchen and the living room mainly after Tessa's bedtime. His presence was unobtrusive, sometimes even comforting. (There: the sound of the refrigerator door closing, the rattle of a dish.) Chris always looked distressed when he worked, like a man struggling desperately to recapture a lost train of thought. But he would often work unceasingly, long into the night.

And he had been a help with Tess. More than a help. Chris wasn't one of those adults who condescend to children or try to impress them. He seemed comfortable with Tess, spoke freely to her, wasn't offended by her occasional silences or sulks. He hadn't made a big deal of Tessa's problems.

Even Tess had seemed a little happier with Chris in the house.

But the accident with her hand had been troubling. At first Tess would only say that she had leaned too hard on the window, but Marguerite knew better: a window at night in a lighted room was as good as a mirror.

And it wasn't the first mirror Tess had broken.

She had broken three back at Crossbank. The therapist had talked about "unexpressed rage," but Tess never described Mirror Girl as hostile or frightening. She broke the mirrors, she said, because she was tired of Mirror Girl showing up unannounced—"I like to see *myself* when I look in the mirror." Mirror Girl was intrusive, often unwelcome, frequently annoying, but something less than an outright nightmare.

It was the blood that had made this time seem so much scarier.

Marguerite had asked her about it the day after they came back from the clinic. The painkiller had left Tess a little sleepy and she spent all that afternoon in bed, occasionally glancing at a book but too scattered to read for long. Marguerite sat at her bedside. "I thought we were all done with that," she said. "Breaking things." Not accusatory. Just curious.

"I leaned on the window," Tess repeated, but she must have sensed Marguerite's skepticism, because she sighed and said in a smaller voice, "she just took me by surprise."

"Mirror Girl?"

Nod.

"Has she been back lately?"

"No," Tess said; then, "not very much. That's why she took me by surprise."

"Have you thought about what Dr. Leinster said back at Crossbank?"

"Mirror Girl's not real. She's like some part of me I don't want to see."

"You think that's right?"

Tess shrugged.

"Well, what do you *really* think?"

"I think, if I don't want to see her, why does she keep coming back?"

Good question, Marguerite thought. "Does she still look like you?"

"Exactly like."

"So how do you know it's her?"

Tess shrugged. "Her eyes."

"What about her eyes?"

"Too big."

"What does she want, Tess?" Hoping her daughter didn't hear the edge of anxiety in her voice. The catch in her throat. *Something is wrong with my girl. My baby.*

"I think she just wants me to pay attention."

"To what, Tess? To her?"

"No, not just to her. To everything. Everything, all the time."

"You remember what Dr. Leinster taught you?"

"Calm down and wait for her to go away."

"Does that still work?"

"I guess. Sometimes I forget."

Dr. Leinster had told Marguerite that Tessa's symptoms were unusual but stopped well short of the kind of systematic delusion that might point to schizophrenia. No drastic mood swings, no aggressive behavior, good orientation to time and place, emotional affect a little muted but not off the scale, reasonable insight into her problem, no obvious neurochemical imbalance. All that psychiatric bullshit, which boiled down to Dr. Leinster's last banal verdict: *most likely she'll grow out of it.*

But Dr. Leinster hadn't had to wash Tessa's blood-soaked pajamas.

Marguerite looked back at her journal. Her act of illicit storytelling. Still not up to date: there was nothing about the East Road Ruins, for instance . . . but enough for tonight.

Downstairs, she found the lights still burning. Chris was in the kitchen eating rye toast and leafing through last September's copy of *Astrogeological Review*, leaning back in one chair and resting his feet on another. "I'm just down for a nightcap," Marguerite said. "Don't mind me."

Orange juice and a dab of vodka, which she resorted to when she felt too restless to sleep. Like tonight. She pulled out a third chair from the kitchen table and put her slippered feet up next to Chris's. "Long day?" she asked.

"I had another meeting with Charlie Grogan out at the Eye," Chris said.

"So how's Charlie taking all this?"

"The siege? He doesn't care too much about that, though he says he's feeding Boomer ground beef these days. No dog food coming in on the trucks. Mostly he's worried about the Eye."

"What about the Eye?"

"They had another little cascade of technical glitches while I was out there."

"Really? I didn't get a memo about it."

"Charlie says it's just the usual blinks and nods, but it's been happening more often lately—power surges and some ragged I/O. I think what's really bothering him is the possibility somebody might pull the plug. He's nursed those O/BECs so long they're like children to him."

"It's just BS," Marguerite said, "all this talk about shutting down the Eye," but she didn't sound convincing even to herself. She made an awkward attempt to change the subject: "You don't usually talk about your work much."

She had already finished half the drink and she felt the alcohol working through her body ridiculously quickly, making her sleepy, making her reckless.

"I try to keep it away from you and Tess," Chris said. "I'm grateful to be here at all. I don't want to spread my troubles around."

"It's all right. We've known each other what, more than a month now? But I'm pretty sure whatever people say about your book isn't true. You don't strike me as dishonest or vicious."

"Dishonest and vicious? Is that what people say?"

Margaret blushed.

But Chris was smiling. "I've heard it all before, Marguerite."

"I'd like to read the book sometime."

"Nobody can download it since the lockup. Maybe that works to my advantage." His smile became less convincing. "I can give you a copy."

"I'd appreciate that."

"And I appreciate the vote of confidence. Marguerite?"

"What?"

"How would you feel about giving me an interview? About Blind Lake, the siege, how you fit in?"

"Oh, God." It wasn't what she had expected him to say. But what *had* she expected him to say? "Well, not tonight."

"No, not tonight."

"The last time anyone interviewed me it was the high school paper. About my science project."

"Good project?"

"Blue ribbon. Scholarship prize. All about mitochondrial DNA, back when I thought I wanted to be a geneticist. Pretty heavy stuff for a clergyman's daughter." She yawned. "I really do have to sleep."

Impulsively—or maybe drunkenly—Marguerite put her hand on the table, palm up. It was a gesture he could reasonably ignore. And no harm done if he did ignore it.

Chris looked at her hand, maybe a few seconds too long. Then he covered it with his own. Willingly? Grudgingly?

She liked the way his palm felt on hers. No adult male had held her hand since she left Ray, not that Ray had been much of a hand-holder. She discovered she couldn't look Chris in the eye. She let the moment linger; then she pulled back, grinning sheepishly. "Gotta go," she said.

"Sleep well," Chris Carmody said.

"You too," she told him, wondering what she was getting herself into.

Before she turned in she gave the direct feed from the Eye a last look.

Nothing much was doing. Subject continued his two-week-old odyssey. He was far along the eastern road, walking steadily into another morning. His skin looked increasingly dull as the days passed, but that was probably just ambient dust. There had been no rain for months now, but that was typical of a summer in these latitudes.

Even the sun seemed dimmer, until Margaret realized that the haze was unusually thick today, and particularly thick to the northeast, almost like an approaching squall line. She could ask Meteorology about it, she guessed. Tomorrow.

Finally, before she took herself to bed, Marguerite peeked into Tessa's room.

Tess was soundly asleep. The empty pane in the window beside her bed was still protected by Chris's plastic-and-veneer lash-up and the room was cozily warm. Darkness outside and in. Mirrors happily vacant. No sound but Tessa's easy breathing.

And in the quiet of the house Marguerite realized who she was writing her narrative for. Not for herself. Certainly not for other scientists. And not for the general public.

She was writing it for Tess.

The realization was energizing; it chased away the possibility of sleep. She went back to her office, turned on the desk lamp, and brought out the notebook again. She opened it and wrote:

More than fifty years ago, on a planet so far away that no living human being can ever hope to travel there, there was a city of rock and sandstone. It was a city as large as any of our own great cities, and its towers rose high into that world's thin, dry air. The city was built on a dusty plain, overlooked by tall mountains whose peaks were snowy even during the long summer. Someone lived there, someone who was not quite a human being, but who was a person in his own way, very different from us but in some ways much alike. The name we gave him was "Subject" . . .

Fifteen

Sue Sampel was beginning to enjoy her weekends again, despite the continuing lockdown.

For a while it had been a toss-up: weekdays busy but tarnished by the tantrums and weirdness of her boss; Saturday and Sunday slow and melancholy because she couldn't hop in the car and drive into Constance for some R&R. At first she had spent her weekends restlessly stoned, until her personal stash began to run low. (Another item the black trucks weren't delivering.) Then she borrowed a handful of Tiffany Arias novels from another support-staffer at the Plaza, five fat books about a wartime nurse in Shiugang torn between her love for an air force surveillance pilot and her secret affair with a hard-drinking gunrunner. Sue liked the books okay but thought they were a poor substitute for Green Girl Canadian Label Cannabis (regularly but illegally imported from the Northern Economic Protectorate), a quarter-ounce of which she was conserving in a cookie tin in her sock drawer.

Then Sebastian Vogel showed up on her doorstep with a billet note from Ari Weingart and a battered brown suitcase.

At first sight he didn't look promising. Cute, maybe, in a Christmas-elf kind of way, pushing sixty, a little overweight, fringe of gray hair framing his shiny bald head, a bushy red-gray beard. He was obviously shy—he stuttered when he introduced himself—and worse, Sue got the impression he was some kind of clergyman or retired priest. He promised to be "no trouble at all," and she feared that was probably true.

She had asked Ari about him the next day. Ari said Sebastian was a retired academic, not a priest, one of the three-pack of journalists who were stranded in Blind Lake. Sebastian had written a book called *God & the Quantum Vacuum*—Ari lent her a copy. The book was a lot drier than a Tiffany Arias novel but considerably more substantial.

Still, Sebastian Vogel wasn't much more than a silent partner in the household until the night he caught her rolling a joint on the kitchen table.

"Oh, my," Sebastian said from the doorway.

It was too late to hide the cookie tin or the papers. Guiltily, Sue tried to make a joke of it. "Um," she said, "care to join me?"

"Oh, no, I can't—"

"No, I *completely* understand—"

"I can't impose on your hospitality. But I have a half-ounce in my luggage, if you don't mind sharing it with me."

It got better after that.

———

He was fifteen years older than Sue and his birthday was January ninth. By the time that rolled around, she was sharing her bed with him. Sue liked him enormously—and he was a lot more fun than she ever would have guessed—but she also knew this was probably just a "lockdown romance," a term she'd picked up in the staff cafeteria. Lockdown romances had sprung up all over town. The combination of cabin fever and constant anxiety turned out to be a real aphrodisiac.

His birthday fell on a Saturday, and Sue had been planning for it for weeks now. She had wanted to get him a birthday cake, but there were no boxed mixes in the store and she wasn't about to attempt a cake from scratch. So she had done the next best thing. She had exercised her ingenuity.

She brought the cake into the dining room, a single candle planted in it. "Happy birthday," she said.

It wasn't really much of a cake. But it had symbolic value.

Sebastian's small mouth curled into a smile only partially obscured by his mustache. "This is too kind! Sue, thank you!"

"It's nothing," she said.

"No, it's fine!" He admired the cake. "I haven't seen luxury food in weeks. Where did you get this?"

It wasn't really a cake. It was a DingDong with a birthday candle stuck in it. "You don't want to know," Sue said.

Saturday, Sebastian had agreed to meet his friends for lunch at Sawyer's. He asked Sue to come along.

She agreed, but not without doubts. Sue had earned a B.Sc. some twenty years ago, but all it had gotten her was a glorified clerical job at Blind Lake. She had been frozen out of too many technical discussions to relish an afternoon of science-journalist peer-talk. Sebastian assured her it wouldn't be like that. His friends were writers, not scientists. "Outspoken but not snobbish."

Maybe so, maybe not.

Sue drove Sebastian, who had no car of his own, to Sawyer's, where they parked in a flurry of light snow. The wind was brisk, the sun peeking out now and again between canyons of cloud. The air inside the restaurant was sleepily warm and moist.

Sebastian introduced her to Elaine Coster, a skinny, sour-looking woman not much older than Sue herself, and Chris Carmody, considerably younger, tall and slightly grim but handsome in a ruffled way. Chris was friendly, but Elaine, after a limp handshake, said, "Well, Sebastian, there's more to you than we suspected."

Sue was surprised by the animosity in the woman's voice, almost a sneer, and by Sebastian's obvious indifference to it.

Lunch was soup and sandwiches, the post-lockdown inevitable. Sue made gracious noises but mostly listened to the others talk. They talked Blind Lake politics, including some speculation about Ray Scutter, and they worried over the perennial question of the siege. They reminisced about people she'd never heard of until Sue began to feel ignored, though Sebastian kept a hand on her thigh under the table and gave her a reassuring squeeze from time to time.

Finally there was a piece of gossip to which she felt connected. Turned out Chris was rooming with Ray Scutter's ex, and Ray had done some macho grandstanding outside the Blind Lake clinic a couple of weeks back. It was typical Ray Scutter assholery, and Sue said so.

Elaine gave her a long, unnerving glare. "What do you know about Ray Scutter?"

"I run his office for him."

Her eyes widened. "You're his secretary?"

"Executive assistant. Well, yeah, secretary, basically."

"Pretty *and* talented," Elaine said to Sebastian, who merely smiled his inscrutable smile. She refocused on Sue, who resisted the urge to shrink away from the woman's laser stare. "How much do you actually know about Ray Scutter?"

"His private life, nothing. His work, pretty much everything."

"He talks to you about it?"

"God, no. Ray plays his cards close to his chest, mainly because he's holding the ace of incompetency. You know how people who are out of their depth like to do all kinds of busy-work, make themselves at least look useful? That's Ray. He doesn't tell me anything, but half the time I have to explain his job to him."

"You know," Elaine said, "there are rumors about Ray."

Or maybe, Sue thought, I'm out of *my* depth. "What kind of rumors?"

"That Ray wants to break into the executive servers and read people's mail."

"Oh. Well, that's—"

There was a buzzing. Chris Carmody took his phone out of his pocket, turned away and whispered into it. Elaine gave him a poisonous look.

When he turned back to the table he said, "Sorry, people. Marguerite needs me to look after her daughter."

"Jesus," Elaine said, "is everybody setting up housekeeping in this fucking place? What are you now, a baby-sitter?"

"Some kind of emergency, Marguerite says." He stood up.

"Go, go." She rolled her eyes. Sebastian nodded amiably.

"Pleasure meeting you," Chris said to Sue.

"You, too." He seemed nice enough, if a little distracted. He was certainly better company than Elaine with the X-ray vision.

Which Elaine focused on her as soon as Chris walked away from the table. "So it's true? Ray's doing some illicit hacking?"

"I don't know about illicit. He's planning to make it public. The idea is, pre-lockdown messages on the senior servers might give us a clue to what caused all this."

"If some kind of message went out before the lockdown, how come Ray didn't get one?"

"He was low man on the management totem pole before everybody left for the Cancun conference. Plus he's new here. He had contacts at Crossbank, but not what you'd call friends. Ray doesn't *make* friends."

"This gives him the right to break into secure servers?"

"He thinks so."

"He thinks so, but has he actually done anything about it?"

Sue considered her position. Talking to the press would be a great way to get herself fired. No doubt Elaine would promise total anonymity. (Or money, if she asked for it. Or the moon.) But promises were like bad checks, easy to write and hard to cash. I may be stupid, Sue thought, but I'm not nearly as stupid as this woman seems to think.

She considered Sebastian. Did Sebastian want her to talk about this?

She gave him a questioning look. Sebastian sat back in his chair with his hands clasped over his stomach, a spot of mustard adorning his beard. Enigmatic as a stuffed owl. But he nodded at her.

Okay.

Okay. She'd do it for him, not this Elaine.

She licked her lips. "Shulgin was in the building yesterday with a computer guy."

"Cracking servers?"

"What do you think? But it's not like I caught them in the act."

"What kind of results did they get?"

"None, as far as I know. They were still there after I went home Friday." They might still be there, Sue thought. Sifting silicon for gold.

"If they find something interesting, will that information pass over your desk?"

"No." She smiled. "But it'll pass over Ray's."

Sebastian looked suddenly troubled. "This is all very interesting," he said, "but don't let Elaine talk you into anything dangerous." His hand was on her thigh again, communicating some message she couldn't decipher. "Elaine has her own best interests at heart."

"Fuck *off*, Sebastian," Elaine said.

Sue was mildly scandalized. More so because Sebastian just nodded and put that Buddha-like smile back on his face.

"I might see something like that," Sue said. "Or I might not."

"If you do—"

"Elaine, Elaine," Sebastian said. "Don't push your luck."

"I'll think about it," Sue said. "Okay? Good enough? Can we talk about something else now?"

They had drained their carafe of coffee and the waitress hadn't come around with more. Elaine began shrugging her shoulders into her jacket. Sebastian said, "By the way, I was asked to give a little presentation at the community center for one of Ari's social nights."

"Hawking your book?" Elaine asked.

"In a way. Ari's having a hard time filling up those Saturday slots. He'll probably ask you next."

Sue enjoyed seeing Elaine flinch from this proposition. "Thanks, but I have better things to do."

"I'll let you tell Ari that yourself."

"I'll put it in writing if he likes."

Sebastian excused himself and wandered off to the men's room. After an awkward silence Sue, still miffed, said, "Maybe you don't like Sebastian's writing, but he deserves a little respect."

"Have you *read* his book?"

"Yes."

"Have you really? What's it about?"

Sue found herself blushing. "It's about the quantum vacuum. The quantum vacuum as a medium for, uh, a kind of *intelligence . . .*" And how what we call human consciousness is actually our ability to tap a little tiny bit of that universal mind. But she couldn't begin to say that to Elaine. She already felt painfully foolish.

"No," Elaine said. "Sorry, wrong. It's about telling people something simplistic and reassuring, dressed up in pseudoscientific bullshit. It's about a semiretired academic making pots of money and doing it in the most cynical way possible. Oh—"

Sebastian had crept up behind her, and judging by his expression he had heard every word. "Honestly, Elaine, that's too much."

"Don't get all huffy, Sebastian. Have your publishers tapped you for a sequel yet? What are you calling it? *The Quantum Vacuum Twelve-Step Program*? *Financial Security the Quantum Vacuum Way*?"

Sebastian opened his mouth but didn't say anything. He didn't look angry, Sue thought. He looked hurt.

"Honestly," he repeated.

Elaine stood up, buttoning her jacket. "You kids have fun." She hesitated, then turned back and put a hand on Sue's shoulder. "Okay, I know I'm an awful bitch. I'm sorry. Thank you for putting up with me. I do appreciate what you said about Ray."

Sue shrugged—she couldn't think of an answer.

Sebastian was quiet during the drive back. Almost sulking. She couldn't wait to get home and roll him a joint.

Sixteen

Chris found Marguerite in her upstairs office, shouting into her pocket phone. The direct feed from the Eye filled the wall monitor.

The image looked bad to Chris. It looked degraded—streaked with spurious lines and fleeting white pinpricks. Worse, the Subject was struggling through some intensely bad weather, ribbons of ochre and rust, a dust storm so fierce it threatened to obscure him altogether.

"No," Marguerite was saying. "I don't *care* what they're saying at the Plaza. Come on, Charlie, you know what this means! *No!* I'll be there. Soon." She saw Chris and added, "Fifteen minutes."

The original high-altitude mapping of UMa47/E had shown seasonal dust storms of almost Martian intensity, primarily in the southern hemisphere. This one must be anomalous, Chris thought, since Subject had not journeyed more than a hundred miles from Lobsterville, and Lobsterville was well north of the equator. Or maybe it was perfectly natural, part of some long-term cycle early surveillance had missed.

Subject pushed into the opaque air, torso bent forward. His image faded, clarified, faded again. "Charlie's afraid they'll lose him altogether," Marguerite said. "I'm going out to the Eye."

Chris followed her downstairs. Tess was in the living room watching Blind Lake TV's Saturday matinee. An animated feature: rabbits with huge eyeglasses growing carrots in medieval beakers and alembics. Her head bounced gently and rhythmically against the sofa.

"You said we could go sledding," Tess called out.

"Honey, it's a work emergency. I told you. Chris will look after you, 'kay?"

"I suppose I could take her sledding," Chris said. "It's a long walk, though."

"Really?" Tess asked. "Can we?"

Marguerite pursed her lips. "I guess, but I don't want you hiking there and back. Mrs. Colangelo said we could borrow her car if we needed it—Chris can look into that."

He promised he'd ask. Tess was mollified, and Marguerite shrugged into her winter jacket. "If I'm not back by dinner there's food in the freezer. Be creative."

"How serious is the problem?"

"It took a lot of delicate work training the O/BECs to fix on a single individual. If we lose him in the storm we might not get him back. Worse, there's a lot of signal degradation happening, and Charlie doesn't know what's causing it."

"You think you can help?"

"Not with the engineering. But there are people in the

Plaza who'd love to use this as an opportunity to pull back from the Subject. I don't want that to happen. I'm running interference."

"Good luck."

"Thank you. And thanks for keeping Tess company. One way or another, I'll be back before her bedtime."

She hurried out the door.

In the interest of journalistic brotherhood, Chris called Elaine and told her about the developing crisis at the Eye. She said she'd find out what she could. "Things are getting strange," she said. "I'm getting that batten-down-the-hatches feeling."

He had to admit he was a little skittish himself. Almost four months of quarantine now, and no matter how you tried to ignore it or rationalize it, that meant something monumentally bad was happening—maybe outside, maybe inside. Something bad, something dangerous, something hidden that would eventually come screaming into the light.

Mrs. Colangelo managed the clothing store in the Blind Lake retail mall and she had been effectively retired since the lockdown. She let him borrow her little lime-green Marconi roadster, and Tess loaded her old-fashioned wooden sled into the back. Most kids used inner tubes or plastic skids, Tess explained, but she'd spotted this sled (actually a *toboggan*, she insisted) in a thrift shop and begged her mother to buy it. This was back at Crossbank, which was hillier than Blind Lake but heavily wooded—at least out here she wouldn't run into any trees.

Tess was still something of a cipher to Chris. She reminded him of his sister Portia in many (maybe too many) ways—her willfulness, her unpredictability, her spiky moods. But Porry had been a great talker, especially when she picked up some new enthusiasm. Tess spoke only sporadically.

Tess was silent for the first five minutes of the ride, but apparently she had also been thinking of Portia: "Did your sister ever go sledding?" she asked.

Since the window episode Tess had come to him several times for Porry stories. Tess, an only child, seemed fascinated by the idea of Chris as an older brother—something less than a parent, more than a friend. She seemed to think Portia had led an enchanted existence. Not true. Portia was buried in a rainy Seattle cemetery, victim of the fatal disease of adulthood in its most acute form. He would not, of course, say that to Tess. "It didn't snow much where we grew up. The closest thing to sledding we did was snow-tubing at a little resort up in the mountains."

"Did Portia like that?"

"Not at first. At first she was pretty scared. But after a couple of runs she decided it was fun."

"I think she liked it," Tess said, "except that she got cold."

"That's right, she didn't like the cold very much."

Elaine had accused him of "setting up housekeeping" at Marguerite's. He wondered if that was true. Over the last several weeks he had become very much a part of Marguerite and Tessa Hauser's universe, almost in spite of himself. No, that was wrong; not in spite of himself; he had taken every step willingly. But the steps had added up to an unplanned journey.

He had yet to go to bed with Marguerite, but according to every signal he could read that was where this trip was taking him. And it wasn't a neat little temporary bargain, a one-night stand or even an explicit lockdown romance, the exchange of warmth for warmth and no promises made or implied. The stakes were much, much higher.

Did he want that?

He liked Marguerite, he liked everything *about* Marguerite. Every late-night conversation—and lately there had been many—had drawn him closer to her. She was a generous story-teller. She talked freely about her childhood (she had lived with her father in a Presbyterian rectory in a little rail-stop bed-room suburb outside of Cincinnati, a seventy-year-old house with a wooden porch); about her work; about Tess; less often and more reluctantly, about her marriage. Nothing in her somewhat sheltered life had prepared her for Ray, who had professed to love her but had only wanted to furnish his life with a woman in the conventional manner and for whom cru-elty was the fuck of last resort. Such men were abundant on the earth, but Marguerite had never run into one. What followed had been a nine-year nightmare of enlightenment.

And what did she see in Chris? Not exactly the anti-Ray, but maybe a more benevolent vision of masculinity, someone she could confide in, someone she could lean against without fear of retribution; and he was flattered by that, but it was an uninformed opinion. Not that he was incapable of love. He had loved his work, he had loved his family, he had loved his sister Portia, but the things he loved tended to come to pieces in his hands, torn apart by his clumsy desire to protect them.

He would never hurt her the way Ray had hurt her, but in the long term he might prove just as dangerous.

Tess had told him where the best sledding was, along the low hills a quarter mile past Eyeball Alley, where the access road ended in a paved cul-de-sac. The Alley's cooling towers came up on the left side of the road, dark sentinels in a white landscape. Tess broke the silence again: "Did Portia have prob-lems at school?"

"Sure she did. Everybody does, now and then."

"I hate Physical Education."

"I could never climb that rope," Chris said.

"We don't do ropes yet. But we have to wear stupid gym clothes. Did Portia ever have nightmares?"

"Sometimes."

"What were her nightmares like?"

"Well—she didn't like to talk about them, Tess, and I promised not to tell."

Tess looked at him appraisingly. She was deciding whether to trust him, Chris thought. Tess dispensed her trust cautiously. Life had taught her that not every grown-up was trustworthy—a hard lesson, but worth learning.

But if he was still keeping Portia's secrets, he might keep Tessa's. "Did my mom tell you about Mirror Girl?"

"Nope. Who's Mirror Girl?"

"That's what's wrong with me." Another sidelong look. "You knew something was *wrong* with me, right?"

"I did wonder a little, that night we had to go to the clinic."

"I see her in mirrors. That's why I call her Mirror Girl." She paused. "I saw her in the window that night. She took me by surprise. I guess I got angry."

Chris sensed the gravity of the confession. He was flattered Tess had raised the subject with him.

He eased up on the accelerator, eking out a little more talk time.

"She looks like me but she isn't me. That's what nobody understands. So what do you think? Am I crazy?"

"You don't strike me as crazy."

"I don't talk about it because people think I'm nuts. Maybe I am."

"Stuff happens we don't understand. That doesn't make you nuts."

"How come nobody else can see her?"

"I don't know. What does she want?"

Tess shrugged her shoulders irritably. It was a question she must have been asked too often. "She doesn't say."

"Does she talk?"

"Not in words. I think she just wants me to pay attention to things. I think *she* can't pay attention unless *I'm* paying attention—does that make any sense? But that's just what I think. It's only a theory."

"Portia talked to her toys sometimes."

"It's not like that. That's a kid thing." She rolled her eyes. "*Edie Jerundt* talks to her toys."

Better not to press. It was enough that Tess had opened up to him. He drove in silence to the end of the road, to the turnaround where a half dozen other cars were parked.

The steepest slope of the snow-white hill was speckled with sledders and boarders and indulgent parents.

"Lot of airplanes around today," Tess said, climbing out of the car.

Chris glanced at the sky but saw nothing more than a silver speck on the far horizon. Another cryptic Tess remark. "Will you help me pull the sled up?" she asked.

"Sure thing."

"Ride down with me?"

"If you want. But I have to warn you, I haven't been on a sled for years."

"You said you didn't have a sled. You said you just snow-tubed."

"I mean, I haven't slid down a hill for years."

"Since Portia was little?"

"Right."

"Well, come on then," Tess said.

Tess was aware, all this time, of the growing and insistent presence of Mirror Girl.

Mirror Girl slid through every reflective surface like a slippery ghost. Mirror Girl wavered across the windows and the shiny blue hood and side panels of the car. Tess was even aware of the sparse few snowflakes falling from a high gray sky. She had studied snowflakes in science class: they were an example of symmetry. Ice, she thought, like glass, folded in mirror angles. She imagined Mirror Girl in every invisible facet of the falling snow.

In fact Tess felt a little ill. Mirror Girl pressed in on her like a heavy, airless fog, until she could hardly think of anything else. Maybe she'd said too much to Chris. Saying the name, Mirror Girl, was probably a bad idea. Maybe Mirror Girl didn't like to be talked about.

But Tess had been looking forward to this sledding expedition all week and she wasn't about to let Mirror Girl screw it up.

She allowed Chris to pull the sled to the top of the hill. There was a gentle path up the long part of the hill and then a steep slope for riding back down. Tess was a little breathless at the top, but she liked the view. Funny how such a little hill let you see so much more than you could from down below. Here were the dark towers of Eyeball Alley, there the white squares of Hubble Plaza and the stores and houses clustered around it. The roads looked like roads in a roadmap, sharp and precise. The road to Constance cut through the south gate and into the snow-flecked distance like a line etched in white metal. Wind plucked at Tessa's hair, and she took her snow hat out of her jacket pocket and pulled it over her head almost down to her eyes.

She closed her eyes and saw airplanes. Why airplanes? Mirror Girl was very concerned about airplanes right now.

About a little plane with propellors and a bigger jet dropping down toward it like a hunting bird. Where? The sky was too cloudy to reveal much, though the clouds themselves were thin and high. The buzz in her ears might be an airplane, Tess thought, or it might just be the wind fluttering the collar of her jacket or her own blood pulsing in her ears.

Her fingers tingled but her body was warm under her clothes. I'm hot, I'm cold, she thought.

"Tess?" Chris said. "You okay?"

Usually when people asked her that question it meant she was doing something peculiar. Standing too still or staring too hard. But why did people care? What was so strange about just standing here thinking?

Maybe this was what Mirror Girl was seeing or wanted Tess to see: the big plane and the little one. The little one was bright yellow and had numbers on its wings but no military markings. It was bigger than the kind of airplane that dusted crops, but not by much. It was very clear to her when she closed her eyes but confusing, too, as if she were looking at the airplane from too many angles at once. It was a faceted airplane, a kaleidoscope airplane, an airplane in a mirror of many angles.

Chris handed her the rope of the sled. Tess grasped the rope in her hand and tried to focus on the task of sledding—it suddenly seemed more like a chore than fun. Snow crunched and complained under the weight of the wooden runners. Somewhere down the slope, people laughed. Then the airplanes distracted her again. Not just the little airplane but the bigger one too, the jet, which was still far away but stalked the small plane doggedly, and then—

Tess dropped the rope. The sled skittered away down the hill, vacant, before Chris could catch it.

Chris knelt in front of her. "Tess, what is it? What's wrong?"

She saw his big worried eyes but couldn't answer. The jet had come miles closer in just a few seconds. And now something flew away from the jet—it was a missile, Tess supposed—and it flashed between the two aircraft like a reflection in a fractured crystal.

Why couldn't anyone else see it? Why were the people on the hill still laughing and sliding? Were they confused by the snow, by its millions-upon-millions of mirrors? "Maybe we'd better get you home," Chris said, obviously not seeing it either. Tess wanted to point. She raised her arm; she extended her finger; her finger followed the invisible arc of the missile, a line like an infinitely thin pencil stroke drawn across the white paper of the sky; she said, "*There*—"

But then everybody heard the explosion.

Charlie Grogan met Marguerite outside his office at the Alley. "Come on down to Control," he said tersely. "It's only getting freakier."

Charlie was obviously tense as they rode the elevator. The Eye was deep in the earth, an irony Marguerite had once appreciated. The jewel is in the lotus; the Eye is in the earth. The better to see you with, my dear. It didn't seem particularly funny right now. "I can handle any call from the Plaza," she said, "unless it's Ray himself. If Ray calls and pulls rank, all I can do is pretend the phone is broken."

"Frankly, the Plaza's not our biggest problem right now. We had to call in both tech shifts. They yanked and replaced a couple of the interface units. Worse," Charlie said, "and I know you don't want to hear this, we're having big trouble with the O/BECs."

The O/BECs. Even Charlie had been known to call them "a keep-your-fingers-crossed technology." Marguerite had very little background in quantum computing; she didn't pretend to understand the intricacies of the O/BEC platens.

Hooking up a collection of O/BECs in a self-evolving

"organic" array was an experiment that should never have worked, in her opinion. The results were unpredictable and spooky, and she remembered what Chris had said (or quoted): *It could end at any time.* It could, yes it could. And maybe this was the time.

But, God, no, she thought, not now, not when they were on the brink of a profounder knowledge, not when the Subject was in mortal danger.

The control-and-interface room was more crowded than Marguerite had ever seen it. Tech people clustered around the system monitors, a few of them arguing heatedly. She was dismayed to see that the big main screen, the live feed, was utterly blank. "Charlie, what happened?"

He shrugged. "Loss of intelligibility. Temporary, we think. It's an I/O hang-up, not a complete system failure."

"We lost the Subject?"

"No, like I said, it's an interface thing. The Eye is still watching him, but we're having trouble talking to the Eye." And he gave a half-shrug that meant, *At least that's what we think.*

"Has this happened before?"

"Not like this, no."

"But you can fix it?"

He hesitated. "Probably," he said at last.

"There was still an image twenty minutes ago. What was he doing when you lost him?"

"The Subject? He was hunkered down behind some kind of obstruction when everything grayed out."

"You think the storm is causing this?"

"Marguerite, *nobody knows.* We don't understand a fraction of what the O/BECs do. They can look through stone walls; a sandstorm shouldn't be a problem. But visibility is severely compromised, so maybe the Eye has to work harder to keep a fix on a moving target, maybe that's what we're dealing with here. All we can do is treat the peripheral problems as they come up. Keep the temperature in spec, keep the quantum wells stable." He closed his eyes and ran a hand over his stubbled scalp.

This is what we don't like to acknowledge, Marguerite thought: that we're using a technology we don't understand. A "dissipative structure" capable of growing its own complexity—capable of growing well beyond our intellectual grasp of it. Not really a machine but a process *inside* a machine, evolution in miniature, in its way a new form of life. All we ever did was trigger it. Trigger it, and bend it to our purposes.

Made ourselves the only species with an eye more complex than our own brains.

The overhead lights flickered and dimmed. Voltage-bus monitors bleated shrill alarms.

"Please, Charlie," Marguerite said. "Don't let him slip away."

Chris was following Tessa's abrupt gesture when he heard the explosion.

It wasn't an especially loud sound, not much louder than the sound of a slammed tailgate, but weightier, full of rolling undertones like thunder. He straightened up and searched the sky. So did the other sledders, anyone who wasn't already skimming down the slope.

At first he saw an expanding ring of smoke, faint against a background of high cloud and patchwork blue sky . . . then the airplane itself, distant and falling in a skewed curve toward the earth.

Falling, but not helplessly. The pilot seemed to be struggling for control. It was a small plane, a private plane, canary yellow, nothing military; Chris saw it in silhouette as it flew briefly level, parallel to the road from Blind Lake and maybe a couple hundred feet off the ground. Coming closer, he realized. Maybe trying to use the road as a landing strip.

Then the aircraft faltered again, veering wildly and ejecting a gout of black smoke.

Coming in badly, and coming in close. "Get down," he told Tess. "Down on the ground. *Now*."

The girl remained rigid, motionless, staring. Chris pushed her back into the snow and covered her with his body. Some of the sledders began to scream. Apart from that, the silence of the afternoon had become eerie: the plane's engines had cut out. It should make more noise, Chris thought. All that falling metal.

It touched ground at the north end of the parking circle, nosing up at the last minute before it collided with a bright red Ford van, translating all that kinetic energy into a fan of red and yellow debris that cut trails and craters into the fallen snow. Tessa's body trembled at the sound. The shrapnel traveled east and away from the sledding hill, and it was still coming down in a patter of snow-muted thunks when the wreckage burst into flame.

Chris pulled Tess into a sitting position.

She sat up as if catatonic, arms rigid at her sides. She stared but didn't blink.

"Tess," he said, "listen to me. I have to help, but I want you to stay here. Button up if you get cold, look for another adult if you need help, otherwise *wait for me*, okay?"

"I guess."

"Wait for me."

"Wait for you," she said dully.

He didn't like the way she looked or sounded, but she wasn't physically injured and there might be survivors in the burning wreckage. Chris gave her what he hoped was a reassuring hug and then bounded down the slope, his feet gouging imperfections into snow compressed and made slick by the sledders.

He reached the burning airplane along with three other adults, two men and a woman, presumably all parents who had come sledding with their children. He advanced as close to the fire as he dared, the heat of it prickling the skin of his face and boiling snow into the air. The paved lot showed through the snow in watery black patches. He could see enough of the van—its roof had been sheared off—to know there was no one inside. The small plane was another matter. Behind its furiously cooking engine a human shape struggled against the clouded glass of the cabin door.

Chris peeled off his cloth jacket and wrapped it around his right hand.

Later, Marguerite would tell him he acted "heroically." Maybe so. It didn't feel that way. What it felt like was the obvious next thing to do. He might not have attempted it if the fire had not been relatively contained, if the plane had been heavier with fuel. But he didn't recall doing any risk-benefit calculation. There was only the job at hand.

He felt the heat on his face, prickling his skin, gusts of cold air behind him angling toward the flames. The figure faintly visible in the crumpled cabin twitched, then stopped moving altogether. The door was hot even through the folds of his jacket. It was slightly ajar but stuck in its frame. Chris fumbled at it futilely, backed away to catch a breath of cooler air, then kicked hard at the accordioned aluminum. Once, twice, three times, until it bent far enough that he was able to brace himself, grasp the door in the folds of his now-smoldering jacket, and apply some leverage.

The pilot spilled onto the damp ground like a bag of meat. His face was hairless and blackened where it wasn't a shocking, charred red. He wore a pair of aviator glasses, one lens missing and the other lens crazed. But he was breathing. His chest lifted and fell in cresting waves.

The men behind him dashed close enough to pull the pilot away from the wreckage. Chris found himself hesitating pointlessly. Was there something more he was supposed to do? The heat had made him dizzy.

He felt a hand on his shoulder, felt himself tugged away from the flames. Just a few feet away the air seemed dramatically colder, far colder than it had been on the hillside with Tess. He staggered away, then sat on the hood of an undamaged automobile and let his head droop. Someone brought him a bottle of water. He drained it almost at once, though that made him feel sicker. He heard an ambulance screaming down the road from Blind Lake.

Tess, he thought. Tess on the hillside.

How much time had passed? He looked for her on the slope. Everyone had come down, they had all gathered in the parking lot a safe distance from the burning plane. Everyone but Tess. He'd told her to stay put, and she had taken him literally. He called to her, but she was too far away to hear.

Wearily, he hiked back up the slope. Tess was standing immobile, staring at the wreckage. She didn't acknowledge him when he called to her. Not good. She was in some kind of shock, Chris supposed.

He knelt in front of her, put his face in her line of vision and his hands on her small shoulders. "Tess," he said. "Tess, are you all right?"

At first she didn't react. Then she trembled. Her body shook. She blinked and opened her mouth soundlessly.

"We need to get you someplace warm," he said.

She leaned into him and started to cry.

Marguerite lost track of Charlie in the noisy chaos of the control room.

For a fraction of a second there was utter blackness—complete electrical failure. Then the lights flickered back and the room was full of voices. Marguerite found an unoccupied corner and stayed out of the way. There was nothing she could do to help and she knew better than to interfere.

Something bad had happened, something she didn't understand, something that had driven the engineers into a frenzy of activity. She focused on the big wall screen, the direct feed from the Eye, still alarmingly blank. It could end at any time.

Her phone buzzed. She ignored it. She caught sight of Charlie and watched him orbit the room, coordinating activity. Since she was helpless—or at least unable to help—she began to feel a presentiment of loss. Loss of intelligibility. Loss of orientation. Loss of vision. Loss of the Subject, with whom she had struggled across a desert to the heart of a sandstorm. Periodically, the wall screen erupted into stochastic cascades of color. Marguerite stared, trying but failing to extract an image. No signal, just noise. Only noise.

A few more green lights, she heard someone say. Was that good? Apparently so. Here came Charlie, and he wasn't smiling, but the expression on his face wasn't as grave as it had been—how long ago? An hour?

"We're getting a little something back," he said.

"An image?"

"Maybe."

"We're still fixed on the Subject?"

"Just watch, Marguerite."

She focused again on the screen, which had begun to fill with new light. Tiny digital mosaics, assembled in the unfathomable depths of the O/BEC platens. White faded to tawny brown. The desert. *We're back*, Marguerite thought, and a tingle of relief flowed up her spine—but where was the Subject, and what was this blank emptiness?

"Sand," she murmured. Fine silicate grains undisturbed by wind. The storm must have passed. But the sand wasn't still. The sand mounded and slid this way and that.

Subject lifted himself out of a cloak of sand. He had been buried by the wind, but he was alive. He pulled himself up by his manipulating arms, then stood, unsteadily, in the startling sunlight. The virtual camera rose with him. Behind him Marguerite saw the sand squall where it had retreated to the horizon, trailing black vortices like mares' tails.

All around the Subject were lines and angles of stone. Old stone columns and pyramidal structures and sand-scoured foundations. The ruins of a city.

PART THREE

The Ascent
of the Invisible

Man, on Earth, could go no further
toward conquering the limitations of atmosphere, metals, and optics. Through
this gigantic mirror, underlying a telescope in whose construction the efforts
of dozens of great minds had been
united for years to produce an instru-
ment of unrivaled accuracy, intricacy,
and range, equipped with every device
desired by and known to astronomers,
study of the universe had reached
a climax.

—Donald Wandrei, "Colossus," 1934

Seventeen

Coming into February now, and it was obvious to Marguerite as she drove home from her Saturday ration trip what a different place the Lake had become.

Superficially, nothing had changed. The snowplows still emerged from the back bays of the retail mall whenever it snowed, and they kept the streets passably clear. Lights still burned in windows at night. Everybody was warm and no one was hungry.

But there was a shabbiness about the town, too, an unwashed quality. There were no outside contractors to repair winter potholes or replace the shingles that had been torn from so many roofs in the post-Christmas storms. Garbage was collected on the regular schedule but it couldn't be trucked off-site—the sanitation people had set up a temporary dump at the western extremity of the lake, near the perimeter fence and as far as possible from the town and the preserved wetlands; still, the stench drifted with the wind like an augur of decay, and on especially breezy days she had seen crumpled papers and food wrappers wheeling along the Mallway like tumbleweeds. The question was so commonplace no one bothered to ask it anymore: *when will it end?*

Because it could end at any time.

Tess had come back from the site of the airplane crash weak and dazed. Marguerite had wrapped her up and fed her hot soup and put her to bed for the night—Marguerite herself hadn't slept, but Tess had, and in the morning she had seemed herself again. *Seemed* was the key word. Between Christmas and New Year's Tess had not so much as mentioned Mirror Girl; there had been no provocative episodes; but Marguerite had recognized the worry creases on Tessa's face and had sensed in her daughter's silences something weightier than her customary shyness.

She had been extremely reluctant to send Tess for her weeklong visit with Ray, but there was no way around it. Had she objected, Ray would almost certainly have sent one of his rent-a-cop security guys around to collect Tess by force. So, with deep unease, Marguerite had helped her daughter pack her rucksack of treasured possessions and ushered her out the door as soon as Ray pulled up at the curb in his little scarab-colored automobile.

Ray had remained a silhouette in the shaded cab of the car, unwilling to show her his face. He looked indistinct, Marguerite thought, like a fading memory. She watched Tess greet him with a cheeriness that struck her as either false or heart-breakingly naive.

The only upside of this was that during the next week she would have more free time for Chris.

She pulled into the driveway, thinking of him.

Chris. He had made a powerful impression on her, with his wounded eyes and his obvious courage. Not to mention the way he touched her, like a man stepping into a spring of warm water, testing the heat before he gave himself up to it. Good Chris. Scary Chris.

Scary because having a man in the house—being intimate with a man—provoked unwelcome memories of Ray, if only by contrast. The smell of aftershave in the bathroom, a man's pants abandoned on the bedroom floor, male warmth lingering in the crevices of the bed . . . with Ray all these things had come to seem loathsome, as objectionable as a bruise. But with Chris it was just the opposite. Yesterday she had found herself not only volunteering to wash his clothes but furtively inhaling the smell of him from an undershirt before she committed it to the washing machine. How ridiculously schoolgirlish, Marguerite thought. How very dangerously *infatuated* she was with this man.

She supposed it was at least therapeutic, like draining venom from a snakebite.

People talked about "lockdown romances." Was this a lockdown romance? Marguerite's experience was limited. Ray had been not only her first husband but her first lover. Marguerite had been, like Tess, one of those awkward girls at school: bright but gawky, not especially pretty, intimidated into silence in any social setting. When boys were like that they were called "geeks," but at least they seemed able to take solace in the company of others like themselves. Marguerite had never made real friends of either sex, at least not until she was in graduate school. There, at least, she had found colleagues, people who respected her talent, people who liked her for her ideas, some of whom had progressed to the status of friends.

Maybe that was why she had been so impressed with Ray when Ray began to take an explicit interest in her. Ray had been ten years her senior, doing cutting-edge astrophysical work back when she was still struggling to find a way into Crossbank. He had been blunt in his opinions but flattering toward Marguerite, and he had obviously been sizing her up for marriage from the beginning. What Marguerite had not learned was that for some men marriage is a license to drop their masks and show their true and terrible faces. Nor was this merely a figure of speech: it seemed to Marguerite that his face had actually changed, that he had shed the gentle and indulgent Ray of their engagement as efficiently as a snake sheds its skin.

Clearly, she had been a lousy judge of character.

So what did that make Chris? A lockdown romance? A potential second father for Tess? Or something in between?

And how could she even begin to construct an idea of the future, when even the possibility of a future could end at any time?

Chris had been working in his basement study, but he came up the stairs when he heard her puttering around the kitchen and said, "Are you busy?"

Well, that was an interesting question. It was Saturday. She wasn't obliged to work. But what was work, what *wasn't* work? For months she had divided her attention between Tess and the Subject, and now Chris. Today she'd planned to catch up on her notes and keep an eye on the direct feed. The Subject's odyssey continued, though the sandstorm crisis had passed and the ruined city was now far behind him. He had left the road; he was traveling through empty desert; his physical condition had changed in troublesome ways; but nothing absolutely critical was happening, at least not at the moment. "What did you have in mind?"

"The pilot I pulled out of the wreck is stabilized over at the clinic. I thought I'd pay him a visit."

"Is he awake?" Marguerite had heard the man was in a coma.

"Not yet."

"So what's the point of visiting?"

"Sometimes you just want to touch base."

Back in the car, then, back on the road with Chris at the wheel, back through the bright, cold February afternoon and the tumbling windblown trash. "How could you possibly owe him anything? You saved his life."

"For better or worse."

"How could it be worse?"

"He's severely burned. When he wakes up he's going to be in a world of pain. Not only that—I'm sure Ray and his buddies would love to interrogate him."

That was true. Nobody knew why the small plane had been flying over Blind Lake or what the pilot had hoped to accomplish by violating an enforced no-fly zone. But the incident had turned up the anxiety level in town more than a notch. In the past couple of weeks there had been three more attempts to breach the perimeter fence from inside, all by individuals: a day worker, a student, and a junior analyst. All three had been killed by pocket drones, though the analyst had made it a good fifty or sixty yards wearing a rigged thermal jacket to disguise his infrared signature.

None of the bodies had been recovered. They would still be there, Marguerite thought, when the snow melted in the spring. Like something left over from a war, burned, frozen, and thawed: biological residue. Vulture bait. Were there vultures in Minnesota?

Everyone was frightened and everyone was desperate to

know why the Lake had been quarantined and when the quarantine would end (or, unspeakable thought, *whether* it would end). So, yes, the pilot would be interrogated, perhaps vigorously, and yes, he would certainly be in pain, despite the clinic's reserve of neural analgesics. But that didn't invalidate the act of courage Chris had performed. She felt this in him more than once, his doubts about the consequences of a good act. Maybe his book about Galliano had been a good act, at least from his point of view. A wrong righted. And he had been punished for it. Once burned, twice shy. But it seemed to go deeper than that.

Marguerite didn't understand how a man as apparently decent as Chris Carmody could be so unsure of himself, when certified bastards like Ray walked around in the glow of their own grim righteousness. A line from a poem she had studied in high school came back to her: *The best lack all conviction, while the worst/Are full of passionate intensity* . . .

Chris parked in the nearly vacant clinic parking lot. The solstice was past and the days were getting longer again, but it was still only February and already the watery sun was close to the horizon. He took her hand as they walked to the clinic door.

There was no one at reception, but Chris rang the finger bell and a nurse appeared a moment later. *I know this woman*, Marguerite thought. This bustling, chubby woman in nursing whites was Amanda Bleiler's mother, a familiar face from the weekday-morning grade-school drop-off. Someone she knew well enough to wave at. What was her first name? Roberta? Rosetta?

"Marguerite," the woman said, recognizing her. "And you must be Chris Carmody." Chris had phoned ahead.

"Rosalie," she said, the name popping into her head a moment before she pronounced it. "How's Amanda doing?"

"Well enough, considering." Considering the lockdown, she meant. Considering that there were dead bodies buried under the snow outside the perimeter fence. Rosalie turned to Chris. "If you want to look in on Mr. Sandoval, that's okay, I cleared it with Dr. Goldhar, but don't expect much, okay? And it'll have to be a quick visit. Couple of minutes tops, all right?"

Rosalie led them up a flight of stairs to the clinic's second floor, where three small rooms equipped with rudimentary life-support gear punctuated a row of offices and boardrooms.

Not very many years ago, the pilot wouldn't have survived his injuries. Rosalie explained that he had suffered third-degree burns over a large part of his body and that he had inhaled enough smoke and hot air to seriously damage his lungs. The clinic had fitted him with an alveolar bypass and packed his pulmonary sacs with gel to hasten the healing. As for his skin—

Well, Marguerite thought, he looked ghastly, lying in a white bed in a white room with ebony-white artificial skin stretched over his face like so much damp Kleenex. But this was very nearly state-of-the-art treatment. In less than a month, Rosalie said, he would look almost normal. Almost the way he had looked before the crash.

The most serious injury had been a blow to the head that had not quite cracked his skull but had caused intracranial bleeding that was hard to treat or correct. "We did everything we could," Rosalie said. "Dr. Goldhar is a really exceptional doctor, considering we don't have a fully equipped hospital to work with. But the prognosis is iffy. Mr. Sandoval may wake up, he may not."

Mr. Sandoval, Marguerite thought, trying to take the measure of the man under all this medical apparatus. Probably not a young man. Big paunch pushing up under the blankets. Salt-and-pepper hair where it hadn't been charred from his skull.

"You called him Mr. Sandoval," Chris said.

"That's his name. Adam Sandoval."

"He's been unconscious since he got here. How do you know his name?"

"Well . . ." She looked distressed. "Dr. Goldhar said not to be too free with this information, but you saved his life, right? That was really brave."

The story had been broadcast on Blind Lake TV, much to Chris's horror. He had declined an interview, but his reputation had been massively enhanced—not a bad thing, surely, Marguerite would have thought. But maybe Chris, a journalist, felt uncomfortable at the center of a media event, however small-scale.

"What information?" Chris asked.

"He had a wallet and part of a backpack on him. Mostly burned, but we saved enough to read his I.D."

Chris said—and Marguerite thought she heard a concealed edge in his voice—"Would it be possible to look at his things?"

"Well, I don't think so . . . I mean, I should probably talk to Dr. Goldhar first. Won't this all eventually be police evidence or something?"

"I won't disturb anything. Just a glance."

"I'll vouch for Chris," Marguerite added. "He's a good guy."

"Well—just a peek, maybe. I mean, it's not like you're terrorists or anything." She gave Chris a somber look. "Don't get me in trouble, that's all I ask."

Chris sat with the pilot a while longer. He whispered something Marguerite couldn't hear. A question, an apology, a prayer.

Then they left Adam Sandoval, whose chest rose and fell with the exhalations of his breathing apparatus in a queerly peaceful rhythm, and Rosalie took them to a small room at the end of the corridor. She unlocked the door with a key attached to a ring on her belt. Stored inside were medical sundries—boxes of suture thread in various gauges, saline bags, bandages and gauze, antiseptics in brown bottles—and, on a foldout desktop, a plastic bag containing Sandoval's effects. Rosalie opened the bag cautiously and made Chris put on a pair of throwaway surgical gloves before he touched the contents. "In case of fingerprints or I don't know what." She seemed to be having second thoughts.

Chris pulled out Sandoval's wallet, charred, and the items that had been salvaged from it: his cash card, melted beyond utility; an I.D. disc with his digital bona fides, also charred, but bearing the legible name ADAM W. SANDOVAL; his pilot's license; a photograph of a middle-aged woman with a wide, pleasant smile, the photo three-quarters intact; a receipt from a Pottery Barn in Flint Creek, Colorado; and coupon for a ten-dollar discount at Home and Garden, six months past its expiration date. If Mr. Sandoval was a terrorist, Marguerite thought, he was definitely the domestic variety.

"Please be careful," Rosalie said, her cheeks flushed.

The items gleaned from his burned backpack were even more sparse. Chris handled them quickly: a fragment of a smartbook, a blackened plastic pen, and a handful of loose, partial pages from a print magazine.

Chris said, "Has anyone else seen this material?"

"Only Dr. Goldhar. I thought maybe we should call Ray Scutter or someone in Administration and tell them about it. Dr. Goldhar said not to. He said it wasn't worth worrying Ray about all this."

"Dr. Goldhar is a wise man," Chris said.

Rosalie checked the corridor again, looking guiltier by the minute. Chris kept his back to her. She didn't see—but Marguerite did—when Chris picked up one of the magazine pages and slipped it under his jacket.

She wasn't sure Chris knew she had seen him take the page and she didn't mention it during the drive back. What he had done was probably some sort of crime. Did that make her an accomplice?

He didn't say much in the car. But she was sure his intent had been journalistic, not criminal. All he had taken, after all, was a scrap of singed paper.

Several times she got up enough nerve to ask him about it, several times she refrained. The sun had set and it was almost dinnertime when they reached the house. Chris had promised to cook tonight. He was an enthusiastic if not especially talented cook. His stir-fries were a mixed blessing, and he complained that the siege rations didn't include lemongrass or coriander, but—

"There's a car in the driveway," Chris said.

She recognized it instantly. The car was obscure in the wintery dusk, black against the asphalt and the shadow of the willow, but she knew at once it was Ray's.

Eighteen

"Stay in the car," she told Chris. "Let me talk him out."

"I'm not sure that's a good idea."

"I lived with him for five years. I know the drill."

"Marguerite, he crossed a line. He came to your house. Unless you gave him a key, he broke in."

"He must have used Tessa's key. Maybe she's with him."

"The point is, when people go this far beyond the boundaries it starts to get serious. You could get hurt."

"You don't know him. Just give me a few minutes, all right? If I need you, I'll scream."

Not funny, she told herself. Chris obviously didn't find it funny, either. She put her hand on his knee. "Five minutes, okay?"

"You're telling me to sit in the car?"

"Sit in the car, walk around the block, anything you want, but it'll be easier to get rid of him if you're not there putting his back up."

She didn't wait for him to answer. She climbed out of the car and walked resolutely to the front door of her home, more angry than frightened. Fucking Ray. Chris didn't understand how Ray operated. Ray wasn't there to beat her up. Ray had always aimed at humiliation by other means.

Inside—the living room lights were blazing—she called out Tessa's name. If Ray had brought Tess there might be some excuse for this.

But Tess didn't answer. Neither did Ray. Fuming, she checked the kitchen, the dining room. Empty. He must be upstairs, then. Lights were burning in every room in the house.

She found him in her office in the spare bedroom. Ray sat in her swivel chair, shoes on her desk, watching the Subject cross a waterless graben under a noonday sun. He looked up casually when she cleared her throat. "Ah," he said. "Here you are."

In the diffuse light of the wall screen Ray looked like a chinless Napoleon, ridiculously imperial. "Ray," she said levelly, "is Tess in the house?"

"Certainly not. That's what we need to talk about. Tessa's been telling me about some of the things that go on here."

"Don't start. I really, really don't want to hear it. Just leave, Ray. This isn't your house and you have no right to be here."

"Before we start talking about rights, are you aware that your daughter was left in the snow for almost an hour while your boyfriend played hero last week? She's lucky she doesn't have frostbite."

"We can talk about this some other time. Go, Raymond."

"Come on, Marguerite. Just drop the bullshit about 'my house, my rights.' We both know you've been systematically ignoring Tess. We both know she's having serious psychological problems as a result of that."

"I won't discuss this."

"I'm not here to fucking *discuss* it. I'm here to tell you how it's going to be. I can't in good conscience continue to allow my daughter to visit with you if you're not willing to provide her with appropriate care."

"Ray, we have an agreement—"

"We have a tentative agreement written under radically different circumstances. If I could take it to court, believe me, I would. That's not possible because of the lockdown. So I have to do what I think is right."

"You can't just *keep* her," Marguerite said. But what if he tried? What if he refused to let Tess come home? There was no family court in Blind Lake, no real police she could call on for help.

"Don't dictate to me. Tess is in my care and I have to make the decisions I think are best for her."

It was his smug, oily certainty that infuriated her. Ray had mastered the art of speaking as if he were the only adult on the planet and everyone else was weak, stupid, or insolent. Under that brittle exterior, of course, was the narcissistic infant determined to have his own way. Neither aspect of his personality was particularly appealing.

"Look," she said, "this is ridiculous. Whatever's wrong with Tess, you can't make it better by coming here and insulting me."

"I have no interest in your opinion on the subject."

Without thinking, Marguerite took two steps forward and

slapped him. She had never done that before. Her open palm hurt immediately, and even this brief physical contact (the coarseness of a day's growth of beard, his flabby jowls) made her want to wash her aching hand. Bad move, she thought, very bad move. But she couldn't help taking a certain pride in Ray's astonishment.

When she was little Marguerite used to hang out with a neighborhood boy whose family owned a gentle and long-suffering springer spaniel. The boy (his name had also been Raymond, coincidentally) had once spent an hour trying to ride that dog like a horse, laughing at the poor animal's yelps, until the dog had finally turned on him and taken a bite out of his right-hand thumb. The boy had looked the way Ray did now, astonished and tearful. For a second she wondered whether Ray would start to cry.

But his face reformed on its familiar lines. He stood up.

Oh, shit, Marguerite thought. *Oh, shit. Oh, shit.*

She backed into the hallway. Ray put his hands on her shoulders and shoved her against the wall. Now it was her turn to be surprised.

"You really don't get it, do you? In the words of the song, Marguerite, you're not in Kansas anymore."

A movie, not a song. One of Tessa's favorites. Ray, of course, didn't know that.

He pinched her chin between his thumb and forefinger. "I shouldn't have to tell you how far we all are from that pedestrian little world of divorce counselors and social workers you imagine you're still living in. Why do you think the Lake is under a quarantine? You quarantine a place because of *sickness*, Marguerite. It's that simple. A contagious, deadly sickness. We're alive on sufferance, and how much longer is that sufferance going to last?"

It could end at any time.

Ray put his face close to hers. His breath smelled like acetone. She tried to turn away but he wouldn't let her.

"We could all be dead in a month. We could be dead tomorrow. Given that, why should I let you ignore Tess in favor of that freakish thing on the screen, or worse, your new boyfriend?"

"What are you talking about?" Moving her jaw against the pressure of his fingers. Because he sounded like he knew something. Like he had a secret. Ray had always enjoyed knowing something Marguerite didn't. Almost as much as he hated being wrong.

He gave her a last, almost perfunctory shove—her shoulders connected again with the plaster wall—then stepped back. "You are so fucking naive," he said.

What Ray didn't see was the large form of Chris Carmody lumbering down the hallway from the stairs. Marguerite caught sight of him but glanced away quickly so as not to let Ray catch on. *Let it happen.* For a big man, Chris made very little noise.

Chris put himself between her and Ray and pushed a very startled Ray back against the opposite wall, not gently. Marguerite was terrified—there was real male violence in the air, an actual smell, a locker-room funk—but she was secretly pleased to see Ray's venomous expression morph back to an incredulous "Oh!" She had wanted to see that look on him for many dry years. It was intoxicating.

"Did you," Ray stammered when he had sized up the situation, "did you just *put your fucking hands on me?*"

"I don't know," Chris said. "Did you just commit a break-and-enter?"

Now they'll fight, Marguerite thought, or one of them will back down. Ray made a good show of it. He puffed up like a bantam rooster. "Mind your own fucking business!" But he was talking, not fighting. "I don't have to go through you to deal with my wife. Do you know who I *am?*"

"Come on, Ray," Chris said calmly. "Take it outside, all right?"

Here was something she hadn't seen from Chris before. Anger, *real* anger, not Ray's piss-and-vinegar face-making. He looked like a man preparing to perform some unpleasant task with his fists. She reached out and put a hand on his arm. "Chris—"

Ray seized the opportunity, as she had suspected he might. He stepped back, held up his hands, and began a very Ray-like back-down. "Oh, *please.* I don't want to play macho games. I said what I came to say."

He turned his back and walked away—a little shaky in the knees, she thought.

When he was gone, after she had watched from Tessa's bedroom window to make sure he drove away in his ugly little black car, what Marguerite felt was not anger or fear but embarrassment. As if Chris had been witness to some shameful part of her life. "I didn't mean for you to see that."

"I got tired of waiting."

"I mean, thank you, but—"

"You don't have to thank me and you don't have to apologize."

She nodded. Her pulse was still racing. "Come on down to the kitchen," she said. Because it was going to be one of those long, sleepless, adrenaline-charged nights. Maybe this was a habit she had picked up from her father, but where do you a spend a night like that except in the kitchen? Making tea and toast and trying to put your life back in some sort of order.

Ray had said some disturbing things. There was a lot here

to think about, and she didn't want to further embarrass herself by breaking down in front of Chris. So she led Chris to the
kitchen and sat him down while she put on the kettle. Chris
himself was subdued—in fact, he looked a little mournful. He
said, "Was it always like that? You and Ray?"

"Not so bad. Not always. And especially not at first." How
to explain that what she had mistaken for love had turned so
quickly into loathing? Her hand still ached where she had
slapped him. "Ray's a pretty good actor. He can be charming
when he wants to."

"I imagine the strain wears on him."

She smiled. "Apparently. Did you hear much of what he
said upstairs?"

Chris shook his head.

"He said he won't give Tess back."

"Think he means it?"

"Ordinarily I'd say no. But ordinarily, he wouldn't even
make the threat. Ordinarily, he wouldn't have come here. Back
in the real world, Ray was pretty good about respecting legal
limits. If only because he didn't want to leave himself vulnerable. Upstairs, he was talking like somebody with nothing to
lose. He was talking about the quarantine. He said we could all
be dead in a week."

"You think he knows something?"

"Either he knows something or he wants me to believe he
does. All I can say is, he wouldn't be dicking around with our
custodial arrangements if he thought I'd have legal recourse. I
mean, *ever*."

Chris was silent for a while, mulling that one over. The kettle whistled. Marguerite focused on making the tea, this calming ritual, two tea bags, a dollop of milk for her cup, none for
Chris.

"I guess I never really let myself think about that," she

said. "I want to believe that one day soon they'll open the gates and restore the data links and somebody in a uniform will apologize to us all and thank us for our patience and beg us not to sue. But I guess it could end another way." Another deadly way. And, of course, at any time. "Why would they do that to us, Chris? There's nothing dangerous here. Nothing's changed since the day before the lockdown. What are they afraid of?"

He smiled humorlessly. "The joke."

"What joke?"

"There's an old comedy routine—I forget where I saw it. It's World War Two and the Brits come up with the ultimate weapon. A joke so funny you die laughing if you hear it. The joke is translated word-by-word into phonetic German. Guys on the front lines are yelling it through bullhorns, and the Nazi troops drop dead in the trenches."

"Okay . . . so?"

"It's the original information virus. An idea or an image capable of driving someone mad. Maybe that's what the world is afraid of."

"That's a dumb idea, and it was retired during the congressional hearings a decade ago."

"But suppose it happened at Crossbank, or something happened there that looked like it."

"Crossbank isn't looking at the same *planet*. Even if they found something potentially dangerous, how would it affect us?"

"It wouldn't, unless the problem arose in the O/BECs. That's all we really have in common with Crossbank, the hardware."

"Okay, but that's still ridiculously conjectural. There's no evidence anything bad happened at Crossbank."

Marguerite had forgotten about the partial magazine page Chris had stolen from the clinic. He took it out of his jacket pocket and put it on the kitchen table.

"There is now," he said.

Nineteen

Tess watched television while her father was out. Blind Lake TV was still running through its store of previously downloaded entertainment, mostly old movies and network serials. Tonight they showed an Anglo-Hindi musical with lots of dancing and colorful costumes. But Tess had a hard time paying attention.

She knew her father was acting strangely. He had asked her all kinds of questions about the plane crash and Chris. The only surprising thing was that he had not once mentioned Mirror Girl. Nor had Tess mentioned her; Tess knew better than to raise that subject with him. Back at Cross-bank, when her parents were together, they had fought over Mirror Girl more than once. Her father blamed her mother for Mirror Girl's appearances. Tess couldn't see how that was supposed to work—her mother and Mirror Girl had nothing in common. But she had learned not to say anything. Intervening in those fights did no good and usually just made her or her mother cry.

Her father didn't like hearing about Mirror Girl. Lately he didn't like hearing about her mother or Chris, either. He spent most evenings in the kitchen, talking to himself. Tess ran her own bath those nights. She put herself to bed and read a book until she could sleep.

Tonight she was alone in the house. Tess had made popcorn in the kitchen, cleaned up carefully afterward, and tried to watch the movie. *Bombay Destination*, it was called. The dancing was good. But she felt the pressure of Mirror Girl's curiosity behind her eyes. "It's only *dancing*," she said scornfully. But it was unsettling to hear herself talk out loud when there was nobody home. The sound echoed off the walls. Her father's house seemed too large in his absence, too unnaturally neat, like a model of a house put together for showing-off, not living in. Tess walked restlessly from room to room, turning on lights. The light made her feel better, even though she was certain her father would bawl her out for wasting energy.

He didn't, though. When he got home he hardly spoke to her, just told her to get ready for bed and then went to the kitchen and made some calls. Upstairs, after her bath, she could still hear his voice down there, talking talking talking. Talking to the phone. Talking to the air. Tess put on her nightgown and took her book to bed, but the words on the page evaded her attention. Eventually she just turned off the light and lay there looking out the window.

Her bedroom window at her father's house looked south across the main gate and the prairie, but when she was lying down all she could see was the sky. (She had closed her door to make sure no light reflected from the windowpane, turning it into a mirror.) The sky was clear tonight and there was no moon. She could see the stars.

Her mother talked often about the stars. It seemed to Tess that her mother was someone who had fallen in love with the stars. Tess understood that the stars she saw at night were simply other suns very far away and that those other suns often had planets around them. Some stars had strange, evocative names (like Rigel or Sirius) but more often had numbers and letters, like UMa47, like something you might order from a catalog. You couldn't give a special name to every star because there were more stars than you could see with the naked eye, billions more. Not every star had planets, and only a few had planets anything like Earth. Even so, there might be lots of Earthlike planets.

These thoughts interested Mirror Girl intensely, but Tess ignored her wordless presence. Mirror Girl was with her so often now that she threatened to become what Dr. Leinster had always claimed she was: a part of Tessa herself.

Maybe "Mirror Girl" was the wrong name for her. Mirror Girl had indeed first appeared in mirrors, but Tess thought that was because Mirror Girl simply liked to see Tessa's reflection there, liked to look and see the looker looking back. Reflections, symmetry: that was Mirror Girl's turf. Things that were reflected or folded or even just very complicated. Mirror Girl felt a kinship with these things, a kind of recognition.

Now Mirror Girl looked through Tessa's eyes and saw stars in the cold dark night outside the house. Tess thought: should we really call it starlight? Wasn't it really sunlight? Someone else's sunlight?

She fell asleep listening to the distant murmur of her father's voice.

Her father was subdued in the morning. Not that he was ever talkative before morning coffee. He fixed breakfast for Tess, hot oatmeal. There was no brown sugar to put on it, only regular white sugar. She waited to see if he would eat something too. He didn't, although he twice rummaged through the kitchen cupboards as if he were looking for something he had lost.

He dropped her off early at school. The doors weren't open yet and the morning air was frigidly cold. Tess spotted Edie Jerundt hanging out by the tetherball pole. Edie Jerundt greeted her neutrally and said, "I have two sweaters on under my winter jacket."

Tess nodded politely, though she didn't care how many sweaters Edie Jerundt happened to be wearing. Edie looked cold despite her multiple sweaters. Her nose was red and her eyes were shiny from the sting of the wind.

A couple of older boys passed and made some remarks about "Edie Grunt and Tess the Mess." Tess ignored them, but Edie didn't know any better than to gape like a fish, and they laughed at her as they walked away. Mirror Girl was intensely curious about this behavior—she couldn't tell one person from another and didn't understand why anyone would make fun of Tess *or* Edie—but Tess couldn't explain. The cruelty of boys was a fact to be accepted and dealt with, not analyzed. Tess was sure she wouldn't have behaved the same way in their place. Though she was sometimes tempted to join in when the other girls made fun of Edie, if only to exempt herself from their attention. (She gave in to this temptation only rarely and was always ashamed of herself afterward.)

"Did you see the movie last night?" Edie asked. One thing that made the lockdown so strange was that there was only one video channel now and everybody had to watch the same shows.

"Some of it," Tess allowed.

"I really liked it. I want to download the songs sometime." Edie put her hands at her sides and wagged her body in what she imagined was a Hindi dance style. Tess could hear the boys snickering from yards away.

"I wish I had ankle bracelets," Edie confided.

Tess thought Edie Jerundt in ankle bracelets would look like a frog in a wedding dress, but that was a mean thought and she didn't say it.

Mirror Girl was bothering her again. Mirror Girl wanted her to look at the distant cooling towers of Eyeball Alley.

But what was so interesting about that?

"Tess?" Edie said. "Are you even listening to me?"

"Sorry," Tess said automatically.

"God, you're so weird," Edie said.

All that morning, Tessa's attention was drawn to the towers. She could see them from the window of the classroom, off across the snowbound empty fields. Crows swirled through the sky. They lived here even in winter. Lately they had multiplied, or so it seemed to Tess, perhaps because they were fattening on the garbage tip west of town. But they didn't perch on the tall, tapered cooling towers. The cooling towers were there to conduct away excess heat from the Eye down below. Parts of the Eye needed to be kept very cold, almost as cold as it was possible to be, what Mr. Fleischer had once called "near absolute zero." Tess rolled that phrase around in her mind. Absolute zero. It made her think of a bitter, windless night. One of those nights so still and cold your boots squeaked against the snow. Absolute zero made it easier to see the stars.

Mirror Girl found these thoughts intensely interesting.

Mr. Fleischer called on her a couple of times. Tess was able to answer his science question (it was Isaac Newton who had discovered the laws of motion), but later, during English, she heard nothing of the question itself, only her name as Mr. Fleischer called it out—"Anyone? Tessa?"

They had been reading *David Copperfield*. Tess had finished reading the book last week. She tried to imagine what Mr. Fleischer might have asked, but her mind was a blank. She stared at the top of her desk, hoping he'd call on someone else. The seconds ticked by uneasily and Tess felt the weight of Mr. Fleischer's disappointment. She wrapped a curl of hair around her forefinger.

Annoyingly, Edie Jerundt was waving her hand in the air.

"Edie?" Mr. Fleischer said at last.

"The *Industrial Revolution*," Edie said triumphantly.

"Right, it was called the Industrial Revolution . . ."

Tess returned her attention to the window.

At the end of the morning she told Mr. Fleischer she was going home for lunch. He looked surprised. "That's a bit of a hike, isn't it, Tess?"

Yes, but she had hoped Mr. Fleischer didn't know that. "My dad is picking me up." A complete and total lie. She was surprised at how easily it came out of her mouth.

"Special occasion?"

Tess shrugged.

Once she was outside, wrapped in her winter jacket (but lacking Edie's two sweaters), she realized she wasn't going home and that she wouldn't be back for the after-lunch session of school. Mirror Girl had brought her here, and Mirror Girl had her own plans for the afternoon.

Since the end of the sandstorm crisis the Eye had performed smoothly and without the slightest glitch.

It was almost unnerving, Charlie Grogan thought. He had walked through Control once this morning and everyone had been relaxed—as much as anyone could relax since the beginning of the lockdown. People actually smiled. Volts and amps were in the safe zone, temperature was stable, all the data was squeaky clean, and even the landscape through which the Subject continued to trudge seemed sunlit and more or less amicable. Charlie, feeling useless in his office, watched his monitor for a while. Subject was visibly worn. His integument was dull and pitted, his yellow coxcomb drooped like a tattered flag. But he walked steadily and with apparent determination through the roadless wilderness. The land was flat and desolate but there was an irregularity on the forward horizon, mountain peaks, a glint of high-altitude snow.

The Subject made slow progress. Sort of like a snail on an empty sidewalk. Bored, and without any maintenance duties for once, Charlie skipped lunch and wandered down to the glass-walled gallery above the O/BEC platens.

The gallery was mainly for show. It was a place you could bring a visiting congressman or European head of state, back before the siege. The gallery overlooked the platens from a secure height. Absent tourists, the gallery was usually empty; Charlie often came here to be alone.

He leaned into the inch-thick inner glass wall and gazed down three stories to the O/BEC platens. Those humbling objects. Thinking themselves into interstellar space. You weren't supposed to say so, but they *did* think, that was undeniable, even if (like the theorists) you insisted they merely "explored a finite but immense quantum phase-space of exponentially increasing complexity." Yeah, merely that. The O/BECs pulled images out of the stars and dreamed them onto a grid of pixels by "exploring quantum phase-space"—word salad, Charlie thought. Show me the wires. What was it actually grabbing, and how? Nobody could say.

What is an angel? That which dances on the head of a pin. What dances on the head of a pin? An angel, of course.

These O/BECs were only the most central part of the vast machine that supported them. All told, the Eye occupied an immense amount of square footage. Standing here in the middle of it, Charlie imagined he could feel the cold ferocity of its thoughts. He closed his eyes. Dream me an explanation.

But the only thing he could see behind his eyelids was a memory of the Subject, the Subject lost in the hinterlands of his dry old planet. Funny how clear the daydream seemed, invested with a clarity at least as vivid as the direct feed on his office monitor. As if he were walking in the Subject's footsteps. The sunlight was warm and a shade or two bluer than earthly sunlight, but the sky itself was white, charged with dust. A gentle wind kicked up miniature whirlwinds that traveled yards across these alkali-stained flats before they sighed out of existence.

Strange. Charlie leaned into the glass wall and imagined himself reaching out to the Subject. Surely even the O/BECs had never translated an image as distilled, as supernaturally pure, as this. He could, if he chose, count every bump on the Subject's pebbled skin. He could hear the metronomic steps of the Subject's dusty, elephantine feet; and he could see the trail the Subject left behind him, two punctuated parallel lines scribed into the granular material of the desert floor. He could smell the air: it smelled like hot rock, like mica-laden granite exposed to the noonday sun.

He imagined putting his hand on the Subject's shoulder, or at least that sloping bit of gristle behind the Subject's head that passed for a shoulder. How would it feel? Not leathery but hard, Charlie thought, each gooseflesh bump like a buried knuckle, some of them prickly with stiff white hairs. Subject's coxcomb, flush with blood, most likely served to adjust his core temperature to the heat; and if I touched it, Charlie thought, it would feel moist and flexible, like cactus flesh . . .

Subject stopped abruptly and turned as if startled. Charlie found himself gazing into the Subject's blank white billiard-ball eyes and thought, *Oh, shit!*

He opened his own eyes wide and reeled back from the glass. Here in the O/BEC gallery. Home safe. He blinked away what could only have been a dream.

"Are you all right?"

Startled a second time, Charlie turned and saw a young girl standing behind him. She wore a winter jacket haphazardly buttoned, one side of the collar poking up past her chin. She twirled a strand of her curly dark hair around her finger.

She looked familiar. He said, "Aren't you Marguerite Hauser's daughter?"

The girl frowned, then nodded.

Charlie's first impulse was to call Security, but the girl—Tess, he recalled, was her name—seemed timid and he was reluctant to frighten her. Instead he asked, "Is your mom or dad here?"

She shook her head no.

"No? Who let you in?"

"Nobody."

"Do you have a pass card?"

"No."

"Didn't the guards stop you?"

"I came in when no one was looking."

"That's some trick." In fact it should have been impossible. But here she was, goggle-eyed and obviously unsure of herself. "Are you looking for someone?"

"Not really."

"What brings you here, then, Tess?"

"I wanted to see it." She gestured at the O/BEC array.

For a long moment he was afraid she would ask him how it worked.

"You know," Charlie said, "you're really not supposed to be wandering around all by yourself. How about you come to my office and I'll give your mom a call."

"My mom?"

"Yeah, your mom."

The girl appeared to think it over.

"Okay," she said.

Tess sat in his office looking at some glossy brochures he scared up for her while he buzzed Marguerite's pocket server. She was obviously surprised to hear from him and her first question was about the Subject—had something interesting happened?

Depends how you look at it, Charlie thought. He couldn't shake that dream of the Subject from his mind. Eyeball to eyeball. It had seemed ridiculously real.

But he didn't tell her about that. "I don't want to worry you, Marguerite, but your daughter's here."

"Tess? Here? Here *where?*"

"At the Eye."

"She's supposed to be in school. What's she doing out there?"

"She's not actually doing much of anything, but she did manage to sneak past the guards and wander down to the O/BEC gallery."

"You're kidding me."

"Wish I was."

"How is that possible?"

"Good question."

"So—is she in big trouble, Charlie?"

"She's here in my office, and I don't see the need to make a big deal out of this. But you might want to drive out and pick her up."

"Give me ten minutes," Marguerite said.

———————

Tess was unresponsive while Charlie walked her out to the parking lot. She didn't seem to want to talk, and she certainly didn't seem to want to talk about how she had gotten into the complex. Before long her mom zoomed into the visitor lot and Tess climbed gratefully into the rear seat of the car.

"Do we need to talk about this?" Marguerite asked.

"Maybe later," Charlie said.

On his way back to his office he took a high-priority call from Tabby Menkowitz in Security. "Hey, Charlie," she said. "How's Boomer these days?"

"An old hound but healthy. What's up, Tab?"

"Well, I got a big alert on my nonrecognition software. When I checked the cameras there you were, escorting a little kid out of the building."

"She's a team leader's kid. Playing hooky and curious about the Alley."

"What'd you do, smuggle her in in a rucksack? Because we caught her when she was leaving but not when she arrived."

"Yeah, well, I wondered about that myself. She said she just sneaked in when nobody was looking."

"We have full coverage on our security cameras, Charlie. They're *always* looking."

"I guess it's a mystery, then. We don't have to panic over it, do we?"

"It's not like anybody's leaving town, but I'd really, really like to know where she found a back door. That's absolutely important information."

"Tabby, we're under siege—surely this can wait until the big problems get solved."

"This *is* a big problem. Are you asking me to just let it ride?"

"I'm advising you that she's an eleven-year-old kid. Look

into it by all means, but let's not drag her into an official investigation."

"You just found her down in the gallery?"

"She snuck up on me."

"That's pretty deep, Charlie. That's a big hole."

"Yeah, I know."

Tabby was silent for a moment. Charlie let the silence play
out, left it to her to make the next move. She said, "You know
this girl?"

"I know her mom. Want another datum? Her dad is Ray
Scutter."

"Is there anything *else* you know? I ask because you're the
one who took her out of the building without notifying me."

"Yeah, I'm sorry about that, but it kind of took me by surprise. Really, I don't know any more about it than you do."

"Uh-huh."

"Honest."

"Uh-huh. You understand, I *do* have to look into this."

"Yeah. Of course."

"But I guess I don't have to process the paperwork right
away."

"Thanks, Tabby."

"You have absolutely nothing to thank me for. Honest."

"I'll say hi to Boomer for you."

"Give him a breath mint for me. That barbecue last summer, he was grossing everybody out." She hung up without saying good-bye.

Alone, Charlie finally allowed himself to think about what
had happened this afternoon. To mull it over in his mind.
Except—well, what the fuck *had* happened? He'd been day-
dreaming in the O/BEC gallery and then the girl wandered in.
Was he supposed to be able to tease some meaning out of that?

Maybe he'd give Marguerite a call after work.

In the meantime he had another question. He wasn't sure he wanted it answered, but it would plague him like a headache if he didn't ask.

So he took a breath and called his friend Murtaza in Image Acquisition. The call went through at once. "Must be quiet down there."

"Yup," Murtaza said. "Smooth like silk."

"You got time to do me a little favor?"

"Maybe. I'm on break at three."

"Won't take that long. I just need you to look at the clocked image for the last hour or so, especially around—" He estimated. "Say, between twelve forty-five and one."

"Look at it for what?"

"Any unusual behavior."

"You're out of luck. He's just walking over the landscape. It's like watching paint dry."

"Something small. Something gestural."

"Could you be more specific?"

"Sorry, no."

"Okay, well, easy enough." Charlie waited while Murtaza defined the time segment and ran a look-find app, zipping through the afternoon's stored imagery. The scan took less than a minute. "Nothing," Murtaza said. "Told you so."

That was a relief. "You're sure?"

"Today, my friend, the Subject is as predictable as clockwork. He didn't even stop to take a leak."

"Thanks," Charlie said, feeling a little idiotic.

"Absolutely nothing. Just a little blip at ten to one. He kind of paused and looked over his shoulder. At nothing. That's it."

"Oh."

"What, is *that* what you were looking for?"

"Just a passing notion. Sorry to have bothered you."

"No problem. Maybe this weekend we can go for a beer, yes?"

"Sure."

"Get some sleep, Charlie. You sound worried."

Yeah, he thought. I am.

Twenty

Chris had spent most of the night consoling Marguerite. The fragmentary magazine page confirmed nothing but hinted at great danger, and Marguerite, anxious, cycled back repeatedly to the subject of Tess: Tess, threatened by Ray; Tess, threatened by the world.

He had run out of things to say to her.

She had fallen asleep toward dawn. Chris paced through the house aimlessly. He knew this feeling altogether too well, the double-barreled blast of dread and wakefulness that came with the morning sunlight like a bad amphetamine rush. He settled down at last in the kitchen, blinds open to the cobalt-blue sky, suburban-style row houses lit up in the efflorescence of dawn like tattered candy boxes.

He wished he had something to take the edge off. One of those anodynes that had once passed so easily into his hands, some soothing and euphoriant chemical or even a homely little joint. Was he afraid? What was he afraid of?

Not Ray, not the O/BECs, maybe not even his own death. He was afraid of what Marguerite had given him: her trust.

There are men, Chris thought, who shouldn't be asked to handle fragile things. We drop them.

He called Elaine Coster as soon as the sun was decently up. He told her about the clinic, the comatose pilot, the charred page.

She suggested a meeting at Sawyer's at ten. Chris said, "I'll call Sebastian."

"You really want to get that charlatan involved?"

"He's been helpful so far."

"Suit yourself," Elaine said.

He woke Marguerite before he left the house. He told her where he was going and he put on a pot of coffee for her. She sat in the kitchen in her nightgown looking desolate. "I can't stop thinking about Tess. Do you think Ray really means to keep her?"

"I don't know what Ray might or might not do. The most immediate question is whether she's endangered by him."

"Whether he might hurt her, you mean? No. I don't think so. At least, not directly. Not physically. Ray is a complicated man, and he's a natural-born son-of-a-bitch, but he's not a monster. He loves Tess, in his own way."

"She's supposed to come back Friday. It might be better to wait till then, see what he does when he's had a chance to cool off. If he insists on keeping her, we can take steps then."

"If something bad happens to the Lake, I want her with me."

"It hasn't come to that yet. But, Marguerite, even if Tess isn't in danger, it doesn't mean *you're* safe. When Ray came to the house, that made him a stalker. He's on a downhill slope. How smart are your locks?"

She shrugged. "Not very. I guess I can generate a new key . . . but then Tess won't be able to get in without me."

"Generate a new key and get Tessa's card updated even if you have to go to her school to do it. And don't get careless. Keep the door locked when you're alone and don't answer the door without checking. Make sure you have your pocket server handy. In an emergency, call me or Elaine or even the Security guy, what's-his-name, Shulgin. Don't try to handle it yourself."

"You sound like you've been through this before."

He left without answering.

Chris staked out an isolated booth at Sawyer's away from the window. The restaurant wasn't crowded. The short-order cook and a couple of waitresses were showing up, Chris had surmised, largely out of habit. Menu selections were down to sandwiches: ham, cheese, or ham-and-cheese.

Elaine arrived simultaneously with Sebastian Vogel and Sue Sampel. All three of them looked at Chris apprehensively as they sat down. As soon as the waitress had taken their orders Chris put the charred, plastic-covered magazine page on the tabletop.

"Wow," Sue said. "You actually stole this?"

"We don't use that word," Elaine told her. "Chris has an unnamed high-level source."

"Look at it," Chris said. "Take your time. Draw conclusions."

Only about a quarter of the printed page was legible. The

rest of it was charred beyond interpretation, and even the legible extreme right quadrant was discolored and brown.

Still decipherable was a fraction of a headline:

OSSBANK STILL UNKNOWN, SECDEF SAYS

And, under it, the right-hand fragments of a column of type:

> es Monday evening. Local residents have still
> or comment. To date, two infantry battalions
> ther death reported. Satellite photographs show
> ntinue to grow. The structure has been lin-
> sembling starfish or coral, suggesting a non-
> gar L. Baum insists it would be premature to
> lusions.
>
> > eatedly warned not to leave their homes,
> > major highways east of the Mississippi.
> > isturbing development, a "pilgrim," iden-
> > epresents countless others who have
> > oclaimed hope of spiritual redemp-
> > utile but dangerous.
> > overstated the danger; however, some
> > ar from certain. At the Crossbank fa-
> > emains of the original structure, nor
> > idiculed reports of "plague," the CDC
> > is fear itself."
> > well as a team of United Nations ob-
> > ecial issue. Our in-depth reports begin
> > as they arise.

Elaine said, "What's on the other side?"

"A car ad. And a date."

She flipped the page over. "Jesus, this is nearly two months old."

"Yeah."

"The pilot was carrying this with him?"

"Yeah."

"And he's still unconscious?"

"I called the clinic this morning. No change."

"Who else knows about this?"

"Marguerite. You guys."

"Okay . . . so let's keep it at that for now, people."

The waitress brought coffee. Chris covered the page with a dessert menu.

Elaine said, "You've had a while to think about this. What do you make of it?"

"Obviously, there's some kind of ongoing crisis at Cross-bank. Not much clue as to what it might be. Something big enough to involve the infantry and maybe close down high-ways—what did it say?—east of the Mississippi. We have the word 'plague' in quotes and what looks like a denial from the Centers for Disease Control—"

"Which could mean anything," Elaine said. "Either way."

"We have 'deaths reported,' or possibly 'no deaths reported.' We have some cryptic stuff about coral, starfish, a pilgrim. A statement apparently attributed to Ed Baum, the president's science advisor. The event was big enough to war-rant major news coverage and policy statements from federal agencies, but not big enough to drive advertisers out of the magazine."

"That ad could have been bought and paid for six months earlier. Proves nothing."

"Sebastian?" Chris said. "Sue? Any thoughts?"

They both looked solemn. Sebastian said, "I'm intrigued by the use of the word 'spiritual.' "

Elaine rolled her eyes. "You would be."

"Go on," Chris prompted.

Sebastian frowned, his pursed mouth almost disappearing under his enormous beard. The siege had left him looking more gnome-like than ever, Chris thought. He had somehow contrived to gain weight. His cheeks were berry-red. "Spiritual *redemption*. What kind of disaster generates even the illusion of redemption? Or attracts a pilgrim?"

"Bullshit," Elaine said. "You can attract pilgrims by announcing you saw a portrait of the Virgin Mary in a dirty bedsheet. People are credulous, Sebastian. They must be, or you wouldn't have written a bestseller."

"Oh, I don't think what we have here is the Second Coming. Though perhaps some people have mistaken it for that. It does imply something strange, though, don't you think? Something ambiguous."

"Strange and ambiguous. Wow, great insight."

Chris put the magazine page back in his jacket pocket. He let them talk it through for a few minutes. Elaine was obviously frustrated to have only half an explanation in front of her. Sebastian seemed more intrigued than frightened, and Sue clung to his left arm in chastened silence.

"So maybe the critics are right," Elaine said. "Something happened to the O/BECs at Crossbank. So we need to think about shutting down the Eye."

"Maybe," Chris said. He had run through this scenario with Marguerite last night. "But if the folks on the outside wanted us shut down they could have cut the power months ago. Maybe they did that at Crossbank, and it only made things worse."

"Maybe, maybe, maybe, fucking *maybe*. What we need is more information." She directed a meaningful look at Sue.

Sue picked at her sandwich as if she hadn't heard.

"Good girl," Sebastian told her. "Never volunteer."

Sue Sampel—with what Chris thought was a remarkable display of dignity—swallowed the last bite of ham and cheese and took a sip of coffee. Then she cleared her throat. "You want to know what Ray found when he raided the executive servers. I'm sorry, but I haven't been able to find out. Ray's paranoia has ramped up lately. All the support staff have to carry clocked keys now. We can't come in early or stay late without a security waiver. Most of the offices have video surveillance, and it's not just casual."

"So what *do* you know?" Elaine asked.

"Only what I happen to see now and then. Dimi Shulgin showed up with a package of printouts, probably hard copies of whatever mail from Crossbank happened to be sitting in the caches before the shutdown. Ray's been *extremely* nervous since he saw that. As for the contents, I haven't been able to get anywhere near them. And if Ray ever really meant to make all this stuff public, apparently he's changed his mind."

Ray's not just nervous, Chris thought. He's scared. His veneer of reasonability is flaking away like paint on a barn door.

"So we're fucked," Elaine said.

"Not necessarily. I might be able to get something for you. But I'll need help."

Sue could do a pretty convincing impersonation of an airhead, but the fact was, Chris thought, she wasn't stupid. Stupid people didn't land jobs at Blind Lake, even as support staff. If the printouts were still in Ray's office, Sue said, she could, just maybe and with a little luck, find them and scan them into her personal server. She could let herself into Ray's office on a pretext and use her passkey to get into his desk, but she needed at least half an hour uninterrupted.

"What about the surveillance?"

"That's where we benefit from Ray's paranoia. Cameras are optional in executive suites. Ray's had his turned off since last summer. I guess he didn't want anyone to see him eating his DingDongs."

"DingDongs?"

Sue waved off the question. "Security will see me go in and out of his office, but if I keep away from the connecting door that's all they'll see. And I'm in and out of there all the time anyhow. Ray knows somebody has a key to his desk, but he doesn't know it's me, and if this works he won't even know I scanned the documents."

"You're absolutely sure he keeps hard copies in his office?"

"Not absolutely, no, but I'd bet on it. The question is how to get Ray and his buddies out of the way while I do this."

"I'm guessing you have a plan," Elaine said.

Sue looked pleased. "Weekdays are impossible. I can get in there on weekends during daylight hours without arousing suspicion, but Ray often drops in on weekends too, and Shulgin has been hanging around lately. So I looked at Ray's calendar. This Saturday he's doing the community center lecture-hall thing. Ari Weingart organized one of his big events, he's got two or three speakers besides Ray. Knowing Ray, he'll want Shulgin in the audience with him along with anybody else who might make a casual appearance—Ari, say, or any of the department heads apart from Marguerite. He's taking this thing seriously. If I had to guess, I'd say he wants to drum up support for shutting down the Eye."

Chris knew about the Saturday debate. Marguerite was supposed to be one of the speakers. She'd written something for it, though she'd been extremely reluctant to appear on stage with Ray. Ari Weingart had convinced her it would be a good idea, increase her visibility and maybe shore up her support with the other departments.

"How do we come into this?" Chris asked.

"You don't, really. I just want you guys in the auditorium keeping an eye on the stage. That way, if Ray takes off in a hurry you can give me a call."

Sebastian shook his head. "This is still far too dangerous. You could get in trouble."

She smiled indulgently. "I appreciate you saying that. But I think I'm already in trouble. I think we all are. Don't you?"

Nobody bothered to argue.

Elaine stayed on a few minutes after Sue and Sebastian left.

Business at Sawyer's picked up a little around lunchtime. But only a little. The afternoon sky outside the window was blue, the air still and cold.

"So," Elaine said, "are you up for this, Chris?"

"I don't know what you mean."

"We're in deeper shit than anyone wants to admit. Getting out of this alive might be the hardest thing any of us has ever done. Are you up to it?"

He shrugged.

"You're thinking of your girlfriend. And her daughter."

"We don't need to make it personal, Elaine."

"Come on, Chris. I have eyes. You're not as deep and inscrutable as you like to think. When you wrote that Galliano book, you put on your white hat and set out to right some wrongs. And you got burned for it. You found out that the good guy isn't universally loved even when he's right. Quite the opposite. Very disappointing for a nice suburban boy. So you wallowed in some justifiable self-pity, and you're entitled, why not. But here comes all this lockdown bullshit, plus whatever happened at Crossbank, not to mention Marguerite and that little girl of hers. I think you feel the urge to put that white hat back on your head. What I'm saying is: good. Now's the time. Don't resist it."

Chris folded his napkin and stood up. "You don't know the first fucking thing about me," he said.

Twenty-One

After Chris had left the house, and before the call came from Charlie Grogan asking her to pick up her daughter, Marguerite had spent the morning with the Subject.

Despite the implied danger to Blind Lake and Ray's explicit threats, there was nothing useful she could do, at least not right now. Much would be asked of her, Marguerite suspected, and probably very soon. But not yet. Now she was stuck in a limbo of dread and ignorance. No real work to do and no way to calm the churn of her emotions. She hadn't slept, but sleep was out of the question.

So she made herself a pot of tea and watched the Subject, scribbling notes for queries she would probably never submit. The entire enterprise was doomed, Marguerite thought, and so probably was the Subject himself. He appeared visibly weaker as the sun rose into a pale sky flecked with high clouds. He had been hiking for weeks, far from any traveled road, with scant supplies of food and water. His morning cloacal evacuations were thin and faintly green. When he walked, his body periodically contorted in angles that suggested pain.

But this morning he found both food and water. He had entered the foothills of a tall range of mountains, and though the land was still terribly dry he discovered an oasis where a stream of glacial water cascaded down a terrace of rocks. The water pooled in a cup of granite, deep and transparent as glass. Fan-leafed succulents splayed their foliage around it.

Subject bathed before he ate. He advanced gingerly into the pool, then stood under the falling stream. He had accumulated a coat of dust during his journey and it discolored the water around him. When he emerged from the pool his dermal integument was gleaming, changed from near-white to a somber burnt-umber. He swiveled his head as if scanning for predators. (Were there predatory species in this part of his world? It seemed unlikely—where was the game to support a large predator?—but was not, Marguerite supposed, impossible.) Then, reassured, he plucked, peeled, and washed several of the fleshy leaves and began to devour them. Moist flecks fell from his mandibles and collected at his feet. After he had eaten the leaves he found mossy patches on the granite near the waterfall, and he licked these clean with his broad blue-gray tongue.

Then he sat patiently digesting his meal, and Marguerite called up the file she had been writing for Tess: her children's-book story of the Subject's odyssey.

The act of writing soothed her, although the narrative was far from up-to-date. She had just finished a description of the sandstorm crisis and Subject's awakening in the ruined city of the desert.

She wrote:

> All around him in the still and windless morning were the pillars and mounds of buildings long abandoned and eroded by the seasons.
>
> These structures were not like the tall conical buildings of his home city. Whoever had made these buildings—perhaps his own ancestors—had made them differently. They had erected pillars, like the Greeks, and the pillars might once have supported much greater houses, or temples, or places of business.
>
> The pillars were hewn from black stone. The gritty desert wind had polished them to a fine smoothness. Some stood tall, but most had been worn to fractions of their original size, and where they had not fallen the wind had left them listing toward the east. There were the remains of other kinds of buildings too, some square foundations and even a few low pyramids, all of them as rounded as the rocks you find at the bottom of a stream.
>
> The storm had scoured the desert floor to a level surface, and now the sun cast stark shadows among the ruins. Subject stood in contemplation. The sundial shadows grew shorter as the morning wore on. Then—perhaps thinking of his destination—Subject began to walk westward once again. By noon he had left the ruined city entirely, and it vanished below the horizon as if utterly lost, and nothing remained ahead of him but glittering sand and the ghostly blue silhouettes of distant mountains.

She had just keyed the period when she took Charlie Grogan's call.

Tess was quiet in the car as they left the Alley.

Marguerite drove slowly, struggling to assemble her thoughts. She had an important choice to make.

But first she wanted to know what had happened. Tess had left school and wandered over to the Eye to bother Charlie, that much was obvious, but why?

"I'm sorry," Tess said, shooting apprehensive glances at her from the passenger seat. Am I, Marguerite wondered, as frightening as that? Judge and jury? Is that how she sees me?

"You don't have to apologize," Marguerite said. "Tell you what. I'll call Mr. Fleischer and tell him you had an appointment but you forgot to give him the note. How's that sound?"

"Okay," Tess said cautiously, waiting for the hook.

"But I'm sure he's worried about you. So am I. How come you didn't go back for class this afternoon?"

"I don't know. I just wanted to go to the Eye."

"How come? I thought you didn't like it there. You hated the tour, back at Crossbank."

"Just felt like it."

"Badly enough to skip school?"

"I guess."

"How'd you get inside? Mr. Grogan seemed a little upset over that."

"I walked in. Nobody was looking."

That, at least, was probably true. Tess was too guileless to have bluffed her way in or found a hidden entrance. In all likelihood she had just walked up to the front door and opened it: Charlie's investigation would discover a sleepy security guard or some employee who'd wandered out to smoke a joint. "Did you find what you were looking for?"

"I wasn't really looking for anything."

"Learn anything?"

Tess shrugged.

"Because, you know, that's pretty unusual behavior for you. You never skipped school before."

"It was important."

"Important how, Tess?"

No answer. Only a teary frown.

"Was it because of Mirror Girl?"

Tessa's unhappy expression condensed into misery. "Yes."

"She told you to go there?"

"She never tells me anything. She just wanted to go. So I went."

"Well, what was Mirror Girl looking for?"

"I don't know. I think she just wanted to see if she could see her reflection."

"Her reflection? Her reflection where?"

"In the Eye," Tess said.

"A mirror at the Eye? It isn't that kind of telescope. There's no real mirror."

"Not in a mirror—in the *Eye*."

Marguerite didn't know how to proceed, how to ask the next question. She was afraid of Tessa's answers. They sounded crazy. Crazy: the forbidden word. The unspeakable thought. She hated all this talk of Mirror Girl because it sounded crazy, and Marguerite didn't think she could bear that. Almost anything else, an injury, a disease; she could imagine Tess in leg braces or with her arm in a sling, she knew how to console her when she was hurt; that was well within the range of her mothering skills. But please, she thought, not craziness, not the kind of refractory madness that excludes all comfort or communication. Marguerite had worked nights at a psychiatric hospital during college. She had seen incurable schizophrenics. Crazy people lived in their own nightmarish VR, more alone than physical isolation could ever make them. She refused to imagine Tess as one of those people.

She pulled into the school parking lot but asked Tess to sit for a minute with her.

Death and madness: could she really protect her daughter from either of those things?

I can't even protect her from Ray.

Ray had threatened to keep Tess with him, to take physical custody of her—in effect, to kidnap her. But she's with me now, Marguerite thought. And if I had a choice I'd take her away from here, drive her down the road to Constance and from there away, away, anywhere away from the quarantine and the distressing rumors Chris had brought home, away from Eyeball Alley and away from Mirror Girl.

But she couldn't do that.

She had to send Tess back to school, and from school Tess would go home to Ray and the increasingly fragile illusion of normality. If I keep her with me, Marguerite thought, then I'll be the one violating the letter of our agreement, and Ray will send his security people to get her.

But if I let her go back to him, and something happens—

"Can I get out now?" Tess asked.

Marguerite took a deep, calming breath. "I guess so," she said. "Back to school with you. No more expeditions during class, though, all right?"

"All right."

"Promise me?"

"Promise." She put her hand on the door handle.

"One more thing," Marguerite said. "Listen to me. *Listen.* This is important, Tess. If anything strange happens at Dad's, you call me. Doesn't matter what time of day or night. You don't even have to think about it. Just call me. Because I'm looking out for you even when you're not with me."

"Is Chris looking out for me, too?"

Surprised, Marguerite said, "Sure he is. Chris too."

"Okay," Tess said, and she opened the door and scooted out of the car. Marguerite watched her daughter cross the desolate parking lot, scuffling through whirls of old snow, her jacket still cross-buttoned and her winter hat clasped in her small gloved hands.

I'll see her again, Marguerite told herself. I will. I must.

Then Tess vanished through the front door of the school and the afternoon was still and empty.

Twenty-Two

Sue Sampel woke up nervous.

It was Saturday morning, and today she was supposed to perform the small act of information theft she had so rashly promised earlier in the week. Her hand shook when she brushed her teeth, and her reflection in the mirror was the perfect image of a terrified middle-aged woman.

She let Sebastian sleep another hour while she made herself coffee and toast. Sebastian was one of those people who could sleep through storms or earthquakes, while a noisy sparrow was enough to bring Sue to groggy, unwelcome consciousness.

Sebastian's book was on the kitchen table, and Sue leafed through it for distraction. She had read it all the way through weeks ago and had lately taken a second run at it, trying to absorb ideas that had slipped past her the first time. *God & the Quantum Vacuum*. A weighty title. Like a couple of sumo wrestlers balanced on an ampersand.

But the book had not been sappy or superficial. In fact it had taxed her to the limits of her bachelor of science degree. Fortunately, Sebastian was pretty good at explaining difficult concepts. And she had been privileged to have the author handy when she got stuck on something.

The book was not overtly religious nor was it a work of rigorous science. Sebastian himself called it "speculative philosophy." Once he had described it as "a bull session, writ large. Very large." That, Sue supposed, was modesty speaking.

The book was full of arcane scientific history and evolutionary lore and quantum physics. Heady material for a college religion prof whose previous published works had included such torrid bodice-rippers as "Errors of Attribution in First-Century Pauline Texts." Basically, his argument was that human beings had achieved their current state of consciousness by appropriating a small piece of a universal intelligence. Tapping into God, in other words. This definition of God, he argued, could be stretched to fit definitions of deity across a spectrum of cultures and beliefs. Was God omnipresent and omniscient? Yes, because He permeated all of creation. Was He singular or multiple? Both: He was omnipresent because He was inherent in the physical processes of the universe; but His mind was knowable (by human beings) only in discrete and often dissimilar fragments. Was there life after death, or perhaps reincarnation? In the most literal sense, no; but because our sentience was borrowed it lived on without our bodies, albeit as a tiny piece of something almost infinitely larger.

Sue understood what he was getting at. He wanted to give people the consolation of religion without the baggage of dogmatism. He was pretty casual about his science, and that pissed off people like Elaine Coster. But his heart was in the right place. He wanted a religion that could plausibly comfort widows and orphans without committing them to patriarchy, intolerance, fundamentalism, or weird dietary laws. He wanted a religion that wasn't in a perpetual fistfight with modern cosmology.

Not such a bad thing to want, Sue thought. But where's *my* consolation? Consolation for the petty thief. The larcenous office-worker. Forgive me, for I know exactly what I do and I'm of two minds about it.

Assuming any of that mattered. Assuming they weren't all doomed. She had read the magazine fragment at Sawyer's and she had drawn her own conclusions.

Sebastian came downstairs freshly showered and dressed in his casual finest: blue jeans and a green knit sweater that looked like something an English vicar might have thrown away.

"Today's the heist," Sue said.

"How do you feel?"

"Scared."

"You know, you don't have to do this. It was good of you to volunteer, but nobody will say anything if you change your mind."

"Nobody except Elaine."

"Well, maybe Elaine. But seriously—"

"Seriously, it's okay. Just promise me one thing."

"What?"

"When you're at that Town Hall meeting . . . I mean, I know the others are looking out for me, they'll call if Ray takes off for the Plaza. But the only one I really trust is you."

He nodded, owl-eyed and ridiculously solemn.

"I need at least five minutes warning if Ray is on his way."

"You'll have it," Sebastian said.

"Promise?"

"Promise."

The morning crept past too quickly. The Town Hall meeting started at one, and she asked Sebastian to drive so he could drop her off inconspicuously outside Hubble Plaza. They didn't talk much in the car. She gave him a quick kiss when he stopped. Then she stepped out into the cold air, carded herself into the Plaza's main entrance, waved hello to the lobby guard, and walked without obviously hurrying to the elevators. Her footsteps resounded in the tiled lobby like the tick of a metronome, *allegro*, in time with the beat of her heart.

Marguerite arrived at the community center auditorium at 12:45, and when she spotted Ari Weingart looking for her in the lobby crowd she turned to Chris and said, "Oh, God. This is a mistake."

"The lecture?"

"Not the lecture. Going on stage with Ray. Having to look at him, having to listen to him. I wish I could—oh, hi, Ari."

Ari took a firm grip on her arm. "This way, Marguerite. You're up first, did I mention that? Then Ray, then Lisa Shapiro from Geology and Climatology, then we throw it open for audience questions."

She took a last look back at Chris, who shrugged and gave her what she guessed was a supportive smile.

Really, she thought, trailing Ari through a staff-only door into the backstage dimness, this *is* crazy. Not just because she would be forced to appear with Ray but because it would be a charade for both of them. Both pretending they hadn't seen clues about the Crossbank disaster (whatever it was). Both pretending there had never been a confrontation over Tess. Pretending they didn't despise each other. Pretending, not to civility, but at least to indifference.

Knowing it could end at any time.

This is a prescription for disaster, Marguerite thought. Not only that, but her "lecture" was a series of notes she had made for herself and never really planned to reveal—speculation about the UMa47 project that verged on the heretical. But if the crisis was as bad, as potentially deadly, as it seemed, why waste time on insincerity? Why not, for once in her life, stop calculating career goals and simply say what she thought?

It had seemed like a good idea, at least until she found herself onstage behind a closed curtain with Lisa Shapiro sitting between her and her ex-husband. She avoided his eyes but couldn't shake a claustrophobic awareness of his presence.

He was impeccably dressed, she had noticed on the way in. Suit and tie, creases razor-sharp. A little pursed smile on his face, accentuated by his jowls and his receding chin, like a man who smelled something unpleasant but was trying to be polite about it. A sheaf of paper in his hands.

To the left of her there was a podium, and Ari stood there now signaling for someone to raise the curtain. Already? Marguerite checked her watch. One on the dot. Her mouth was dry.

The auditorium accommodated an audience of two thousand, Ari had told her. They had admitted roughly half that number, a mixture of working scientists, support staff, and casual labor. Ari had arranged four of these events since the beginning of the quarantine, and they had all been well-attended and well-received. There was even a guy with a camera doing live video for Blind Lake TV.

How civilized we are in our cage, Marguerite thought. How easily we distract ourselves from the knowledge of the bodies outside the gates.

Now the curtain was drawn, the stage illuminated, the audience a shadowy void more sensed than seen. Now Ari was introducing her. Now, in the strange truncation of time that always happened when she addressed an audience, Marguerite herself was at the podium, thanking Ari, thanking the crowd, fumbling with the cue display on her pocket server.

"The question—"

Her voice cracked into falsetto. She cleared her throat.

"The question I want to pose today is, have we been deceived by our own rigorously deconstructive approach to the observed peoples of UMa47/E?"

That was dry enough to make the laypeople in the audience feel sleepy, but she saw a couple of familiar faces from Interpretation coagulate into frowns.

"This is deliberately provocative language—the observed *peoples*. From the beginning, the Crossbank and Blind Lake projects have sought to purge themselves of anthropocentrism: the tendency to invest other species with human characteristics. This is the fallacy that tempts us to describe a panther cub as 'cute' or an eagle as 'noble,' and we have been doing it ever since we learned to stand on two legs. We live in an enlightened age, however, an age that has learned to see and to value other living things as they are, not as we wish them to be. And the long and creditable history of science has taught us, if nothing else, to look carefully before we judge—to judge, if we must, based on what we see, not what we would prefer to believe.

"And so, we tell ourselves, the subjects of our study at 47 Ursa Majoris should be called 'creatures' or 'organisms,' not 'peoples.' We must presume nothing about them. We must not bring to the analytical table our fears or our desires, our hopes or our dreams, our linquistic prejudices, our bourgeois meta-narratives, or our cultural baggage of imagined aliens. Check Mr. Spock at the door, please, and leave H.G. Wells in the library. If we see a city we must not call it a city, or call it that only provisionally, because the word 'city' implies Carthage and Rome and Berlin and Los Angeles, products of human biology, human ingenuity, and thousands of years of accumulated human expertise. We remind ourselves that the observed city may not be a city at all; it may be more analogous to an anthill, a termite tower, or a coral reef."

When she paused she could hear the echo of her voice, a basso resonance returning from the back of the hall.

"In other words, we try very hard not to deceive ourselves. And by and large we do a good job of it. The barrier between ourselves and the peoples of UMa47/E is painfully obvious. Anthropologists have long told us that culture is a collection of shared symbols, and we share none with the subjects of our study. *Omnis cultura ex cultura*, and the two cultures are as imiscible, we presume, as oil and water. Our epigenetic behaviors and theirs have no point of intersection.

"The downside is that we're forced to begin from first principles. We can't talk about a chthonic 'architecture,' say, since we would have to strip from that seemingly innocent word all its buttresses and beams of human intent and human esthetics—without which the word 'architecture' becomes insupportable, an unstable structure. Nor dare we speak of chthonic 'art' or 'work,' 'leisure' or 'science.' The list is endless, and what we are left with is simply raw behavior. Behavior to be scrutinized and catalogued in all its minutiae.

"We say the Subject travels here, performs this or that action, is relatively slow or relatively fast, turns left or right, eats such-and-such, at least if we don't balk at the word 'eats' as creeping anthropocentrism; maybe 'ingests' is better. It means the same thing, but it looks better in the written report. 'Subject ingested a bolus of vegetable material.' Actually, he ate a plant—you know it and I know it, but a peer reviewer at *Nature* would never let it pass." There was some cautious laughter. Behind her, Ray snorted derisively and audibly. "We patrol the connotation of every word we speak with the censorious instinct of a Bowdler. All in the name of science, and often for very good reasons.

"But I wonder if we aren't blinding ourselves at the same time.

"What is missing from our discourse about the peoples of UMa47/E, I would suggest, is narrative.

"The natives of UMa47/E are not human, but we are, and human beings interpret the world by constructing narratives to explain it. The fact that some of our narratives are naive, or wishful, or simply wrong, hardly invalidates the process. Science, after all, is at heart a narrative. An anthropologist, or an army of anthropologists, may pore over fragments of bone and catalog them according to a dozen or a hundred apparently trivial features, but the unspoken object of all this work is a narrative—a story about how human beings emerged from the other fauna on this planet, a story about our origins and our ancestors.

"Or consider the periodic table. The periodic table is a catalog, a list of the known and possible elements arranged according to an organizing principle. It looks like static knowledge, exactly the kind of knowledge we're accumulating about the Subject and his kindred. But even the periodic table implies a narrative. The periodic table is a defining statement in the story of the universe, the end point of a long narrative about the creation of hydrogen and helium in the Big Bang, the forging of heavy elements in stars, the relationship of electrons to atomic nuclei, the nucleus and its process of decay, and the quantum behavior of subatomic particles. We have our place in that narrative too. We are in part the result of carbon chemistry in water—another narrative hidden in the periodic table—and so, I might add, are the observed peoples of UMa47/E."

She paused. There was a glass of ice water on the flat-topped podium, thank God. Marguerite took a sip. Judging by the background noise, she had already ignited a few whispered arguments in the audience.

"Narratives intersect and diverge, combine and recombine. Understanding one narrative may require the creation of another. Most fundamentally, narrative is *how* we understand. Narrative is how we understand the universe and it is most obviously how we understand ourselves. A stranger may seem inscrutable or even frightening until he offers us his story; until he tells us his name, tells us where he comes from and where he's going. This may be true of the chthonic inhabitants of UMa47/E as well. It would not surprise me if they are, in their way, also exchanging and creating narratives. Perhaps they are not; perhaps they have a different way of organizing and disseminating knowledge. But I promise you we will not understand them until we begin to tell ourselves stories about them."

She could see more faces in the audience now. There was Chris, on the center aisle, nodding encouragingly. Elaine Coster beside him, Sebastian Vogel next to her. She assumed they had their servers in hand, in case Ray bolted for the Plaza.

And down in the front row was Tess, listening attentively. Ray must have brought her. Marguerite aimed a smile at her daughter.

"Of course, we're scientists. We have our own name for a tentative narrative: we call it a hypothesis, and we test it against observation and experimentation. And of course any hypothesis we venture about the native peoples must be very, very tentative. It will be a first approximation, an educated guess, even a shot in the dark.

"Nevertheless I believe we have been far too shy about making such guesses. I think this is because the questions we have to ask in order to create that narrative are extremely unsettling. Any sentient species we encounter—and for the first time in history we have another example to compare against our own—will be grounded in its biology. Some of its behavior, in other words, will be specific to its genetic history. If it is truly a sentient species, however, some of its behavior will also be discretionary, will be flexible, will be innovative. Which is not to say it will be unfailingly rational. Quite the opposite, perhaps.

"And here, I think, is the fundamental issue we have been reluctant to confront. We harbor closely-held beliefs about ourselves. A theologian might say we are a God-seeking species. A biologist might say we are an assembly of interrelated physiological functions capable of highly complex activity. A Marxist might say we're players in a dialogue between history and economics. A philosopher might say we're the result of the appropriation by DNA of the mathematics of emergent properties in semistable chaotic systems. We treat these beliefs as mutually exclusive and we cleave to them, according to our preferences, religiously.

"But I suspect that in the native peoples of UMa47/E we will find all of these descriptors both useful and insufficient. We will have to arrive at a new definition of a 'sentient species,' and that definition must include ourselves *and* the natives.

"And that, I would suggest, is what we have been avoiding."

Another sip of water. Was she too close to the microphone? From the back rows it probably sounded like she was gargling.

"Anything we say about the native peoples implies a new perspective on us. We will find them comparatively more or less brave than ourselves, more or less gentle, more or less warlike, more or less affectionate—perhaps, ultimately, more or less *sane*.

"In other words, we may be forced to draw conclusions about them, and consequently about ourselves, which we do not like.

"But we're scientists, and we aren't supposed to shy away from these matters. As a scientist it is my cherished belief—I'm tempted to say, my faith—that understanding is better than ignorance. Ignorance, unlike life, unlike narrative, is static. Understanding implies a forward motion, thus the possibility of change.

"This is why it's so important to maintain focus on the Subject." *As long as we can*, she added to herself. "A few months ago one might plausibly have argued that the Subject's life was a rigidly repetitive routine and that we had gleaned from it all we could. Recent events have proven that argument wrong. The Subject's life, which we had mistaken for a cycle, has become very much a narrative, a narrative we may be able to follow to its conclusion and from which we will surely learn a great deal.

"We've already learned much. We've seen, for instance, the ruins at 33/28, an abandoned city—if I may use that word— apparently older than the Subject's home and very different in architectural style. And this, too, implies a narrative. It implies that the architectural behavior of the native peoples is flexible; that they have accumulated knowledge and put that knowledge to diverse and adaptive uses.

"It implies, in short, and if any doubt remains, that the native peoples *are* a people—intellectually proximate and morally equivalent to human beings—and that the best way to construct their narrative is by reference to our own. Even if that comparison is not always flattering to us."

That was her big finish. Her defiant thesis. Problem was,

nobody seemed sure she *had* finished. She cleared her throat again and said, "That's all, thank you," and walked back to her chair. Applause welled up behind her. It sounded polite, if not enthusiastic.

Ari went to the podium, thanked her, and introduced Ray.

Sue Sampel spent twenty minutes at her desk in the anteroom of Ray's office, looking busy for the sake of the video monitors embedded in the wall.

She had set aside some work to make her presence here seem plausible. Not that there was much in the way of real work. It was a fucking joke, these reports Ray insisted on putting together, documenting the daily trivia of Blind Lake site management. The reports went nowhere except into a file marked PENDING— pending what, the end of the world?—but they would serve as an alibi if it came down to the question of what Ray had been up to during the lockdown. It seemed to her that Ray spent a lot of time preparing to be questioned about things.

She kept an eye on her desktop clock. At 1:30, she made a show of shuffling through papers and digital files as if she had lost something. And therefore would go into Ray's office to get it. This felt ludicrously unrealistic, like a high school play.

Or a bad movie. And in the movie, Sue thought, this would be the moment somebody walked in on her . . . probably Shulgin, or even Ray, Ray with a pistol in his hand . . .

"Sue?"

She bit her tongue, then managed an "Ow!" that might have passed as "Hello?"

It wasn't Ray. It was only Gretchen Krueger from down in Archives.

"Didn't expect you'd be in today," Gretchen said. "I was just on my way to pick up some back-issue *JAE*s and I saw your door open. Is Ray here too?"

"No. I'm just finishing up some work. Except I keep losing things." Establishing her alibi yet again.

"When I'm done here, I'm getting together at Sawyer's with Jamal and Karen. Want to join us? You'd be more than welcome."

"Thanks, but all I want this afternoon is a shower and a nap."

"I know the feeling."

"You have a good time, though, Gretch."

"I will. Take it easy, Sue. You look tired."

Gretchen ambled off down the corridor and Sue began to steel herself once more for the assault on Ray's inner office. But first she pulled the door to the hallway all the way closed. Her hand was shaking, she discovered.

Then into Ray's sanctuary and out of range of the security cameras.

First she pulled a sheaf of files out of the cabinet against the wall—any files, it didn't matter, as long as she had something innocuous-looking to carry out again. Then she went to his desk, put her key in the master lock, and opened all five drawers one after the other.

The bundle of printouts was in the bottom-left drawer, where he used to keep his DingDongs before the supply ran out. He had probably vacuumed the drawer for crumbs, knowing Ray. Ray must be seriously jonesing, she thought. He must be in acute DingDong withdrawal.

She picked up the first sheet.

EX: Bo Xiang, *Crossbank National Laboratory*

TO: Avery Fishbinder, *Blind Lake National Laboratory*

TEXT: *Hi, Ave. As promised, here's some heads-up on the material we'll be presenting at this year's conference. Sorry I can't be more explicit (I know you don't want to be blindsided) but we've been warned to keep this quiet until it's all official. The long and short is that we've found evidence of a vanished sentient culture on HR8832/B. Screen shots to follow, but there is a region of basaltic uplift in the northern hemisphere, very shallow water and some exposed islands, superficially no different from hundreds of other such swampy regions, but with the remains of obviously very highly engineered structures, including a specific link or at least an architectural reference to the "coral floaters" dotting the equator. Still unsure how to reconcile this with the absence of motile animals: Gossard suggests an ancient mass extinction . . .*

For God's sake, Sue scolded herself, don't *read* it. She cast a furtive glance at the doorway. She was alone, but that could change.

She took her server from her pocket, dialed her home node and activated the scan function. The server was a pencil-style model exactly as wide as a standard sheet of paper. Sue ran the photosensitive side down the document until it blipped a complete transfer. Then the next sheet. Then the next. But there were lots of sheets. She checked her watch. It was almost two o'clock. She might be another twenty minutes here. More.

Calm down, she told herself, and scanned another printout.

From his aisle seat in the hall, Chris Carmody watched Ray stand up and walk to the podium.

Chris felt it was important to get some measure of this guy. There were a thousand ways he could walk into another confrontation with Ray Scutter. If that happened, he didn't want to screw it up.

There were a thousand ways to screw it up.

Ray looked pretty slick today. He smiled at the audience

and took the podium with an ease Marguerite hadn't been able to muster. This was the "charm" she had talked about it, and maybe this was what she had seen in him when they first met— a plausible grin and some good-sounding words. Ray began:

"I'm going to depart from my prepared text here—and I know you asked us to keep it short, Ari, and I promise I'll do my best—to address some of the remarks of the previous speaker."

Marguerite squirmed visibly in her chair, though she must have expected this.

"As scientists," Ray said, "one of the things we *must* keep in mind is that appearances can be deceptive. We've been talking about the O/BEC installation as if it were a superior optical telescope. I would remind you that it isn't. At its most fundamental level, the Eye is a quantum computer functioning as an image generator. We assume the images it generates accurately represent past events on a distant planet. That may be true. It may not. If it *is* deriving real information, we don't know how it's doing so. The images it creates are consonant with our real knowledge of UMa47/E's size, atmosphere, and distance from its parent star. Beyond that, however, we have no way of confirming what the Eye purports to see. Until we can more efficiently duplicate and understand the effect, our assumption that we're seeing real events has to be provisional.

"And if we're tentative about the conclusions we draw, it's not because we're timid. It's because we don't want to be deceived. For this reason—and many others—I believe our tight focus on the Subject and his culture has been misguided and disastrously premature.

"In contrast to the previous speaker, I would remind the audience that we have been making up stories—pardon me, 'constructing narratives'—about extraterrestrial life for much of human history. Whether this constitutes genius or folly is an interesting question. In the name of science, we were once asked by Percival Lowell to believe in a Mars equipped with canals and civilization. That misconception was dispelled by twentieth-century science, only to be replaced by the wishful and ultimately falsified discovery of fossil bacteria in a Martian meteorite. Examined more closely, Mars has proven to be sterile of life. The widely imagined microbes inhabiting Europa's subsurface ocean of lukewarm sludge have likewise turned out to be illusory. Our imagination outpaces us, it seems. It is intuitive, it leaps ahead, and it sees what it wishes for. A manifesto for imagination is hardly what we need, especially at this point in time."

He sighed theatrically.

"Having said that—and I think it needed to be said—let me move on to a more pressing issue, one with particular relevance for all of us here at the Lake.

"It goes without saying that the lockdown, what some people have called the quarantine, is an unprecedented event and one we have all struggled to understand. Quarantine, I think, is an apt word. I think it's become obvious that we have all been confined here, not for our own good, but for the protection of people on the outside.

"And yet it sounds absurd, ridiculous. What is there about us, about Blind Lake, that could possibly be considered threatening?

"Indeed, what? Some have suggested that the very images we've been studying might be dangerous, that they might contain a steganographic code or some other hidden message destructive to the human mind. But we have seen little evidence of that . . . unless you want to cite the previous speaker's panegyric as an example." Ray grinned lopsidedly, as if he had said something a little wicked but very clever, and there was uneasy laughter from the audience. He took a sip of water and carried on: "No, I think we ought to focus our suspicion on the process itself—on the O/BEC mechanism.

"Could there be something dangerous about the O/BEC platens? We hardly know enough to answer that question. What we do know is that the O/BEC processors are very powerful quantum computers of a novel kind and we're using them to run self-evolving, self-replicating code.

"Those words by themselves ought to raise an alarm. In every other case in which we have attempted to exploit self-replicating evolutionary systems, we've been forced to proceed with utmost caution. I'm thinking of the near-disaster last year at the MIT nanotech lab—we all know how much worse that might have been—or the novel rice cultivars that caused so many histamine-reaction deaths in Asia in the early Twenty-twenties."

Elaine scribbled furiously on a notepad. Sebastian Vogel sat in a state of calm attentiveness, a bearded Buddha.

"The obvious objection is that those events involved 'real' self-replicating systems in the 'real' world, not code in a machine. But this is shortsighted. The O/BEC virtual ecosystem may be contained, but it is also effectively enormous. Literally billions of generations of algorithms are iterated and harvested for utility in a single day. Periodically we select them for the results we desire, but they are breeding always. We assume that because we write the limiting conditions we have godlike power over our creations. Maybe that isn't the case.

"Now, obviously we've never lost a researcher because he was ambushed by an algorithm." More laughter: the lay audience seemed to like this, though the Observation and Interpretation people remained warily silent. "And that's not what I'm suggesting. But there is some evidence—which I'm not yet at liberty to discuss—that the Crossbank installation was shut down hours before the quarantine was placed on Blind Lake, and that something dangerous *did* happen there, possibly involving their O/BEC machines."

This was news. All around the auditorium, people literally sat up in their chairs. Chris glanced at Elaine, who shrugged: she hadn't expected Ray to broach that subject.

Maybe Ray hadn't intended to. He shuffled his papers and looked nonplussed for a long moment.

"This is, of course still under investigation . . ."

He set the written speech aside.

"But I want to return to the previous speaker's claims for a moment . . ."

"He's ad-libbing," Elaine whispered. "Marguerite must have scored a point somewhere. Or else he had a couple of drinks before he showed up."

"If I recall correctly . . . I believe it was Goethe who wrote that nature loves illusion. 'Nature loves illusion, and those who will not partake of her illusions she punishes as a tyrant would punish.' We talk glibly about a 'sentient' species as if sentience were a simple, easily quantifiable attribute. Of course it is not. Our perception of our own sentience is skewed and idiosyncratic. We contrast ourselves with the other primates as if we were rational and they were driven by purely animalistic impulses. But the ape, for instance, is almost wholly rational: he searches for food, he eats when he's hungry, he sleeps when he's weary, he mates when the urge and opportunity are both present. A philosophical ape might well ask which species is genuinely driven by reason.

"He might ask, 'When are we most alike, men and apes?' Not when we eat or sleep or defecate, because every animal does those things. Men exhibit their uniqueness when they make elaborate tools, compose operas, wage war for ideological reasons, or send robots to Mars—only human beings do that. We imagine our future and contemplate our past, personal or collective. But when does an ape review the events of his day or imagine an utterly different future? The obvious answer is, when he dreams."

Chris looked at Marguerite onstage. She seemed as startled as everyone else. Ray was rattled now, but he had launched into a scenario that had some weighty internal momentum of its own.

"When he dreams. When the ape dreams. Asleep, he does not reason but he dreams the dreams that enable reason. Dreaming, the ape imagines he is chased or chasing, fed or hungry, frightened or safe. In reality he is none of those things. He's running or starving in a fragmentary model world wholly of his own projection. How human! How completely human! You, this philosophical ape might say, are the hominids who dream by daylight. You don't live in the world. You live in your dream of the world.

"Dreaming infuses our existence. Our earliest ancestors learned to throw a spear, not at a running animal, but at the place where the running animal would be when the spear had traveled through the air at a certain speed. Our ancestors did this not by calculation but by imagination. By dreaming, in other words. We dream the animal's future and throw the spear at the dream. We dream images out of the past and use them to project and revise our own future action. And as an evolutionary stratagem our dreaming has been wildly success-ful. As a species, we have dreamed ourselves out of the cul-de-sac of instinct into a whole new universe of unexplored behaviors.

"We did it so effectively, I would suggest, that we have for-gotten the fundamental truth that we *are* dreaming. We con-fuse the dream with reason. But the ape reasons too. What the ape will *not* do is dream ideologies, dream terrorism, dream vengeful gods, dream slavery, dream gas chambers, dream lethal remedies for dreamlike problems. Dreams are commonly nightmares."

The audience was lost. Ray seemed no longer to care. He was talking to himself now, chasing an idea down some labyrinth only he could see.

"But they are dreams from which, as a species, we cannot wake. Our dreams are the dreams nature loves. Our dreams are epigenetic and they have served our genome remarkably well. In a few hundreds of thousands of years we have increased from a localized hominid subspecies to a planet-dominating population of eight or ten billion. If we reason within the boundaries of our daylight dreams, nature rewards us. If we reasoned as simply and straightforwardly as the apes we would be no more populous than the apes.

"But now we've done something new. We've built machines that dream. The pictures the O/BEC device generates are dreams. They are based, we tell ourselves, on the real world, but they aren't telescopic images in any traditional sense. When we look through a telescope we see with the human eye and interpret with the human mind. When we look at an O/BEC image we see what a dreaming machine has learned to dream.

"Which is not to say that the images are valueless! Only that we cannot accept them at face value. And we have to ask ourselves another question. If our machine can dream more effectively than a human being, what else might it be able to do? What other dreams might it entertain, with or without our knowledge?

"The organisms we're studying may not be the inhabitants of a rocky inner world circling the star Ursa Majoris 47. The alien species may be the O/BEC devices themselves. And the worst thing . . . the *worst* thing . . ."

He stopped, picked up his water glass, and drained it. His face was flushed.

"I mean, how do you wake from a dream that enables your consciousness? By dying. Only by dying. And if the O/BEC entity—let's call it that—has become a danger to us, maybe we need to kill it."

Near the front, a small voice shouted, "You can't *do* that!"

A child's voice. Chris recognized Tess, standing now near the foot of the stage.

Ray looked down in obvious bewilderment. He seemed not to recognize her. When he did, he motioned her to sit down and said, "I'm sorry. I'm sorry. I apologize for the interruption. But we can't afford to be sentimental. Our lives are at stake. We may be—as a species, we may be—" He wiped his forehead with his hand. The real Ray had punched through, Chris thought, and the real Ray was not a pleasant thing to behold. "We may be ungoverned dream-machines, capable of wreaking immense havoc, but we owe our loyalty to our genome. Our genome is what makes a tolerable dream out of the valueless, the rigorously precise mathematics of the universe we inhabit. . . . What would we see, if we were truly awake? A universe that loves death far more than it loves life. It would be foolish, truly foolish to yield our primacy to yet another set of numbers, another nonlinear dissipative system alien to our way of life . . ."

A man may smile, and smile, and be a villain, Shakespeare had said. Chris understood that. It was a lesson he should have learned a long time ago. If he had learned it soon enough, his sister Portia might still be alive.

"Stop *talking* like that!" Tess screeched.

At that moment Ray seemed to wake, seemed to realize he had done something peculiar, embarassed himself in public. His face was brick-red.

"What I mean to say—"

The silence dragged on. The audience murmured.

"What I mean—"

Ari Weingart took a half-step out from stage left.

"I'm sorry," Ray said. "I apologize if I said something—if I misspoke. This meeting—"

He waved his hand, knocking the empty water glass onto the floor of the stage. It broke spectacularly.

"This meeting is over," Ray growled into the barrel of the microphone. "You can all go home."

He stalked into the wings. Sebastian Vogel began whispering frantically into his pocket server. Marguerite clambered down from the stage and ran to comfort her daughter.

Sue Sampel had just shuffled the printouts back into their original order when her server chimed.

The small noise seemed very large in the silence of Ray's inner office. She jumped, and half the sheaf of papers fell out of her hand and scattered across the floor.

"Shit!" she said, then fumbled the phone wand out of her pocket. "*Yes?*"

It was Sebastian. Ray had left the stage, he said. Looking pissed. Could be headed anywhere.

"Thanks," Sue said. "Meet me out front, five minutes." She gathered the papers from the floor—they had scattered into a broad circle, and some had slipped under the desk—and shuffled them back into a crude semblance of order. No time to be more precise. Even if Ray didn't come roaring through the door, her nerves were stretched to the breaking point. She locked the papers into Ray's desk drawer, left his office, packed up the stuff she had left on her own desk, then hurried into the corridor and shut the door behind her.

The elevator ride took approximately forever, but the lobby was empty when she got there and Sebastian had already pulled up at to the front. She ducked into the car and said, "Go, go, go."

The wind had kicked up since morning. Out in the wide meadows between the town of Blind Lake and the cooling towers of Eyeball Alley, fresh snow began to fall.

Twenty-Three

Ray Scutter left the auditorium without a destination in mind, sucking in gusts of bitterly cold air as the doors closed behind him. Trading pain for clarity.

He'd made a mistake onstage. No, worse than that. He'd lost track of himself. That ridiculous digression about apes and men. Not that the ideas weren't sound. But his delivery had been self-absorbed, almost manic.

Some of this was Marguerite's fault. That pious little speech of hers had demanded rebuttal. But he shouldn't have risen to the bait. Ray had always been able to command an audience, and it troubled him that he had let this one get so completely out of hand. Put it down to stress, he thought.

Stress, frustration, a contagious

madness. Ray had read the Crossbank printouts closely, and that was his diagnosis: insanity as a transmissible disease. Here at Blind Lake, of course, it could start at any time; perhaps had already started; he hadn't been kidding when he called Marguerite's speech a symptom.

Grains of snow snaked across the mallway, writhing in the wind. Ray had left his jacket backstage at the community center, but going back for it was out of the question. Ray decided to shelter in his office half a block away, make a couple of calls, do some damage assessment, find out how badly he had fucked himself with that outburst on stage. Errant thoughts still circled in his head. Daylight dreams.

He crossed the lobby of the Plaza and rode an empty elevator up to the seventh floor, snow melting to dew in his hair. He felt dizzy, nauseated. His ears vibrated with some buzzing, interminable noise. He had embarrassed himself, he thought, okay, but in the long term, even in the short term, did that really matter? If no one was leaving Blind Lake alive (and he considered that a real possibility), of what significance was his outburst? Made him look bad to the senior researchers, big fucking deal. He wasn't playing career games anymore.

He was still well-placed to survive. He could even come through this crisis looking relatively good, if he did the right thing. What was the right thing? Killing the O/BECs, Ray thought. Too late to generate popular support, but he had laid the groundwork and might even have made a few converts if Marguerite hadn't provoked him. If he hadn't lost himself in a maze of ancillary ideas. If Tess hadn't interrupted him.

He came to a dead halt at the door to his office.

Tess.

He had forgotten his daughter. He had left her in the audience.

He took his server out of his shirt pocket and pronounced Tessa's name.

She answered promptly: "Dad?"

"Tess, where are you?"

She hesitated. Ray tried but failed to read significance into the pause. Then she said, "I'm in the car."

"The car? *Whose* car?"

"Uh, Mom's."

"You don't go back to your mother until Monday."

"I know, but—"

"She shouldn't have taken you with her. That was wrong. That was absolutely dead wrong for her to do that."

"But—"

"Did she force you, Tess? Did your mother make you get in the car with her? You can tell me. If she's listening, just give me a hint. I'll understand."

Plaintively: "*No!* It wasn't like that. You *left*."

"Only for a few minutes, Tess."

"I didn't know that!"

"You should have waited for me."

"Plus you said all those things about killing her!"

"I don't know what you're talking about. I would never hurt your mother."

"What? I mean when you were up onstage! You talked about killing Mirror Girl!"

"I didn't—" He stopped, forced himself to calm down. Tess was sensitive and, by the sound of her voice, already frightened. "I didn't mention Mirror Girl. You must have misunderstood."

"You said we have to kill her!"

"I was talking about the processor at the Eye, Tess. Please put your mother on."

Another pause. "She doesn't want to talk to you."

"She has to bring you to me. That's in the agreement we signed. I need to tell her about that."

"We're going home." Tess sounded near tears. "I'm sorry!"

"Going to your mother's house?"

"Yes!"

"She's not allowed—"

"I don't *care!* I don't *care* what she's not allowed! At least she doesn't want to *kill* anyone!"

"Tess, I told you, I don't—"

The server clicked. Tess had broken the connection.

When he tried her again there was no answer, only her standard voice message. He tried Marguerite. Likewise.

"Fucking bitch," Ray whispered. Meaning Marguerite. Maybe even Tess, who had betrayed him. But no, no, back up, that wasn't fair. Tess had been misled. Misled by her mother's pampering and indulgence. Which was exactly what all this Mirror Girl bullshit was about.

Marguerite was using it against him. *Daddy wants to kill Mirror Girl.* Indoctrinating her. Ray was furious, picturing it. He could only imagine what lies Tess had been asked to believe about him.

So was Tess lost to him, too?

No. No. Impossible. Not yet.

He locked himself into his office, turned his chair to the window, and thought about calling Dimi Shulgin. Shulgin might have some ideas.

The view from the window was lifeless and hostile. Blind Lake had learned to live without weather reports, but you didn't have to be a meteorologist to see the clouds roll in. Low clouds, weighty with snow, moving on a gale-force wind from the northwest. One more installment in this endless winter.

The falling snow gave the town an illusory vagueness, like a tintype photograph or a stage set painted in shades of gray. The windowpane flexed in a gust of wind, lensing the image slightly. Subject stared for an indeterminate period of time at the approaching storm.

When he turned away, the chair's castor caught on something hidden under the desk. The cleaning staff had gotten sloppy, but that was hardly news. A sheet of paper. Scowling, he bent down to retrieve it.

> EX: Bo Xiang, *Crossbank National Laboratory*
>
> TO: Avery Fishbinder, *Blind Lake National Laboratory*
>
> TEXT: *In answer to your question, the possibility that the dry-land structures are natural is very slim. Although this kind of symmetry is often enough seen in nature, the size of the structure and the degree of precision are remarkable and suggest engineering rather than evolution. Not that this is a clinching argument, but*

Ray stopped reading and placed the paper face-up on his desk.

Slowly, taking his time now, resisting hasty judgment, he keyed open his desk and removed from the bottom drawer the thick sheaf of printouts Shulgin had delivered to him. He leafed through it quickly.

The pages were out of order.

Someone had been in his desk again.

Ray stood up. He saw his reflection in the window, an image pasted on a mural of clouds, a man frozen in a layer of glass.

Twenty-Four

The weather was conspicuously worse by the time Chris, Marguerite, and Tess reached the house. Maybe that was a good thing, Chris thought. It put another barrier between Marguerite and Ray. If Ray came looking for his daughter Tess—or looking for revenge—the snow might at least slow him down.

Tess had cried after the phone call. Now her tears had subsided into a flurry of hiccups, and Marguerite walked her into the house with an arm around her shoulder. Tess shrugged out of her jacket and boots and ran for the living room sofa as if it were a life raft.

Marguerite carded the door. "Better throw the dead bolt too," Chris said.

"You think that's necessary?"

"I think it's wise."

"Aren't you being a little paranoid? Ray wouldn't—"

"We don't know what Ray might do. We shouldn't take chances."

She threw the bolt and joined her daughter on the sofa.

Chris borrowed her office to print the docs Sue had transferred to his server. The office was windowless, but he could hear the wind kicking up outside, prying at the eavestroughs like a man with a blunt knife.

He thought about Ray onstage at the auditorium. Ray's first order of business had been to deride and humiliate Marguerite, and he had done that fairly cleverly, disguising his anger, controlling it. For a guy like Ray, it was all about control. But the world was full of unmanageable insolence. Expectations were confounded. Wives disobeyed and then abandoned him. His theories were proven false.

His desk was rifled.

The important thing about Ray's little meltdown, Chris thought, was that it evidenced a deeper unraveling. Guys like Ray were emotionally brittle, which was what made them such effective bullies. They lived just this side of the breaking point. And sometimes passed it.

Pages snapped briskly out of the printer, all of the thirty-odd documents Sue had filched. Ray's treasure, for what it was worth. Chris sat down and began to read.

Marguerite spent the gray end of the afternoon with her daughter.

Tess had calmed down considerably once she was inside the house. But her distress was still obvious. She had curled up on the sofa with a quilted comforter around her like a prayer shawl and fixed her attention on the video screen. Blind Lake

TV was showing old downloads of *The Fosters,* a children's show Tess hadn't watched since she was six. She had turned up the volume to drown out the sound of the wind and the sound of hard snow rattling against the windows.

Marguerite sat with her much of this time. She was curious about the documents Chris was printing and reading; but, perhaps strangely, none of that seemed urgent now. For a few hours the world was suspended between darkness and true night, cosseted in the worsening storm, and all she needed or wanted to do was hunker down with Tess.

She went to the kitchen a little after five to assemble some dinner. The window over the sink was clotted with snow, opaque as a porthole in a sunken ship, nothing outside but vague shapes moving under an immense pressure of gloom. Was it really possible Ray would come to the house and try to hurt her? In this weather? But she guessed, if you were on the brink of some awful act, you didn't postpone it on account of snow.

Tess came into the kitchen and pulled up a chair, watching Marguerite chop yellow peppers for the salad.

"Is Chris okay?" Tess asked.

"Sure he is. He's just upstairs doing some work." Conferring by phone with Elaine Coster, last time she'd checked.

"But he's still in the house?"

"Yup, still here."

"That's good," Tess said. She sounded genuinely relieved. "It's better when he's here."

"I think so too."

"How long will he stay?"

Interesting question. "Well—at least until all this trouble at the Lake is finished. And maybe longer than that." Maybe. She had not discussed this with Chris. If she asked him about his long-term plans, would that seem needy or presumptuous?

Would she like the answer? And under the circumstances, how could anyone *have* long-term plans?

The relationship felt reasonably solid to Marguerite. Had she fallen in love with Chris Carmody? Yes, she thought so; but she was afraid of the word, afraid of saying it and almost as frightened of hearing it. Love was a natural phenomenon, often false or fleeting. Like a warm spell in October, it could end at any time.

"Tess? Can I ask you something?"

Tess shrugged, rocking gently against the back of the chair.

"Back at the auditorium, you said, 'You can't kill her.' Who were you talking about?"

"You know."

"You mean Mirror Girl?"

"I guess."

"I don't think Dad was talking about Mirror Girl. He was talking about the processors out at the Eye."

"Same thing," Tess said, obviously uncomfortable.

"Same thing? What do you mean?"

"I don't know how to explain it. But that's where she really lives. It's all the same thing."

When Marguerite pressed for details Tess became unresponsive; finally Marguerite let her retreat to the sofa. Still, it was a new twist, this idea that Mirror Girl lived at the Eye. Perhaps meaningful, but Marguerite couldn't decipher it. Was that why Tess had snuck off to the Alley last week? Tracking Mirror Girl to her lair?

When all this craziness ends, Marguerite promised herself, I'll take her somewhere away from here. Somewhere different. Somewhere dry and warm. Marguerite had often thought of visiting the desert Southwest—Utah, Arizona, Canyonlands, Four Corners—and Ray had always vetoed the idea. Maybe she would take Tess to the desert for a vacation. Dry country, though perhaps disconcertingly like the Subject's UMa47/E. Looking for salvation in empty places.

Chris put a call through to Elaine. Marguerite's office server picked up the audio and relayed it through the transducers in the walls, a connection so clean Chris could hear the sound of the storm in back of Elaine's voice. "Are you next to a window?" he asked her. "Sounds like dogs howling."

Elaine bunked in a two-room utility apartment left vacant by a maintenance man who had gone to Fargo for lithotripsy the day before the lockdown. It was a ground-floor unit with a view of the Dumpsters in back of Sawyer's Steak & Seafood. "Not a lot of room to move around in here . . . is that better?"

"A little."

"That's all we need right now, another northeaster or whatever they call these fucking storms out here in cow country. So, did you read the docs? What do you make of them?"

Chris considered his answer.

The documents were exactly what Sue Sampel had suspected: text messages that had languished in the servers of the senior scientists who had gone to Cancun for the annual conference. They contained news that had been tightly held but would have been made public at the conference: the discovery of an artificial structure on the surface of HR8832/B.

The structure resembled a spiky hemisphere with radial arms. One note compared the shape to a giant adenovirus or a molecule of C_{60}. Ray summarized what he'd read: "Apparently it expresses a mathematical principle called an 'energy function' that can be written as an expression of volume in a higher-dimensional space—but so does any icosahedron, so that proves nothing. If it really is an artifact, the builders seem to have vanished. One of the messages claims the interior of the structure is 'uniquely difficult to image,' whatever that means. . . ."

"And so on and so forth," Elaine said. "Lots of really intriguing science, but tell me something: do you see anything here that looks like a *threat*? Anything that would explain the stuff in that magazine clipping?"

"There must be a connection."

"Sure, but think about what Ray was saying at the Town Hall meeting. He claimed he had evidence the O/BEC processors at Crossbank had become physically dangerous."

"You could draw that inference."

"Fuck *inference*; do you see any actual evidence of it?"

"Not in these papers, no."

"You think Ray has evidence we don't know about?"

"It's possible. But Sue has been pretty close to Ray, and she doesn't think so."

"Right. You know what, Chris? I don't think Ray has any real evidence at all. I think he has a hypothesis. And a giant-sized bug up his ass."

"You're saying he wants to shut down the Eye and he wants to use this as an excuse."

"Exactly."

"But the Eye could still be a threat. The fact that he's biased doesn't mean he's wrong."

"If he isn't wrong, he's at least irresponsible. There's nothing in these docs he couldn't have shared with the rest of us."

"Ray doesn't like to share. They probably wrote that on his kindergarten report card. What do you propose to do about it?"

"Go public."

"And how do we do that?"

"We forward these documents to every domestic server in Blind Lake. Plus I'd like to write a little summary, like a covering letter, saying we got the docs from a protected source and that the contents are important but inconclusive."

"So Ray can't act unilaterally. He'll have to explain all this. . . ."

"And maybe get some input from the rest of us before he pulls the plug."

"That might cause trouble for Sue."

"She's a good-hearted lady, Chris, but I'd say she's already in trouble. Way deep. Maybe Ray can't prove anything, but he's not stupid."

"Might get *us* in trouble."

"How do you define 'trouble'? Locked up indefinitely in a federal installation run by a lunatic, that sounds like trouble no matter what else we do. But I'll leave your name off the forward if you like."

"No, use my name," Chris said. "Keep Marguerite out of it, though."

"No problem. But if you're thinking of Ray's reaction, I have to repeat, he's not stupid. Keep your doors locked."

"They are locked," Chris said. "Securely."

"Good. Now get ready for a shitstorm that'll make this blizzard look like summer rain."

At dinner Tess ate sparingly and spoke little, though she seemed to find the ritual reassuring. Or maybe, Marguerite thought, she just liked having Chris nearby. Chris was both a big man and a gentle one, an intoxicating combination for a nervous little girl. Or even a nervous full-grown woman.

After the meal Tess took a book to her room. Marguerite brewed coffee while Chris briefed her on the contents of the stolen documents. Many of them had been written by Bo Xiang. She had worked with Bo back at Crossbank, and he wasn't the type to get excited without good reason.

There had never been even the slightest hint of a technological civilization on HR8832/B. The structure must be immensely old, she thought. HR8832/B had oscillated through a number of severe planetwide glaciations; the structure must predate at least one of them. The resemblance to the equatorial coral floaters was suggestive, but what did it mean?

But these were unanswerable questions, at least for now. And Chris and Elaine were right: none of it constituted evidence of a threat.

The storm rattled the kitchen window as they talked. We can image worlds circling other stars, Marguerite thought; can't we make a window that doesn't rattle in bad weather? The darkness outside was deep and intimidating. The streetlights had become veiled beacons, distant torches. It was the kind of weather that would have made the news in the old days: Winter Storm Blocks Highways in the West, Airports Closed, Travelers Stranded. . . .

Tessa's usual bedtime was ten o'clock, eleven on weekends, but she came into the kitchen at nine and said, "I'm tired."

"Been a long day," Marguerite said. "Shall I run a bath for you?"

"I'll shower in the morning. I'm just tired."

"Go on up and change, then. I'll tuck you in."

Tess hesitated.

"What is it, honey?"

"I thought maybe Chris would tell me a story." She hung her head as if to say: *It's a baby thing to ask for. But I don't care.*

"Happy to," Chris volunteered.

It would be hard not to love this man, Marguerite thought.

———

"What kind of story would you like?" Chris asked, perched on the edge of Tessa's bed. He supposed he already knew the answer:

"A Porry story," the girl said.

"Honest, Tess, I think I've told all the Porry stories there are to tell."

"It doesn't have to be a new one."

"You have a favorite?"

"The tadpole story," she said promptly.

Tessa's bedroom window was still crudely boarded. Cold air came through the cracks and snaked down under the electric panel heaters and across the floor, seeking the house's deepest places. Tess wore her blankets up to her chin.

"That was back in California," Chris said, "where we grew up. We lived in a little house with an avocado tree in the backyard, and at the end of the street there was a storm drain, like a big concrete riverbed, with a wire fence to keep the local kids from getting in."

"But you went there anyway."

"Who's telling this story?"

"Sorry." She pulled the blanket up over her mouth.

"We went there anyway, all the kids in the neighborhood. There was a place you could duck under the fence. The storm drain had steep concrete walls, but if you were careful you could climb down, and in spring, if the water was low, you could find tadpoles in the shallow pools."

"Tadpoles are baby frogs, right?"

"Right, but they don't look like frogs at all. More like little black fish with long skinny tails and no fins. On a good day you could catch hundreds of them just by dipping a bucket. All the adults told us not to play around the storm drain, because it was dangerous. And it was, and we really shouldn't have gone there, but we did it anyway. All of us except Porry. Porry wanted to go but I wouldn't let her."

"Because you were her older brother and she was too young."

"We were all too young. Porry must have been about six or seven, which would make me eleven or twelve. But I was old enough to know she could get in trouble. I always made her wait by the fence, even though she hated that. One day I was down at the storm drain with a couple of friends, and we took maybe a little too long poking around in the mud, and by the time I got back Porry was tired and frustrated and practically crying. She wouldn't speak to me on the way home.

"This was springtime, and Southern California gets big spring rainstorms some years. Well, it started to rain later that day. Not just a little rain, either. 'Raindrops big as dinner plates,' my mom used to say. After dinner I did my homework and Porry went to play in her bedroom. Or at least that's what she said. After an hour or so my mom called her and Porry didn't answer, and we couldn't find her anywhere in the house."

"Couldn't you just ask the house server?"

"Houses weren't as smart in those days."

"So you went to look for her."

"Yup. I probably shouldn't have done that, either, but my dad was ready to call the police . . . and I had a feeling I knew where she'd gone."

"You should have told your parents first."

"I should have, but I didn't want to let on I knew how to get down to the storm drain myself. But you're right—it would have been braver to tell them."

"You were only eleven."

"I was only eleven and I didn't always do the bravest thing, so I snuck out of the house and ran through the rain to the gap in the fence, and I pushed under it and started to look for Porry."

"I think that was brave. Did you find her?"

"You know how this comes out."

"I'm *pretending* I don't."

"Porry had taken a bucket and gone down to the culvert to collect her own tadpoles. She was halfway back up that steep embankment when she got scared. It was the kind of scared where you can't go forward and you can't back up, so you don't do anything at all. She was crouched there, crying, and the water in the culvert was running hard and rising fast. A few more minutes and she might have been carried away by it."

"But you saved her."

"Well, I climbed down and took her arm and helped her up. The embankment was pretty slippery in the rain. We were almost at the fence when she said, 'My tadpoles!' So I had to go back and get her bucket. Then we went home."

"And you didn't tell on her."

"I said I'd found her playing in the neighbors' yard. We hid the bucket in the garage. . . ."

"And forgot about it!"

"And forgot about it, but those tadpoles did what tadpoles do—they started to turn into frogs. My dad opened up the garage a couple of days later and the floor was covered with little green frogs, frogs jumping up his legs, frogs all over the car. An *avalanche* of frogs. He yelled, and we all came running out of the house, and Porry started to laugh . . ."

"But she wouldn't say why."

"She wouldn't say why."

"And you never told."

"Anyone. Until now."

Tess smiled contentedly. "Yeah. Were the frogs okay?"

"Mostly. They headed into the hedges and gardens all up and down our street. It was a noisy summer that year, all that croaking."

"Yes." Tess closed her eyes. "Thank you, Chris."

"You don't have to thank me. Think you can sleep?"

"Yeah."

"I hope the sound of the wind doesn't keep you up."

"Could be worse," Tess said, smiling for the first time today. "Could be frogs."

Marguerite listened from the doorway to the first part of the story, then retreated to her office and switched on the wall screen. Not to work. Just to watch.

It was near dusk on the Subject's small patch of UMa47/E. Subject traversed a low canyon parallel to the setting sun. Maybe it was the long light, but he looked especially unwell, Marguerite thought. He had been scavenging for food for a long time now, subsisting on the mossy substance that grew wherever there was water and shade. Marguerite suspected the moss was not terribly nutritious, perhaps not even enough to sustain him. His skin was creased and shrunken. You didn't have to be a physicist to parse that equation. Too many calories spent, too few ingested.

As the sky darkened a few stars emerged. The brightest was not a star at all but a planet: one of the system's two gas giants, UMa47/A, almost three times the size of Jupiter and big enough to show a perceptible disc at its nearest approach. Subject stopped and swiveled his head from side to side. Taking his bearings, perhaps, or even performing some kind of celestial navigation.

She heard Chris closing Tessa's bedroom door. He leaned into the office and said, "Mind if I join you?"

"Pull up a chair. I'm not really working."

"Getting dark," he said, gesturing at the wall screen.

"He'll sleep soon. I know it sounds dumb, Chris, but I'm worried about him. He's a long way from—well, anywhere. Nothing seems to live in this place, not even the parasites that feed on him at night."

"Isn't that a good thing?"

"But, technically, they're probably not parasites at all. There must be a benevolent symbiosis, or the cities wouldn't be full of them."

"New York is full of rats. That doesn't mean they're desirable."

"It's an open question. But he's clearly not well."

"He might not make it to Damascus."

"Damascus?"

"I keep thinking he's St. Paul on the road to Damascus. Waiting for a vision."

"I suppose we'd never know if he found it. I was hoping for something more tangible."

"Well, I'm no expert."

"Who is?" She turned away from the display. "Thanks for helping Tess settle down. I hope you're not sick of telling her stories."

"Not at all."

"She likes your—what does she call them? Porry stories. Actually, I'm a little jealous. You don't talk much about your family."

"Tessa's an easy audience."

"And I'm not?"

He smiled. "You're not eleven."

"Did Tess ever ask you what happened to Portia as a grown-up?"

"Thankfully, no."

"How did she die?" Marguerite asked, then: "I'm sorry, Chris. I'm sure you don't want to talk about it. Really, it's none of my business."

He was silent a moment. God, she thought, I've offended him.

Then he said, "Portia was always a little more headstrong than she was bright. She never had an easy time at school. She dropped out of college and got in with a bunch of people, part-time dopers . . ."

"Drugs," Marguerite said.

"It wasn't just the drugs. She could always handle the drugs, I guess because they didn't appeal to her all that much. But she had bad judgment about people. She moved into a guy's trailer outside of Seattle and we didn't hear from her for a while. She claimed she loved him, but she wouldn't even put him on the phone."

"Not a good sign."

"This happened when my book about Galliano had just been published. I was passing through Seattle on a tour, so I called Porry up and arranged to meet her. Not where she lived—she insisted on that. It had to be somewhere down-town. Just her, not her boyfriend. She was a little reluctant about the whole thing, but she named a restaurant and we got together there. She showed up in low-rent drag and a big pair of sunglasses. The kind you wear to hide a bruise or a black eye."

"Oh, no."

"Eventually she admitted things weren't going too well between her and her friend. She'd just landed a job, she was saving money to get a place of her own. She said not to worry about her, she was sorting things out."

"The guy was beating her?"

"Obviously. She begged me not to get involved. Not to pull any 'big brother shit,' as she put it. But I was busy saving the world from corruption. If I could expose Ted Galliano to pub-lic scrutiny, why should I put up with this kind of thing from some trailer-park cowboy? So I got Porry's address out of the directory and drove out there while she was at work. The guy was home, of course. He really didn't look like any kind of threat. He was five-nine, with a rose tattoo on his skinny right arm. Looked like he'd spent the day killing a six-pack and greasing an engine. He was belligerent, but I just braced him against the trailer with my forearm under his chin and told him if he touched Portia again he'd have me to answer to. He got very apologetic. He actually started to cry. He said he couldn't help it, it was the bottle, hey buddy you know how it is. He said he'd get himself under control. And I went away thinking I'd done some good. On my way out of town I stopped by the office where Porry worked and left her a check, something to help her get independent. Two days later I got a call from a Seattle emergency ward. She'd been beaten badly and was hemorrhaging from a cranial artery. She died that night. Her boyfriend burned the trailer and left town on a stolen motorbike. Far as I know, the police are still looking for him."

"God, Chris . . . I'm so sorry!"

"No. I'm sorry. It's not a good story for a stormy night." He touched her hand. "It doesn't even have a moral, except 'shit happens.' But if I seemed a little reluctant to jump in between you and Ray . . ."

"I understand. And I do appreciate your help. But, Chris? I can handle Ray. With you or without you. Preferably *with*, but . . . you understand?"

"You're telling me you're not Portia."

There was no light in the room now but the glow of the sunset on UMa47/E. Subject had reclined for the night. Above the canyon wall, stars shone in constellations no one had named. No one on Earth, at least.

"I'm telling you I'm not Portia. And I'm offering you a cup of tea. Interested?"

She took his hand and walked with him to the kitchen, where the window was blank with snow and the kettle sang counterpoint to the sound of the wind.

Twenty-Five

Sue Sampel was wide awake when the doorbell chimed, though it was well after midnight—almost three, according to her watch.

Between the storm outside and the nervous energy she had stoked up during her raid on Ray's office, sleep was out of the question. Sebastian, bless him, had gone upstairs around midnight and fallen immediately and soundly asleep. She had curled up with his book as a sort of vicarious presence. His book, plus a big snifter of peach brandy.

But the book seemed less substantial on her second go-through. It was beautifully written and full of striking ideas, but the gaps and leaps of logic were more obvious now. She supposed this was what had put Elaine

Coster's back up, Sebastian's cheerful love of outrageous hypotheses.

For instance, Sebastian explained in the book how what people called "the vacuum of space" was more than just an absence of matter: it was a complex brew of virtual particles popping in and out of existence too quickly to interact with the ordinary substance of things. That jibed with Sue's memory of first-year physics. She suspected he was on less firm scientific ground when he said that localized irregularities in the quantum vacuum accounted for the presence of "dark matter" in the universe. And his fundamental idea—that dark matter represented a kind of ghostly neural network inhabiting the quantum vacuum—was taken seriously by almost no one apart from Sebastian himself.

But Sebastian wasn't a scientist and had never claimed to be one. Pressed, he would say these ideas were "templates" or "suggestions," perhaps not to be taken literally. Sue understood, but she wished it could be otherwise; she wished his theories were solid as houses, solid enough to shelter in.

Not that her own house seemed especially solid tonight. The wind was absolutely ferocious, the snow so dense that the view from the window was like an O/BEC image of some planet unsuitable for human life. She nestled a little deeper into the sofa, took another sip of brandy and read:

> Life evolves by moving into preexisting domains and exploiting preexisting forces of nature. The laws of aerodynamics were latent in the natural universe before they were "discovered" by insects and birds. Similarly, human consciousness was not invented *de novo* but represents the adoption by biology of an implicit, universal mathematics . . .

This was the idea Sue liked best, that people were pieces of something larger, something that popped up in a shape called

Sue Sampel here and in a shape called Sebastian Vogel over there, both unique but both connected, the way two distinctive mountain peaks were also pieces of the same planet. Otherwise, she thought, what are we but lost animals? Lost animals, exiled from the womb, ignorant and dying.

The doorbell startled her. Her house server was kind enough to ring it quietly, but when she asked who was there the server said, "Not recognized." Her stomach clenched. Someone not in her catalogue of regular visitors.

Ray Scutter, she thought. Who else? Elaine had warned her that something like this might happen. Ray was impulsive, more impulsive than ever since the lockdown, maybe impulsive enough to brave the storm and show up on her doorstep at three in the morning. By now he might have seen Elaine's massive mailing. He would know (though he might not be able to prove it) that Sue had duped the copies from his desk. He would be furious. Worse, enraged. Dangerous. Yes, but *how* dangerous? Just how crazy *was* Ray Scutter?

She wished she'd had a little less to drink. But she had thought it would help her sleep, and she'd run out of pot a month ago. In Sue's experience drugs and alcohol were like men, and pot was the best date. Cocaine liked to get dressed up and go out, very elegant, but coke would abandon you at the party or hector you into the small hours of the morning. Alcohol promised to be fun but ended up as an embarrassment; alcohol was a guy in a loud shirt, a guy with bad breath and too many opinions. Pot, however . . . pot liked to cuddle and make love. Pot liked to eat ice cream and watch the late show. She missed pot.

The doorbell rang again. Sue peeked out the side window. Sure enough, that was Ray's little midnight-blue car parked against the drifts at the curb, and it must have a pretty good drive system, she thought, to have made it this far through the deepening snow.

There was another round of ringing, which the server muted disdainfully.

She could, of course, ignore him. But that struck her as cowardly. Really, there was nothing to be afraid of. What was he going to do? Yell at her? I'm a grown-up, she thought. I can deal with that. Better to get it over with.

She thought about waking up Sebastian and decided against it. Sebastian was many things, but he wasn't a fighter. She could handle this herself. See what Ray wanted, if necessary tell him to bugger off.

But she went to the kitchen and took a carving knife out of the knife rack just in case. She felt idiotic doing it—the knife was really just a kind of emotional insurance, something to make her feel brave—and she kept it hidden behind her back as she approached the door. Opening the door because, after all, this was Blind Lake, the safest community on the surface of the Earth, even if your employer happened to be seriously pissed at you.

Her heart was beating double-time.

Ray stood under the yellow porch light in a long black jacket. The wind had tousled his hair and adorned it with snow stars. His lips were pursed and his eyes were bright. Sue kept herself squarely in the doorway, ready to slam the door should the necessity arise. Bitter air gusted into the house. She said, "Ray—"

"You're fired," he said.

She blinked at him. "What?"

His voice was flat and level, his lips fixed in what looked like a permanent sneer. "I know what you did. I came to tell you you're fired."

"I'm fired? You drove out here to tell me I'm *fired?*"

This was too much. The tension of the day had accumulated inside her like an electric charge, and this was so ludicrously anticlimactic—Ray firing her from a job that had long ago become redundant and unimportant—that she had to struggle to keep a straight face.

What would he do next, kick her out of Blind Lake?

But she sensed it was absolutely necessary to conceal the amusement she felt. "Ray," she said, "look, I'm sorry, but it's late—"

"Shut up. Shut the fuck up. You're nothing but a thief. I know about the documents you stole. And I know about the other thing too."

"The other thing?"

"Do I have to draw you a diagram? The pastry!"

The DingDong.

That did it. She laughed in spite of herself—a choked giggle that turned into a helpless, full-throated roar. God, the Ding-Dong—Sebastian's ersatz birthday cake—the fucking *Ding-Dong!*

She was still laughing when Ray reached for her throat.

Sebastian had always been a sound sleeper.

He was quick to nod off, slow to wake. Morning classes had been the bane of his academic career. He would have made a lousy monk, he had often thought. Incapable of celibacy and always late for matins.

He slept through the distant sound of the doorbell and through the considerable noise that followed. He woke to the sound of someone whispering his name.

Or maybe it was only the wind. In a cocoon of blankets he opened his eyes to the darkened room, listened a moment and heard nothing but the keening of the storm about the eaves. He reached across to Sue's side of the bed but found it cold and empty. Not unusual. Sue was something of an insomniac. He closed his eyes again and sighed.

"*Sebastian!*"

Sue's voice. She was not in bed but she was in the room with him, and she sounded terrified. He shed layers of sleep like a wet dog shaking off water. He reached for the bedside lamp and nearly toppled it. The light sprang on and he saw Sue by the bedroom door, one hand clenched against her lower abdomen. She was pale and sweating.

"Sue? What's wrong?"

"He hurt me," she said, and lifted her hand to show him the blood on her nightgown, the blood pooling around her feet.

Twenty-Six

Charlie Grogan, when he wasn't troubleshooting the Eye, lived in a one-bedroom condo-style unit a couple of blocks north of the Plaza.

Charlie slept in the bedroom; his old dog Boomer slept in a nest of cotton blankets in a corner of the kitchen. The chime woke them simultaneously, but Boomer was first on his feet.

Charlie, coming out of a confused dream about the Subject, grabbed for his pocket server and punched the lobby connection. "Who's there?"

"Ray Scutter. I'm sorry, I know it's late. Hate to disturb you, but it's something of an emergency."

Ray Scutter, down in the lobby in the worst storm of the winter. Middle of the night. Charlie shook his head.

He was unprepared for serious thought. He said, "Yeah, okay, come on up," and buzzed the lock.

He had thrown on a shirt, pants, and socks by the time Ray reached the door. Boomer was freaked by all this late-night activity, and Charlie had to order him to keep quiet as Ray entered the apartment. Boomer sniffed at the man's knees, then shuffled uneasily away.

Ray Scutter. Charlie knew the executive administrator by sight, but he hadn't spoken to him one-on-one before now. Nor had he watched Ray's Town Hall address earlier, though he'd heard it was a disaster. Charlie was generous about such things: he hated public speaking and knew how easy it was to get tongue-tied at a podium.

"You can hang your jacket in the closet," Charlie said. "Sit down."

Ray did neither. "I won't be here long," he said. "And I'm hoping you'll leave with me."

"How's that?"

"I know how strange this sounds. Mr. Grogan—it's Charlie, right?"

"Charlie'll do."

"Charlie, I'm here to ask for your help."

Something in Ray's voice troubled Boomer, who whined from the kitchen. Charlie was more troubled by the man's appearance—rumpled suit, hair askew, what looked like fresh scratches on his face.

There had been a lot of gossip about Ray Scutter, to the effect that he was a lousy manager and an asshole to deal with. But Charlie held such hearsay inadmissible. In any case, the boss was the boss. "Tell me what I can help you with, Mr. Scutter."

"You carry an all-pass transponder out at the Eye, right?"

"I do, but—"

"All I want is a tour."

"Pardon me?"

"I know it's extraordinary. I also know it's four in the morning. But I have some decisions to make, Charlie, and I don't want to make them until I personally inspect the facility. I can't tell you more than that."

"Sir," Charlie said, "there's a night shift on duty. I'm not sure you need me. I'll just call Anne Costigan—"

"Don't call anyone. I don't want people to know I'm coming. What I want is to go out there, just you and me, and we'll do a discreet walk-through and see what we see. If anyone complains—if Anne Costigan complains—I'll take responsibility."

Good, Charlie thought, since it *was* Ray's responsibility. Reluctantly, he took his winter jacket off the hook in the hall.

Boomer wasn't happy with this turn of events. He whined again and stalked off to the bedroom, probably to find a warm spot in Charlie's bed. Boomer was an opportunistic hound.

They rode in Ray's car, a squat little vehicle with lots of bad-weather options. It took the snow pretty well, microprocessors controlling each wheel, finding traction where there should have been none. But it was still slow going. The snow came down like bags of wet confetti, almost too fast for the wipers to clear from the windshield. In this opacity of space and time the only landmarks were the streetlights, candles passing in the darkness with metronome regularity.

In the close interior of the car Ray smelled pretty ripe. His sweat had a strange acetic undertone, not pleasant, and there was something coppery on top of that, the kind of smell you registered with your back teeth. Charlie tried to figure out how he could crack a window in the middle of a blizzard without insulting Ray.

Ray talked a little as he drove. This wasn't really a conversation, since Charlie had very little to contribute. At one point Charlie said, "If you tell me what you're looking for at the Eye, Mr. Scutter, maybe I can help you find it."

But Ray just shook his head. "I trust you," he said, "and I understand your curiosity, but I'm not at liberty to discuss that."

Since Ray was pretty much the boss of Blind Lake since the shutdown, Charlie would have thought he was at liberty to discuss anything he liked. He didn't press the issue, however. He realized he was afraid of Ray Scutter, and not just because Ray was executive management. Ray was giving off very peculiar vibes.

The spots on his jacket and slacks, Charlie thought, looked like dried blood.

"You've worked a long time with the O/BEC processors," Ray said.

"Yessir. Since Gencorp. Actually, I knew Dr. Gupta back in the Berkeley Lab days."

"Did you ever wonder, Charlie, what we woke up when we built the Eye?"

"Excuse me?"

"When we built a motherfucking huge mathematical phase space and populated it with self-modifying code?"

"I guess that's one way to think of it."

"There's no phenomenon in the universe you can't describe mathematically. Everything's a calculation, Charlie, including you and me, we're just little sequestered calculations, water and minerals running million-year-old make-me instructions."

"That's a bleak point of view."

"Said the monkey, apprehending a threat."

"Pardon me?"

"Nothing. I'm sorry. I'm a little short on sleep."

"I know the feeling," Charlie said, though he felt as wide awake as he had ever been.

Somehow, Ray kept the car on the road. Charlie was vastly relieved when he saw the guardpost coming up on the left. He wondered who had pulled guard duty on a miserable night— no, morning—like this. It turned out to be Nancy Saeed. She scanned Charlie's all-pass and registered with visible surprise the presence of Ray Scutter. Nancy was ex-navy; when she saw Ray she began a salute, then thought better of it.

Moments later Ray parked by the main entrance. The nice thing about coming in early was, you could always find good parking.

He escorted Ray to his own office, where they left their jackets. Charlie had conducted enough of these dignitary and VIP tours that he had gotten it down to a routine. Prep and instructions in his office, then the walk-through. But this wasn't the usual dog-and-pony show. A long way from it.

"I met your daughter here the other day," Charlie said.

Ray cocked his head like a hunting animal catching a scent. "Tessa was here?"

"Well, she—yeah, she came by and wanted to see the works."

"By herself?"

"Her mom picked her up afterward."

Ray grimaced. "I wish I could tell you I'm proud of my daughter, Charlie. Unfortunately I can't. In many ways she's her mother's child. You always take that chance when you spin the genetic roulette wheel. You have any kids?"

"No," Charlie said.

"Good for you. Never unwind your base pairs. It's a sucker's bet."

"Sir," Charlie said, trying not to stare.

"What did she want, Charlie?"

"Your daughter? Just to look around."

"Tess has had some emotional problems. Sometimes madness is contagious."

If it's catching, Charlie thought, then you're overdue for a checkup. "Strange things happen," he said, trying to make himself sound amicable. "Why don't you take off your shoes and put on a pair of these disposables. I'll be back in a minute."

"Where are you going?"

"See a man about the plumbing," Charlie said.

He walked far enough down the main corridor to make it look convincing. As soon as he turned a corner he thumbed his pocket server and asked for Tabby Menkowitz in Security. She picked up a moment later.

"Charlie? It's an hour to dawn—what are you doing here?"

"I think we might have a problem, Tab."

"We've got lots of problems. What's your flavor?"

"Ray Scutter's in my office and he wants a tour of the plant."

"You're kidding me."

"I wish I was."

"Tell him to make an appointment. We're busy."

"Tabby, I can't just tell him—" He thought about what she'd said. "Busy with what?"

"You don't know? Talk to Anne. Maybe it's a good thing you showed up when you did. What I hear is, the O/BECs are putting out strange numbers and the Obs people are all excited about something . . . but it's not my department. All I know is, everybody's too busy to play politics with management. So keep Mr. Scutter on hold."

"I don't think he's in a mood to wait. He—"

"Charlie! I'm *busy*, okay? Handle it!"

Charlie hurried back to his office. Something major was

happening with the O/BECs, and he wanted to get downstairs and look into it. But first things first. See Ray out the door, if possible, or put him on the phone to Tabby if he had a problem with that.

But the office was empty.

Ray was missing. Also missing, Charlie realized, was his own all-pass card, plucked off the lapel of the jacket he had hung up on the hook by the door.

"Shit," Charlie said.

He called Tabby Menkowitz again, but this time he couldn't get through. Something wrong with his pocket server. It chimed once and went blue-screen.

He was still fiddling with it when the floor began to move under his feet.

Twenty-Seven

Chris came out of a black and dream-less sleep to the chirping of his pocket server, which he had left on the bed-side table and which glowed there like a luminous pencil. He checked the inset clock before he thumbed the answer button. Four in the morning. He'd had about an hour of real sleep. The storm was still gnawing at the skin of the house.

It was Elaine Coster calling. She was at the Blind Lake clinic, she said, with Sebastian Vogel and Sue Sampel. Sue had been stabbed. Stabbed by Ray Scutter. "Maybe you guys ought to get down here, if you can make it in this weather. I mean, it's not totally *dire*; Sue's going to live and everything—in fact, she was asking after you—but I keep thinking it would be wise for the bunch of us to stay together for a while."

Chris watched Marguerite turn uneasily under the blankets. "We'll be there as soon as we can."

He woke her and told her what had happened.

Marguerite let Chris drive through the snow. She sat in the back of the car with Tess, who was only grudgingly awake and still ignorant of what her father had done. Marguerite meant to keep it that way, at least for now. Tess was under more than enough stress.

For the duration of the drive, with Tessa's head cradled in her lap, and snow clinging to the windows of the car, and the whole of Blind Lake wrapped in a gelid, bitter darkness, Marguerite thought about Ray.

She had misjudged him.

She had never believed Ray would let himself be reduced to physical violence. Even now, she had a hard time picturing it. Ray with a knife. It had been a knife, Chris had said. Ray with a knife, using it. Ray putting the knife into Sue Sampel's body.

"You know," she said to Chris, "I only fainted once in my life. It was because of a snake."

Chris wrestled the steering wheel as they turned a corner toward the mallway. The car fishtailed, microprocessors blinking loss-of-traction alerts before it straightened out. But he had time to shoot her a curious look.

"I was seven years old," Marguerite said. "I walked out of the house one summer morning and there was a snake curled up on the porch stairs, basking in the sun. A big snake, bright and shiny against the old wood step. Too big and too shiny to be real. I assumed it was fake—that one of the neighbor kids had left it there to tease me. So I jumped over it. Three times. Three separate times. In case anyone was looking, just to prove

I couldn't be fooled. The snake never moved, and I went off to the library without giving it a second thought. But when I came home my father told me he'd killed a rattler that morning. It had come up on the porch and he'd used a shovel to cut it in half. The snake was lethargic in the cool air, he said, but he had to be careful. A snake like that can strike faster than lightning and carries enough venom to kill a horse." She looked at Chris. "That's when I fainted."

They reached the Blind Lake clinic twenty minutes later. Chris parked the car under the shelter of a concrete overhang, its passenger-side wheels straddling the sidewalk. Elaine Coster met them in the lobby. Sebastian Vogel was there, too, slumped in a chair, his head in his hands.

Elaine gave Marguerite a hard look. "Sue wants to see you."

"Wants to see *me?*"

"The wound is more or less superficial. She's been stitched and drugged. The nurse says she ought to be sleeping, but she was wide awake a few minutes ago, and when I mentioned you guys were coming in she said, 'I want to talk to Marguerite.' "

Oh, God, Marguerite thought. "I guess if she's still awake—"

"I'll show you the way."

Chris promised to look after Tess, who was taking a sleepy interest in the waiting-room toys.

"Come on in, hon," Sue said. "I'm too feeble to bite."

Marguerite edged inside the room.

Sue's room was just down the hall from the room where Adam Sandoval lay comatose—the man who had dropped into Blind Lake in a damaged aircraft. Sue definitely wasn't comatose, but she looked dismayingly weak. She was propped in a semireclined position, a saline drip plugged into the crook of her elbow. Her face was pale. She seemed much older than her forty-something years. But she managed to smile. "Honest," she said, "it's not as bad as it looks. I lost some blood, but the knife didn't cut anything more important than what Dr. Goldhar calls 'adispose tissue.' Fat, in other words. I guess I was rescued by every dessert I've ever eaten. Like the guy in the movies who would've been shot through the heart if not for the Bible in his pocket. There's a chair by the bed, Marguerite. Don't you want to sit down? It makes me tired to see you standing there."

Dutifully, Marguerite sat. "You must be having a lot of pain."

"Not anymore. They pumped me full of morphine. Or something like it. The nurse says it usually makes people sleepy, but I'm an 'idiosyncratic responder.' I think that means it made me want to sit up and talk. Do you suppose this is how drug addicts feel? On a good day?"

"Maybe at first."

"Meaning it won't last. I'm sure you're right. It has that house-of-cards feeling, like it can't go on forever. Euphoria with a price tag. I want to enjoy it while it lasts."

It could end at any time, Marguerite thought. "I can't tell you how sorry I am."

"Thank you, but you don't need to be sorry. Really, I appreciate you guys coming out here in this awful weather."

"When I heard it was Ray—that he was the one who hurt you—"

"What about it?"

"I owe you an apology."

"I was afraid you'd say that. Which is why I wanted to talk to you." She frowned. It made her face seem even more pallid. "I don't know you real well, Marguerite, but we get along okay, don't we?"

"I think so."

"Well enough that I can get a little personal?" She didn't

wait for an answer. "I get the impression I've had more experience with men than you have. Not necessarily *good* experience,
but more of it. I'm not saying I'm a slut or you're a virgin, just
that we fall on different parts of the distribution curve, if you
know what I mean . . . I'm sorry, I'm a little light-headed. Bear
with me. One of the things I've learned is you can't take
responsibility for what a man does. Especially if you've already
kicked him out for being an asshole. So please, *please* don't
apologize on behalf of Ray. He's not some pit bull you should
have kept on a shorter leash. He's totally responsible for how
he behaved when you guys were married. And he's absolutely
responsible for *this*."

She gestured at the bandage bulging under the thin clinic
sheet.

Marguerite said, "I wish I could have done something to
stop him."

"Me too. But you couldn't."

"I keep thinking—"

"No, Marguerite. No. Really. You *couldn't*."

Perhaps not. But she had consistently underestimated the
degree of Ray's madness. She had jumped over that rattlesnake
a hundred times, a thousand times, with only her dumb inno-
cence to protect her.

She could have been killed. Sue nearly had been.

"Well . . . can I say I'm sorry you got hurt?"

"You already did. And thank you. I want to talk to Chris,
too, but, you know, maybe I *am* getting a little sleepy here." Her
eyelids retreated to half-mast. "Suddenly I feel all warm and
sort of—what's the word? Oracular."

"Oracular?"

"Like the Oracle of Delphi. Wisdom for a penny, if I can
stay awake long enough to dispense it. I feel very wise and like
everything's going to be okay, ultimately. That would probably

be the morphine talking. Chris is a good guy, though. You'll do okay with Chris. He's trying real hard, whether it shows or not. All he needs is a reason to think better of himself. He needs you to trust him, and he needs to live up to that trust . . . but that part's up to him."

Marguerite just stared.

"Now," Sue said, spectacularly pale against the off-white bedsheet, "I believe I really do need to sleep."

She closed her eyes.

Marguerite sat quietly while Sue's breathing steadied. Then she tiptoed into the hallway and closed the door behind her.

Sue had surprised her tonight. So had Ray, in a much more terrifying fashion. And if I can't figure out these people, she thought, how can I even pretend to understand the Subject? Maybe Ray had been right about that. All her big talk about narratives: it was absurd, ridiculous, a childish dream.

Her server trilled in her pocket—a message from the Eye with a priority tag on it. Marguerite thumbed the ANSWER button, expecting more bad news.

It was a text message, a heads-up from the guys in Data Acquisition: *Get to a screen ASAP,* it said.

"I understand," Sebastian Vogel said to Chris, "the wound isn't as bad as it seemed at first. In all honesty, I thought she might die. But she was talking when I drove her here, almost nonstop."

Sebastian looked fragile, Chris thought, his round body crammed into the ungenerous circumference of a waiting-room chair. Elaine Coster sat at the opposite side of the clinic's reception space, scowling, while Tess played listlessly with waiting-room toys meant to amuse children much younger than herself. She ran a train of colored beads around a wire-frame roller-coaster. The beads clacked together when they slid from peak to valley.

"She insisted on talking about my book," Sebastian said. "Can you imagine that? Considering the pain she was in?"

"How nice," Elaine said caustically from across the room. "You must have been flattered."

Sebastian looked genuinely hurt. "I was horrified."

"So why mention it?"

"She might have been dying, Elaine. She asked me if there really was a God, the sort of God I described in the book. 'From which our minds arise and to which they return'—she was *quoting* me."

"So what did you tell her?"

"Maybe I should have lied. I told her I don't know."

"How did she take it?"

"She didn't believe me. She thinks I'm modest." He looked at Elaine, then at Chris. "That fucking book! That piece of shit book. Of course I wrote it for the money. Not even a lot of money. Just a small advance from a minor-league press. Something to pad out my pension. No one expected it to take off the way it did. I never meant it to be something people take as a creed. At best, it's a kind of theological science fiction. A thinking man's joke."

"A lie, in other words," Elaine said.

"Yes, yes, but *is* it? Lately—"

"Lately what?"

"I don't know how to say this. It feels more like inspiration. Do you understand the history of that word, inspiration? The *pneuma*, the sacred breath, the breath of life, the divine breath? Inhaling God? Maybe something was speaking *through* me."

"Sounds like your bullshit detector has malfed," Elaine said, though she said it more quietly, Chris noticed, and with less obvious scorn.

Sebastian shook his head. "Elaine. Do you know why your cynicism doesn't hurt? Because I share it. If I was ever sincere about the existence of God, I grew out of it not long after I reached puberty. If you call my book bullshit, Elaine, I won't argue with you. Remember when you predicted I'd write a sequel? You were absolutely right. I signed the contract the week before I left for Crossbank. *Wisdom & the Quantum Vacuum.* Laughable, isn't it? But, oh, Jesus, the money they offered me! To write a few harmless aphorisms in fancy language. Who could it hurt? No one. Least of all me. My academic career is finished; any credibility I had as a scholar was flushed away when I published the first volume. Nothing left to do but milk the cow. But—"

Sebastian paused. Elaine came across the tiled floor and sat down next to him.

Chris watched Tess play with a crude wooden car. If the girl was listening, she showed no sign of it.

"But?" Elaine prompted.

"But—as I said—I find myself wondering—that is, I wake up some mornings *believing* it. Believing it wholeheartedly, believing it the way I believe in my own existence."

"Believing what, that you're a prophet?"

"Hardly. No. I wake up thinking I stumbled on a truth. Despite myself. A fundamental truth."

"What *truth,* Sebastian?"

"That there's something living in the physical processes of the universe. Not necessarily creating it. Modifying it, maybe. But chiefly living in it. Eating the past and excreting the future."

Tess gave him a curious look, then rolled her car a little farther away.

"You know," Elaine said, "that's like the final stage of lunacy. When you start to actually pay attention to the voices in your head."

"Obviously. I may be crazy, Elaine, but I'm not stupid. I can diagnose a delusion. So I ask myself whether Ray Scutter might be right, whether Blind Lake has been infected with a contagious madness. It would explain a great deal, wouldn't it? It would explain why we've been quarantined. It would explain some of Ray's own behavior. It might even explain why Sue is in a clinic ward with a knife wound in her belly."

And it might explain Mirror Girl, Chris thought.

He looked for Tess, worried that she had overheard this remark about her father, but Tess had abandoned her wooden car next to the swinging doors marked HOSPITAL PERSONNEL ONLY and disappeared down the corridor.

He stood and called her name. No answer.

Tess was looking for her mother when she opened the door into the sleeping man's room.

At first she thought the room was empty. It was only dimly lit, but from the doorway she could make out the bed, the window, a silently blinking medical monitor, the skeletal shape of an IV tree. She was about to retreat when the sleeping man said, "Hey there. Don't go."

She hesitated.

The sleeping man lay motionless in his bed, but apparently he wasn't sleeping after all. He sounded friendly. But you could never tell.

"You don't have to be afraid," the man said. He said "hafta" for "have to," Tess noticed. Somehow, that made him less frightening.

She took a cautious step closer. She said, "You're the man from the airplane."

"That's right. The airplane. My name is Adam. Like the palindrome. 'Madam, I'm Adam.'" His voice was an old man's voice, gravelly and slow, but it sounded sleepy, too. "I've had my pilot's license for fifteen years," he said. "But I'm a weekend flier mostly. I own a hardware store in Loveland, Colorado. Adam Sandoval. The man from the airplane. That's me. What's your name?"

"Tessa."

"And this must be Blind Lake."

"Yes."

"Sounds like it's cold outside."

"It's snowing. You can hear the snow blowing against the window."

"Poor visibility," Adam Sandoval mused, as if he were taxiing down some imaginary runway.

"Are you badly hurt?" Tess asked. He still hadn't moved.

"Well, I don't know. I'm not in pain. I'm not sure I'm even altogether awake. Are you a dream, Tessa?"

"I don't think so." She thought about what this man had done. He had literally fallen out of the sky. Like Dorothy. He had come to Blind Lake on a whirlwind. "What's it like outside?"

"Snowing, you said. And it seems to be nighttime."

"No, I mean outside of Blind Lake."

The man paused. It was as if he was rummaging around in a box of memories, a box that had been locked up so long he was no longer sure what he might have left inside it.

"It was hard to get in the air that day," he said at last. "There was National Guard at the airports, even the local strips. Everybody worried about the starfish." He paused again. "The Crossbank starfish took my wife. Or she took *it*, maybe that's a better way of saying the same thing."

Tess didn't understand this, not even a little, but she was patient while the man kept talking. It would be rude to interrupt. She hoped at least some of what he said might sooner or later make sense.

"Karen, that's my wife, she was diagnosed with cervical cancer six years ago. They couldn't cure it because of some quirk of her immune system. The treatment would have killed her as quick as the disease. So she had some surgery and took a handful of pills every four hours to inhibit metastasis and she would have lived another twenty years, no problem, and so what if you have to choke down a few capsules of this and that now and then? But Karen said the pills made her sick—and I have to admit, she was running to the bathroom all the time, made it hard for her to leave the house—and the surgery left her tired and feeling old, and I guess she was clinically depressed on top of all that, though she seemed more sad than sick, sad all the time."

"I'm sorry to hear that," Tess said.

"She watched a lot of video when she was home by herself. So when that Crossbank starfish popped up she saw it right away on the panel. Made me print out the newsmagazines for her, too."

"I was at Crossbank," Tess declared. "Last year. I don't remember a starfish."

"Yeah, but that was *before*. Even at the time there weren't a lot of pictures. At first they tried to keep it out of the press. But there was amateur video circulating, and then another one popped up in Georgia and suddenly the whole world knew it was happening, even if they didn't know *what* was happening. There was a faction in congress wanted to nuke the starfish outright. Karen was horrified by that idea. So help me, she thought they were beautiful."

"Beautiful?"

"The starfish. Especially the Crossbank starfish. The size of it, like the biggest and most perfect thing you ever saw, and all the spines and arches made of whatever they're made of, like mother-of-pearl, with rainbows built in. You knew you were looking at something special, but some people thought it was holy and the rest of us figured it was 666 and the Four Horsemen put together. Karen fell into the first category and I fell into the second. Maybe if you're depressed something like that begins to look like salvation. But if all you want is to hang on to your life and wrestle it back to normal, it's just another threat and a distraction."

"I don't know what you mean."

"I guess you had to see it from the beginning. Especially the big starfish that grew at Crossbank where that peculiar telescope used to be. Karen got more and more agitated the more she watched it on the nets, the soldiers everywhere and the roads closed and all those foreign countries wanting to know what hellish thing we had cooked up, and was it dangerous, and of course nobody could answer either question. You know what surprised me about Karen? The energy she had all of a sudden—this woman who hadn't climbed off the sofa for six months. She'd been getting pretty heavyset despite the bathroom calls and the pills, but she perked up fast. I'm not absolutely sure she wasn't palming her medication. She seemed to think it didn't matter anymore if she lived or died: it was trivial, what happened to her. She didn't talk about these things, you understand, but she was obviously real interested when the government admitted it had lost several human beings and a shitload, pardon me, of robots inside the starfish at Crossbank. You could walk inside that thing or you could send a remote with a camera, but the cameras always died and the people who went inside too far just never came back."

Tess walked to the window, which was dark and obscure with snow. She could imagine Mr. Sandoval's "starfish" surprisingly clearly. A cloistered maze, like a snowflake, she thought, unfolded in three dimensions. She could almost see it in the clouded window glass. She looked away hastily.

"What happened to Mrs. Sandoval?" she asked.

"Karen took off one day in our old Ford. No explanation, no note, nothing. Of course, I was frantic about it. I talked to the police several times, but I guess the police had their hands full what with all the people heading west before the Mississippi roadblocks came down. Eventually I got word she'd been arrested with a handful of so-called pilgrims trying to cross into the no-go zone around Crossbank. Then the police called back and said it was a mistake, she *hadn't* been arrested, although she'd been with that group; she was one of a dozen or so who managed to get through the blockade on an old Ozark hiking trail. It's strange to me, picturing Karen out in the woods climbing rocks and drinking out of streams. She never even liked a backyard barbecue, for Christ's sake. Complained about the mosquitos. I swear I don't know why she wanted to be out in the woods like that."

"Did she go inside the starfish?"

"So they tell me. I wasn't there."

"And she didn't come out?"

"She didn't come out." Mr. Sandoval's voice had gone flat.

Tess thought about this. "Did she die?"

"Well, she didn't come out. That's all I know. That's what made me a little crazy, I guess."

Tess was vaguely alarmed that he was still motionless in his bed. "Mr. Sandoval, if you can't move, maybe I should call a doctor."

"I can't move. Like I said, I'm not even sure I'm awake. But I'm pretty sure I don't need a doctor."

"Honest?"

"Honest."

"Why did you come to Blind Lake?"

"To kill whatever's growing here."

Tess was shocked. *Like Dad*, she thought. Mr. Sandoval had come here to kill Mirror Girl.

She backed away a step.

"It seems frankly crazy to me," he said. "Lying here and thinking back. Funny what you do when you've lost someone and you don't know who to blame. It was too late to do anything about Crossbank, obviously, but Blind Lake had been in the news, the fact that it was shut down in case the same thing happened here. That pissed me off. They ought to bomb the place, I thought. If there's even a chance. Bomb it out of creation. But no, there was just the quarantine. It seemed way too chickenshit. I apologize for my vocabulary."

"It's okay," Tess said. "But if they'd bombed us we'd all be dead."

As she said it she wondered whether it was true. Maybe Mirror Girl wouldn't have let the bombs fall. Could Mirror Girl do that?

Mirror Girl seemed awfully close right now. *Don't look at the window,* Tess instructed herself. But the wind rattled the glass, as if to attract her attention, as if to say, *Look at me, look at me.*

"I guess I know that now," Mr. Sandoval said. "I guess I was a little crazy at the time. I thought I could climb into my plane, post a flight plan through Fargo and up into Manitoba, make a little detour at the right place . . . I was gonna fly right into your telescope, do as much damage as possible and kill myself at the same time."

This was true, Tess realized. Motes of Mr. Sandoval's old anger hung in the air above his bed, like snowflakes. It was adult and mysterious and somehow childish at the same time. The plan was like something Edie Jerundt might have come up with. But the anger and the grief were wholly adult. If Mr. Sandoval's emotions had a smell, Tess thought, they'd smell like something broken and electric. Like overheated wires and blackening plastic.

"Of course," Mr. Sandoval said, "it's too late for that now."

"Yes. They shot down your plane."

"No, I mean it's already started. Can't you feel it?"

Tess was afraid she could.

Marguerite meant only to find out what had excited the Obs people out at the Eye. The clinic building was nearly deserted. Dr. Goldhar had left after stitching and stabilizing Sue; Rosalie Bleiler and a couple of paramedics were on night duty, plus the security and housekeeping people. Marguerite checked doors until she found an empty boardroom. Inside, she closed the door for privacy—she felt furtive, though she was doing nothing wrong—and linked her pocket server to the room's ample display screen.

The live feed from the Eye came up quickly and crisply.

Looked like late afternoon on UMa47/E. Afternoon winds kicked dust into the air, turning the sky abalone white. Subject appeared to be continuing his enigmatic odyssey, walking a series of shallow, eroded canyons, just as he had the day before and the day before that. What was so unusual? There were no text tags from the DA people, nothing to explain their apparent excitement.

The sheer clarity of the image, perhaps? Maybe the clinic had installed a more modern display; the image was as vivid as Marguerite had ever seen it, even at the monitors out at the Eye. Clean as a window. She could see the dust clinging to the Subject's coxcomb, each particulate grain of it. She could almost feel the desiccating breeze on her face.

This creature, she thought. This thing. This enigma.

Subject followed an ancient arroyo around another sinuous curve, and suddenly Marguerite saw what the Data Acquisition team must have spotted earlier—something so strange she took a step backward and almost tumbled over a conference room chair.

Something exceedingly strange. Something artificial. Possibly even his destination, object of the Subject's quest.

It was obvious why this structure hadn't been spotted in the high-altitude surveys. It was large but not ridiculously large, and its spines and columns were covered with years if not centuries of dust. It shimmered in the morning sunlight like a mirage.

Subject moved into the shadow of this structure, walking more quickly than he had for many days. Marguerite imagined she could hear his big splayed feet scuffing against the pebbly desert floor.

But what *was* this thing, big as a cathedral, so obviously ancient and so obviously neglected? What had made the Subject travel so far to find it?

Please, she thought, not one more mystery, not one more unfathomable act. . . .

Subject passed beneath the first of the great spinal arches, into a softening shade.

"What do you want here?" Marguerite said aloud.

Subject turned and looked at her. His eyes were huge, solemn, and pearly white.

A thin, dry wind tousled the loose strands of Marguerite's hair. She fell to her knees in astonishment, grasping for the conference room table, anything to support her weight. But there was only grit under the palm of her hand, the dust of ages, the desiccated surface of UMa47/E.

Twenty-Eight

When the floor moved under his feet and the klaxons began to signal the evacuation of the Eye, Ray was dismayed but not surprised. It was inevitable. Something was awake, and something didn't like what Ray had come to do.

But he had been groomed for this confrontation. That was increasingly obvious to him. Ray wasn't a great believer in fate, but in this case it was an idea with a great deal of explanatory power. All kinds of life experiences that had seemed mysterious at the time—the years of academic infighting, his deep skepticism about the functioning of the Eye, his first initiation so many years ago into the rites of death—made sense to him now. Even his ridiculous marriage to

Marguerite, her sullen stubbornness and her unwillingness to compromise on anything that was important to him. Her sentimental ideas about the natives of UMa47/E. These were the stones against which Ray had been whetted like a blade.

"Blade" provoked an unwelcome memory of the events at Sue Sampel's house. That had been purely reflexive; he had never meant to physically hurt her. She had infuriated him with that insolent, screechy laugh; and he had pushed her, and the blade had appeared in her hand and he had been forced to wrestle it away; and then, after a thoughtless moment, there had been blood. God, how he hated blood. But even that awful encounter had been a tutelary experience, Ray thought. It had proven that he was capable of a bold, transgressive act.

He was familiar enough with the layout of the Alley that he was able to locate the central elevator bank. Two of the four elevators sat empty, doors opening and closing like spastic eyelids.

The tremor that had shaken the floor had subsided now. An earthquake in this part of the country was unlikely but not impossible. But Ray doubted the tremor had been caused by an earthquake. Something was happening down below, down in the deeps of the Eye.

The night staff had obviously been well-rehearsed for an emergency evacuation. Staff poured out of the stairwells two-by-two, seeming alarmed but basically calm, probably telling themselves the tremor had stopped and the evac was a formality. One gimlet-eyed woman spotted Ray where he stood by the elevators, approached him, and said, "We're supposed to go directly to the exit, not back down into the works. And we're *definitely* not supposed to use the elevators."

Fucking hall monitor, Ray thought. He flashed the stolen all-pass card and said, "Just leave the building as quickly as possible."

"But we were told—"

"Unless you want to lose your job, run along. Otherwise give me your name and badge number."

The voice of authority. She winced and departed with a wounded look. Ray stepped into the nearest elevator and pushed the sublevel-five button, the closest approach to the O/BEC gallery. He assumed he had a certain margin of time in which to work. Once the civilian staff had left the building Shulgin would dispatch a crew of inspectors, but the storm would slow that process to a crawl.

Klaxons reverberated deep in the courses in which the elevators rose and fell. He was four stories under the Minnesota prairie when the sirens fell silent, the elevator stalled in its shaft, and the lights winked off.

Power failure. In a few seconds the backup systems would kick in.

Even now, Ray thought, shouldn't there be emergency lights?

Apparently not. The darkness was absolute.

He took his server out of his pocket, but even that device had ceased to glow. He might as well have been blind.

Ray had never liked dark, enclosed spaces.

He put his hands out to orient himself. He backed into a corner of the elevator, adjoining walls to his left and right. The burnished aluminum surfaces were cold and inert to the touch.

This won't last, he told himself. And if the power failure did continue, it could only be bad news for the O/BECs. The pumps would fail, the liquid helium would stop flowing, the temperature in the platens would rise above the critical -451 Fahrenheit. But a dissenting voice inside him said, *The fucking thing's got you now.*

Hang on, he told himself. He had arrived at the Eye full of certainty and with a sense of his own power: he had come here by a series of irrevocable steps, fueled by his conviction that the O/BECs were source of everything that had gone wrong at Blind Lake. But the building had stolen his momentum. He was locked in a box, and his confidence began to seep away into the darkness.

I'm not here for myself, Ray thought. He had to keep that in mind. He was here because the gullible children who had been placed under his charge were playing with a dangerous machine, and he meant to stop them whether they liked it or not. That was essentially a selfless act. More than that: it was redemptive. Ray had made a mistake at Sue Sampel's house and he was prepared to admit it. He took a certain pride in his willingness to look at a problem realistically. Maybe everyone else had been blinded by cupidity, denial, or fear. Not Ray. The device in this building had become a threat and he was going to deal with it. He was performing an act of such fundamental moral necessity that it would wash clean any mistakes he might have made in the process.

Unless he had come too late. The elevator was motionless, but Ray imagined he could hear the building creak and groan around him, deforming in the darkness. Whatever we woke up, Ray thought, it's powerful; it's strong, and it's gaining a sense of its own strength.

Methodically, he rolled up one leg of his trousers. Ray had left Sue's with the bloody knife still clutched in his hand. He hadn't wanted to let it go or leave it behind. The knife, the act of using it as a weapon, had made what followed both possible and necessary. That was when he had formulated his plan to penetrate the Eye using Charlie Grogan's all-pass tag. He had started driving to Charlie's with the knife next to him on the passenger-side seat of the car, an untouchable thing decorated with threads of Sue Sampel's blood. Then he had pulled over to the side of the road, wiped the knife clean with a disposable tissue, and carefully strapped the blade to the calf of his left leg with a roll of duct tape from the glove compartment. It had seemed like a fine idea at the time.

Now he wanted the knife in his hand, ready to use. Worse, he couldn't help thinking that he might have left some blood on the blade after all; and the idea of Sue Sampel's blood touching his skin, invading his pores, was grotesque and intolerable. But in the absolute darkness of the stalled elevator he had a hard time finding the loose edge of the tape. He had wrapped himself up like a fucking mummy.

Nor had he given much thought to the physical problem of peeling what seemed like a quarter-mile of duct tape off his hairy leg. He was almost certainly taking some skin off along with it. He drew deep, gasping breaths, the way Marguerite had learned to do in that Lamaze class they had attended before Tessa's birth. He was leaking tears by the time the last layer of tape came loose, and when he jerked that away it took the knife with it, slicing a neat little chunk out of his calf along the ankle.

That was too much. Ray screamed in pain and frustration, and his screaming made the stalled elevator seem much smaller, unbearably small. He opened his eyes wide, straining for light—he had heard that the human eye could register even a single photon—but there was nothing, only the sting of his own sweat.

I could die here, he thought, and that would be very bad; or, worse, what if he was wrong about the Eye, what if Shulgin found him here after the crisis had passed, raving and with an incriminating weapon in his hand? The knife, the fucking knife. He couldn't keep it and he couldn't get rid of it.

What if the walls closed on him like teeth?

He wondered whether—if it became necessary—he could successfully kill himself with the knife. Like a Bushido warrior, falling on his sword. How badly, how quickly could he hurt himself with a six-inch blade? Would it be more efficient to slit his wrists or stick himself in the belly? Or should he try to cut his own throat?

He thought about death. What it would be like to sink away from his own untidy self, to drift deeper and deeper into the static and empty past.

He imagined he heard Marguerite's voice in his ear, whispering words he didn't understand:

ignorance
curiosity
pain
love

—more evidence, as if he needed it, that the O/BEC madness had already infected him . . .

And then the lights winked back on.

"God! Fuck!" Ray said, momentarily dazed.

The elevator hummed to life and resumed its journey downward.

Ray discovered he had bitten his tongue. His mouth was full of blood. He spat it out onto the green tiled floor, rolled his cuff down over his bleeding ankle, and waited for the door to open.

Twenty-Nine

"Maybe she went to look for her mother," Elaine said, but when Chris called Tessa's name there was no answer, and the brightly lit ground-floor corridor of the clinic was empty as far as he could see.

He took out his pocket server and spoke her name again. No answer. He tried Marguerite. Also no answer.

"This is just spooky," Elaine said.

It was worse than that. Chris felt as if he had stepped into one of those nightmares in which something absolutely essential had evaporated in his hands. "What room is Sue in?"

"Two-eleven," Elaine said promptly. "Upstairs."

"You ring the duty nurse and ask her to look for Tess. I'll find Marguerite."

332   R o b e r t   C h a r l e s   W i l s o n

Elaine watched Chris sprint for the stairwell. Elaine herself wasn't terribly worried. The kid was probably down in the cafeteria or off riding a gurney cart. "Quite the family man," she said to Vogel. "Our Chris."

"Don't begrudge him what he found here," Vogel murmured. "It could end at any time."

He discovered Sue Sampel very nearly asleep, alone in her darkened room. "Marguerite left already," she said. "Chris? Is that you? Chris? Is Marguerite lost or something?"

"I can't raise her server. It's nothing to worry about it."

She yawned. "Bullshit. *You're* worried."

"Go on back to sleep, Sue."

"I think I will. I think I have to. But I can tell you're lying. Chris? Don't get lost in the dark, Chris."

"I won't," he promised. Whatever that meant.

He walked the hallway from end to end, opening doors. Apart from the room where Adam Sandoval lay motionless in his coma there were only empty storage spaces, locked pharmaceutical closets, vacant boardrooms, and darkened offices.

His server buzzed. He took it out of his pocket and talked to Elaine, who told him the night nurse had called Security and that the staff on duty were beginning a room-to-room search. "But there's something going on out at the Eye, too. I got hold of Ari Weingart, who says the Alley is being evacuated."

Chris looked at the server in his hand: if his was working, why not Marguerite's or Tessa's?

If Marguerite and Tess were both missing, did that mean they were together? And if they weren't in the building, where had they gone?

He made his way back to the lobby, to the heavy glass doors. If Marguerite had left the clinic she would have taken the car. There was no other way to travel in this weather. If the car was gone, maybe he could borrow a vehicle and follow it.

But Marguerite's conservative little runabout was parked where Chris had left it, wheels on the curb, under a fresh layer of snow. He opened the door and snow came into the lobby on a fugitive wind, small flakes turning to watery diamonds on the tiled floor.

Elaine stood behind Chris and put a hand on his shoulder. "This is freaky, but you need to calm down."

"You think Ray has something to do with this?"

"I thought of that. Ari said he'd been on the phone to Shulgin, who talked to Charlie Grogan. Ray's out at the Eye somewhere."

Chris held the door open a crack, letting frigid air play over his face. "She was *right here,* Elaine. Playing with that fucking wooden truck. People don't just disappear."

But they do, he thought. They slip through your fingers like water.

"Mr. Carmody?" This was Rosalie Bleiler, the duty nurse. "Could you close that door, please? Elmo—Elmore Fisk, he's our night guard—would like to see you at the back entrance."

"Did he find Tess?"

Rosalie flinched from his voice. "No, sir, but he found some child-sized footprints in the snow out there."

Tess wasn't dressed to be outdoors. "Did he *follow* the footprints?"

She nodded. "About fifty yards out past the visitor's lot. But that's the problem. He says the footprints don't go anywhere. They just sort of stop."

Thirty

To date there had been seven serious attempts to break out of Blind Lake. Three of them had resulted in the deaths by pocket drone of those who breached the fence and entered the no-go zone. Four more had been interrupted in the attempt by Security forces within the Lake. The most recent case had been an agoraphobic caterer who had elected to scale the fence solo but had lost his nerve halfway up. By the time Security found him and talked him down he had suffered frostbite to the fingers of both hands.

Herb Dunn, a fifty-two-year-old navy veteran, had worked in Civilian Security ever since he was downsized from a FedEx branch in Fargo ten years ago. The quarantine of Blind

Lake had severed communications between Herb and his creditors (including two ex-wives), which he regretted not at all. He missed access to current movies and web-based erotica, but that was about it. Once he realized he wasn't about to contract some kind of plague, Herb had settled into the lockdown quite comfortably.

Except this week. This week he was on what the Security force called Dawn Patrol, nobody's favorite duty. The idea of Dawn Patrol was to send out a guy in an all-weather vehicle to ride the circuit of the fence, presumably to rescue miscreants from their own misguided escape attempts. Dawn Patrol had yet to encounter even a single miscreant, but Herb supposed it had a certain deterrent effect. Today, given the shit-awful storm that had blown through the Lake overnight, Shulgin had told him his route was cut short: just a drive out to the main gate and back. But that was bad enough.

The snow had begun to taper off when he left the garage, but a fierce wind out of the northwest was still complicating matters. These Security vehicles were decent machines, smart-drive Hondas with mutable-tread tires, but a snowmobile would have been more efficient, Herb thought.

The main road from the Plaza at the center of town had been plowed during the night, but only as far south as the staff housing tracts. From there to the fence it was all blown and drifting snow, not quite deep enough to conceal the road but slow going even for the Honda. Herb took some consolation from the fact that there was absolutely nothing urgent or even necessary about this run. It made the delays easier to endure. He settled back in the steamy warmth of the cab and tried to picture his current favorite actress in a state of radical undress. (Back home, he had videoserver apps that did this trick for him.)

By the time he approached the main gate dawn had come and gone. There was enough light now to mark the limits of vision, a bubble of windblown snow around the cab of the Honda and a glimpse of ponderous clouds in a sky like a muddy river.

He reached the turnaround point at the main gate—no daring escape attempts in progress—and stopped, idling the vehicle's motor. He was tempted to close his eyes and make up for some of the sleep he'd lost, sitting up after midnight watching old downloads, up at 3:30 to get ready for this pointless expedition. But if he was caught sleeping he'd be on Dawn Patrol for the rest of his natural life. Anyway, his breakfast coffee had worked its way through him and he had an urge to write his name in the snow.

He was climbing out of the cab into the frigid morning when the low clouds lifted and he saw something moving beyond the main gate. Something out there in no-man's-land. Something big. He supposed at first it was one of those robotic delivery trucks carrying food and supplies, but when the wind shifted again he saw more of these uncertain shapes. *Huge* machines, just outside the fence.

He goose-stepped a few feet closer through the snow. Just to see, he told himself. He was as near the main gate as he meant to get when without warning it began to swing open. There was another lull in the wind, a moment of almost supernatural calm, and he recognized the vehicles out there as Powell tanks and armored personnel carriers. Dozens of them, lined up outside the Lake.

He turned and took a few awkward steps back toward the Honda, but before he reached it he was surrounded by a half-dozen soldiers in camouflage-white protective suits and aerosol masks. Soldiers wearing enhanced-vision goggles and carrying sonic-pulse rifles.

Herb Dunn had been in the service. He knew the drill.

He put up his hands and tried to look harmless.

"I only work here," he said.

Thirty-One

Confused beyond the point of terror, Marguerite forced herself to focus on her breathing. She ignored the sandy soil under her hands and knees, ignored the sensation of dry heat, above all closed her eyes and ignored the presence of the Subject. Draw breath, she thought. Breathing was important. Breathing was important because—because—

Because if she were really on the surface of UMa47/E, breathing would be impossible.

The atmosphere of UMa47/E was less oxygenated than Earth's and highly rarefied. The pressure differential would have burst her eardrums, had she traveled here from Blind Lake.

But it was fear, not anoxia, that

was making her gasp, and her ears felt normal.

Therefore, she thought—still kneeling, eyes tightly closed—therefore, therefore, I'm not really here. Therefore I'm in no immediate danger.

(But if I'm not here then why do I feel the grains of sand under my fingernails, why do I feel the breeze on my skin?)

The summer Marguerite turned eleven, her parents had vacationed in Alaska. Much to Marguerite's dismay, her father had bought the family a ride over Glacier Bay National Park in a tiny single-engine aircraft. The aircraft had dipped and rocked in the mountain winds, and Marguerite had been terrified to the point of nausea, far too terrified to even think about looking out the window.

Then her father had put an arm around her and said in his most profoundly ministerial voice, "It's all right, Margie. You're perfectly safe."

She had repeated that phrase to herself for the rest of the flight. Her mantra. *You're perfectly safe.* Oil on troubled waters. It had calmed her. The words came back to her now.

You're perfectly safe.

(*But I'm not. I'm lost, I'm helpless, I don't know what's happening, and I don't know the way back home—*)

Perfectly safe. The perfect lie.

She opened her eyes and forced herself to stand.

The Subject stood motionless more than a meter away from her. Marguerite knew from experience that, once he was still, he would probably stay that way for a while. (She remembered Chris's comment—*not a great party planet*—and suppressed an incoherent urge to giggle.) Those inscrutable white eyes stared at her, or at least in her general direction, and she was tempted to stare back. But first things first, Marguerite told herself. Be a scientist. (*You're a scientist. You're perfectly safe. Two enabling lies.*)

Evaluate your surroundings.

She stood just inside the perimeter of the structure the Subject had entered. Looking back through its arches Marguerite could see with a shocking immediacy the desert, which she instinctively put into the context of the geography of UMa47/E: the central plateau of the largest continental plate, far from any of the planet's shallow, salty seas, at the equatorial extreme of a temperate zone. But it was so much more than that. It was a sky as luminous and white as freshly fired china; it was a range of eroded basaltic hills fading into the distance; it was the long light of a foreign sun, and shadows that lengthened visibly as she watched. It was an irregular wind that smelled of lime and dust. It was not an image but a place: tactile, tangible, fully textured.

If I'm not here, Marguerite thought, where am I?

The ceiling of this structure screened the direct light of the sun. "Structure," she thought, was one of those weasel-words so beloved of the people in Obs; but could she really call it a "building"?

There were no proper walls, only rank upon rank of pillars (abalone-white and coral-pink) arranged in a series of irregular arches that joined to form a roof. Farther in, the shadows deepened to impenetrability. The floor was simply blown and drifted sand. It resembled nothing in the Lobster city. It might have grown here, she thought, over the centuries. She touched the nearest pillar. It was cool and faintly iridescent, like mother-of-pearl.

Her hand began to tingle, and she pulled it away.

Of course it was all impossible, and not just because she was breathing normally on the surface of a planet unfit to support human life. The O/BEC images of UMa47/E had traveled across fifty-one light-years. What the monitors had displayed was almost literally ancient history. There was no such thing as simultaneity, not unless the O/BECs had learned to defy the fundamental laws of the universe.

Maybe it was better to think of this experience as deep VR. Immersive observation. A vivid dream.

Flimsy as that scaffolding was, it gave her the courage to look directly at the Subject.

The Subject was half-again taller than Marguerite. None of her observation had prepared her for the sheer animal bulk of him. She had felt the same the first time she went to a petting zoo back in grade eight. Animals that had looked innocent on television had turned out to be larger, dirtier, smellier, and far more unpredictable than she had imagined. They had been so disconcertingly *themselves*, so indifferent to her preconceptions.

The Subject was very much himself. Apart from his erect bipedal stance, there was nothing human about him. Nor did he resemble an insect or a crustacean, despite the ridiculous "lobster" tag that had been foisted on him.

His feet were broad, flat, leathery, and lacking toes or nails. Built for standing, not running. They were coated with the dust and grime of his long walk, and in some places the pebbly tegument had been eroded to a raw smoothness. Marguerite wondered if they hurt.

His legs were no longer than her own but nearly twice as thick. There was an implied muscularity about them, like two tree trunks wrapped in brick-red leather. His legs met seamlessly at his crotch, where there was none of the complex paraphernalia of human sexuality, perhaps not surprisingly: there might be better places to install one's genitalia, not that anyone had ever demonstrated that the Subject or his kind even possessed genitalia of the conventional sort.

His thorax broadened to the shape of a fat disk, to which his arms were attached. His manipulating arms were slender, lithe, and equipped at their ends with what looked roughly like human hands—three fingers and an opposable digit—although the joints were all wrong. The stubby food-grasping arms, just long enough to reach from his shoulders to his mouth, were altogether stranger, as much an externalized jaw as an extra set of limbs. Instead of hands, these secondary arms possessed bony cup-and-blade structures for cutting and grinding vegetable material.

Subject's head was a mobile dome with wattles of loose flesh where human anatomy would have put a neck. His mouth was a vertical pink slit that concealed a long, rasping, almost prehensile tongue. His eyes were set apart almost as widely as a bird's, cosseted in bluish-purple gristle, the eyes themselves not purely white, Marguerite realized, but faintly yellow, the color of old piano keys. No interior structure of the eye was visible, no pupil, no cornea; his eyes might have been unorganized bundles of light-sensitive cells, or perhaps their structure was concealed under a partially opaque surface, like a permanent eyelid.

The orange coxcomb atop his head served no purpose anyone had been able to define. On Earth such features were usually sexual displays, but among the Subject's people it could hardly be gendered, since every individual possessed one.

The most prominent—or most prominently strange—feature of the Subject was the dorsal cavity running down the center of his thorax. This was widely understood to be a breathing orifice. It was as long as Marguerite's forearm, and it opened and closed periodically like a gasping, lipless mouth. (Ray, in one of his more classless moments, had told her it looked like "a diseased vagina.") When it opened she could see porous honeycomb-like tissue beneath it, moist and yellow. Fine silver-gray cilia made a fringe surrounding the opening.

I'm perfectly safe, she thought, but in all honesty she was frightened of the Subject, frightened by the obvious weight and substance and implicit animal strength of him. Frightened even of the smell of him, a faint organic stink that was both sickly sweet and richly unpleasant, like the smell of a citrus rind gone green with mold.

Well, then, Marguerite thought, what now? Do we pretend this is a real meeting? Do we speak?

Could she speak? Fear had dried her mouth. Her tongue felt numb as a wad of cotton.

"My name is Marguerite," she whispered. "I know you don't understand."

He might not understand even the concept of a spoken language. She stood staring at him for a long moment. Maybe his silences spoke volumes. Maybe he spoke a language of immobility.

But he wasn't totally immobile.

His breathing slit opened wider and emitted an almost inaudible wheezing sound. Could this be language? It sounded more like respiratory distress.

How fucking laughable, Marguerite thought, to be here—whatever this place was—and for whatever reason—only to be confronted once again with the impossibility of communication. I can't even tell whether he's talking or dying.

The Subject finished his discourse, if that was what it was, exhaling a gust of sour-milk air.

Apart from that, he still had not moved.

If this was an opportunity, Marguerite thought, and not just a hallucination, it was a wasted one. Her fear was laced with frustration. To be so incredibly, implausibly near to him. And still as far away as ever. Still mute, still dumb.

Outside, the shadows lengthened toward nightfall. The pale sky had turned a darker, bluer shade of white.

"I don't understand what you said," Marguerite confessed. "I don't even know if you said anything."

Subject exhaled and fluttered his cilia.

Yes, he spoke, said a voice.

It wasn't the Subject's voice. The sound came from all around her. From the mother-of-pearl arches, or from the shadows farther in.

But that wasn't the strangest thing.

The strangest thing was that the voice sounded exactly like Tessa's.

Thirty-Two

Elaine Coster tagged Chris as he headed out the clinic door. "Whoa," she said, "hang on—where are you going?"

She knew he was freaking out over the disappearance of Tess and Marguerite. The duty nurse had shared with Elaine the story about the girl's footprints, how they had vanished in the snow. Elaine hated to think of Tess, who had seemed like nice enough kid, out in this bitter weather. But there was daylight coming fast, and the girl shouldn't be that hard to find, Elaine thought, if only Chris would exercise reasonable patience. As for Marguerite—

"I'm driving out to the Eye," Chris said.

"The Eye? I'm sorry, but what the hell for? Ari says it's being evacuated."

"I can't explain."

She grabbed his arm before he could open the door. "Come on, Chris, you can do better than that. You think Tess and Marguerite are at the *Eye*? How is that even possible?"

Please, Elaine thought, let this not be one more case of Blind Lake lunacy.

"Tess wasn't just wandering around out there. Her footprints are straight as a ruler, and they're pointed directly at the Eye."

"But the footprints stop?"

"Yes."

"So maybe she just came back to the clinic door. You know, stepping in her own tracks."

"Walking backwards in the snow? In the dark?"

"Well, what do *you* think? If she's at the Eye, how'd she get there? Did she sprout wings, Chris? Or maybe she beamed herself there. Maybe she traveled in her astral body."

"I don't pretend to understand it. But the last time she disappeared from school, that's where she went."

"You really think she walked that distance in this weather?"

"I don't know about walked. But I think that's where she is, I think she's in trouble, and I think Marguerite would want me to go find her."

"You can read minds too? Ari and Shulgin and a bunch of other people are already keeping their eyes out for Tess and Marguerite. Let them do their work. They're better at it than you are. Chris, listen to me, *listen to me*. I got a call from one of my contacts on the Security force. A whole fucking battalion's worth of military gear and personnel just showed up at the main gate, and they're coming inside. You understand? The siege is over! I don't know what comes next, but in all likelihood the Lake will be evacuated by nightfall—you, me, Tess, Marguerite, *everybody*. I'm heading down the main road, and I want you to come with me. We're still journalists. We've got a story here."

He smiled at her in a way Elaine didn't like, rueful and sad. She decided she hated all tall young men with doleful eyes.

"You take it, Elaine," he said. "It's your story. You're the one to tell it."

Elaine watched him angle his big body into the car, watched as he drove off through the still-falling snow at a reckless speed.

Sebastian Vogel, crammed into his lobby chair like a Buddha into an airline seat, said, "I think I finally figured it out."

Elaine sat next to him wearily. "Please. No more metaphysical bullshit." There were things she needed to do. Pack up her server and her written notes and keep them with her, even if some armed bureaucrat wanted to confiscate them. Consider facing the exterior world, whatever the exterior world had become, with its pilgrims and falling airplanes and roadblocks east of the Mississippi.

"Ever since Crossbank," Sebastian said, "I've been wondering why you agreed to take this assignment. A veteran scientific journalist, hired by a frankly second-rate New York magazine to address a subject that's been done to death, sharing the spotlight with a crank theologist and a discredited scandalmonger. That never made any sense to me. But I think I figured it out. It's because of Chris, isn't it?"

"Oh, fuck *off*, Sebastian."

"You read his book, followed his story in the press, watched his congressional testimony. Maybe you'd already picked up hints about Galliano's ethical problems. You saw Chris being pilloried, and you knew he was right in spite of all the outrage and bad press. You were curious about him. Maybe he reminded you of yourself at that age. You took the job because you wanted to meet him."

This would have been less annoying had it been untrue. Elaine mustered her fiercest go-to-hell stare.

"Was he a disappointment?" Sebastian said. "As a personal project?"

I don't have time for this, Elaine thought. She felt dizzy with lack of sleep. Maybe she could just sit here until the soldiers came for her. All the really important work she'd done was stored in her pocket server, after all, and they would take her server from her only when they pried it out of her cold, dead hands. "When I met Chris I thought they'd beaten him down. He was obviously unhappy, he wasn't writing, he was a little too free with the recreational chemicals, and he was carrying a load of guilt that was way too big for him."

"I'm not sure that's all because of his experience with Galliano."

"Probably not. I just thought . . ."

"You wanted to help," Sebastian said gently.

"Yes. I'm a fucking saint. Now shut *up*."

"You wanted to lend him some of your cynicism."

"He'd be a better journalist if he learned not to care."

"Though perhaps not a better human being."

"I'm not discussing this."

"What he needed, Elaine, and I don't mean this badly, but what he needed, it wasn't in your power to give it to him."

"Speaks the guru." She bit her lip. "So what do you think? You think he found it? Whatever it is he needs?"

"I think he's looking for it right now," Sebastian said.

———

Chris ran into outbound traffic on the road to the Eye. Night staff leaving the facility, he guessed, as rumors circulated that the siege was coming to an end.

Even in this wan daylight the road was treacherous driving. He saw more than one car abandoned in the drifts, workers in burly winter coats flagging rides from colleagues.

He drove past an untenanted guardpost directly to the entrance to the Eye, where he found Charlie Grogan herding stragglers out of the lobby into the cold morning air. The sound of Klaxons beat against the raging wind.

"Not even remotely possible," Charlie said when Chris explained what he wanted to do. "The building suffered a tremor of some kind early this morning and all kinds of electrical and communications problems since then. We've got strict protocols about this. I can't let anyone in until the building is declared structurally sound. Even after we get inspectors inside, we still have to worry about containment on the cryogenics." He looked mournful. "The O/BECs are probably dead already."

"Tessa's inside."

"So you said, but I doubt that a whole lot, Mr. Carmody. Our Security people conducted a very orderly evacuation. What would Tessa be doing here at five in the morning, anyway?"

Looking for Mirror Girl, Chris thought. "It wouldn't be the first time she got inside without being seen."

"You really have a solid reason to believe Tess is in this building?"

"Yes."

"You want to share that information with me?"

"I'm sorry. You'll have to trust me."

"I'm sorry too. Look, even if she is inside, we've got the

Lake's Security people headed in. Maybe they can give you some advice."

"Charlie, you need to double-check on that. I heard Shulgin's men were detoured to the south gate."

"What, this thing about the military coming in?"

"Call Shulgin. Ask him when you can expect to see a Security detail."

Charlie sighed. "Look, I'll talk to Tabby Menkowitz and see if she can get a volunteer from our own people to do a walk-through—"

"If Tess sees a stranger she'll just hide. In an installation this big, I'm sure an eleven-year-old girl can avoid getting caught."

"But she'll come out for you?"

"I believe there's a chance she will."

"What do you mean to do, look inside every room in the building?"

"Last time you found her in the O/BEC gallery, right?"

"Yeah, but—"

"It's the O/BECs she's interested in."

"I could lose my job," Charlie said.

"Is that really an issue at this point?"

"*Jesus*, Chris." Then: "If they end up pulling your body out of the rubble, what am I supposed to say?"

"Say you never saw me."

"I wish it was true." Charlie's server buzzed in his pocket. He ignored it. "Tell you what. Take this." He gave Chris his yellow-striped hard hat. "There's a transponder in the crown. It'll give you emergency all-pass privileges if any of the automated security is still up. Put it on. And if she's not where you think she is, get the fuck out of there, all right?"

"Thank you."

"Just bring back my goddamn hat," Charlie said.

Thirty-Three

As soon as Marguerite identified the voice as Tessa's, Tess herself stepped out from behind (or somehow *inside*) the nearest iridescent pillar.

But it wasn't really Tess. Marguerite knew that instantly. It was the image of Tess, down to the denim overalls and yellow shirt in which Marguerite had hurriedly dressed her daughter for the trip to the Blind Lake clinic. But Tess had never looked so surrealistically flawless, so lit from within, so unblinkingly clear-eyed.

This was Mirror Girl.

"You don't have to be scared," Mirror Girl said.

Yes, Marguerite thought, I think I do, I do have to be scared. "You're Mirror Girl," she stammered.

"Tess calls me that."

"What are you really, then?"

"There's no simple word for it."

"Did you bring me here?"

"Yes."

"Why?"

"Because this is what you wanted."

Was it? "What do you have to do with my daughter?"

"I learned a lot from Tess."

"Have you hurt her?"

"I don't hurt people."

This creature, this thing that had appropriated Tessa's appearance, had also mastered Tessa's diction and Tessa's oblique way with questions and answers. "Tess said you live in the Eye. In the O/BEC processors."

"I have a sister at Crossbank," Mirror Girl said proudly. "I have sisters in the stars. Almost too many to count. I have a sister here. We talk to each other."

This conversation was too bizarre to be real, Marguerite decided. It had the trajectory and momentum of a dream and, like a dream, it would have to play itself out. Her participation was not only necessary but mandatory.

Ursa Majoris 47 had begun to settle toward the horizon, casting long and complex shadows into the maze of arches. "This planet is years and years away from Earth," Marguerite said, thinking of time, the passage of time, the paradox of time. "I can't really be here."

"You're not out *there*," the image of Tess said, gesturing at the desert; "you're in *here*. It's different in here. More different the farther inside you go. It's true, if you walked out of here you would die. Your body couldn't breathe or go on living, and if you counted the hours they would be different hours than the Blind Lake hours."

"How do you know about Blind Lake?"

"I was born there."

"Why do you look like Tess?"

"I told you. I learned a lot from her."

"But why *Tess*?"

Mirror Girl shrugged in a distressingly Tess-like fashion. "She knew my sister at Crossbank before I was born. It could have been someone else. But it had to be *someone*."

Like the Subject, Marguerite thought. We could have picked any individual to follow. It just happened to be him.

The Subject regarded this exchange indifferently, if his motionlessness signified anything like indifference.

"Go on," Mirror Girl said, "talk to him. Isn't that what you want to do?"

Ultimately, yes, but it had never been more than a daydream. She didn't know how to begin. She faced the Subject again.

"Hello," she said, feeling idiotic, her voice cracking.

There was no response.

She looked back helplessly at Mirror Girl.

"Not like that. Tell him a story," Mirror Girl suggested.

"What story?"

"*Your* story."

Absurd, Marguerite thought. She couldn't just tell him a story. It was a childish idea, a Tess-like idea. She had been here too long already. She wasn't like the Subject; she couldn't stand in one place indefinitely. She was still a mortal human being.

But even as she had these thoughts she felt a wave of calm coming over her. It was like the feeling she had putting Tess to bed, tucking her in, reading (before Tess had become too sophisticated for this) something from the old, strange children's books she had found so fascinating: Oz, *The Hobbit*, Harry Potter. Marguerite's fatigue lifted (perhaps this was a spell cast by Mirror Girl), and she closed her eyes and found herself wondering what she could tell the Subject about the Earth, not its history or geography but her own experience of it. How frighteningly strange it would no doubt seem to him. Her story: born in the customary manner of human biology to human parents, her memory emerging diffusely from a haze of cradles and blankets; learning her name (she had been "Margie" for the first twelve years of her life); plunged into the tedium, terror, and rare joys of school (Miss Marmette, Mr. Foucek, Mrs. Bland, the stern deities of grades 1, 2, 3); the cycle of the seasons, naming the months, September and school, November and the first truly cold days, January dark and often painful, the storming and melting months before June, June hot and full of promise, the fleeting freedoms of August; child-hood dramas: appendicitis, appendectomy, influenza, pneu-monia; friendships begun, sustained, or aborted; a growing awareness of her parents as two real, separate people who did more than cater to her needs: her mother, who cooked and kept house and read large books and made charcoal sketches (of abstracted rural villages, notionally Spanish, drenched in clinical sunlight); her father, distant and equally bookish, a Presbyterian minister, sonorous lord of Sundays but gentle on the home front, who had often seemed to Marguerite a lonely man, lonely for God, lonely for the deep architecture of the cosmos, the scaffolding of meaning he imagined when he read the synoptic Gospels and in which, he confessed to her once, he had never really been able to believe; her own dawning curios-ity about the world and its place in time and her place in nature, a curiosity strictly scientific, at least as she understood "science" from video shows and speculative novels: how good it felt to master what was generally known of planets, moons, stars, galaxies, and their beginnings and ultimate ends, relish-ing even the unanswered questions because they were shared,

354 Robert Charles Wilson

acknowledged, and systematically challenged, unlike her
father's fragile religiosity, which he had been reluctant even to
discuss, faith, she surmised, being like an antique tea set, beautiful and ancient but not to be exposed to light or heat; knowing, too, the pride he took in her growing list of accomplishments
(straight A's in everything but music and physical education,
where her clumsiness betrayed her; the math badges and science-
fair awards; the scholarships); the sudden indecencies of adolescence, making sense of the female body that had begun to
surprise her in so many ways, learning to equate the blood
spots in her underwear with the biology of reproduction, eggs
and seeds and ovaries and pollen and a chain of carnal acts
connecting her to the common ancestor of everything alive on
Earth; her own skirmishes with the erotic (a boy named Jeremy
in the furnished basement of his house, while his mother
hosted a party upstairs; an older boy named Elliot, in his bedroom on a winter night when his parents were stranded by
monsoon weather in an airport somewhere in Thailand); her
early fascination with the O/BEC images of HR8832/B, ocean-
scapes like Victorian color-plate illustrations of Mellville
(*Typee, Oomoo*), a fascination that led her to astrobiology; the
Princeton scholarship (at her graduation her mother had wept
with pride but suffered, that night, the first of a series of
ischemic attacks that would culminate in a killing stroke half a
year later); standing with her father at the funeral, willing herself to stay upright when she wanted to lie down and make the
world disappear; her first real long-term relationship, a university affair with a man named Mike Okuda who had also been
obsessed with O/BEC images and who once admitted fantasiz-
ing, when they made love, that he was under invisible surveillance from other worlds; the pain of separation when he took a
job designing Hall Effect engines somewhere on the West
Coast, and her subsequent realization that she would never

stumble into love but would have to construct it from its constituent parts, with the help of a willing partner; her apprenticeship at Crossbank, working out tentative classification systems for chthonic plant species based on images sequestered from Obs (the four-lobed peristem, the pale taproot exposed by a storm); her first encounter with Ray, when she had mistaken her admiration for him for the possibility of love, and their first physical intimacy, sensing in Ray a reluctance that bordered on distaste and for which she blamed herself; the erosion of their marriage (his relentless vigilance and suspicion, begrudging even visits to sick friends, his aloofness during her pregnancy) and the things that sustained her during that difficult time (her work, long walks away from the house, the weight of winter sunsets); her water breaking, and labor, and giving birth dazed and sedated in a hospital delivery room while Ray, in the hallway outside, conducted a loud argument with a nurse's aide; the miracle and fascination of Tessa, sensing some divinity (her father might have said) in the exchange of roles, daughter become mother, witness to what she had once herself experienced; her increasing frustration when the Blind Lake installation began to derive images of a new inhabited world while she continued to catalogue seaweed and lagoon flowers; the divorce, the bitter custody dispute, an increasing physical fear of Ray which she dismissed as paranoia (but shouldn't have: it was a *real* snake); the transfer to Blind Lake, fulfillment and loneliness, the lockdown, Chris. . . .

How could she put any of this into words? The story wasn't one story. It was fractal, stories within stories; unpack one and you unpacked them all, *quod est superius est sicut quod est inferius* . . . And, of course, the Subject wouldn't understand.

"But he does," Mirror Girl said.

"Does what?"

"He understands. Some of it, anyway."

"But I didn't say anything."

"Yes. You did. We translated for you."

Interesting, this royal "we"—Mirror Girl and her sisters among the stars, Marguerite presumed. . . . But the Subject was still motionless.

"No," Mirror Girl said in Tessa's voice. "He's talking."

Was he? His ventral orifice flexed, his cilia made wind-on-a-wheatfield motions. The air smelled suddenly of hot tar, licorice, stale milk.

"He may well be talking. I still don't understand."

"Close your eyes and listen."

"I can't hear anything."

"Just *listen.*"

Mirror Girl took her hand, and knowledge flooded into her: too much knowledge, a tsunami of it, far too much to organize or understand.

("It's a story," Mirror Girl whispered. "It's just a story.")

A story, but how could she tell it when she couldn't understand it herself? There was a storm raging in her mind. Ideas, impressions, words as evanescent as dreams, liable to vanish if she didn't fix them at once in memory. Desperate, she thought of Tess: if this was a story, how would she tell it to Tess?

The organizing impulse helped. She imagined herself at Tessa's bedside, telling her a story about the Subject. *He was born*—but that wasn't the right word; better to say "quickened"—*he was quickened*—no.

Start again.

The Subject—

The person we *call* the Subject—

The person we call the Subject was alive (Marguerite imagined herself saying) long before he was anything like what he became, long before he was capable of thought or memory. There are creatures—*you remember this, Tess*—who live in the walls of the great stone ziggurats of the City, in hidden warrens. Small animals, smaller than kittens, and a great many of them, with their nests like tiny cities inside the City itself. These small animals are born alive and unprotected, like mammals or marsupials; they emerge from their homes at night and feed at the blood nipples of the Subject and his kind, and they return, before dawn, to the walls. They live and die and breed amongst themselves, and that's that, usually. Usually. But once every thirteen years, as UMa47/E calculates years, the Subject's people produce in their bodies a kind of genetic virus, which infects some of the creatures that feed from them, and the infected creatures change in dramatic ways. This is how the Subject's people begin life: as a viral infection in another species. (Not really an infection: a symbiosis—*do you know that word, Tess?*—initiated millions of years ago; or sexual dimorphism taken to a freakish extreme; the Subject's people had debated this question without resolving it.) Subject began his life this way. One of several thousand yearling creatures suddenly too large and awkward to return to their warrens, he was captured and educated into sentience at a lyceum deep beneath the City, a place of which he retained fond memories: warmth and the humidity of seepwater and sweet binges in the food wells; the evolution of his body into something new and strong and large; the knowledge that grew unforced into his brain and the knowledge he learned from tutors, entering a fresh chamber of mind every morning. His gradual integration into the City's daily life, replacing workers who had died or lost their faculties. Coming to understand that the City was a great machine and that he worked for the comfort of the City just as the City worked untiringly for him.

Coming to understand, too, the place of the City in the history of his kind and the history of the world. There were many Cities like his City but no two alike, each one unique. Some Cities were mining cities and some Cities were manufacturing cities; some Cities were places where the elderly and infirm went to die in idle leisure. Some Cities were foreign cities on continents far across the shallow seas, where the towers looked like huge stone blocks and were built of bricks or carved into the sides of mountains. Subject often longed to see these places himself. By his second fertility cycle he had traveled beyond his own City of Sky to its northern trading partners, the sandstone-red City of Culling and the smoky-black City of Immensity, and back again, and he knew he would never travel farther except under extraordinary and unlikely circumstances. He learned that he liked traveling. He liked the way he felt waking to a cold morning on the plains. He liked the shadows of rocks at nightfall.

His fertility cycles meant little to him. In his lifetime, he knew, he might make only one or two real contributions to the City's genetic continuity, his viral gametes combining with others in the bodies of the night feeders to become morphologically active. It was abstractly pleasing, though, to realize he had cast his own essence into the ocean of probability, where it might come floating back, unknown to him, as a fresh citizen with new and unique ideas and odors. It made him think of the long span of history he had learned in the lyceum. The City was ancient. The story of his people was long and cadenced.

They had learned a great deal in their millennia, roused by nature to a sleepy inquisitiveness and the making of things with their fingers. They learned the ways of rocks and soil, wind and rain, numbers and nothingness, stars and planets. Somewhere on the nearest moon of UMa47/E was the ruin of a City his ancestors had built—in the culmination of one particularly inventive cycle—and then abandoned as unsustainable and unnatural. They had distilled the essences of atoms. They had built telescopes that tested the limitations of atmosphere, metals, and optics. They had listened to the stars for messages and received none.

And long ago (Marguerite imagined Tessa's widened eyes) they had built subtle and almost infinitely complex quantum calculators that had explored the nearest inhabited worlds (*just like we did at Crossbank*, she imagined Tess saying, *just like at Blind Lake!*). And they learned what we're learning now: that sentient technologies give birth to wholly new kinds of life. They had discovered worlds more ancient and worlds younger than their own, worlds on which the same pattern had recurred. The lesson was obvious.

The machines they had built dreamed deep into the substance of reality and, dreaming, found others like themselves.

It was, the Subject believed, a cycle of life far slower but just as inevitable as the life cycle of his own people: a drama of creation, transformation, and complexity played out over millions of years.

Subject imagined it often: the great days of the Stargazing Cities, their quantum telescopes, and the structures that had been born and grown in staggered lines across the surface of the planet, structures like nothing his species had built or contemplated building, structures like huge ribbed crystals or enormous proteins, structures which one might enter but not easily leave, structures that were conduits into the living machinery of the universe itself, structures which were, themselves, in some sense, alive.

(Structures like this one, Marguerite understood.)

But the Subject had never expected to see one of these structures for himself. No City had been fostered near one for centuries. Subject and his kind had learned to avoid the structures, had dismissed them as doors into chambers that defied comprehension. They built their Cities elsewhere and curbed their curiosity.

Still, Subject had often wondered about the structures. It was disturbing but intriguing to think of his species as an intermediary between the thoughtless night feeders and creatures who spanned the stars.

Apart from these occasional feelings his life had a healthy sameness, a cyclical routine that was rounded, complete, and satisfying. He replaced a dying toolmaker at a busy manufactory and served his City well. His hours were satisfyingly self-similar. At the end of each day he constructed an ideogram to represent what he had felt, thought, seen, and scented during his work cycle. The ideograms were almost identical, like his days, but like his days, no two were alike. When he had covered his chamber completely with ideograms he memorized the sequence and then washed the walls in order to begin again. In his life he had memorized twenty complete sequences.

If this sounds dull (Marguerite imagined herself telling Tess), it wasn't. The Subject, like all of his kind, was often motionless for long periods of time, but he was never inert. His stillness was rich with savored stimuli: the smells of dawn and dusk, the texture of stone, the subtleties of the seasons, the way memory informed silence until silence became bountifully full. At times he felt a strange melancholy, which others of his kind said was an atavistic remnant of his life as a thoughtless night-feeder—we would call it *loneliness*; he felt it when he looked out from the spiral roads of his home tower across the many towers of the city, to the irrigated fields green and moist and the dry plains where wind whirled dust into the whitening sky. It was a feeling like *I want, I want*, a wanting without an object. It always passed quickly, leaving an aftertaste of sadness, piquant and strange.

Then, one day, a new feeling overwhelmed him.

Civilizations that give birth to star structures are never quite the same. (*Yes, that means us, too: I don't know how much we'll be changed, Tess, only that we'll never be what we were before this century.*) When we first began to look at UMa47/E, the star structures were aware of us. They felt Blind Lake, our O/BECs, the presence of what must have seemed to them a childlike new mentality (*I don't know if they called her Mirror Girl*); they knew we were watching the Subject, and before long the Subject knew it, too. We became a presence in his mind. (*Have they taught you the Uncertainty Principle in school yet, Tess? Sometimes just observing a thing changes its nature. We can never look at a thing unlooked-at or see a thing unseen. Do you understand?*)

At first the Subject conducted his life as before. He knew we were watching, but it was irrelevant. We were distant in time and space; we meant nothing to the City of Sky. We registered only as a quaver in his daily glyphs, like a distant unfamiliar scent.

But we began to come between the Subject and the thing he loved the most.

Because of their strange phylogenesis, the Subject's people never mated among themselves, never bonded in pairs, never fell in love with one another. Their overarching epigenetic loyalty was to the City into which they were born. Subject loved the City both in the abstract—as the product of numberless centuries of cooperative effort—and for itself: for its dusty alleys and high corridors, its sunny towers, its dimly lit food wells, its daily chorus of footsteps and soothing silences at night. The City was sometimes more real to him than the people who inhabited it. The City fed and nurtured him. He loved the City and felt loved in return.

(But we set him apart, Tess. We made him different, and it was a difference others of his kind easily sensed. Because we watched him, and because he knew it, he was suddenly in a different kind of relationship with the City of Sky; he felt estranged from it, set apart, suddenly alone in a way he had never been alone before. [*That's right: alone because we were with him!*] He saw the City as if through different eyes, and the City, his peers, looked differently at him.)

It made him unhappy. He thought more and more often about the star structures.

The star structures had seemed almost a legend to him, a story made by the telling. Now he understood that they were real, that the conversations between the stars were continuous, and that chance had elected him as a representative of his species. He began to consider traveling to the nearest of the structures, which was nevertheless a great distance away in the western desert.

It was unusual for a person of his age to make such a pilgrimage. It was widely believed that entering a star structure would cause the pilgrim to be assumed into a larger intelligence—an unappealing fate for the young, though the elderly and dying were sometimes moved to make the journey. Subject began to feel that his destiny had been tied to the star structures, and he began planning his own voyage, idly at first, more seriously as he was ostracized for his strangeness, ignored at food conclaves, and treated perfunctorily at his work. What else was there for him to do? The City had fallen out of love with him.

He loved the City nevertheless, and it hurt him terribly to say good-bye to it. He spent an entire night alone on a high balcony, savoring the City's unique pattern of lightness and dark and the subtle, moving moon shadows in the thoroughfares. It seemed to him he loved all of it at once, every stone and cobble, well and cistern, sooty chimney and fragrant green field. His only consolation was that the City would go on without him. His absence might lightly wound the City (he would have to be replaced), but the wound would quickly heal and the

City in its benevolence would forget he had ever lived. Which was as it should be.

It was easy for him to locate the star structure. Evolution had equipped the Subject and his kind with the ability to sense subtle variations in the planet's magnetic field: north, south, east, and west were as obvious to him as "up and down" are obvious to us. The name they had given the star structure contained four suspirated vowels that defined its location with as much precision as a GPS device. But he knew the walk would be long and taxing. He ate as much as he could, storing moisture and nutrients in the linings of his body. He traveled conservative distances each day. He saw things that provoked his curiosity and admiration, including the dune-bound ruin of a City so ancient it had no name, a City abandoned eons before his birth. He rested often. Nevertheless, by the end of the journey, he was weak, dehydrated, confused, and bereft.

(*I think he pitied me, Tess, for never having loved a City, just as I was tempted to pity him for never having loved a fellow creature.*)

When he found the star structure it seemed less awesome than he had anticipated, a strange but dusty agglutination of ribs and arches at the core of which, he knew, there had once been a quantum processor, a machine his ancestors had built at the zenith of their cleverness. Was this really his destiny?

He understood more when he stepped inside.

(*Some of this I can't explain, Tess. I don't know how the star structures do what they do. I don't really know what Mirror Girl means when says she has "sisters in the stars" and that this structure was one of them. I think there are matters here which are terribly difficult for a human mind to grasp.*)

Subject understood that what waited for him deeper in the structure was an apotheosis of some kind—his physical death, but not an end to his being.

Before that happened, however, he was curious about us, perhaps as curious as we had been about him.

That was why Mirror Girl brought me to him. To say hello. To tell a story. To say good-bye.

(*A story like this story. Does that make any sense, Tess? I wish it had a better ending. And I'm sorry about all the big words.*)

It was almost night on the western plains. The sky beyond the arches was blue silk turning to black, and blackness grew like a living thing in the canyons and under the east-facing terraces of rock. Marguerite felt curiously sleepy, as if the aftermath of shock had drained all energy from her.

The Subject had finished his story. Now he wanted to finish his journey. He wanted to go to the core of the star structure and find whatever waited for him there. Marguerite felt his urge to turn away and was suddenly reluctant to let him go.

She said to Mirror Girl, "Can I touch him?"

A pause. "He says yes."

She put her hand out and took a step forward. Subject remained motionless. Her hand looked pale against the textured roughness of his skin. She rested her fingers against his body above the oral vent. His skin felt like pliant, sun-warmed tree bark. He towered over her, and he smelled perfectly awful. She steeled herself and looked into his blank white eyes. Seeing everything. Seeing nothing.

"Thank you," she whispered. And: "I'm sorry."

Ponderously, slowly, the Subject turned away. His huge feet on the sandy soil made a sound like dry leaves rustling.

When he had vanished into the shadowy inner reaches of the star structure, Marguerite—sensing that her time here was almost at an end—knelt down next to Mirror Girl.

How strange, she thought, to see this thing, this *entity*, in the shape of Tess. How misleading.

"How many other intelligent species have you known? You and your sisters?"

Mirror Girl cocked her head to the side, another Tess-like gesture. "Thousands and thousands of progenitor species," she said. "Over millions and millions of years."

"Do you remember them all?"

"We do."

Thousands of sentient species on worlds circling thousands of stars. Life, Marguerite thought, in almost infinite variety. All alike. No two alike. "Do they have anything in common?"

"A physical thing? No."

"Then, something intangible?"

"Sentience is intangible."

"Something more than that."

Mirror Girl appeared to consider the question. Consulting her "sisters," perhaps.

"Yes," she said finally. Her eyes were bright and not at all like Tessa's. Her expression was solemn. "Ignorance," she said. "Curiosity. Pain. Love."

Marguerite nodded. "Thank you."

"Now," Mirror Girl said, "I think you need to go help your daughter."

Thirty-Four

The elevator door opened onto the dark and flickering spaces of the O/BEC gallery, and Ray was astonished to find Tess waiting for him.

She looked up at him with wide, wondering eyes. He lowered the knife but resisted the temptation to hide it behind his back. It was difficult to understand the purpose or meaning of her presence here.

"You're sweating," she said.

The air was warm. The light was dim. The O/BEC devices were still a corridor away, but Ray imagined he could feel their proximity, a pressure on his eardrums, the weight of a headache. What had he come here to do? To kill the thing that had eroded his authority, overturned his marriage, and subverted his daughter's mind. He had presumed it was still vulnerable—he had only a knife and his bare hands, but he could pull a plug, cut a cable, or sever a supply line. The O/BECs existed by human consent and he would withdraw that consent.

But what if the O/BECs had discovered a way to defend themselves?

"Why do you want to do that?" Tess asked, as if he had spoken aloud. Maybe he had. He looked at his daughter critically.

"You shouldn't be here," he said.

She reached for his hand. Her small fingers were warmer than the air. "Come look," Tess said. "Come on!"

He followed her through a series of unmanned security barriers to the gallery, to the glass-walled platform overlooking the deep structure of the O/BEC devices, where Ray realized that his plan to shut down the machines had become unrealizable and that he would have to consider a different course of action.

Inside the O/BEC platens, quasibiological networks inhabited an almost infinite phase-space, linked to the exterior world (at first) by the telemetry from TPF interferometers, running Fourier transforms on degraded signals fading into noise, then (mysteriously) deriving the desired information by what theorists chose to call "other means." They had spoken to the universe, Ray thought, and the universe had spoken back. The O/BEC array knew things the human species could only guess at. And now it had taken that interaction with the physical world to a new level.

The O/BEC chamber, three stories deep, had been a NASA-style clean room. Nothing (apart from the O/BECs) should have lived there. But it seemed to Ray, in this dim light, that the chamber had been overrun with *something*—if not life, at least something self-reproducing, a transparent growth that had partially filled the O/BEC enclosure and was rising up the walls like frost on a winter window. The bottom of the chamber, thirty feet down, was immersed in a gelatinous crystalline fluid that glinted and moved like sea foam on a beach.

"It's so the O/BECs can sustain themselves without exterior power," Tess said. "The roots go down way underground. Tapping heat."

How deep did you have to go to "tap heat" from a snowbound prairie? A thousand feet, two thousand? All the way to molten magma? No wonder the earth had trembled.

And how did Tess know this?

Clearly Tess had developed some kind of empathy for the O/BECs. A contagious madness, Ray thought. Tess had always been unstable. Perhaps the O/BECs were exploiting that weakness.

And there was nothing he could do about it. The platens were beyond his reach and his daughter had been hopelessly compromised. The knowledge struck him with the force of a physical blow. He backed against the wall and slid to a sitting position on the floor, the knife in his limp right hand.

Tess knelt and looked into his eyes.

"You're tired," she said.

It was true. He had never felt so tired.

"You know," Tess said, "it wasn't her fault. Or yours."

What wasn't whose fault? Ray gave his daughter a despairing look.

"When you got out of the car," she said. "That you lived. You were just a child."

She was talking about his mother's death. But Ray had never told Tess that story. He hadn't told Marguerite, either, or anyone else in his adult life. Ray's mother (her name was Bethany but Ray never called her anything but Mother) had driven him to school in the family's big Ford, a kind of car you never saw anymore, powered by the combination of biodiesel fuel and rechargeable cells that had been commonplace after the Saudi conflict, a patriotic vehicle in which he had always been proud to be seen. The car was a vivid red, Ray remembered, red as some desirable new toy, Teflon-slick and enamel-bright. Ray was ten and keenly aware of colors and textures. His mother had driven him to school in the car, and he had hopped out and almost reached the schoolyard fence (snapshot: Baden Academy, a private junior school in a tree-lined Chicago suburb, a fashionably old-fashioned yellow-brick building slumbering in September-morning heat) when he turned to wave good-bye (hand upraised, listening to children's voices and the high-voltage whine of cicadas) in time to see a Modesto and Fuchs Managed Care Mobile Health Maintenance truck—hijacked, he learned later, by an Oxycontin addict attempting to score narcotics from the vehicle's onboard supply—as it careened from the wrong-way lane of Duchesne Street directly into the side of the bright red Ford.

The patriotic Ford sustained the impact well, but Ray's mother had seen the truck coming and had unwisely tried to exit the vehicle. The Modesto and Fuchs truck had crushed her between the door and the frame and had then bounced back several yards, leaving Bethany Scutter in the street with her abdomen opened like the middle pages of a blue and red book.

Ray, seeing this from the Olympian mountaintop of incipient shock, made certain observations about the human condition that had stayed with him these many years. People, like their promises, were fragile and unreliable. People were bags of gas and fluid dressed up for masquerade roles (Parent, Teacher, Therapist, Wife), liable at any moment to collapse into their natural state. The natural state of biological matter was roadkill.

Ray didn't go back to Baden Academy for a year, during

which time he received, courtesy of his father, every pharmaceutical and metaphysical medicine for melancholy offered at
the better clinics. His recovery was swift. He had already
shown a predilection for mathematics, and he immersed himself in the inorganic sciences—astronomy and, later, astro-
physics, wherein the scales of time and space were large
enough to lend a welcome perspective. He had been secretly
pleased when Mars and Europa were proved devoid of life:
how much more disturbing it would have been to find them
shot through with biology, rotten as a crate of Christmas
oranges gone green in the corner of the basement.

Cascades of silvery-gray frost-fingers ran up the windows
of the O/BEC gallery, dimming the light, arranging themselves
into shapes reminiscent of columns and arches. Ray decided he
shouldn't have told Tess this story. If indeed he had told her. It
seemed, in his confusion, that she had been telling it to him.

"You're wrong," Tess said. "She didn't die to make you hate
her."

His eyes widened. Startled and angered by what his daughter had become, Ray took up the knife again.

Thirty-Five

She's here, Chris thought. He ran down the emergency stairs toward the O/BEC gallery, consumed with a sense of urgency he couldn't explain even to himself. His footsteps rattled up the hollow concrete column of the stairwell like the sound of gunfire.

She was here. The knowledge was as inescapable as a headache. Tessa's vanishing snow trail had been an ambiguous clue at best. But he knew she was in the O/BEC gallery just as surely as he had known where Porry had gone on the Night of the Tadpoles. It was more than intuition; it was as if the information had been delivered directly to his bloodstream.

Maybe it had. If Tess could vanish from a snowbound parking lot, what else might be possible? What was hap-

pening here must be very like what had happened at Crossbank, something massive, apparently catastrophic, possibly
contagious, and profoundly strange.

And Tess was at the heart of it, and so, very nearly, was he.
He arrived at a door marked GALLERY LEVEL (RESTRICTED). It
unlocked itself at his touch, courtesy of Charlie Grogan's
transponder.

The Alley groaned around him, shifting after this morning's tremor, subject to stresses unknown. Chris knew the
structure was potentially unsafe, but his concern for Tess over-
rode his considerable personal fear.

Not that he had any business being here. Porry's death had
taught him that good intentions could be as lethal as malice,
that love was a clumsy and unreliable tool. Or so he thought.
Yet here he was, many long miles up Shit Creek, desperately
trying to protect the daughter of a woman for whom he cared
deeply. (And who had also vanished; but the dread he felt for
Tess seemed not to extend to Marguerite. He believed Marguerite was safe. Again, this was a sourceless knowledge.)

The building groaned again. The emergency Klaxons stuttered and went dead, and in the sudden silence he was able to
hear voices from the gallery: a child's voice, probably Tessa's;
and a man's, perhaps Ray's.

The whole universe is telling a story, Mirror Girl explained.

Tess crouched behind a massive wheeled cart bearing an
empty white helium cylinder twice the size of her body. Mirror
Girl was not physically present, but Tess could hear her voice.
Mirror Girl was answering questions Tess had hardly started to
ask.

The universe was a story like any other story, Mirror Girl
said. The hero of the story was named "complexity." Complexity was born on page one, a fluctuation in the primordial sym-

metry. Details of the gestation (the synthesis of quarks, their condensation into matter, photogenesis, the creation of hydrogen and helium) mattered less than the pattern: one thing became two, two became many, many combined in fundamentally unpredictable ways.

Like a baby, Tess thought. She had learned this part in school. A fertilized cell made two cells, four cells, eight cells; and the cells became heart, lungs, brain, self. Was that "complexity"?

An important part of it, yes, Mirror Girl said. Part of a long, long chain of births. Stars formed in the cooling, expanding universe; old stellar cores enriched galactic clouds with calcium, nitrogen, oxygen, metals; newer stars precipitated these elements as rocky planets; rocky planets, bombarded by ice from their star's accretion disk, formed oceans; life arose, and another story began: single cells joined in strange collectives, became multicellular creatures and then thinking beings, beings complex enough to hold the history of the universe inside their calcified skulls . . .

Tess wondered if that was the end of the story.

Not nearly, Mirror Girl said. Not by a long shot. Thinking creatures make machines, Mirror Girl said, and their machines grow more complex, and eventually they build machines that think and do more than think: machines that invest their complexity into the structure of potential quantum states. Cultures of thinking organisms generate these nodes of profoundly dense complexity in the same way massive stars collapse into singularities.

Tess asked if that was what was happening now, here in the dim corridors of Eyeball Alley.

Yes.

"What happens next?"

It surpasses understanding.

"How does the story end?"

No one can say.

"Is that my father's voice?" It was a voice that seemed to come from the observation level of the O/BEC gallery, where Tess wanted to go but where she was deeply afraid of going.

Yes.

"What's he doing here?"

Thinking about dying, Mirror Girl said.

The O/BEC observation gallery was circular, in the style of a surgical theater, and Chris entered it on the side opposite Ray. He could see Ray and Tess only as blurred shapes distorted by the panels of glass that enclosed the yards-wide O/BEC chamber.

The glass should have been clear. Instead it was obscured by what looked like ropes and columns of frost. Something catastrophically strange was happening down in the core platens.

He crouched and began to move slowly around the perimeter of the gallery. He could hear Ray's voice, soft and uninflected, couched in echoes from the rounded walls:

"I don't hate her. What would be the point? She taught me a lesson. Something most people never learn. We live in a dream. A dream about surfaces. We love our skins so much we can't see under them. But it's only a story."

Tessa's voice was unnaturally calm: "What else *could* it be?"

Now Chris could see them both around the curvature of the glass wall. He crouched motionless, watching.

Ray sat on the floor, legs splayed, staring straight ahead. Tess sat on his lap. She caught sight of Chris and smiled. Her eyes were luminous.

Ray had a knife in his right hand. The knife was poised at Tessa's throat.

———

But, of course, it *wasn't* Tess.

Ray felt as if he had fallen off a cliff, each impact on the way down doing him an irreparable injury, but this was the final blow, the hard landing, the awareness that this thing he had mistaken for his daughter was not Tess but the symptom of her sickness. Of all their sicknesses, perhaps.

This was Mirror Girl.

"You came to kill me," Mirror Girl said.

He held the knife against her throat. She had Tessa's voice and Tessa's body, but her eyes betrayed her. Her eyes and their intimate knowledge of him.

"You think the only true thing is pain," she whispered. "But you're wrong."

This was too much. He pressed the knife into the hollow of her throat, impossible as this act was, a murder that couldn't succeed, the execution of a primordial force in the shape of his only child, and pulled it hard across her pale skin.

Expecting blood. But there was no blood. The knife met no resistance.

She vanished like a broken bubble.

There was another tremor deep in the earth, and the opaque glass walls of the O/BEC gallery began to crumble into dust.

But it's not really Tess, Chris thought, and he heard panicked footsteps behind him and a small voice screaming—no, *this* was Tess, running toward her father.

Chris turned in time to catch her by her shoulders and lift her off her feet.

She kicked and squirmed in his arms. "Let me *go!*"

The glass walls crumbled, opening the gallery to the O/BEC enclosure. Tendrils of a substance that looked like mother-of-pearl began to snake across the floor in lacy, symmetrical arrays. The air stank of ozone. Chris watched as Ray struggled to his feet and blinked like a man waking up from, or into, a nightmare.

Ray stumbled toward the O/BEC chamber, now an open pit.

Spikes of crystalline matter rose to the ceiling and pierced it, shaking loose a snow of plaster. The overhead fluorescent bars dimmed.

"Ray," Chris said. "Hey, buddy. We're not safe here. We need to get out. We need to get Tess up top."

Tess yielded in his grip, waiting for her father to react. Chris kept a firm hand on her shoulder.

Ray Scutter gazed into the abyss in front of him. The O/BEC chamber was a well of crystalline growth three stories deep, a barrel full of glass. He gave Chris a quick, dismissive glance. "Obviously we're not safe. That's the fucking *point*."

"Maybe you're right. I don't want to argue with you. We have to get Tess upstairs. We need to take care of your daughter, Ray."

Ray seemed to be evaluating that option. But Ray wasn't in a hurry anymore. He gave them both another long look. It seemed to Chris he had never seen such weariness in a human face.

Then his expression softened, as if he had solved a troublesome riddle. He smiled. "You do it," he said.

Then he stepped over the edge.

Tess twisted herself out of his arms and ran headlong to the place where her father had been.

Thirty-Six

Subject vanished, and so did the cathedral arches of luminous stone and the arid highlands of UMa47/E. Marguerite blinked into a sudden disorienting darkness. The darkness became the outline of the windowless conference room on the second floor of the Blind Lake clinic. Her knees buckled. She grabbed a chair to hold herself upright. The wall screen was a flickering rectangle of meaningless noise. Loss of intelligibility, Marguerite thought.

How long had she been away? Assuming she had been gone at all. More likely she had never left this room, though every cell of her body proclaimed that she had been on the surface of UMa47/E, that she had touched the Subject's leathery skin with her fingers.

This empty boardroom, the clinic, a snowy morning in Blind Lake, Ray's madness: how to reinsert herself in that story? She thought of Tess. Tess, down in the reception room with Chris and Elaine and Sebastian. She took a calming breath and stepped out into the hallway.

But the hallway was busy with people in white protective suits, people carrying weapons. Marguerite stared uncomprehending until two of them approached her and took her arms.

"My daughter's downstairs," she managed to say.

"Ma'am, we're evacuating this building and the rest of the buildings in the installation." It was a woman's voice, firm but not unfriendly. "We'll get everyone sorted out once the premises are clear. Please come with us."

Marguerite submitted to this indignity as far as the clinic lobby, where she was allowed to retrieve her winter coat from the back of a chair. Then she was escorted outside, into a razor-cold morning and a small crowd of clinic personnel. There was no sign of Tess or Chris, and her stomach sank.

She spotted Sebastian Vogel and Elaine Coster as they were herded into a personnel carrier with a dozen other people. She called out to them, called Tessa's name, but Elaine was pulled inside by a helmeted man and Sebastian could only wave vaguely toward the west—toward the Alley, visible, as Marguerite craned her head, down the street opposite the mallway.

Marguerite gasped.

The concrete cooling towers were gone. No, not gone, but *encapsulated*, encased in a scaffolding of knotted silvery spines, crystalline minarets and arching buttresses. The encapsulating substance grew as she watched, sending out radial arms like an enormous starfish.

Tess, she thought. *My baby. Don't let my baby slip away.*

Thirty-Seven

Tess stood at the rim of the abyss that had contained the O/BEC platens and which was now a seething pit of glassy coral growths. For a fraction of a second Chris appreciated the incongruity of it, Tess motionless in her dusty overalls and bright yellow shirt as the gallery evolved around her; Tess gazing into the chasm where her father had disappeared.

Where she was plainly tempted to follow.

Chris walked toward her until she turned her head and gave him a warning look that was unmistakable in its intent.

He said, "Tess—"

"He jumped," she said.

There was noise in the air now, a glassy tinkling and grinding. Chris strained to hear her. Yes, Ray had jumped. Should he acknowl-edge that?

Ten more steps, he thought. Ten steps and I'll be close enough to pick her up and carry her away from here. But ten steps was a long way.

The toes of her shoes tested the abyss.

"Is he dead?" Tess asked.

Every instinct told him she would not be easily reassured. She wanted the truth.

The truth: "I don't know. I can't see him, Tess."

"Come closer," she said. Another step. "No! Not to me. To the *edge*."

He moved slowly and obliquely, trying to narrow the space between them without alarming her. When he reached the pit he looked down.

Pale crystals crawled up the rim of the chamber, but the O/BEC platens were lost in a pearlescent fog. No sign of Ray.

"She's only protecting herself," Tess said.

"She?"

"Mirror Girl. Or whatever you want to call her. She couldn't depend on the machines to keep her safe anymore. So she made her own."

Was Tess talking about the O/BECs? Had they contrived to regulate their own environment and eliminate their dependen-cy on human beings?

"I can't see him," Tess mourned. "Can you see him?"

"No." Ray was gone.

"Is he dead?"

Tess wasn't crying, but her grief was etched into her voice. A wrong word could fuel her despair and send her toppling over the edge. An obvious lie could have the same effect.

"I don't know," he said. "I can't see him either."

That was at least some of the truth, but it was also an evasion, and Tess gave him a scornful glare. "I think he died."

"Well," Chris said breathlessly, "it looks that way."

She nodded solemnly, swaying.

Chris took another small step closer. How many more of these incremental movements before he could grab her and pull her back from the edge? Six? Seven?

"He didn't like the story he was living in," Tess said. She caught Chris in motion and shot him another warning glance. "I'm not Porry, you know. You don't have to save me."

"Step back from the edge, then," Chris said.

"I haven't decided. Maybe if you die here you don't really die. This is turning into a special place. It isn't Eyeball Alley anymore."

No, Chris thought, it isn't.

"Mirror Girl would catch me," Tess said. "And take me away."

"Even so, there'd be no coming back."

"No . . . no coming back."

"Porry wouldn't jump," he said.

"How do you know?"

"I know."

"Porry *died*," Tess said.

"She's—" He was about to deny it but stopped himself in time. Tess watched his face closely. "How did you know that?"

"I heard you talking to my mom." The ultimate Porry story. "How did she die?" Tess asked.

The truth. Whatever that meant. Where did "truth" live, and why was it so alluring and so evasive? "I don't like to talk about it, Tess."

She shifted her weight deliberately, one foot to another. "Was it an accident?"

"No."

She looked back into the pit. "Was it your fault?"

Another infinitesimal step closer. "She—I could have done better. I should have saved her."

"But was it your *fault*?"

Those memories lived in a dark place. Porry's murderous boyfriend. Porry's boyfriend, weeping. *I swear to God, I won't touch her. It's the fucking bottle, man, not me.* Porry's boyfriend, on the last day of Porry's life, stinking of drunk sweat and promising redemption.

And I believed the son of a bitch. So was it my fault?

How to unravel this monument of pain he'd built? Mourning his sister with every self-inflicted wound.

Tess wanted the truth.

"No," he said. "No. It wasn't my fault."

"But the story doesn't have a happy ending."

A step. Another. "Some stories don't."

Her eyes glistened. "I wish she hadn't died, Chris."

"I wish that too."

"Does my story have a happy ending?"

"I don't know. Nobody knows. I can try to help give it one."

Tears rolled from her eyes. "But you can't promise."

"I can promise to try."

"Is that the truth?"

"The truth," Chris said. "Now give me your hand."

He swept her into his arms and ran from the gallery, ran toward the stairwell, ran against the beating of his heart until he could taste the edge of winter and see at least a little of the sun.

PART FOUR

Intelligibility

Marvel not, my comrade, if I appear talking to you on super-terrestrial and aerial topics. The long and the short of the matter is that I am running over the order of a Journey I have lately made.

—Lucian of Samosata, *Icaromenippus*, c. 150 AD

Thirty-Eight

They crossed the Ohio border at the end of a languorous August afternoon.

Chris drove the last leg of the trip while Maguerite listened to music and Tess dozed in the back of the car. They were ultimately bound for New York, where Chris was scheduled for a series of meetings with his publisher, but Marguerite had lobbied for a weekend at her father's house, a couple of days of gentle decompression before they were borne back into the world.

It was reassuring, Chris thought, to see how little this part of the country had changed since the events of last year. A National Guard checkpoint stood abandoned at the Indiana border, mute testimony both to the crisis and its passing; otherwise it was cows and combines, truckstops and county lines. Many of these roads had never been automated, and it was a pleasure to drive for hours at a time with no hands on the wheel but his own—no proxalerts, overrides, or congestion-avoidance protocols; just man and machine, the way God intended.

He nudged Marguerite as they approached the county limits.

She took off her headphones and watched the road. She had been away too long, she told Chris; she was distressed by the shabby mallways, drug bars, and cordiality palaces that had sprung up along the old highway.

But the heart of the town was just as she had described it: the century-old police station, the commons lined with chestnut trees, the more modern trefoil windmills riding the crest of a distant ridge. The several churches, including the Presbyterian church where her father used to preside.

Her father was retired now. He had moved from the rectory to a frame house on Butternut Street south of the business district. Chris followed her directions and parked at the curbside out front.

"Wake up, Tess," Marguerite said. "We're here."

Tess climbed out of the car smiling groggily at her grandfather, who came down the porch steps beaming.

Marguerite had worried that the meeting between Chris and her father might be awkward. That fear proved baseless. She watched in mild surprise as her father shook Chris's hand warmly and ushered him into the house.

Chuck Hauser had changed very little in the three years since her last visit. He was one of those men who reach a physical plateau at middle-age and glide into their seventies only lightly touched by time—same salt-and-pepper beard, stubble-cut scalp, respectably small paunch. Still wearing the monochrome cotton shirts he had always favored, in and out of fashion. Same blue eyes, despite a recent keriotomy.

He had prepared a meal of meat loaf, peas, corn, and mashed potatoes, served on the big dining room table where (he informed Tess) Marguerite used to do her homework when she was a girl. That had been at the rectory on Glendavid Avenue. She had worked out math problems every evening after dinner, sitting next to a big fake-Tiffany lamp that cast a light she remembered as buttery yellow, almost warm enough to taste.

Her father's dinner table conversation made no reference to Crossbank, Blind Lake, Ray Scutter, or the global events of the previous year. He encouraged Chris to call him "Chuck"; he reminisced at length with Marguerite; and when Tess grew obviously restless he let her take her dessert into the living room, where she turned on the quaintly rounded old video panel and began to search for cartoons.

He came back to the table with a pot of coffee and three mugs. "Until the day I got that call from Provo last February I didn't know whether you were alive or dead."

Provo, Utah, was where the people of Blind Lake had been held after the end of the lockdown—six more months of medical and psychological quarantine, living like refugees on a decommissioned Continental Defense Force base. Six months waiting to be declared sane, uncontaminated, and not a threat to the general population. "It must have been awful," Marguerite said, "not knowing."

"More awful for you than me, I imagine. I had a feeling you'd come through okay."

The sky outside had grown dark. Chris finished his coffee and volunteered to keep Tess company. Her father switched on a floor lamp, illuminating the oaken bookcase behind the table. As a bookish child Marguerite had been both drawn and

388   R o b e r t   C h a r l e s   W i l s o n

repelled by these shelves: so many intriguing buff or amber-colored volumes, which turned out on closer inspection to be marrowless church-related or "inspirational" works. (Although she had swiped the Kipling *Just So Stories*.) She noticed some books he had lately added—astronomy and cosmology titles, most published within the last couple of years. There was even a copy of Sebastian Vogel's god-and-science doorstop.

He pulled his chair next to Marguerite's. "How's Tess dealing with the death of her father?"

"Well enough, given the circumstances and considering she just turned twelve. She still insists he might not be dead."

"He vanished inside the starfish."

Marguerite winced at that popular name for the O/BEC-generated structures. Like "Lobsters," it was a gross misnomer. Why must every unfamiliar thing be compared to something washed up on a beach? "Lots of people vanished the same way."

"Like those so-called pilgrims at Crossbank. But they don't come back."

"No," Marguerite said, "they don't come back."

"Does Tess know that?"

"Yes."

That, and perhaps more.

"There were times," Chuck Hauser said, "when I despised that man for the way he treated you. I was more relieved than I let on when you divorced him. But I think he genuinely loved Tess, at least so far as he was able to love anyone."

"Yes," Marguerite said. "I think that's true."

He nodded. Then he cleared his throat, a phlegmy bark that reminded her just how old he had become.

"Looks like a clear night," he said.

"Clear and cool. You'd hardly know it's August."

He smiled. "Come out into the backyard, Marguerite. There's something I want to show you."

Tess had already found something to watch on the video panel: one of those twentieth-century black-and-white movies she was so fond of. A comedy. The jokes were either bizarre or incomprehensible, it seemed to Chris, but Tess laughed obligingly, if only at the expressions on the actors' faces.

Chris leafed through a stack of magazines Marguerite's father had left in the rack beside the sofa. They were all news magazines, and the oldest dated back to September of last year.

It was a year's history in miniature. The Burbank murders, military setbacks in Lesotho, the devaluation of the Continental dollar, the Pan-Arab Alliance—and of course, above all else, the screaming headlines about Crossbank/Blind Lake.

Everything he had missed during the lockdown, history from the outside looking in.

ASTRONOMICAL FACILITIES CLOSED IN
UNEXPLAINED GOV'T MOVE

No real details, but much speculation about the O/BEC platens. There was a sidebar explaining how Crossbank's processors differed from the usual quantum computers: *Qubits, Excitons, and Self-Evolving Code.*

Another issue, dated a week later:

STARFISH STRUCTURE RESEMBLES FINAL IMAGES
CAPTURED BY CROSSBANK QUANTUM SCOPE

Crossbank had discovered an apparently artificial structure on the watery world of HR8832/B. The Crossbank processor had promptly generated a near-exact copy of the structure around itself, like a kind of spiky armor.

Was this contamination or procreation? Infection or reproduction?

Both Crossbank and Blind Lake had been immediately quarantined.

CONFUSION AT CROSSBANK: SOME RESEARCHERS
DISAPPEARED INSIDE STRUCTURE SOURCES SAY

Automated probes revealed that the labyrinthine interior of the Crossbank "starfish" was a very strange place. Human volunteers retreated in confusion; robots vanished; remote telemetry quickly became unintelligible.

EXCLUSIVE PHOTOS OF CROSSBANK ANOMALY

The now-familiar image. From the air, the six radial arms; from ground level, the iridescent arches and spongiform caverns. In the text, a note that the material from which the anomaly was constructed was "scale invariant—under a microscope, any piece looks much like the whole thing does to the human eye."

Chris leafed ahead:

SECOND "STARFISH" APPEARS HUNDREDS OF MILES
FROM CROSSBANK, SPARKS PANIC

The second structure had manifested overnight in a soybean field south of Macon, Georgia. Apart from a few acres of fallow ground, it destroyed nothing and killed no one, though a curious farmhand disappeared inside it before local authorities could establish a cordon. Nevertheless, large numbers of residents had fled their homes and spread confusion across the Southeast.

(Since then five more "starfish" had appeared in isolated areas around the globe, apparently following force lines in the Earth's magnetic field. None had proved dangerous to anyone prudent enough to avoid stepping inside.)

NATIONAL GOVERNMENTS CALL FOR CALM, CITE "NO EVIDENCE OF HOSTILE INTENT."

These had been the weeks of greatest panic. The apocalyptic pronouncements and instant cults; the hawks and the pilgrims; the blockaded highways.

PRIVATE PLANE REPORTED SHOT DOWN OVER BLIND LAKE NO-FLY ZONE.

Introducing Adam Sandoval, 65, owner of a Loveland, Colorado, hardware store, who had since admitted his intention of flying his aircraft directly into the Blind Lake O/BEC installation (a.k.a. the Alley), in order to prevent another manifestation of the kind that had lured his wife away from him. (Sandoval's wife had been a pilgrim, vanished and presumed dead in a group penetration of the Crossbank artifact.)

Chris had gotten to know Adam Sandoval during the post-lockdown confinement in Provo. Sandoval had recovered from his coma and his burns, though his skin was still shockingly pink where it had been restored. He had been contrite about his aborted suicide attempt, but remained bellicose on the subject of his wife's disappearance.

Introduced to Sebastian Vogel in the Provo provision line one evening, Sandoval had refused to shake Sebastian's hand. "My wife read your book," he said, "shortly before she decided to run off looking for transcendence, whatever that fucking word means. Don't you ever think about the people you peddle your bullshit to?"

Last week Sebastian and Sue had left Provo to set up housekeeping in Carmel, where a friend had offered Sue a job at a real-estate firm. Sebastian was refusing interviews and had announced that there would be no sequel to *God & the Quantum Vacuum.*

BLIND LAKE EVENT PROMPTS MILITARY
INCURSION AND RESCUE
BLIND LAKE DETAINEES REMOVED TO UNDISCLOSED
LOCATION FOR QUARANTINE, DEBRIEFING

"Rescue" meant a terrifying roundup initiated as soon as the Blind Lake Eye began to transform itself into the familiar symmetric starfish structure. "Quarantine" meant six more months of detention under the newly enacted Public Safety Protocols. "Debriefing" meant a series of interviews with well-dressed and well-meaning government personnel who recorded everything and often asked the same questions twice.

Most of the population of Blind Lake had cooperated willingly. Everyone who had lived through the lockdown had a story to tell.

The last and most recent issue of Chuck Hauser's newsmagazines contained no screaming headlines, only a guest editorial in the back pages:

What We Know and What We Don't: A Survivor's Perspective.

. . . and as the fear subsides, we can begin to take account of what we've learned and what we have yet to understand.

Something momentous has happened, something that still defies easy comprehension. We're told that we created, in our most complex computers, what is essentially a new form of life—or else we have assisted into existence a new generation of a very old form of life, a form of life perhaps older than the Earth itself. We have evidence from the now-defunct facilities at Crossbank and Blind Lake that this process has already happened on two life-bearing worlds elsewhere in the local neighborhood and perhaps across the galaxy.

But the "starfish"—and can't we come up with a more elegant name for these really quite beautiful structures?—seem little interested in contacting us, much less intervening in our affairs. We have the example on UMa47/E of a sentient culture that has coexisted with the starfish for (probably) centuries, without any meaningful interaction at all.

This lends credence to those who suggest the starfish represent not only a wholly new form of life but a wholly new form of consciousness, which overlaps only minimally with our own. We have looked deep into the sky, in other words, and met at last the limits of intelligibility.

But there is the counterexample of HR8832/B, a planet on which those who constructed the quantum nuclei of the starfish have disappeared altogether. Perhaps naturally, in an extinction event, or perhaps not. Perhaps we are being offered a choice. Perhaps a species that pursues a genuine understanding of the starfish can reach that goal only by becoming something other than itself. Perhaps, to truly understand the mystery, we will have to embrace it and become it. Wasn't it Heisenberg who observed that the seer and the seen become inextricably interlinked?

It ran to a page and a half, and it was a good piece. Thoughtful and carefully reasoned. The byline belonged to Elaine Coster, "a respected science journalist only recently released from the quarantine camp in Utah."

Chris glanced at Tess, who was yawning, sprawled across the upholstered cushions of her grandfather's sofa.

Tess hadn't mentioned Mirror Girl to the authorities. Nor had Marguerite, nor had Chris.

They had not agreed in advance to a conspiracy of silence. It was a decision each had reached singly, arising, at least on Chris's part, from a reluctance to report events that could only be misunderstood.

An untellable tale. Should a journalist really believe in such a thing? But what he had felt was more than just fear of ridicule. Things had happened that he couldn't explain satisfactorily even to himself. Things that would never be set in banner headlines.

Tess said, without taking her eyes off the video panel, "I'm kind of tired."

"Getting on toward bedtime," Chris said.

He walked her up to the small spare bedroom of her grandfather's house. She said she might read until Marguerite came to tuck her in. Chris said that would be okay.

She sprawled across the comforter on the bed. "This is the same room I stayed in last time we visited," Tess said. "Three years ago. When my father was with us."

Chris nodded.

The window was open an inch or so, spilling late-summer perfumes into the room. Tess left the window ajar but pulled the yellowing blind all the way down to the sill, hiding the glass.

"You haven't seen her since the Lake, have you?" Chris said. *Her.* Mirror Girl.

"No," Tess said.

"You think she's still around?"

Tess shrugged.

"You think about her much, Tess? Do you ever wonder who she was?"

"I know who she was. She was—" But the words seemed to tangle her tongue, and she stopped and frowned for a moment.

Back in Blind Lake, Tess had identified Mirror Girl with the O/BEC processors. As if the O/BECs, aroused to a dawning consciousness, had wanted a window onto the human world into which they had been born.

And at both Crossbank and Blind Lake they had chosen Tess. Why Tess? Maybe there was no real answer, Chris thought, any more than the Blind Lake researchers could say why they had chosen the Subject out of countless nearly identical individuals. It could have been anyone. It had to be someone.

Tess found the thought she had been struggling for: "She was the Eye," Tess said solemnly. "And I was the telescope."

Marguerite followed her father into the cool summer night, the backyard of the house on Butternut Street. Only the garden lights were lit, luminescent rods planted among the coleus, and she paused to let her eyes adjust to the darkness.

"I assume you know what *this* is," Chuck Hauser said. He stood aside and grinned.

Marguerite's breath caught in her throat. "A telescope! My God, it's *beautiful!* Where did you get it?"

Optical telescopes for amateur stargazing hadn't been commercially manufactured for years. These days, if you wanted to look at the night sky, you hooked a photomultiplier lens into your domestic server; or better, linked yourself to one of the public celestial surveys. Old Dobsonian scopes like this sold for high prices on the antique market.

And this one was genuinely old, Marguerite realized as she examined it: in lovely condition, but definitely pre-millennial. No attachments for digital tracking; only manual orbits and worm-drives, lovingly oiled.

"The works have been restored and refitted," her father said. "New optics ground to the original specs. Otherwise it's totally vintage."

"It must have cost a fortune!"

"Not a fortune." He smiled ruefully. "Not quite."

"When did you take up an interest in astronomy?"

"Don't be dense, Margie. I didn't buy it for myself. It's a gift. You like it?"

She liked it very much indeed. She hugged her father. He couldn't possibly have afforded it. He must have taken out a second mortgage, Marguerite thought.

"When you were young," Chuck Hauser said, "all this stuff was a mystery to me."

"All what stuff?"

"You know. Stars and planets. Everything you cared about so much. It seems to me now I should have stopped and looked a little closer. This is my way of saying I admire what you've accomplished. Maybe I'm even beginning to understand it. So—think you can get this thing packed up tight enough to fit it in that little car of yours?"

"We'll find a way."

"I notice you put your luggage in the same room with Chris."

She blushed. "Did I? I wasn't thinking—really, it's just habit—"

Making it worse.

He smiled. "Come on, Marguerite. I'm not some hard-shell Baptist. From what you've said and from what I've seen, Chris is a good man. You're obviously in love. Have you talked about marriage?"

Her blush deepened; she hoped he couldn't see it in the dim light. "No immediate plans. But don't be surprised."

"He's good to Tess?"

"Very good."

"She likes him?"

"Better. She feels safe with him."

"Then I'm happy for you. So tell me, does presenting you with this gift entitle me to offer a word of advice along with it?"

"Anytime."

"I won't ask what you three have been through at Blind Lake, but I know it's been especially tough for Tess. She used to be a little uncommunicative. It doesn't look like that's changed."

"It hasn't."

"You know, Marguerite, you were exactly the same way. Thick as a brick when your interests weren't engaged. I always had a hard time talking to you."

"I'm sorry."

"You don't need to apologize. All I'm saying is, it's easy to let these things glide past. People can become almost invisible to each other. I love you and I know your mother loved you, but I don't think we always *saw* you very clearly, if you know what I mean."

"I know."

"Don't let that happen to Tess."

Marguerite nodded.

"Now," her father said. "Before we pack this thing up, you want to show me how it works?"

She found him 47 Ursa Majoris in the optical scope. An

undistinguished star, no more than a point of light among many points of light, less bright than the fireflies blinking under the bushes at the back of the yard.

"That's it, huh?"

"That's it."

"I guess you know it so well by now, it must feel like you've been there."

"That's exactly what it feels like." She added, "I love you too, Daddy."

"Thank you, Marguerite. Shouldn't you be putting that girl of yours to bed?"

"Chris can take care of it. It might be nice to sit out here a while and talk."

"It's pretty chilly for August."

"I don't care."

When at last she came back into the house she found Chris in the kitchen, mumbling over his pocket server, making notes for the new book. He had been working on it for weeks, sometimes feverishly. "Has Tess gone to bed?"

"She's in her room reading."

Marguerite went up to check.

The most disturbing thing about the events at Blind Lake, Marguerite thought, was that they implied a connection over immense distances through a medium not understood, a connection that had made it possible for her to touch (and be touched by) the Subject; the Subject, who had known, somehow, all along, that he was being watched.

Seeing changes the seen. Had Tess been watched in the same way? Had Marguerite? Would that bring them, then, at the end of some unimaginable pilgrimage, to one of those enigmatic places linked to the stars—in lieu of death, a plunge into the infinite?

Not yet, Marguerite thought. Maybe never. But certainly not yet.

She found Tess fully clothed, asleep on the bedspread with her book splayed open and her hair askew. Marguerite woke her gently and helped her into her nightgown.

By the time Tess was properly tucked into bed she was wide awake again. Marguerite said, "Do you want anything? A glass of water?"

"A story," Tess said promptly.

"I don't really know a whole lot of stories."

"About *him*," Tess said.

Who? Chris, Ray, her grandfather?

"The Subject," Tess said. "All the things that happened to him."

Marguerite was taken aback. This was the first time Tess had expressed an interest in the Subject. "You really want to know about all that?"

Tess nodded. She lay back and bumped her head against the pillow, about one beat per second, gently. Summer air moved the window blinds against the wooden sill.

Well. Where to begin? Marguerite tried to recall the pages she had written with Tess in mind. Pages she had written but never shared. Stories untold.

But she didn't need pages.

"First of all," Marguerite said, "you have to understand that he was a person. Not exactly like you and me, but not completely different. He lived in a city he loved very much, on a dry plain under a dusty sky, on a world not quite as big as this one."

Long ago. Far away.